EARTH FIRE

EARTH FIRE

EARTHRISE, BOOK IV

Daniel Arenson

CHAPTER ONE

There it was—the source of the distress signal. A black planet orbiting a red dwarf. A world lost in blackness. A colony deep in the demilitarized zone. It floated ahead. Hell.

As if to mock the crew, the Mayday call repeated on the starship's speakers, crackling with static, broken with pain.

Help. Help. In Hell. Help.

"Turn it off," said Captain Einav Ben-Ari, struggling not to shudder. "I've heard enough."

Her lieutenant flipped a switch, and the recording died. The only sound now was the familiar engine hum of the HDFS *Saint Brendan*. Aboard the small, stealthy starship they flew: a captain, a pilot, and thirteen infantrymen. A few humans venturing into realms no humans should ever enter. Into no man's land. Into the darkness past the frontier, the remnants of the scum's empire which no race had yet claimed. The Human Defense Force called it the demilitarized zone. Among the troops, they called it Ghost Town.

"What the hell are they doing out here?" Ben-Ari whispered. Standing on the bridge, she stared ahead at the dark planet. It was a rocky world, smaller but denser than Earth, all black mountains and craggy canyons, its star dim and cold. "We shouldn't be here. Nobody should."

From the dark viewport, her ghostly reflection gazed back at her, hovering above the planet. Despite herself, Ben-Ari's eyes refocused on her astral mirror image. A young officer with dark blond hair, a pale face, and green eyes that had seen too much, that looked too old, too hurt for a woman of twenty-five. Eyes that had seen too much war. Too many friends fall. Her black battle fatigues faded in her reflection, and her head seemed disembodied, floating in darkness, and now Ben-Ari couldn't stop herself. She shivered.

It's been five years since the war against the scum, Ben-Ari thought. *Five years since we defeated the alien horde. Yet I still wake up screaming most nights. When I gaze into space, I still see the creatures.*

The *Saint Brendan*'s engines changed gears. The ship gave a little jolt, and outside the viewport, the dark planet snapped back into focus. It seemed to mock Ben-Ari, to stare at her with its dark craters like arachnid eyes, a canyon on its surface leering like a mouth. Across the ship, the others felt it too. When Ben-Ari glanced behind her, she saw her infantry squad in the hold, thirteen warriors clad in black, hands tightening around their guns.

"Sorry for the turbulence, ma'am," said Lieutenant Kemi Abasi, the ship's pilot. The young woman winced, hitting buttons on her control panel. "I'm not used to these stealth engines. This ship works very differently than a Firebird starfighter."

The two officers could not have been more different. Ben-Ari had grown up an army brat, the daughter of an Israeli colonel, her childhood spent traveling from base to base. Kemi had grown up in Canada, the granddaughter of Nigerian immigrants, and had never known war until enlisting in Julius Military Academy five years ago, then fighting the scum as a pilot. Kemi's skin was dark while Ben-Ari was pale, her hair was curly and black while Ben-Ari's was smooth and blond, and she smiled readily while Ben-Ari struggled to still find joy in this cosmos. And yet over the past few years, the two had become more than just crew, more than just captain and pilot. They had become, perhaps, even more than friends. Kemi was like a sister.

Dón't let me lose my sister today, Ben-Ari prayed silently, gazing out into the demilitarized zone. Ghost Town. *I lost too many friends and family already.*

The recording had been turned off, but the distress call still echoed in Ben-Ari's ears.

Help. Help. In Hell.

"What's that?" Ben-Ari said, squinting at the planet. "There, in that crater. Is that a natural structure?"

She frowned, trying to see more clearly. She could make out only jagged black shapes like ancient ruins.

"I'm not detecting any electromagnetic energy, ma'am," said Kemi. "No radio signals, no movement. Let me zoom in."

The lieutenant hit a few buttons, and the viewport displayed a larger image of the crater. Ben-Ari's frown deepened.

"It's . . . a building," she said. "No, not a building. A *hive*."

"It just looks like a pile of boulders to me, ma'am," said Kemi.

"In the middle of a crater?" Ben-Ari shook her head. "Run a heat scan, Lieutenant."

Kemi nodded. On the viewport, the image glowed, blue around the edges, reddish in the center.

"Trace amounts of heat," the lieutenant said. "Maybe geothermal activity. A volcano or—"

"Life," said Ben-Ari. "Warm bodies." She nodded. "The distress signal came from there. Take us down, Lieutenant. And be careful. Keep scanning the area."

"Scanning for what, ma'am?"

"Anything," said Ben-Ari, her hand instinctively clutching her rifle.

The *Saint Brendan* was not a large ship, not a powerful ship, her cannons small. But she was stealthy and fast. All smooth, black surfaces, she reflected and emitted no light. Highly advanced technology—most of which Ben-Ari barely understood—rendered the *Saint Brendan* invisible to the best telescopes and scanners.

As they sailed toward the planet, Ben-Ari kept watching the viewports, seeking . . . she wasn't sure what. Scum pods? The scum, foul alien centipedes, had lost their empire years ago. They no longer occupied this space. Other alien ships? This was the demilitarized zone, forbidden for anyone to enter.

Yet we're *here,* Ben-Ari thought. *And down there, on the surface, in that strange dark structure—life. Life in danger. Life that calls for us. Life in Ghost Town.*

The *Saint Brendan* jolted as they slipped into the thin atmosphere, a haze of carbon dioxide with splashes of nitrogen. Ben-Ari watched the surface stream below them, a black desert of boulders, dunes, mountains, and canyons plunging into darkness. The starmaps simply called this place TSR7b, too insignificant for a proper name. It should be a lifeless world, just a desolate rock like the billions that filled this corner of the galaxy. And yet . . .

With a crackle, the Mayday recording came back to life, emerging from the speakers far too loudly, echoing through the starship.

Help. Help. In Hell. Help. They're everywhere. They—

The words morphed into a scream of pure agony. It was so loud that Ben-Ari started and the soldiers in the hold cursed.

"Sorry, Captain!" said Kemi, flipping switches, and the speakers shut off, leaving an echo. "I don't know why it just turned on like that." She shook her head, her hair bouncing. "There's something weird seeping out of this planet. It's mucking up our instruments."

Ben-Ari cursed inwardly, her knees weak. She pointed. "Just so long as you can land us in that crater. Take us down right by the structure."

She had almost said *alien structure*, but she couldn't jump to conclusions yet. Perhaps Kemi had been right. Just the jagged mouth of a volcano. Likely, here were just outlaws or adventurers who had ventured too far, had gotten lost in Ghost Town, had crash landed on this world. Perhaps that was all, just a shelter for some lost, frightened humans where no humans should tread.

Kemi directed the *Saint Brendan* down into the crater. They hovered for a moment, then landed with barely a sound.

For a long moment, Ben-Ari stood silently, waiting. The structure loomed outside the viewport. It seemed so much larger from down here, dwarfing their ship, a black edifice, all jumbled, jagged stones.

A hive, she thought. *An alien hive.*

In the deepest chasms of her mind, the scum still scurried, massive centipedes, larger than humans, leaping toward her. Her soldiers screamed. Her soldiers died. The claws dug into her, and—

Enough! Ben-Ari told herself. *Stop.* She inhaled deeply. *You are a captain in the Human Defense Force. You are the commander of this ship and its warriors. You will act like it.*

Shoving the memories aside, she turned away from the viewport.

"Come, Lieutenant," she said to her pilot. Ben-Ari walked off the bridge, and Kemi followed close behind.

They entered *Saint Brendan*'s hold, a rectangular room where a squad of warriors—all members of the prestigious Erebus Brigade—were waiting.

"Officers on deck!" said Sergeant Murphy, the squad commander, a burly man with brown skin and a thick mustache. He and his warriors stood at attention, clad in black, holding T58 assault rifles.

Ben-Ari stared at them. Tough warriors. Elite commandos. Brothers, sisters, children, parents.

The scum are breaking in! echoed a voice.

Run! shouted one of her soldiers, silenced as the tunnels collapsed onto him.

Ben-Ari inhaled sharply. *Stop. Enough. Do not let your memories interfere with your duty, Einav. Not now. Not here.*

"Several hours ago, our base received a distress call," Ben-Ari said to the squad. "It was garbled. There was so much static we couldn't make out more than a few words. But it was a human voice. And it requested help. There is a structure outside this ship—whether human, alien, or naturally formed, we don't know. We've detected lifeforms within. If there are humans here, our job is to get them out."

"And blast any space bug we see!" said a private, a towering man with a square jaw, bulging muscles, and a blond crew cut. His actual surname was Johnson, but they all called him Private Johnny.

Ben-Ari shook her head. "Not if we can avoid it. We're deep in the demilitarized zone. Any shots fired here could be interpreted as an act of war. According to galactic law, only urgent humanitarian missions are allowed here."

"Hey, we're humanitarians!" Private Johnny hefted his assault rifle. A grenade launcher was attached to the barrel. "We're here to make sure humans squash the bugs."

"We don't know there are bugs," Ben-Ari said. "The scum empire fell years ago. This might all be just a few miners trapped in a tunnel."

Private Johnny sighed. "It's space bugs. It's always fucking space bugs."

"Watch it, Johnny," rumbled Sergeant Murphy, "or I'll personally feed your ass to the next Betelgeusian cockroach we meet."

"Sergeant Murphy, take the vanguard with me," Ben-Ari said. "Lieutenant Abasi, walk behind us with your scanners. Johnny, you take the rear."

"What? I—" the burly private began, but under the withering glare of his sergeant, he stiffened and saluted. "Yes, ma'am."

Ben-Ari sighed. "And don't salute indoors, Private. Did they teach you nothing at basic?" She grabbed a helmet from the wall. "Helmets on. Visors down. Magazines in."

They stepped out of the *Saint Brendan*, two officers and thirteen soldiers, all in black, all holding assault rifles. Ben-Ari had considered bringing plasma guns on this mission, but they were more destructive than mere bullets—*too* destructive. Her mission was to find whoever had sent the Mayday and bring them home, not burn down the place.

The structure towered before them. It looked like a mountain of boulders and pebbles glued together with tar. When Ben-Ari stepped closer, she frowned.

"What is that?" Kemi said, staring with her. "Is that a net?"

Ben-Ari stepped closer to the structure. Black strands clung to the tarry surface. She reached out, hesitated, then touched one strand. It was springy.

"Alien G-strings?" said Private Johnny, walking up toward them.

"A web," Ben-Ari whispered, looking at thousands of other strands that coated the structure, glued to the stone. "Like a spider web."

Johnny nodded and cocked his gun. "Space bugs. Knew it."

Sergeant Murphy approached, grabbed the private, and shoved the man back with a scowl. When he turned toward Ben-Ari, his scowl vanished, and his eyes grew solemn. "Ma'am, Private Johnson may have shit for brains, but in this case, he may be right. This looks like a typical Type Three organic alien infestation. Big one too. This structure is nearly half a kilometer long, and my scanner's showing organic material all over the damn place. We'll need backup. An orbital bombing campaign, then a couple platoons of marines with flamethrowers and chem-sprayers. In short, ma'am, this is a bug extermination job."

"No, Sergeant." Ben-Ari shook her head. "Not here. If we were in human territory, yes. But this is the demilitarized zone. We're not supposed to even be here, let alone attack a potential new alien civilization. We don't know what alien species is here. We don't know if they're intelligent or not. We don't want to antagonize them and the rest of the sentient galaxy. We sneak in. We find whatever humans are alive in there. We sneak them out. That's it. This is a rescue operation, not a bug hunt."

Like Corpus was a rescue operation? whispered a voice in her mind. *Like the place where you led your platoon, Einav? Where your friends died, where you escaped while they rotted, where—*

She shoved that voice down again. She refused to let that terror seize her now, refused to show weakness. If anyone knew of her shell shock, she would lose her position as the *Saint Brendan's* captain, perhaps even be discharged. There would be time later to deal with her trauma, to listen to her old classical music collection, to paint with her watercolors, to meditate, to calm the storm. Right now, she needed to keep sailing through that storm.

"Captain, ma'am!" A corporal rushed toward her. "Private Komagata found something. A doorway, we think."

Ben-Ari nodded and followed the soldier. Flashlights mounted onto their helmets lit the way. As she walked, she kept scanning the area, gun raised, seeking some hint of the aliens who had built this hive. Nothing. If she was lucky, the aliens had left ages ago. The cosmos was an old place. Most worlds were billions of years old. Most alien structures were mere ruins, lingering long after their builders had gone extinct.

Just a few human adventurers stuck under something heavy, she told herself. *A simple, quick job, and we'll be back in human territory.*

They finally reached Private Ayumi Komagata, a young Japanese woman, smallest in the squad but among the fiercest. She stood with her legs in a wide stance, gun pointed at what looked like a cave in the structure's wall. Beyond lay shadows.

"The gates of Hell," the young warrior muttered.

"Then let us be angels," said Ben-Ari. "I'll lead the way. Follow me, guns raised, but keep your safety switches on and your fingers far from your triggers. Let's do this without violence if we can."

Private Johnny smirked. "I don't need bullets to kill space bugs. I got big feet." He stomped on the ground, then leaned toward Private Komagata. "And you know what they say about men with big feet, right, Komagata?"

"That they feel the need to boast because of their tiny cocks?" she said.

As Sergeant Murphy scolded the two rookies, Ben-Ari stepped into the cave. A tunnel delved into darkness. She walked, rifle held before her, her flashlight barely able to pierce the shadows. Lumpy strands covered the floor and walls, and suddenly they reminded Ben-Ari less of a web and more of veins. A terror leaped in her that this was a great corpse, a massive alien who had fossilized on this planet.

"Captain." Kemi approached her, staring at a handheld monitor. "Scanners show . . . air. This place is full of air. Twenty-two percent oxygen, seventy-seven percent nitrogen, one percent water vapor . . . small amounts of toxins but nothing we can't handle. Earth air or close to it. We can breathe this." The lieutenant pulled open her visor, inhaled deeply, then grimaced. "It stinks. But it's breathable."

Ben-Ari raised her own visor, and she nearly gagged. *Stinks* was an understatement. This place reeked of rot, of death. She pulled her visor back down and inhaled the clean air that flowed from the tank on her back. "Breathable? That's debatable. Still, it raises some interesting questions. The atmosphere outside is hostile. Why is the air in here so different, suited not just to life—but to human life?"

Private Komagata raised her visor too, then turned green and quickly shut her helmet again. "Alien stench. Worse than Johnny's giant feet."

Kemi pulled down her own visor, apparently having suffered enough of the miasma. She looked around at the veined walls of the tunnel. "What is this place?"

"Do you still detect heat signatures, Lieutenant?" Ben-Ari said.

Kemi checked her monitor again and nodded. "Yes, ma'am. From deeper in the structure."

"Let's keep going," Ben-Ari said.

They plunged deeper down the tunnel. Ben-Ari's visor was closed, but she still smelled that stench. The stench of space. Many back on Earth thought that space had no smell, but it did— a burning, metallic smell, and this place was rank with it.

We should never have come here, Ben-Ari thought. *We don't belong here. Not in the demilitarized zone. Not in space. There is such darkness here. Such coldness. Such evil.*

The tunnel delved deep, twisting, coiling through the innards of this stone structure. The webs along the walls thickened, black, bristly, and it seemed to Ben-Ari that the strands were living beings, serpents that crawled and grabbed and built.

"What is that?" Kemi whispered, pointing ahead. "Is that a person?" She squinted. "Is that a kid?"

Ben-Ari stared and her heart burst into a gallop. It hung from the ceiling, gently turning. A bundle. A cocoon. No—a figure trapped in a web.

"What the fuck?" Private Johnny said, rushing forward.

"Wait!" Ben-Ari grabbed him, pulled him back. "Slowly. Behind me."

The soldiers crowded behind Ben-Ari in the tunnel, gazing forward, beams of light piercing the dusty shadows. Ben-Ari inched toward the dangling figure. A bundle of webbing, like a fly in cobwebs but larger, large as a child. Ben-Ari drew her knife and began sawing. The web was thick. Even with Kemi helping, it was long moments before they cut an opening in the web.

"Fur?" Ben-Ari said.

Kemi made a gagging sound. "I can smell it even through my visor." She shuddered. "There are worms."

Ben-Ari kept cutting the web, revealing more fur, a fang, a maggoty eye socket, and—

The creature fell from the torn web and slammed onto the ground. Its belly burst, spilling rot.

Private Johnny burst into laughter. "Fuck, that thing scared me. Just a dog."

Ben-Ari knelt, eyes narrowed. A dog. A German Shepherd. It had been dead for a while by the looks of it. A collar still rotted around its neck. She leaned down to lift the collar, to examine the dog tag, and—

A shriek tore through the air.

"Fuck!" Johnny shouted.

Ben-Ari started and raised her gun. A shadow lurched and—

"Die, fucker!" Private Johnny shouted, firing his gun.

"Die!" cried Private Komagata, firing too. Bullets rang.

"Hold your fire!" Ben-Ari shouted. "Damn it, soldiers, hold your fire!"

A few more bullets rang out, and the soldiers lowered their guns, panting. Private Johnny gave a "woo!" that sounded half exhilarated and half terrified.

"Damn it, soldiers, I told you this is a rescue op, not a raid," Ben Ari said.

"Sorry, ma'am." Private Komagata, at least, had the grace to blush. "I thought I saw something. A shadow."

"A fucking alien shadow, that's what," Private Johnny said.

Ben-Ari had seen it too. A small, scurrying creature, no larger than a house cat, and maybe it *was* a house cat. If dogs, why not cats?

"Next time you jump at a shadow," rumbled Sergeant Murphy, "shoot your own balls off, Johnny. Save us from a future generation of idiots."

Ben-Ari looked back at the dog, but a bullet had shattered its tag.

Bad luck, she thought. *Bad luck in this whole damn place. That's what this stench is. Bad luck.*

"Bad luck," whispered Private Komagata.

Ben-Ari spun toward her. "What's that, Private?"

"I . . ." The young Japanese warrior paled. "I thought I heard you say that . . ." She shook her head. "No. You said nothing. If dogs, why not cats, right?"

Ben-Ari frowned, then shook her head and looked away. "Come on, squad. And no more firing at shadows."

They traveled deeper. The air thickened, full of mist and dust, and wet strands hung from the ceiling like lichen. A rumble rose in the darkness. Noises sounded in the deep. Clicks. Clatters. Deep breathing that soon vanished. Pattering feet. Deep in the underground things were moaning, moving, exhaling, waiting, perhaps ancient machinery, perhaps ancient life that hungered. Another shadow raced across the ceiling, too fast to see clearly, then vanished ahead. Rumbling laughter sounded in the deep, and distant metal clanged and crashed and somebody screamed.

"Fuck this shit," Private Johnny whispered. "I changed my mind. Let's get the hell out of here."

"Soldier, keep it together," said Sergeant Murphy.

"This place is fucked, man," Johnny said. "Got a bad vibe. I say we fucking bolt and call in the cavalry, man. Nuke the whole place from space."

"There's at least one human prisoner here, soldier," Ben-Ari said. "Maybe more. We're not nuking anything. Now man up, toughen up, and shut up."

"Just don't fuck up," muttered Private Komagata.

Deeper they went, and that clattering kept sounding in the depths, the bowels of this place, the forgotten machinery, awakening perhaps after a million years of slumber. Somebody was alive here. Somebody, some*thing*, had trapped that dog, had sent out a distress call. The aliens must have heard the gunfire. Why didn't they attack?

They're luring you deeper. The thought came unbidden into Ben-Ari's mind. *You know this. They're calling you, sucking you into the darkness. They're intelligent. You can feel it. You can feel them watching. Listening. They can feel you.*

Ben-Ari realized that the webs were tighter down here, that as she stepped on them, they quivered, that as the warriors brushed against the dangling strands, the tremors ran into the deep.

"They can feel us through the strands," she whispered. "They know we're coming. This is a spiderweb, and we're the flies."

Private Johnny took a deep breath. "Fuck. This. Shit." He turned and began to leave, only for his comrades to grab him and pull him back.

"Tiny cock and tiny balls," muttered Komagata. "Knew it."

"Load your weapons," whispered Ben-Ari. "Keep a bullet in the chamber, the safety off, your fingers on the triggers."

"Ma'am, are you sure?" said Sergeant Murphy. "Rescue op, remember?"

Only Ben-Ari wasn't sure this *was* a rescue op anymore. This was a web. This was a trap. The words echoed.

Help. Help. In Hell.

"What the hell?" whispered Kemi, stepping forward. She brushed dirt and webs aside. "It's a door."

The others approached. Ben-Ari helped clear aside the grime. Indeed—it was a door. Human-made, by the looks of it, thick and metallic. Something had clawed at this door, digging into the iron. A few letters were still visible.

ELL B 7

"What does it mean?" Kemi said. "Ell B 7?"

"Hell," whispered Komagata, standing behind them.

The door was unlocked but rusted, dented, and jammed shut. It took several soldiers to finally push it open. It groaned and shrieked in protest, showering rust.

A cavernous hall awaited them, large as a church nave, drenched in filth. Webs hung everywhere. Countless black, quivering strands covered the place, curtains that soared to a craggy, organic ceiling. A cathedral. An alien cathedral, rotten and infested.

"What the hell is this place, Captain?" Johnny asked.

Kemi's eyes widened. "My God." She ran forward. "Oh my God."

Ben-Ari cursed inwardly. "Lieutenant, wait!"

Yet Kemi wouldn't slow down, and Ben-Ari ran after her.

A hill rose before them in the center of the hall. A hill of naked corpses.

Ben-Ari grimaced and struggled not to vomit in her helmet.

There must have been hundreds of corpses here. Human corpses. Their limbs were slung together, holding the hill in place. They were naked, cadaverous, and all of them seemed to be adult males.

"Fuck, fuck, fuck," Private Johnny said when he reached them. "We got to get out of here, man. Come on, man. There are shadows moving in the webs, man. There are things here. We're fucked. We're fucked. We're—"

"Hold it together!" said Sergeant Murphy. "Take a time out, Johnny. Go sit." He shoved the private aside, then turned toward Ben-Ari. "Ma'am, I suggest we clear the area, report back to base, then bomb this whole place from the air. There are no survivors left. But the hostiles are still here. I can hear 'em." The beefy, mustached sergeant scowled. "I can smell 'em."

Ben-Ari was ready to agree with him. This place was wrong. This had gone too far.

We have to get out.

The voices from her past.

They're everywhere!

The echoes of the Scum War.

"Who did this?" Ben-Ari whispered. "This isn't a scum hive. Scum eat their victims. These bodies are—"

For the first time, Ben-Ari saw it.

She clenched her jaw.

Again she nearly vomited.

In the shadows, she had not seen it at first. She leaned closer to one corpse, its mouth open in anguish, its gray skin already rotting. The skull had been carved open with surgical precision. The brain was gone.

Shuddering, Ben-Ari looked from corpse to corpse. Each had suffered the same disfigurement. Each man's skull had been neatly sawed open, the brain removed, the corpse then discarded here.

"Captain, take a look at this," said Kemi, lifting a corpse's arm.

Ben-Ari walked toward her and leaned closer. Her flashlight illuminated the pale arm.

Another shock rattled Ben-Ari.

A swastika was tattooed onto the man's arm.

"Nazis," whispered Kemi. "Goddamn Nazis. This one too." She pointed at another corpse, its chest tattooed with Sig runes, a favorite symbol of the Third Reich. "Captain, what's going on here?"

Ben-Ari inhaled sharply through clenched teeth, gripping her gun. Two hundred years ago, her Jewish ancestors had fled the concentration camps, had fought the Nazis in the forests of Eastern Europe. Kemi, of African descent, doubtlessly hated the bastards just as much.

"Did we come here to save a bunch of white supremacists, Captain?" Kemi asked. "Because if so, I say to hell with them."

"Wait. No. Look at this corpse. It has different tattoos." Ben-Ari frowned. "It looks like . . . Japanese?"

Private Komagata approached, lifted her visor, and spat. "I recognize those tattoos. The Blood Lotus. Pacific gangsters. I fucking *hate* those guys."

"Look at this one," said Kemi. "See this corpse's tattoos? *La Familia*. That's Spanish. Mexican mafia. What the hell was going on here? Some top secret convention of evil henchmen?"

Ben-Ari thought back to the words on the door. *ELL B 7*.

"Of course," she whispered.

Leaving the pile of corpses, Ben-Ari headed toward the side of the hall, where sticky black webs hung like tapestries. She worked with her knife, cutting the thicker strands, then pulled webs aside like drawing curtains.

Behind the webs rose rusted bars.

A small cell. A cell with only a concrete bed, a concrete desk, a rusted toilet. A prison cell.

"Ell B 7," Ben-Ari said. "Cell Block 7. It's a prison."

Kemi approached her, eyes dark. "What is a prison doing inside an alien structure on a forgotten world in the demilitarized zone?"

Ben-Ari knelt and lifted a tattered prison uniform. Dried blood and grime darkened the orange fabric. She brushed aside flecks of blood, revealing a logo printed onto the uniform.

She dropped the fabric.

"Damn," she whispered.

A crude snake, eating its own tail, was drawn onto the uniform. Ben-Ari recognized that symbol, and it scared her more than any of the tattooed gang signs. She had seen this symbol on

Corpus, the moon overtaken by the scum. She had seen it on countless military vehicles, from tanks to starship engines.

"Chrysopoeia Corporation," she said.

Kemi opened her mouth, and she seemed ready to speak when a scream rose from deep in the prison.

A human scream.

Ben-Ari ran.

The others joined her, running close behind. They raced through the cell block, shoving aside the dangling strands. The webs trembled around and above them, and shadows scurried. Leaving the hill of corpses, they reached the end of the cell block. A cavernous archway loomed before them, woven of bones and black webs. The scream sounded again, weaker now. Deep laughter rumbled. Feet clattered. The sounds came from beyond the archway.

"Ma'am, wait, let me—" Sergeant Murphy began, but Ben-Ari didn't listen. She raced through the archway, bones crunching beneath her boots.

She burst into a towering chamber, larger than the cell block. It was a mess hall, or had been long ago. She could still see a few tables and the remains of a serving counter, all draped with webs and grime. Shadows cloaked the ceiling, the lights long gone. Only the squad's flashlights lit the room.

A moan sounded ahead.

Ben-Ari inhaled sharply, pointed her flashlight, and felt the blood drain from her face.

A man sat in the center of the mess hall. He was gaunt, naked, and strapped into a metal chair with a coil of webs.

"Help," he whispered. "Please . . . Help . . ."

The top of his skull had been surgically removed. The brain was exposed, quivering and red.

"Help . . . me . . ." Tears streamed down his cheeks.

"Fuck, fuck, fuck," Private Johnny whispered.

"We have to help him!" Kemi darted forward.

"Wait." Ben-Ari grabbed her lieutenant. "Wait!"

They all froze, guns raised, staring.

"Ma'am, we—" Kemi began.

"Wait!" Ben-Ari whispered.

The webs in the room were quivering.

A shadow was moving above.

Ben-Ari's head spun, her breath quickened, and her heart pounded.

Bait, she thought. *The man—bait in the center of the web. The distress call. All of this. A trap.*

"Help me," whispered the strapped prisoner.

"Hold still," Ben-Ari whispered, and the squad all stood still, arranged in a semicircle, guns raised.

Deep, rumbling laughter sounded in the shadows above.

A shadow began descending from the ceiling, moving down on a black strand.

Ben-Ari's eyes watered.

No, she thought. *Oh God, no. No.*

At first, she thought this creature was a great spider, an arachnid the size of a grizzly bear. But no. Instead of eight legs like a spider, it had six serrated limbs, each tipped with claws. The alien's jaws were massive, large enough to swallow a man, lined with teeth like swords. A red scar trailed across the creature's face, a deep canyon, and a crest of horns topped its head. Hundreds of skulls clung to its back, the tops sawed off, forming clattering armor, the eye sockets gazing vacantly.

"Goddamn fucking space bug!" Private Johnny shouted, aiming his rifle. "I—"

"Stop!" Ben-Ari pulled his barrel down. "Hold your fire. All of you. Hold your fire! That's an order."

She stared ahead. The alien kept descending, inch by inch, and its jaws—God, the size of them—opened in a lurid grin. Four black eyes stared at Ben-Ari, and she could see intelligence there. She could see amusement. This wasn't just a dumb bug. This creature was calculating.

It wants something, Ben-Ari thought. *It wants us to shoot it. It wants us to start a war in the demilitarized zone. This isn't a trap to kill us.* She understood. *This is a trap to get us to kill.*

The alien lowered itself until it hovered over the bound prisoner. Its front legs moved out, clasping the prisoner's head. A tongue unfurled from the alien's leering mouth—small teeth lined that tongue like the teeth on a chainsaw. The tongue dipped into the open skull. It happened so quickly Ben-Ari could barely grasp it. The alien scooped out the brain like a man shucking an oyster, pulling the quivering organ into its waiting mouth. The creature swallowed, and the prisoner's head tilted forward, brainless, lifeless.

"Hold your fire!" Ben-Ari shouted as soldiers aimed their guns.

"Hold your fire!" Sergeant Murphy echoed her call.

Ben-Ari stared at the alien. It still dangled before her on its web, saliva dripping down its fangs onto the dead prisoner. All the flashlights were on it, leaving the rest of the hall in shadow.

"You understand me, don't you?" Ben-Ari said. "Who are you? *What* are you? What do you want from us?"

A clattering emerged from the alien's mouth, eerily like laughter. Its body throbbed, and the human skulls on its back clanked, a rancid armor of death. And then it spoke. Its voice was deep, unearthly, a voice like stones rumbling, like echoes in caves, like wind through a graveyard.

"We . . . are . . . *marauders*." Its jaw stretched into a grin, and the clattering in its throat grew louder. "We . . . want . . . your pain."

"It can talk," whispered Private Johnny, and tears flowed down his cheeks. "Oh God, how can it talk?" The beefy soldier let out a howl. "Die, you son of a bitch! Die!"

"No!" Ben-Ari shouted, but it was too late.

The private fired his gun.

Bullets rang out, slamming into the alien.

Skulls shattered on its back. Bullets ricocheted off its teeth. The creature laughed, and its claws rose, pointing at the soldiers.

"Die, fucker!" shouted Private Komagata, firing too, and suddenly they were all firing their guns, and a hailstorm of bullets slammed into the alien, into the prisoner beneath it, into the webbing that draped across the mess hall.

The alien stretched out its legs like an arachnid Christ, laughing even as the bullets tore into it. Its rumbles echoed through the prison.

And from the shadows above, more creatures descended.

"Fuck, they're everywhere!" shouted Komagata.

"Kill them all!" Private Johnny was shouting, tears still on his cheeks, firing in automatic mode, emptying magazine after magazine. "Die!"

The creatures were descending everywhere, cloaked in shadows, reaching out their claws. The flashlight beams reflected in their fangs, their mocking eyes. Dozens of them. Hundreds.

"They're covering the ceiling!" shouted a corporal.

"Die, bugs!" Private Johnny was spinning in a circle, firing his gun at the ceiling. "Die—"

A marauder lowered itself on a strand. Bullets slammed into it, rebounding off its legs. One of those legs reached down, and claws yanked Johnny's rifle from his hands. Other claws grabbed the soldier's arm, tugging him up.

"Help me!" Private Johnny shouted. "God, help me, somebody! Kill it!"

They all fired their guns. Bullets slammed into the alien, shattering skulls on its back, but could not slay the beast.

Holding the private several meters above the floor, the alien yanked off Johnny's helmet.

The claws cut deep. Carving. Sawing through the skull. The alien pulled off the skull's top like a lid. Private Johnny was still screaming as the alien scooped out his brain. The screams died as his lifeless body crashed onto the floor.

"Run!" Ben-Ari shouted.

They ran back toward the archway of bones. A marauder descended from the ceiling, grabbed a corporal, and pulled the man into the shadows. The soldier screamed above, and blood and guts rained down, followed by the sawed-off top of a skull. Private Komagata reached the archway first, only for a marauder to leap from the shadows. Massive jaws grabbed the soldier, ripping her apart, scattering limbs. The alien screeched, legs outstretched, blocking the exit.

Ben-Ari fired her rifle, hitting the alien's head. Bullets shattered and whizzed. A fragment of bullet hit Ben-Ari's thigh, tearing the skin, and she screamed. She kept firing. More marauders kept descending. Others scurried behind her. The aliens grabbed a man, tore him open, and feasted on the brain.

Ben-Ari emptied a magazine, loaded another, fired again. Bullets could not harm these creatures' hardened skin. She inhaled deeply, aimed through her scope . . .

She hit a marauder's eye.

The alien howled in pain.

Kemi fired again, hit another eye, and the marauder scurried backward, knocking into its comrades.

"Run!" Ben-Ari shouted. "Hurry!"

She raced through the archway. Kemi ran close behind. The surviving soldiers followed.

As they raced through the cell block, the marauders leaped from the walls, from the prison cells, from the ceiling. Webs shot out, grabbed a soldier, and pulled him up into the shadows. Blood showered. Another web caught Doc, the squad's medic, and yanked him into a cell. The marauder cracked Doc's skull open and slurped out the brain.

Ben-Ari kept firing bullets as she ran. A web shot from a cell, grabbed her foot, and began pulling her toward waiting jaws. She fired—not at the alien but at the black strand, severing it. She leaped up and kept running. A claw grabbed Kemi's helmet and began squeezing. Ben-Ari fired, hit the alien's eyes, and pulled Kemi free. They raced around the pile of bodies. A soldier screamed as a marauder tore open her belly, and entrails spilled. Another soldier crawled forward, legs severed, only for a marauder to rip off her arms and devour them as the soldier screamed.

They left the cell block and ran through a tunnel. Only four or five soldiers remained. The marauders chased. Webs shot out, grabbing soldiers, pulling them back into the snapping jaws. Ben-Ari fired over her shoulder, trying to hit the eyes, but the creatures kept scurrying. Bullets shattered the human skulls coating their backs, and the aliens laughed—deep, demonic laughter. They raced forth at incredible speed on their six clawed legs.

Finally the soldiers burst out onto the planet's dark surface. Ben-Ari's spacesuit was torn at the leg, exposing her skin to the planet's thin nitrogen atmosphere. Already the exposed skin turned gray and hardened. She wouldn't survive long here without a proper suit. Kemi and one more soldier—the brawny Sergeant Murphy—emerged from the prison. They were the last survivors of the mission.

Ahead, the marauders were already encasing the HDFS *Saint Brendan* with black webs.

The three soldiers raced toward the starship. Countless marauders emerged from the prison behind them.

Several marauders stood on the roof of the *Saint Brendan,* hissing down at the three humans. Ben-Ari fired, hit one in the eye, and knocked it down. The other two screeched and kept wrapping webs around the ship.

"Into the *Brendan!*" shouted Ben-Ari. "We'll tear them off as we fly!"

A marauder leaped toward them across the landscape, blocking their passage. Sergeant Murphy tossed a grenade.

"Down!" he cried.

They knelt, covered their heads, and shrapnel hailed around them. One shard ripped Ben-Ari's suit at the arm. Another cracked her helmet. She struggled for breath. Her oxygen began leaking out.

"More behind us!" Kemi shouted. "Captain, watch out!"

The pilot fired her rifle. Bullets whistled over Ben-Ari's head and slammed into marauders behind her. Kemi was no longer trying to reach the starship; instead she stood in place, firing at the enemy.

Hundreds of marauders were emerging from the prison. One of the creatures leaped toward Kemi, and the pilot kept firing, but she couldn't stop the assault.

The alien opened its jaws wide, engulfing her gun.

Kemi fired into its mouth.

Unperturbed, the marauder snapped its jaws shut around her wrist. It yanked its head back, swallowing both the gun and Kemi's hand.

Kemi fell to her knees, screaming.

Her arm ended at the wrist, spurting blood.

Sergeant Murphy tossed another grenade into the crowd of marauders. It burst and several alien legs flew.

"Get her into the ship, Captain!" the sergeant shouted. "I'll hold them off. Go!"

As the sergeant kept lobbing grenades, Ben-Ari cursed. She grabbed the wounded Kemi.

"Captain," Kemi whispered, tears in her eyes. She was losing blood fast.

"I've got you, Lieutenant," Ben-Ari said. "You're all right."

She lifted the lieutenant and slung her across her shoulders. She ran toward the *Saint Brendan*. It was barely visible now through the coating of black, sticky webs. Behind her, Ben-Ari could hear Murphy still shouting, and grenades burst, and shrapnel—both the shards of grenades and chunks of marauders—fell all around, sizzling hot, cutting Ben-Ari. Her last oxygen seeped away. She couldn't breathe. She ran on whatever air was left in her lungs.

She reached the ship. Before she could climb aboard, a marauder leaped from the roof. Ben-Ari fired, hit its head, fired again, finally hit an eye. It screeched and scuttled away, blinded.

She sawed through webbing and opened the airlock. She climbed into the ship, Kemi still slung across her shoulders. Ben-Ari gasped for air, then turned back toward the landscape.

Her heart sank.

Sergeant Murphy stood alone before the infested hive. Countless marauders were racing toward him. He emptied his last magazine. He was still far away. Too far to make it.

"Sergeant!" Ben-Ari cried. "Run!"

He looked over his shoulder at her, holding a grenade.

"Fly, Captain!" he cried back to her. "It was an honor."

Lips tight, Murphy saluted, then grabbed a second grenade from his belt.

Marauders leaped onto him, burying the man.

The grenades burst.

Clawed legs, swordlike fangs, and human flesh flew.

Ben-Ari closed the airlock door. She laid Kemi down, took off her helmet, and inhaled deeply. Using a cable, she applied a tourniquet to Kemi's stump, then raced onto the bridge.

She was no pilot, but she knew enough to kick-start the engines. They rumbled and died. Ben-Ari gritted her teeth, hitting buttons, diverting power from shielding and stealth to the engines, then started them again. The ship shuddered as the engines roared.

But the *Saint Brendan* struggled to rise, still caught in the webs. Through the viewport, Ben-Ari could see the strands tightening, holding the ship down, could see a thousand marauders racing toward them, more webs shooting out. A few marauders grabbed the hull, claws scratching the metal.

Ben-Ari leaned toward another control panel, hit buttons, and photon bolts burst out from the ship's cannons. Webs burned and tore.

The ship soared, casting off webs and marauders alike.

They blasted into the sky.

They emerged from the thin atmosphere within moments, and the stars spread out above. Webbing still burned and fell off the dented ship. Ben-Ari trembled on the bridge, losing blood, her leg and arm cut.

Again, death. Again, losing soldiers under her command. Again, terror in the dark.

"We should never have come here," she whispered. "Not to this world. Not into space. We awoke too many monsters in the shadows."

Kemi shuffled onto the bridge, clutching her arm. The stump still leaked blood, even with the tourniquet. She needed proper medical attention—soon.

"Kemi!" Ben-Ari said. "You need to rest, you—"

"Captain," the lieutenant whispered, looking at a viewport. "They're following."

Ben-Ari saw them. Ships. Jagged alien ships rising from the planet below. They reminded her of metal flowers, their petals closed, or like drills ready to burrow through stone. No, she decided. Not flowers or drills. Here were great *claws*—claws of steel. Red plasma burned within their grips, and the ships soared toward the *Saint Brendan*. Five of them, then six, then a hundred.

The metal claws on the alien ships opened like uncurling fists, exposing the flames within.

Balls of plasma shot out.

This was a fight she could not win, Ben-Ari knew.

She grabbed a joystick. She flew away from the world below, away from the enemy ships, away from the corpses of her men, from the nightmares.

But she knew that those nightmares would never leave her. Even if she escaped today, they would linger in her mind. The visions of the marauders emerging from the shadows. Cracking open skulls. Slurping. Consuming. Laughing.

"Captain!" Kemi cried, and an instant later a blast hit the *Saint Brendan*.

Fire raged outside the viewports.

The ship shook madly.

"Kemi, can you still fly this thing?" Ben-Ari cried.

The pilot nodded, reached for the controls with one hand, but then fell. She lay on the floor, her tourniquet loosening, and began to convulse.

She's going into shock, Ben-Ari thought. *Damn it, we need—*

Another blast hit the ship. They jolted. Smoke filled the bridge and alarms blared. A robotic voice intoned about a hull breach at the crew quarters.

Sitting at the helm, Ben-Ari fired the rear cannons, sending out photon bolts, knowing it was not enough. She diverted energy away from the guns, away from the stealth motors, leaving just the bare minimum for survival. The oxygen levels dropped. The air turned frigid. She kept diverting more power, putting everything into the engines. Into speed.

They blasted forward in space.

Their azoth engine—a warp drive capable of bending spacetime—began to warm up. Through the viewport, she could see its blue glow.

We're a small ship, she thought. *We're weak. We're alone. But we're fast.*

She shoved the throttle forward.

The warp drive roared into action, and the stars stretched into streams of light, and they burst into warped space.

And the marauder ships followed.

Ben-Ari could see them in the rear viewports, great metal claws, soaring after her through the funnel of warped spacetime.

"So they have warp technology," she muttered. "Great."

Kemi moaned, convulsing, her eyes sunken. The low oxygen level wasn't helping. The pilot needed urgent care and probably a blood transfusion. Ben-Ari only had time to kneel and tighten the tourniquet, then return to the controls.

Sorry, Kemi, I can't help you any more right now.

Another blast of enemy plasma flew, and Ben-Ari yanked on the joystick, dodging the assault. The plasma roared overhead, searing the roof of the ship. Built for stealth, the *Saint Brendan* wasn't particularly sturdy. Already they were leaking air. One more blow, and the whole ship was likely to collapse.

Ben-Ari inhaled deeply.

Oh to hell with it.

She flipped more switches, shutting down the life support system, diverting even that power to the engines.

The lights shut off. The air stopped circulating. Even the control panels shut down.

The only sound came from the engines—roaring, thrumming, shaking the dark ship. The only light came from their blue glow, the streaks of starlight, and the enemy fire.

They flew.

They flew like a falcon after prey, like fire in the deep, like light in the dark, like a woman fleeing old horrors and guilt, faces of dying friends, terrors that would not die. They flew, a single ship of humanity, fleeing the darkness.

And there ahead, Ben-Ari saw it. A point of light in the tunnel of curved spacetime. The star Achernar. The border of humanity's territory in the Orion Arm of the Milky Way galaxy.

A hundred streams of plasma burst out from the enemy ships behind her.

Ben-Ari could not breathe, but she shouted.

She shoved down against the throttle, as if her own body, her own willpower could give the ship extra speed.

She charged toward the star and shut down the azoth warp engine.

She crashed out of warped space, the stars slamming into dots around her.

She returned power to life support and gasped for air.

Fire raged.

She yanked the ship down, pulled it sideways, then dived. The blasts of plasma lit space around her. One grazed the wing, tossing the *Saint Brendan* into a tailspin. She managed to steady the ship, finding herself facing the marauder fleet.

A hundred ships, maybe more, floated in space before her. They did not advance farther.

The enemy vessels hovered just across the border, still within the demilitarized zone. With the lights off on the *Saint Brendan*, Ben-Ari felt as if she were floating through space with no ship around her, lost in the darkness.

She knelt by Kemi and touched her cheek. The pilot was still alive, still conscious, but growing cold. They stared out the viewport together.

Before them, one enemy ship floated a little closer, hovering right at the border. A massive ship, large enough to swallow the *Saint Brendan*, formed of a hundred blades curving inward. That claw opened, blooming like an iron flower, exposing the innards of the ship. There, behind a porthole like an eye, lurked one of the aliens.

There was barely any power left in the *Saint Brendan*. The ship was cracked, leaking, burnt. Ben-Ari jiggled the controls, sending a last fleck of power to her viewport, zooming in on the enemy ship, on its arachnid captain.

He stared at her. She recognized him. Yes, it was a *him*—not an *it*, not a dumb bug, but a sentient being. A cruel being. The first marauder she had seen, the one with the red scar and crest of horns, the one who had spoken to her.

The alien stared at her across the border. He smiled—a lurid, drooling, toothy smile, human blood in his jaws.

Ben-Ari hit a button, opening a communication channel.

"Who are you?" she whispered.

His voice emerged through her ship's speakers, guttural, clattering. "Call . . . me . . . Malphas."

"Where are you from?" she said. "What do you want from us? What—"

"Sleep well, Einav Ben-Ari," the alien hissed. "We will meet again. The nightmares are coming."

With that, the claws on the ship closed, hiding him from view. The alien vessel turned and flew away, and the others followed, vanishing into the darkness of the demilitarized zone.

Ben-Ari held the wounded Kemi close.

He knows my name, she thought.

"Captain," Kemi whispered, eyes sunken, barely able to speak. "Divert . . . power from the auxiliary batteries . . . should be enough . . . to return to base."

The lieutenant's eyes closed, and she lost consciousness.

As the *Saint Brendan* limped back toward its port of call, a small colony on a nearby world, the words kept echoing in Ben-Ari's mind.

We will meet again. The nightmares are coming.

CHAPTER TWO

It was a lot tougher to leave the army than join it.

After five years of service in the Human Defense Force, Staff Sergeant Marco Emery stood in the crowded room, barely able to breathe. Hundreds of other soldiers, all anxious for their release papers, crammed together.

"Fucking place is more crowded than a whorehouse on half-off Tuesdays," Addy muttered.

Marco tried to shove her aside. "Addy! For chrissake, your elbow is digging out my kidney."

She shoved back. "I got nowhere to go! Besides, you have two kidneys, you can lose one." Her elbow jabbed back into him.

Marco sighed. She was right. It was a large hall but packed to the gills. The soldiers were squeezed together like scum eggs in a hive. Addy was pushing up against Marco's right side; strangers pressed against the rest of him. Most were sergeants, having risen in the enlisted ranks for five years. Others were younger soldiers, injured in the wars, eligible for early discharge; some were missing limbs, others were missing faces, while some peered with the dead eyes of shell shock. Everyone was sweaty and annoyed. The temperature felt hot enough to kill tardigrades, and Marco had read that the little buggers could withstand nuclear blasts.

"They torture us when we join," Marco muttered, thinking back to RASCOM on his enlistment day five years ago. "And they give us one last good torturing when we leave."

"I'll keep torturing you forever." Addy knuckled his head. "It keeps me busy."

Marco sighed, looking at Addy. She was his foster sister. His sister-in-arms. His best friend. Tall, blond, and bluff, she had been with him during his darkest hours: the night his parents had died, the morning of their enlistment, their battles against the scum, and now here, as they left the military and began a new life. He thought back to the girl he had known on their enlistment, an eighteen-year-old full of piss and vinegar, more bluster than brains. Over the past five years, fighting in the depths of space and training new recruits here on Earth, Addy Linden had grown into a wise, sensitive woman, kinder, softer, and—

She elbowed his ribs—hard. "Shove the fuck over, Poet! You stink like a whore's crotch in July."

Marco groaned. Kind and soft, at least, when they weren't crammed with a thousand soldiers all clamoring for their military discharges.

"It's not me who stinks," Marco said. "It's the soldiers around me, and—"

When the brute in front of him—a towering sergeant of pure muscle and sweat—turned around and scowled, Marco swallowed his words.

Finally, a door at the back of the chamber opened. A single soldier stepped out, clutching his release papers. Another soldier stepped in.

A thousand more kept waiting.

"Hurry up!" shouted a soldier.

"For fuck's sake, I gotta pee, hurry!" roared another sergeant.

After what seemed like ages, the door opened, and another soldier moved forward in line.

Marco groaned. It would be a long day.

As the hours stretched by, as the heat and stink of sweat spun his head, Marco thought back over the past five years. An era was ending. Half a decade in the military—by the end of today, it would be his past.

I joined this army as a terrified teenager, he thought. *And I'm just as terrified to leave.*

Five years. By far, the first had been the hardest. He had joined at the worst of times, at the height of the Second Galactic War, the great struggle against the *scolopendra titaniae*, the aliens most folk just called the scum. After a hellish ten weeks in boot camp, Marco had fought the aliens. On Earth. In the mines of Corpus, a dark moon in the depths of space. And eventually on the aliens' own homeworld, finally killing their emperor. That first year still haunted Marco's nightmares, leaving him drenched in cold sweat most nights.

The following four years had, blessedly, been easier. At first, Marco had joined Addy and Lailani—his two closest friends—in training new recruits. The three corporals had been heroes to the young ones, the trio that had defeated the scum emperor himself. But after Lailani had left the basic training base, accepting a mysterious mission in the Oort Cloud, Marco too had requested a transfer. After a couple months of intense training, he had then spent three years as a computer analyst—querying databases, pulling reports, writing software, and trying to ignore the nightmares and echoing screams. The job had been easy; forgetting had been harder.

And now it all ends, Marco thought. *Now we can be together again. Me. Addy. Lailani.* He looked around him, still hoping—as he had been hoping all day—to see Lailani enter this room, to be discharged with them. All three had enlisted on the same day. All three should be discharged here together. Yet he hadn't seen Lailani in almost a year, not since their last Christmas break, and she had never revealed details of her mission.

You better be waiting for me back at the library, Lailani, he thought. *I miss you.*

In the heat, sweat, and suffocating crowd, the thought of seeing Lailani kept Marco going. He wanted to pull the little Filipina into his arms, to kiss her, to never let her go again. Five years ago, he had fallen madly in love with her. Now that they were leaving the army, he intended to marry her.

Finally, after what seemed like a whole other five years in this room, Marco and Addy reached the doorway at the back. It opened to reveal a lieutenant at a desk, bespectacled and balding despite his youth.

"Lieutenant, what the hell?" shouted a sergeant from the back of the line. "Hurry up!"

The officer looked over the crowd. "Wait your turn, soldier."

"Fuck that!" shouted the sergeant. "Half my cousins outrank you. You think you're somebody because of your butter bars?"

The lieutenant sighed and gave Marco and Addy an apologetic look. He called Marco in first.

"Come, soldier. You're up."

"Good luck, Poet!" Addy whispered, patting his bottom as he entered the room. Marco tried to ignore the snickering soldiers outside as he closed the door.

The lieutenant rifled through his papers. "Staff Sergeant Linden, yes?"

"Emery, sir," he said. "Marco Emery. Linden is that tall blond oaf outside the door."

The lieutenant cleared his throat, placed aside Addy's file, and lifted Marco's instead. He spent a moment looking through the papers, then paused. His eyes widened, and he looked up at Marco.

"You're him," the lieutenant said. "Marco Emery."

Marco nodded. "Yes, you got the right file this time."

The lieutenant's jaw nearly hit the tabletop. "You're Marco Emery."

"Last time I checked," Marco said, "though I'm starting to think I might be Linden after all."

"You fought the scum on Abaddon!" The lieutenant walked around the table, grabbed Marco's hand, and shook it. "You killed the scum emperor himself and blasted the damn buggers back into the Stone Age! Exterminated their entire empire. Damn good work, man."

Marco gently extricated his hand. He wasn't so sure he wanted to be congratulated for exterminating anything, let alone an entire species.

"Thank you, sir," he simply said. "Now, about my discharge papers—"

The lieutenant continued as if he hadn't heard. "If you ask me, we need to nuke *all* the damn aliens back into the Stone Age. The Guramis, the Silvans, the fucking Klurian blobs—blast 'em all. Space bugs, all of them. Only way we'll be safe, you know?" He patted Marco on the shoulder. "A man to my liking, you are! Proud to have met you. My brother fought at Abaddon. Flew a landing craft under heavy fire. I can't wait to tell him I shook your hand."

Marco cleared his throat, wishing the floor would swallow him. "The papers, sir?"

The lieutenant nodded. "Of course, of course." He stamped a few papers, gave Marco a quick salute—probably the only time a lieutenant had ever saluted a sergeant—then a pat on the shoulder.

And with that, Staff Sergeant Marco Emery became Marco Emery, civilian. With that, one life ended. With that, another life began.

He stepped out of the room. Addy was waiting there, a huge grin on her face.

"Move it, civilian," she said.

Marco looked at her. A tall warrior in olive fatigues. The woman who had fought with him against the alien invasion. Who had been fighting at his side since they had been eleven, since the scum had killed his mother and both her parents. A best friend. A soldier.

But can we ever go back? Marco thought. *Can we ever be who we were?*

"Hurry up!" shouted a soldier behind them.

With an elbow to Marco's ribs, Addy entered the room and closed the door.

Marco walked away slowly, feeling empty, feeling confused, not sure who he was now, who he could become, whether his old life—his childhood, his youth—still awaited him.

When Addy emerged from the lieutenant's office, she pulled Marco into a storage room on the base. They removed their uniforms and stuffed them into their duffel bags. Addy pulled on denim shorts and a Maple Leafs hockey jersey. Marco pulled on corduroy pants and a T-shirt featuring Einstein sticking out his tongue.

They stared at each other. For a moment, they were silent.

Then they burst out laughing.

"You look like a right nerd!" Addy said.

Marco rolled his eyes. "You look like a hockey hooligan."

"Good! I *am* a hockey hooligan!" She grabbed his arms. "Poet. It's over, Poet. It's over."

And suddenly she was crying. And Marco was crying too. And they embraced, tears falling, and for long moments they could say nothing.

"It's over," he finally whispered, holding her close. His best friend. His Addy.

She pulled back from him, sniffling, and mussed his hair.

"Stop being a crybaby, Poet. Come on." She took his hand in hers. "Let's go home."

They stepped out of the base. They wore civilian clothes. They held no weapons. A highway stretched before them through the desert, leading to a dusty horizon and beyond it the unknown.

* * * * *

They hitchhiked.

They hitchhiked across the desert, the sun beating down on them.

The HDF didn't pay its soldiers. They had no money. All they had were their thumbs.

They wore no more uniforms, held no more guns, and those drivers who often braked for soldiers roared by, covering them with clouds of dust. Finally a mustached old man stopped his truck, and Marco and Addy climbed into the back and sat among migrant workers. They rattled down the highway between the rocky plains and dunes toward yellow mountains.

They wandered through a strange city in a strange land, a place with no trees, where raw concrete buildings rose around them, where camels and donkeys fled from fighter jets that flew low in the sky. When a boy tried to mug them, Addy tossed a stone at him, and he fled. They bought street meat. They drank from a tap they found by a trough. They were on Earth but they were still so far from home.

They elbowed their way through a crowded airport, the ceiling fans doing little to alleviate the heat. When a few soldiers walked by, robed locals saluted them, and somebody cried out a blessing in a foreign tongue. Marco gazed at the soldiers walking by. To the crowds, they were warriors, defenders of the Earth. But Marco saw young boys and girls. Mere privates. Teenagers. Afraid. He looked away, and even Addy lost her smile and remained solemn for long moments.

They flew.

They flew over the desert, sea, and forest. They flew over the frozen wilderness of Greenland, heading home.

They did not fly in a suborbital carrier, a military rocket that could launch into Earth's orbit, then land anywhere on Earth within half an hour. They were no longer soldiers. They flew in a civilian atmospheric jet, its fuselage crammed with five hundred passengers. Civilians. Weary souls. Veterans.

Addy sat beside Marco, her knees pulled to her chest, her head against his shoulder. She was deep in slumber, snoring and drooling on him. Somehow, even in sleep, her elbow managed to keep jabbing his ribs.

Marco looked at her for a moment, then gazed out the window. The snowy land sprawled below, all piny mountains and sheets of snow and icy rivers. The wilderness of the world.

The mountains gave way to water, then land again, and he saw Toronto below.

The city's glory days were gone. Many of the old skyscrapers had fallen in the wars. Many people had died here. But today the city bustled with new life, home to three million people, a hive of highways and apartment blocks and factories pumping out smoke. City of metal, concrete, wood, and snow. City of memories. Of books. Of family. Home.

It was unusually cold for early November; snow was already falling. Marco and Addy stood on the wet roadside, thumbs raised. The cars roared by, splashing them with sludge, and the wind shrieked, lashing them with sleet. They shivered. They had no jackets, no money. The military had given them their plane tickets; the rest was down to hitchhiking.

"Fuck this shit," Addy said, breath frosting. "I preferred the desert."

Marco's teeth chattered. "Soon we'll be home in the library. Soon we'll sit with Dad by the fireplace, drinking hot cocoa."

Addy spat. Her spit froze. "Fuck that, I'm having a beer."

And maybe Lailani will be waiting for us, Marco thought, and that thought warmed him in the cold.

He hadn't seen Lailani in eleven months. He had barely seen her at all during the past three years, ever since she had accepted a secret mission in the Oort Cloud, two light-years away from Earth. He still thought about her every day. As he lay in bed at night, he imagined her by his side. He ached to hold her, to kiss her, to stroke her black hair, to laugh at the silly faces she made, to read her his short stories, to simply be happy with her. To feel right. He always felt right with Lailani in his arms.

Be here, he thought. *Be here, Lailani.*

A car finally stopped on the roadside, and the driver rolled down the window.

"Need a ride?" the young man asked.

Addy stepped toward the back door. "Thanks, man. We just got discharged. First day as civvies. We—"

"Fucking fascists!" The man spat out the window and drove off, spraying Marco and Addy with mud.

"Yeah, well, electric cars are for pussies!" Addy shouted after him, waving her fist.

Marco sighed and wiped sludge off him. "Actually, Addy, electric cars are responsible and protect the environment, and—"

"Don't make me punch you."

Finally another driver pulled over, and they crammed into the back of a van between carpet cleaning equipment.

An hour later, they hopped out outside the library.

After years of war and want, they were home.

Not for a Christmas visit. Not for just a few days of anxious silence before returning to the military. They were home, back at the library, forever.

Yearning to see his father, have a hot shower, and mostly sleep, Marco rushed toward the library door.

It was padlocked.

Marco froze and frowned.

"What the hell is this?" Addy said, yanking the chains around the door.

The wind moaned, spraying them with snow. Marco's heart sank. A piece of paper had been plastered to the door, soggy with snow. He could just make out a few of the words.

"It's closed," he said, throat tight. "They're tearing it down. They're building a condo tower here instead."

"What the fuck?" Addy tore the paper off the wall, stared at it, then ripped it to shreds. "Fuck this shit!" She tossed the shreds of paper into the wind, then pounded on the door. "Carl! Carl, open up, damn it! You in there?"

"Dad!" Marco shouted, but no reply came from within.

"Fuck, I'm pissed off, I haven't showered in three days, and I could eat a horse," Addy said.

"In short, your usual state," Marco said, dodging her punch.

They trudged through snow toward a window, brushed aside the ice, and peered inside. The library was dark, and when they stepped back and gazed toward the apartment above, they saw no light there either. Carl Emery, it seemed, no longer lived here.

"Why didn't Dad write me?" Marco said. The kindly librarian used to send Marco's base a letter every couple weeks, but Marco hadn't received any communication for over a month now, no word of the library closing.

Addy and Marco hurried into the convenience store across the street, the place where they had often bought sweets and rented movies during their youth. The same shopkeep still manned the cash register, a graying Korean man who, it seemed, stood at his post day and night, year after year, more dedicated than any guard in the HDF.

"Myung," Marco said, shivering. "How are you?"

The shopkeep looked up from his game of sudoku. "Marky! You're home. Welcome home. How goes bug killing business?"

Marco cringed inwardly. He had spent the past three years in the military at a desk, not killing space bugs, and preferred being remembered for his slick database queries than the number of aliens he had killed. But right now, he was too cold, hungry, and worried to explain any of that.

"Myung, what happened to the library? To my father?" The convenience store was warm, but suddenly Marco was shivering more than ever. "I just got back."

"And we're starving," Addy said. "Mind if I steal this bag of Hickory Chips? I'll pay you back later." She began to munch.

Myung's eyes darkened, and he placed down his sudoku book. "Oh, Marky . . . They never told you, did they? They just sent you back like this?"

Marco stepped closer and leaned over the counter. "Myung. Tell me."

The wind rattled the windows and the fluorescent lights flickered. Marco and Addy stood silently for long moments, listening to Myung speak of the government cutting funding to libraries, then selling the land to developers, of Carl Emery so consumed with stress that his heart failed. Of the old librarian recovering from his heart attack, only to suffer a stroke, to finally pass away three weeks later from a second heart attack in a hospital room. To be buried quietly, only two old friends in attendance.

"They never told us," Addy whispered. "Why didn't those sons of bitches in the army tell us? Why—"

"Because we were bouncing from base to base," Marco said softly. "Because of bureaucracy. And it doesn't matter to them. Because he's gone. He's gone, Addy. And we never got to say goodbye."

He lowered his head, and for the second day in a row, he shed tears.

"Myung," Addy said, voice hoarse. "Before Carl died, he was taking care of our dog. Sergeant Stumpy. Did . . ."

"I took the dog in myself," Myung said. "I fed him, walked him every day. But he grew sick. He passed away two weeks after

Carl. Vet said it was just old age, but I know it was a broken heart."

Marco and Addy left the shop, silent.

They climbed the escape ladder in the alleyway, and Marco jiggered open the window to their apartment above the library. Once this small home had been full of light, of comfort, of love. Today it was cold, no heat in the vents, no power in the outlets, no water in the taps, no father in his rumpled vest sitting in his armchair, rising to greet them, hugging them close.

"We'll light a fire," Addy said.

She turned toward the fireplace, added a log, and worked in silence for long moments, but the fire wouldn't start. She cursed, slammed the log down, and stood still, shoulders tense, fists tightened. When Marco approached, he saw that she was crying.

"Addy—" he began.

"It's not fair," she said. "Why did he have to die? Just as we were getting out. Why do they just toss us out like this? Like we're trash. Like we didn't fight the scum. Like we didn't land on their planet light-years away. Like we didn't go underground and kill the bugs. Like we're not scarred. Like we're not hurt. Like we don't wake up with nightmares every night. Like we're old uniforms, just thrown away, too old for use." Her tears rolled. "What are we going to do, Poet?"

Marco wiped his eyes. "First, start this fire. Then sleep. Then figure things out tomorrow."

He knelt by the logs and got the fire started, earning an elbow from Addy.

"I warmed up the logs," she said. "Show-off." Her voice softened. "Marco, I'm sorry for your dad. Our dad. He was like a father to me too." She held his hand. "I love you."

They carried their mattresses from their bedrooms into the living room, laid them by the hearth, and lay down. Marco had not slept in thirty-something hours, but no sleep found him. In the fireplace, he kept seeing the flames of burning Abaddon, homeworld of the scum. In the shadows, he kept seeing the infested mines of Corpus. As the logs crackled, he kept hearing the clattering scum claws, and when a police siren sounded outside, Marco remembered the screams of his dying friends.

The thought struck him: *I'm an orphan.*

A shadow shifted beside him, and Marco tensed, instinctively reaching under his pillow for his gun, forgetting that he was no longer armed, and images of the scum flashed before him. But it was only Addy. She wriggled off her mattress and onto his.

"Make room," she mumbled, eyes closed, and nestled against him. Soon she was snoring and drooling on him again. And once more, her elbow was poking him.

Marco sighed and wrapped his arms around her. With Addy against him, he finally slept. But in his dreams, he was back in the mines of Corpus, riding the rusted mine carts, lost in darkness, traveling for hours, seeking a way out.

CHAPTER THREE

Ben-Ari stood in the Dome, the hub of humanity's might in the darkness, facing the most powerful man in space.

They hadn't even given her time to change her bloody uniform.

"Sir!" She pressed her heels together and saluted. "Captain Einav Ben-Ari, reporting for duty as requested, sir."

Blood trickled down her arm, through a tear in her suit, and onto the carpet.

Admiral Komagata stood ahead, his back to her. He did not turn around. He stared out into the darkness.

Since the invasion over four years ago, Ben-Ari had not been invited here to the Dome, to the command center of Nightwall. The transparent bubble perched like a dewdrop atop Space Station One, a massive military base that orbited a dark, starless planet. Standing here, Ben-Ari had a 360 degree view of space. If she turned around, she would face Sol, Earth's star, shining too dimly to see with the naked eye. Ahead of her shone the star Achernar, only a light-year away—the end of the Human Commonwealth and the beginning of the demilitarized zone where the scum had once reigned.

A dozen warships idled outside Space Station One, silvery vessels large enough to transport marine battalions to battles on distant worlds. A squadron of Firebirds, single-pilot starfighters, was flying on patrol, zipping between the larger starships. A few cargo craft were rising and descending, ferrying supplies between the starships and the military bases that covered the planet like barnacles. Nightwall—the center of Space Territorial Command. The great guardian of Earth's might in the darkness of space. Defending the border of humanity's empire.

And it's a shell of what it once was, Ben-Ari thought, still holding her salute.

She remembered serving here during the Second Galactic War. Back then, thousands of warships had been stationed here, not a mere dozen. Millions of troops had mustered here to fight the scum, not a few thousand. Thousands of Firebirds had circled the dark planet, not a handful of squadrons. Ten space stations had orbited the planet, full of humanity's best scientists and engineers and generals, not just Space Station One. But that had been a different time, under different leadership. That had been before millions of soldiers had died in the war. Before Earth had been left bankrupt, reeling from destruction, struggling to rebuild and rise again from the ruins.

We won the war, Ben-Ari thought. *We beat the scum. But we'll pay for that victory for the rest of our lives. So will our children.*

Finally Admiral Hiroki Komagata turned toward her. He was a small man, but his face was stone. His eyes were hard, thick grooves framed his mouth, and his hair was still jet black despite his age. Service ribbons from the Second Galactic War bedecked his chest, and two golden phoenixes spread wings on each of his shoulders. Born in Japan sixty years ago, Komagata had risen through the ranks despite his lack of family influence in the HDF. He was the first intelligence officer who had risen to lead Space Territorial Command, ending a long line of famous, cocky pilots.

The previous admiral—the famous Evan Bryan—had filled the Dome with memorabilia of the First Galactic War: his first rifle in a glass case, a shard from the first scum ship he had shot down, and the dog tags of fallen comrades. The new admiral had removed those mementos. Hiroki Komagata had filled the Dome with his own artifacts. A bonsai tree coiled on a table. An ancient katana, its hilt wrapped with blue silk, stood on a stand. An original Hokusai *ukiyo-e* painting, showing Mount Fuji and cherry blossoms, hovered over a pillar: a priceless work of art.

Admiral Komagata admires art as much as he admires war, Ben-Ari thought. *Perhaps that's a quality every good admiral needs.*

Ben-Ari's arm was hurting by the time Komagata returned her salute. Gratefully, she lowered her arm.

He stared at her, silent. Ben-Ari was of average height for a woman, and he stood no taller, but his eyes were blades. He had none of Admiral Bryan's charm, but—this Ben-Ari dared to hope—more integrity.

"Sir," she said, breaking the awkward silence. "I would like to attend the infirmary. To check on my lieutenant. To—"

"She was my daughter, you know." Finally he spoke. "The young soldier under your command. The soldier who died in the demilitarized zone."

Ben-Ari opened her mouth, closed it. Her head spun.

"Private Komagata?" she whispered. "I . . . The surname is common, I never . . ."

"She never wanted anyone to know," said Admiral Komagata, and now a flicker of pain filled those hard, cold eyes of his. "She wanted to succeed on her own merit, not her family name. I offered to send her to the best military academies, and she refused, preferring to join the enlisted." He took a step closer to Ben-Ari, and his eyes reddened. "My eldest daughter is dying of cancer. Now I've lost my youngest child to war. Tell me, Captain. Why do you stand here before me while my daughter never came home?"

"Sir." She lowered her head. "I'm deeply sorry for your loss. I don't know how to offer proper condolences, how—"

"Tell me how she died and how you and your lieutenant lived, Captain." And now fury trembled in his voice.

"We encountered something, sir." Ben-Ari looked up and met his eyes. "A terror in the darkness. Creatures. Monsters. Alien life. There were other humans there. Prisoners. A prison colony in the demilitarized zone. We tried to help, but the creatures were everywhere. They killed my squad. They—"

"Captain, you are incorrect," said Admiral Komagata. "What actually happened is that the *Saint Brendan* crash landed on the planet, where you found a group of outlaws who had starved to death. You and your lieutenant managed to repair the ship and fly back to Nightwall, though your squad did not survive the crash."

Ben-Ari gasped. "Sir! The alien lifeforms I encountered are something new. Something powerful. A threat to humanity. We cannot cover this up, we—"

"Captain, are you familiar with the story of Edwin Hubble?"

She stiffened. "Yes, sir, but—"

"He is considered by many to be the greatest cosmologist. The man who let us gaze into the darkness. Years after his death, the Hubble telescope, named in his honor, discovered countless galaxies beyond our own. For the first time, we realized the true enormity of the universe." Admiral Komagata walked toward the transparent dome that encircled his office. He stared out into space. The spiral arm of the Milky Way spread before him. "To this day, centuries since Hubble's death, we still cannot grasp the sheer size of the cosmos."

"It's a big one, sir," Ben-Ari said.

He continued as if he hadn't heard. "We still don't know how many alien species exist in our own galaxy, let alone the cosmos. Even with all our might, all our knowledge, we've explored only a corner of this single spiral arm. According to our estimates, there are ten thousand intelligent, space-faring civilizations in the Milky Way. Some of them are millions of years older than us, have moved beyond physical bodies, and have become beings of pure consciousness not unlike gods. Others are just starting their journey, just reaching out to their local moons. And some—hundreds of them, maybe thousands—are where we are now. Exploring the stars. Seeking to grasp a piece of power. To build empires." He reached toward space and clenched his fist, as if he could grab the stars. "The *scolopendra titaniae* have left a power vacuum, and space hates a vacuum. Across the galaxy, creatures stir."

"Sir, with all due respect, these creatures have done more than *stir.*" Ben-Ari came to stand beside him, gazing with him at Achernar, the last human star. "They are a danger we must face."

She looked at him, and she was surprised to see tears on his cheeks.

"Captain, we cannot afford another war. We cannot afford more deaths." Komagata turned toward her, and suddenly all the fury was gone from his eyes, replaced with grief. "I have three more children serving in the military. I cannot lose them too."

"Then we must strike, sir," she said. "We must defeat this menace before it can strike us. We—"

"We are still rebuilding our strength, Captain. The military is a shadow of what it once was. The days of massive fleets, of thousands of human starships flying together, are over. Too many have been decommissioned to cover the costs of rebuilding our ravaged planet. No. We will not fight again. We will not panic the troops. We will not be warmongers. We will remain as we are, watching the darkness. Aware of the danger. But keeping it in the darkness."

"And if the marauders muster for war while we wait, sir?" she said.

And now she saw something new in his eyes. Not just grief.

Fear.

"Ben-Ari, what waits out there . . . You cannot imagine its might. Its cruelty. There are terrors in the darkness that would freeze your blood. I know." He gazed out into space, and his voice dropped to a whisper. "I know . . ." He inhaled deeply and squared his shoulders. "What happened on your mission, Captain, and the creatures you encountered—those are highly classified. Should you or your lieutenant ever speak of them again, you know what that would entail."

Ben-Ari knew. Leaking classified information was a good way of skipping prison entirely and leaping right to the firing squad.

She wanted to argue. She wanted to rail against him. She wanted to demand to reveal this information to the public. To put pressure on politicians. To gain more funding. To build more starships. To do *something*, not just sit here, not just cover this up.

But the admiral dismissed her.

Ben-Ari left the Dome, weary and cold, the alien's warning echoing in her mind. *The nightmares are coming.*

CHAPTER FOUR

Marco stood in the cemetery, gazing down at his father's grave. There was no tombstone, just a small marker. There was no epitaph, just a simple name and date. There were no words on Marco's lips, just silence, just despair.

For a long time, he simply stared, silent. He said goodbye.

Finally he turned around. Addy stood there, a step away. Trees rose around them, draped with ice and snow. For so many years, serving in the desert overseas, Marco had barely seen trees, had forgotten their beauty.

"It's a beautiful place," he said. "I used to come here with Kemi. We'd walk along the paths. There are trees of many kinds here, brought from across Ontario, and their leaves all rustle in the spring. There were hawks and foxes here then, and flowers around the fountains, and children played."

"Strange place to play," Addy said. "Strange place to walk with your girl. Gives me a bit of the creeps, to be honest."

"Not many green places left in the world," Marco said. "Here is one. Back then, I never saw cemeteries as sad places. I thought they were serene places for the dead to rest, for their families to find solace. In many ways, I preferred the silent company of the dead over the loud, bustling crowds of the living.

But it all seems different now. This cemetery. This city. Everything. Me."

"I'm the same old Addy, at least."

He looked at her. "No you're not. None of us are the same." He looked at the snowy tombstones around them. "We left too many behind. All of us who were out there, who came home—we left something behind too."

Addy lowered her head. "I know."

He thought about his fallen friends. About Caveman, who had died on the tarmac at Fort Djemila in North Africa. About Beast, Elvis, Corporal Diaz, Sergeant Singh, his friends who had fallen in the mines of Corpus in the depths of space. About millions who had fallen in the great battle for Abaddon, homeworld of the scum.

"How was I any different?" he said softly. "We were all just kids. Just dumb eighteen-year-olds. I wasn't any stronger or braver than them. I was weaker." His eyes dampened. "Beast was a hero, holding back the scum to let us escape. Diaz and Singh always charged right into battle. I always stayed behind, I never sacrificed my safety, and now they're dead, and—"

Addy grabbed his arms, fingers tight, painful. She glared at him. "Enough, Marco. We were all scared, and we were all stupid, and we were all heroes. We were lucky, you and I. That's all. Just lucky. A claw might have thrust just a few centimeters in another direction, and it would be my body left in space. And Elvis, or Beast, or any one of the others would be here now. Just fucking bad luck for them." She wiped her eyes. "We were lucky, so let's not forget that. Let's do something with this luck."

"Like what, Addy?" His voice was weak. "What do we do now?"

"Get a bite to eat," Addy said. "I know we don't have much money. Just whatever cash we found in the apartment. But I say we spend it on a plate of pancakes the size of my ass."

"With bacon," Marco said.

"And fried eggs." Addy nodded. "And lots of maple syrup. That's not bad, right?" She wiped away a last tear. "That's something worth being lucky for."

They headed through the cemetery back toward Yonge Street, the city's main thoroughfare. The foreclosed library was only a twenty-minute walk away. They still had a few days—according to the notice outside, at least—before it was torn down.

Before we need a backup plan, Marco thought.

They stepped between the last tombstones and found the street blocked.

Hundreds of people, maybe thousands, were marching down Yonge Street.

"No more war!" they chanted, waving signs. "No more war!"

Marco and Addy stood at the cemetery gates, staring.

"What the hell?" Addy said.

Marco shrugged. "It's a nice sentiment."

Countless cardboard signs rose from the crowd. Marco read a few of them.

Bring our boys home!

Close down the colonies!

End humanity's war of aggression!

Tear down the human empire!

Alien killers to prison!

No more genocide!

As the protesters marched, they kept shouting, faces red, undaunted by the cold. One man, young and spindly, walked at their lead. His brown hair and beard flowed, and he wore round spectacles.

"It's like John Lennon bred with a stick insect," Addy muttered, looking at the wiry man.

"That's not very nice," Marco said.

"I'm not nice," Addy said.

The gangling man spoke through a megaphone. "We will dismantle Earth's violent empire in space! We will close every last colony and withdraw every last human from alien worlds. Never more will human aggression victimize innocent alien lifeforms! Every soldier who killed an alien will be imprisoned. No mercy for alien killers!"

The crowd cheered. The signs rose higher. Drums beat and faces twisted in rage.

"This is bullshit!" Addy said. "Innocent alien lifeforms? The scum—victims? Did these people forget that the scum destroyed our cities, murdered billions of us before we fought back?"

Marco placed a hand on her shoulder; she looked ready to charge into the crowd and swing punches.

"Forget it, Addy. They mean well. They want peace. That's a worthy cause."

"I wanted peace too." Addy fumed. "I wanted peace when we were stuck in the goddamn mines in Corpus. I wanted peace when thousands were dying around us in Abaddon. But aliens were killing us, so I picked up my gun instead of a goddamn cardboard sign, and—"

"Addy, pancakes, remember?" Marco said. "Pancakes the size of your ass, and that's a sizable meal."

She growled at him. "Watch it, or your ass will meet my foot." But some anger left her eyes.

They walked along the sidewalk, careful to avoid rubbing elbows with the protesters marching down the road.

"No more humans in space!" a young woman shouted.

"Stop alien killers!" shouted another protester.

"Stop human aggression against innocent alien life!"

Addy's face reddened, her fists tightened, and she seemed ready to leap into the crowd. Marco held her waist, guiding her forward, whispering "pancakes" over and over into her ear to calm her.

They had almost reached their intersection when a protester stared at them. She was a topless woman with curly hair, and letters were painted onto her breasts, spelling out, "Kill Soldiers." She frowned at Marco and Addy, and then her eyes widened, and she pointed.

"It's them!" she cried. "Marco Emery! Addy Linden! The war criminals who murdered the alien king!"

Other protesters turned toward them. The crowd erupted in boos.

"Nazis!" somebody shouted.

"How would you feel if somebody butchered your families?" a protester called out, tears in his eyes.

"They *did*!" Addy said. "The scum did. That's why we fought them!"

"Stop using slurs!" somebody cried in the crowd. "Xenophobes!"

The crowd began to pelt them with coffee cups, with empty wrappers, with snow, with stones.

This time Marco couldn't stop her. Addy tore free from his grip and leaped toward the crowd, fists flying.

"Addy, no!" He tried to grab her. "It's not worth it. Back, Addy!"

Somebody shoved her. Addy shoved back, and the man fell. The crowd mobbed them.

"Call the cops!" somebody shouted. "Arrest them! Arrest the fascists!"

"You fucking scum-loving pieces of—" Addy began.

"Addy!" Marco managed to grab her waist and pull her back. She bled from her lip. "Come on. Let's go. They're just kids. They mean well. Let's go eat, Addy."

The cries of fury followed them.

"Arrest the war criminals!"

"Don't let them get away!"

"Put them on trial for war crimes!"

Hands reached out to grab Marco and Addy, and people were dialing the cops, when a voice rang out from a megaphone.

"Let them go, friends!" It was the tall man with long brown hair, standing at the head of the protest. "They're not our enemies. They were only pawns in the war. Our enemies are the puppet masters. The corporations. The corrupt politicians. The greedy CEOs who profited from the war. Let these two poor souls go. They too suffered at the hands of the warmongers, turned into weapons of war. Do not hate them. Pity them."

"I don't need your goddamn pity!" Addy shouted. As Marco kept dragging her away, she flipped off the crowd, spat at them, and cursed all the way toward the pancake house.

Soon they were sitting in the warm restaurant, pancakes piled up before them. Addy ate sullenly, muttering between bites, and Marco had lost his appetite and picked at his food. Even the bacon, those little strips of paradise, tasted stale today.

"Can you believe them?" Addy said. "Defending the scum? We were there, fighting, seeing our friends killed, and—"

"Addy, forget it." Marco poured more maple syrup onto his pancakes, hoping to add some flavor. His tongue felt lifeless, everything bland. "Right now we have other things to worry about. We only have a few days until they tear down the library and begin raising that condo building. What do we do?"

"March into city hall and punch the mayor's big fat face," Addy said.

"Not every problem can be solved with violence."

"That's how I solve things!" Addy said.

"Then you'll only prove those protesters right." Marco finally pushed his plate aside, giving up on his appetite. "You want my pancakes?"

Addy added his meal to hers. She spoke between mouthfuls. "What we need is Lailani. We always worked best as a trio. The Three Musketeers. Well, we were more like the Three Stooges most of the time, but we still got shit done. She'd think of something. Where the hell is she?"

"She needs more time," Marco said. "Last I heard, she was stationed in the Oort Cloud. That's a couple light-years away. It might take her a few days, maybe even weeks, to get back from there, depending on what starship she hitches a ride on. I just hope she has a home waiting when she arrives. The library is her home now, as much as ours."

Addy's eyes lit up. "Hey, Poet. Since we lived in the apartment over the library, once they build that condo tower, does that mean we get a free condo?" She gasped. "The penthouse? Because we owned that land, right?"

Marco loved Addy. Truly he did. But sometimes he wondered if she was more stomach than brains.

"Sorry, Ads." He poured another sugar packet into his coffee. "My dad only rented the apartment. Our family never owned land."

Addy groaned. "Nor mine. My fucking dad, man. In and out of prison. Drunk driving. Drugs. Fucker. Land? He didn't even own the dirt beneath his fingernails. I loved him, but goddamn, he and my mom—they left me with nothing but a hockey stick, big hips, and probably some side effects of fetal alcohol syndrome I'll find out about in a few years."

"Don't forget the big nose," Marco said.

Addy raised her fist. "When I'm done with you, your nose will be flatter than these pancakes."

Marco pulled bills out from his pocket. It felt strange, paying with money he had found in the coffee tin on the top shelf at home—his father's money. But he imagined that dear old Carl Emery would've wanted his son and foster daughter to enjoy this meal.

"He always made us pancakes on Sunday mornings," Marco said. "Do you remember?"

Addy's face softened, and she lowered her fist. "I remember. He used to add blueberries and those little peanut butter drops, like chocolate chips but made out of peanut butter. I loved those."

"Remember when we were in sixth grade, and we woke up early one morning, and we tried to make pancakes, and we set off the fire alarm?"

Addy laughed. "They were still good, once we scraped off the burnt parts. Damn alarm was always too sensitive."

Marco found himself laughing too. "Dad thought it was a scum attack. He put on his gas mask and everything."

"With the amount of smoke in the apartment, not a bad thing!" She was laughing so hard now her eyes watered. "Damn, I miss the old man. I loved him."

"I did too," Marco said quietly.

"Hey, Poet, remember that time at boot camp when Elvis stole a bunch of packets of jam, then stuffed them into his boots to stop the blistering?"

"I thought it was slices of Spam," Marco said.

"Mmm, Spam." Addy licked her lips. "I love it. I wish they served Spam here."

Marco groaned. "I never want to taste it again."

"I have my lucky can back in the apartment," Addy said. "Stole it from boot camp. Carried it with me for five years in the army. Never going to eat it, though. That sucker is gonna be my army souvenir."

Marco had his own souvenir at home—a severed scum claw. He thought that Addy's memento from the war was far more pleasant.

"I miss it sometimes," Marco said. "Boot camp. I hated it when we were there. I was miserable. I thought it was the worst time of my life. But now I look back on it fondly. It was difficult but we had no responsibilities. Other people looked after us, taught us, fed us, sheltered us. Our friends were still alive. I miss it. Just hanging out at the mess, with Elvis, Lailani, Caveman, all the others. I miss Ben-Ari. I'd give up this bacon and pancakes and eat Spam again if we could be back there, together again, all of us."

Addy nodded, head lowered. "Me too."

Marco stood up. "Come on, Ads. We fought the bloody scum. We can face city hall. Let's go raise some hell."

She pounded the tabletop. "That's more like it. Punching time!" She leaped to her feet. "We're going to punch the fuck out of them!"

Several families turned to stare. Marco winced and shushed Addy before the waitress could toss them out.

An hour later, they found themselves stuck in a line as long and exhausting as anything in the military.

Hundreds of people filled the waiting room in city hall, covering the seats, standing in the aisles, lining up in the corridors. There were people in business suits, mothers with crying children, farmers wearing overalls and straw hats, and Marco could swear he even saw a chicken at one point. He and Addy took a number, but given that their number was in the hundreds, and the clerk had just called the eighth person of the day, it wasn't looking good.

"I don't even know what we'll tell them," Marco said. "That we're war heroes, so please fund public libraries?"

Addy grumbled, shifting her weight from foot to foot. There were no chairs left. "I'll grab the clerk by the collar and won't release her until we get our home back."

The hours stretched by. The room got more and more crowded. Finally, at 5:00 PM, the clerk shuffled away from her desk.

"Hey, we haven't talked to anyone yet!" Addy cried, and others in the crowd moaned in protest.

"Come earlier tomorrow!" the clerk said. "We open at 6:00 AM."

"Can we keep our number?" Marco called after her, but the clerk left the room, followed by a chorus of moans and complaints.

Next morning, Marco and Addy arrived at five in the morning, only to find hundreds of people already cramming the halls.

"Been coming here for three days," a heavyset woman told them. "Finally camped overnight in the hallway. Damn city turned my gas off a week ago, winter and snow and all. Ever since the last big war, everything breaks, and there's no money to fix it." She hefted the child she held. "At least coming here keeps the little one warm."

"They should hire more clerks," Marco said.

"No money," replied the woman. "War took everything we had."

Marco thought about his time in the war, flying in a fleet of starships between the stars. The invasion of Abaddon had been humanity's most expensive endeavor, more than reaching the moon, more than building the pyramids, probably more than all of World War Two. A hundred thousand ships had carried millions of soldiers across hundreds of light-years to defeat the scum on their planet. Earth won. Earth was left bankrupt.

It was something we had to do, Marco told himself. *The scum attacked us. We had to fight back.*

Yet more and more, those words seemed hollow. He remembered the corruption of Admiral Bryan, a man consumed with vengeance for the scum, leading the fleet on a personal vendetta. He remembered seeing the Chrysopoeia Corporation logo on every weapon and starship in the fleet. He considered the trillions of dollars its shareholders must have earned from the war. He thought of the words the man with the megaphone had spoken—calling him a pawn.

I never wanted to be part of any of this, Marco thought. *I never wanted to be hero nor pawn. I just wanted to stay in my library and write.*

So why did such guilt fill him?

Fifteen minutes before closing time, their number was finally called. They sat before the clerk—a stocky woman with bags under her eyes, a cold sore, and a frown.

"Ma'am, we recently found that our home is foreclosed, that it'll be torn down," Marco began. "We'd like to speak to somebody who—"

"Fill out this form." The clerk yawned and shoved a piece of paper his way. "You'll receive a reply within six to eight weeks."

Addy growled, and Marco had to hold her back.

"Ma'am," he said, "our home will be torn down in *a few days*. There must have been some mistake. It's a library, and—"

"City Council has voted unanimously to cut funding to all public libraries, parks, preschools, and drug rehabilitation centers." The clerk seemed to be reciting the words, stifling another yawn. "If you wish to register a complaint, please fill out a Schedule 15b." She shoved another paper their way. "You'll receive a reply within—"

"Six to eight weeks?" Marco offered.

"See? You figured it all out." The clerk rose to her feet. "Closing time."

"We didn't even fill out the form yet!" Addy said.

"Is there anywhere we can mail it to?" Marco called after the clerk, but he had barely completed his sentence before she left the room, again to a chorus of groans from the crowd that still waited.

He filled out the form and left it on the clerk's desk.

"I bet she's got a black hole back there somewhere," Addy said, "where all these forms go."

"That or some paper-eating alien," Marco said. He rubbed his temple. "This was a waste of time. Let's go home. While we still have a home."

They stepped outside into the cold, and Marco winced in sudden pain. His war wounds had been throbbing lately. He had spent most of his service in the deserts of North Africa and the Levant, and the heat had dulled the pain. Here in Canada, the snowy winds stabbed his old wounds like fresh scum claws. He saw Addy tighten her jaw, but she otherwise gave no sign of her own pain. Both still carried the scars of battle, even years after the war. A chunk the size of an avocado pit was missing from Marco's thigh where a claw had stabbed him, and skin grafts covered one of his arms, still rough to the touch. Addy's limbs and torso bore long, thin scars too. Both still complained of ringing in their ears, and Marco had trouble hearing from his right ear. But neither had lost organs or limbs. They were the lucky ones. But both had taken their share of ugly flesh wounds that still hurt if so much as a bedside fan blew on them.

But I'd take a hundred more scars over the nightmares I still have every night, he thought. He wasn't looking forward to tonight. He knew that he would be there again. Lost in the scum hives, racing through the darkness, seeking a way out.

These past few nights, he had dreamed of the fleshy bundle they had found on Corpus. The round, living creature wrapped in skin. The thing that had grown his face. Back in the mines, Addy had melted the abomination in a cauldron. But in his dreams, the creature emerged from the molten metal, dripping, crawling toward him, begging for the pain to stop. Marco's own face melted upon it. He had seen many horrors on Corpus. Humans and scum stitched together. Hybrids built in alien labs. Thousands of monsters in the dark. But it was that ball of flesh with his face that haunted Marco the most.

He and Addy walked home through the snow, bundled up in their old jackets from high school. Marco remembered walking down this very street twelve years ago, fighting the snow, on the night his mother had died, on the night Addy had come into his life. He had carried a gas mask then. He had carried a gas mask for most of his life. It still felt strange to walk here without one. Without a gun. Without a helmet. He felt naked, exposed.

The scum are defeated, he told himself. *The war is over. We're safe now. We're safe.*

Yet still, when a motorcycle roared by, Marco started and nearly dived for cover. Still he kept reaching for his rifle, a phantom limb.

They were a block away from their library when they heard the protests again.

"No more war!"

"War criminals to trial!"

"Justice for aliens!"

Marco and Addy rounded the corner and saw them there.

"Great," Marco muttered. "Our friends are back."

A crowd of hundreds surrounded the library, blocking any passage. There would be no reaching the fire escape Marco and Addy had been using to access the apartment above the library. The signs rose and news reporters were filming. A woman—the same one who had marched topless yesterday, though today she wore a jacket—stood on a platform, speaking into a megaphone.

"We demand that the war criminals Marco Emery and Addy Linden stand trial!" Cheers erupted in the crowd. "No mercy for war criminals! Humans have no business in space. We antagonized the aliens. We called them scum. We invaded their territory." The protester's voice cracked with passion. "Can we blame them for lashing back, for defending themselves? And finally Emery and Linden toppled their civilization and killed their queen!" Tears flowed down the protester's cheeks. "The aliens can never recover from such genocide. Emery and Linden must face justice!"

"Lock them up!" somebody called in the crowd. "Lock them up!"

The chant gained more voices. "Lock them up! Lock them up!"

"Get the fuck out of our way!" Addy leaped into the crowd. She began shoving and elbowing protesters aside. "Get lost, pests."

"It's them!" somebody shouted. "The war criminals!"

"Fascists!"

"Xenophobes!"

"Alien killers!"

Somebody spat on Addy, and she lunged at him, fists flying. Marco tried to reach her. Chaos descended, and the news cameras kept rolling.

"Let me through or I'll fucking kill every last one of you fuckers!" Addy cried.

"She confessed she's a murderer!"

"Lock them up! Lock them up!"

A protester tried to grab Addy. She punched his face. Blood spilled. Suddenly everybody was brawling, and Marco was caught in the swarm. Hands grabbed him, pulled him, and tore his clothes. Faces spun around him, twisted with rage, shouting. Somebody spat on him.

The scum raced around him.

The claws grabbed him.

He was fighting through the hive, trying to break free. Addy was shouting in pain as the aliens cut into her.

Beast was roaring, and grenades tore him apart.

Caveman died on the tarmac.

Everywhere—the faces of the aliens, swimming around him, and no way out, no way out.

Marco fell to his knees. He rose. He tried to move between them. His heart pounded and he was blind, he was losing consciousness, his hands were shaking, and sweat drenched him even in the cold.

"Back off, assholes!" Addy was shouting somewhere in the distance. "He's sick. Back off!"

He saw her through the storm. Addy shoved protesters aside, reached Marco, and helped him rise. He stood beside her, panting, his chest aching. It felt like a heart attack. His ribs pressed together, and his heart felt like grinding stones, struggling with each pump. Sweat covered him. He and Addy stood back to back. The sea of protesters surrounded them, hissing with rage.

Beyond them, on the makeshift stage, Marco saw him. The bearded man with the long brown hair and round spectacles. The man who had led the march down the street yesterday.

"Talk to us!" Marco cried out. "Come here. Pull back your people. Talk to us."

The man stared at him through those round lenses, looking like a cross between Harry Potter and Jesus. Their eyes met, and Marco didn't see cruelty there, didn't see the mindless fury in the crowd around him.

This one isn't just a follower, he thought. *This one can see some reason.*

"Let them through!" said the bearded man.

"Lock them up!" the crowd chanted. "Lock them up!"

"Let me speak to them," said the man. "Bring them to me."

Rough hands grabbed Marco and Addy, manhandling them toward the library. The long-haired man stepped off the stage and approached them. They stood outside the padlocked library door. Protesters surrounded them, blocking off any escape.

"Hello," said the man. "My name is James. I apologize if my flock got rough with you. I don't condone violence."

"Your *flock?*" Addy said. "So you admit they're sheep?"

"And I'm their shepherd." James smiled. "As I said yesterday morning when our paths crossed, I wish you no harm."

"Aside from making sure we end up in prison?" Marco said.

James sighed. "An unfortunate escalation, and not a path I condone. There are those who must be imprisoned for their crimes in the Second Galactic War. The admirals and generals who led our fleet to exterminate the alien civilization. The politicians who funded them. The CEOs who profited from the violence. We will make sure they all stand trial. But you, Marco. You, Addy. You two were mere corporals in the war, mere marionettes. And I don't wish to see you languish for the rest of your lives in prison because of how you were manipulated."

"So call off your goons," Addy said, "and get the fuck out of our lives."

James sighed. "That I can't do. Because though you were marionettes, the old defense of 'just following orders' has never applied to those guilty of war crimes. But perhaps . . . we can work out a deal." He leaned forward, eyes shining. "Join us, Marco and Addy. Join the Never War movement. You will rise high here, become the poster children of our struggle. The world will see that Marco Emery and Addy Linden, the so-called heroes of the war, the warriors who destroyed the alien civilization—that they oppose the violence! That they support withdrawing all humans from space! That they support sending their officers to prison! Join us, and I'll protect you from both harassment and legal action."

"Hmmm." Addy stroked her chin. "I have a counteroffer. Why don't you go fuck yourself?"

James's smile tightened. "This attitude might have served you in the war, Sergeant Linden. But it won't win you many friends on Earth. And right now, you need all the friends you can get."

"Right now you need to get the fuck out of my way before I plant my boot up your ass," said Addy.

"James," Marco said, stepping between the two. "We just got home a few days ago. We're tired. We're cold. We're jet-lagged. Give us a few days to consider your offer. Give us space. A ceasefire, if you'll forgive a military term. Then we'll talk again."

It was, perhaps, the best Marco could hope for now. He needed time to gather his thoughts, to come up with a plan—a plan to deal with his library foreclosing, with Lailani still missing, with his father's death, with the Never War movement, with his own guilt and confusion, with this new civilian life that already was looking like another war. He could deal with all this. He could face it. He just needed time to calm the damn shakiness, to ease that pain in his chest, the flashbacks that still haunted him. Perhaps, once his thoughts were clear, he could find peace with this movement, with the city, with his own tormented soul.

James tightened his lips, seeming to consider. Finally he sighed, opened his mouth, and—

Chants rose from down the street, interrupting him.

"Earth power! Earth power! Hail to the heroes!"

Marching boots thudded in unison. Deep voices filled the street.

"Earth power! Hail to the heroes!"

Marco turned toward the sound and his heart, already in his stomach, sank to his pelvis.

"Fuck," he whispered.

Dozens of men were marching toward the library, their heads shaved. They did not carry signs, but they raised flags, the red fabric emblazoned with iron crosses. A few men displayed swastika tattoos on their foreheads. One banner displayed the words *Earth Power* over smaller letters that spelled out *Death to Alien Scum.*

James scowled. "Are these your friends, Marco?"

"No." Marco bristled. "I do *not* associate with them. I—"

One of the Earth Power marchers raised a megaphone. "Hail to the heroes!" He was a tall, muscular man, his bald head massive, and he spoke with an English accent. He raised his hand in a Nazi salute. "Earth rises!"

Behind him, his dozens of followers raised their own hands. "Earth rises!"

The men marched like an army. They were fewer than the Never War protesters, but taller, wider, their boots tipped with steel, and Never War fell back before them. When one peace protester fell, the boots stomped him, and blood leaked into the snow.

"Behold the scum-lovers!" said the British skinhead, pointing at James and the other protesters.

"Traitors to humanity!" shouted a man in a leather trench coat.

"Alien-fuckers!" cried another.

"Hail Hunt!" the skinheads chanted, giving their leader Nazi salutes. "Hail Hunt!"

Hunt—presumably the burly Brit—paced the street, speaking into his megaphone. A few of the Never War protesters tried to shout him down, but Hunt's voice washed over them.

"The alien scum devastated Earth!" said Hunt. "They invaded our world, determined to impregnate our women, to infest pure humanity with their insect DNA." He spoke over his men's roars of hatred. "And these Never War weaklings betrayed our race. They scheme to surrender Earth to the next space vermin that fills the power vacuum. They plot to destroy the pure Human Empire that is destined to colonize the galaxy. But here stand true heroes!" He pointed at Marco and Addy. "Here stand two brave Aryan soldiers, exemplifying humanity at its purest, who defeated the alien scum! Hail the heroes!"

His men all raised their open hands in salute. "Hail the heroes!" The Iron Cross flags rose higher.

Marco felt like he was about to throw up. As much as the Never War movement loathed him, they now seemed the kinder alternative; he'd prefer their hatred over the adulation of Earth Power any day.

"Fascists!" shouted a Never War woman with flowers in her hair.

"Nazi pigs!" cried a man with dreadlocks.

Stones began to fly. Steel-tipped boots kicked. Fists slammed into teeth.

Soon the protests devolved into an all-out brawl. In one camp stood Never War, protesters with beards, braided hair, dreadlocks, beads, and tie-dyed shirts. In the other camp roared the Earth Power thugs, wearing black, heads shaved, many sporting swastika or iron cross tattoos, their boots tipped with steel. A few men drew knives and clubs. Rocks flew. Blood spilled. A skinhead grabbed a woman's hair and tugged her down, and her friends launched onto the man, kicking and punching. Police sirens wailed and Marco could see the cop cars racing from down the road.

"Come on, Addy, let's get out of here." Marco grabbed her and began pulling her away from the brawl.

"This is our home!" she said, pointing at the library, but access was now blocked. The only way they'd reach the fire escape was to fight their way through. "Where will we go?"

"Anywhere but here!" Marco said, already imagining the evening news showing his and Addy's mugshots.

She groaned but let him drag her away. They hurried down the road as cops leaped out from their cars and began handcuffing protesters from both camps.

They were a block away when Marco's stomach twisted. He raced into an alleyway and lost his pancakes behind a trash bin.

Addy wrapped an arm around him, and he leaned against her. The snowfall intensified and the wind shrieked. They walked down the streets, hunched over, only a few spare dollars in their pockets.

"Do we have enough money for a hotel tonight?" Marco said. "Maybe just a hostel? I wish I had taken more cash. There's still a bit in the apartment, but God knows when we'll be able to get back inside, if ever. Those idiots seem determined to keep us out until the wrecking ball arrives." He sighed. "Some homecoming."

"I'd even welcome an army tent now," Addy said.

Marco felt close to tears. Throughout his time in the war, in the bowels of the scum hive, he would think about home, draw strength from the memory. In the darkest nights, he would imagine lying in his bed at home, living with his father again. That had taken him through rough days and long nights in the army. Now he was a civilian again, and he had come home, but everything was different. Everything was wrong.

"We can find an all-night coffee shop," Marco said. "Drink lots of caffeine to stay awake, then come back in a few hours, and—"

"No," Addy said. "We're down to our last few bucks, and I need a mattress or couch beneath me. I know a place."

They trudged for half an hour through the sludge. Apartment buildings rose at their sides, the metal balcony railings weeping rust onto the raw concrete. A TV blared in an apartment, and gunshots sounded from the program, and Marco started. Finally Addy led them into one apartment building's lobby.

"We'll find a hideout here." Addy reached for the intercom.

"Addy, wait." Marco grabbed her wrist. "This isn't *his* place, is it? Your ex-boyfriend's?"

She bristled. "And what if it is?"

"You said he was a dope!" Marco said.

"He is! So? He'll also have a couch to crash on."

Marco sighed. He remembered the brute—a hulking hockey player who towered over Marco, who had stolen his lunch once in elementary school, who had begged to copy Marco's homework in high school.

"What's his name again?" Marco said. "Butch? Buck? Bubba?"

"You know his name is Steve." Addy scowled. "Marco, stop being a jealous baby."

"What do I have to be jealous about? You're like a sister to me."

She stared at him for a second too long, and Marco knew what she was remembering. It was a memory he didn't like to dredge up, a memory four years old now. They had been nineteen, just kids, terrified, haunted, lost in the war and completely alone. Their wounds from Corpus had not yet healed, and already they were lurching toward another battle, and all their friends had been taken away. In their loneliness and fear, Marco and Addy had made love—a night of tears, embraces, terror, sweat, sex. A night that had occurred only once, that still crept into Marco's dreams sometimes, into his memories when he watched Addy do something trivial—grab a beer from the fridge with the ghostly light upon her, or watch a bird take flight, or laugh, or look inward. At those times, Marco remembered that night with her, remembered the time he had loved her as more than a friend, more than a sister, but as a woman.

But she can't be that to me, he thought. *Not again.*

Their fates had been entwined for too long. Ever since that day in the snow, not far from here. That day when they had been children. When their parents had died. When Addy had moved into the library, an eleven-year-old with skinned knees, a foul mouth, and the stench of cigarettes already on her breath. A girl from a family of criminals, a girl he had always feared at school, who would knuckle his head, twist his arm. A girl who became his foster sister, his dearest friend, his sister-in-arms. And for one night only, something she could never be again.

"All right then," Addy said. "So no problem." She turned away, blinked, and hit the intercom.

They climbed the stairs to the fourth floor, knocked on the door, and it swung open. Steve stood there, wearing nothing but boxer shorts. Crossing hockey sticks were tattooed onto his chest.

"Addy Fucking Linden!" he roared, pulling her into an embrace. "Where the fuck have you been these past five years?"

"Killing scum while you were hiding under your desk," she said.

"Fuck I was! I was fixing antennae out in the mountains. If you think this is cold weather, try climbing a three-hundred-meter tower in the goddamn Siberian mountains and welding metal for five hours." He pulled back from Addy, holding her at arm's length, and examined her. "Fuck me, you've barely changed. Still hot. Still got great tits."

"Fuck you, asshole." She shoved him aside. "My tits are frozen solid. I'm here to warm them up. Some fuckers took over our old place and kicked us out."

For the first time, Steve seemed to notice Marco standing at the doorway. His eyes widened.

"Rico!" he said, crushed Marco in one arm, and knuckled his head. "Got any lunch money for me?"

"It's Marco," he muttered, shoving the man off. "You might have seen me in the news. War hero and all that."

"Forget it, Poet," Addy said. "Steve only watches *Robot Wrestling*."

"Fuck yeah!" Steve nodded. "It's on now, as a matter of fact. Come on in, grab a beer. Exterminator is about to smash The Claw."

They shuffled into the apartment. The living room was small, cluttered, and thick with the smell of weed. Dirty clothes, a couple acoustic guitars, hockey gear, footballs, dirty dishes, and a collection of bongs covered every surface.

"Hey, Stooge, move over!" Steve kicked the couch.

Marco realized that a man lay on the couch. He was so covered with potato chips, laundry, candy wrappers, and beer bottles that he blended into his surroundings. The bearded man fell to the floor, moaned, and shuffled into the corner, where he found a bag of cookies and began to munch.

"Yo, Stooge," Addy said. "Still working on your music career?"

The man mumbled something incoherent, then lay down and began snoring.

Lovely, Marco thought. *And we could have gone to a nice, cozy homeless shelter.*

"Yeah, I've been back for a few months now," Steve was saying, grabbing beers from the fridge. "Hurt my ankle in the mountains so they let me out early. Stooge held down the fort while I was away. Life's good. My old man got me a gig installing air conditioners. Not much business in winter, but I've been fitting in lots of hockey games. You should play with us tomorrow, Ads."

"Got to fight the man tomorrow," she said, accepting a bottle of beer.

"Stickin' it to the man!" Steve clanged his bottle against hers.

That night, Addy crept into Steve's bedroom to sleep, and the two closed the door. Marco lay on the living room couch, a blanket pulled over him. Stooge was still snoring on the floor; Steve had assured them that his bearded roommate spent most nights there anyway. The couch smelled of smoke, of old pizza crusts, of a thousand nights of Stooge passed out in front of infomercials. Marco closed his eyes, trying to ignore the snoring coming from the bearded man in the corner, to ignore the smells, to ignore the fear.

Marco didn't know how much time passed before he heard the moan from the bedroom.

Silence. A moment later—another moan.

The scum. They're racing through tunnels. They're—

"Oh God," Addy said from behind the bedroom door. "Oh God! God, Steve. *God!*"

Steve only moaned. Lying on the couch, Marco could hear their bed rattling.

He pulled a pillow over his head, but he could still hear it. Addy kept crying out to God, to Steve, then God again, growing louder and louder. Steve, never one for big words, simply kept groaning. Finally Addy screamed—an actual scream, and Marco remembered the screams of his dying friends. And he hated it, hated those memories, hated the thought of Addy and Steve, hated the jealousy, that horrible, nonsensical jealousy. And he hated the tears in his eyes.

Finally he found some fitful sleep, waking up every few moments, until the sun rose and another day of this new war began.

CHAPTER FIVE

When Ben-Ari returned to her quarters, desperate for a shower, a meal, and eight hours in bed, a stranger was waiting there for her.

She froze, hand reaching toward her gun.

They had given her a private chamber in Space Station One, a rare luxury for a junior officer, a luxury she had earned with years of dedicated service and daring missions. She had led the platoon that slew the scum emperor. Her face was famous across human civilization. The other junior officers—ensigns, lieutenants, and even captains—shared bunks here on the frontier, living barely better than the enlisted. Not she. Not the famous Captain Einav Ben-Ari, daughter of a colonel, a war heroine. Here was her reward: a small room, barely larger than a closet, a mansion in this crowded space station at Nightwall. A bed. A desk. Best of all, her own private shower. A palace.

And at her desk, he sat. A young man in a suit, dark shades hiding his eyes, his hair spiked with gel. He rose and extended a hand to shake.

"Captain Ben-Ari! Lovely to meet you in person at last."

She stood in place, her hand a centimeter from her pistol. "Tell me your name before I blast off your head."

The man laughed heartily. "So the stories about you are true. A soldier through and through." He kept his hand extended. "My name is Erik Pike, Senior Headhunter and Human Resource Manager at Chrysopoeia Corporation Space Territorial Command Outreach Program. A mouthful, I know. My friends just call me the Pikemaster." When she still wouldn't clasp his hand, he lowered it, never losing his smile. "Would you like some coffee or tea? I just boiled a kettle."

"I would like you to get the hell out of my bunk," she said.

Pike tossed his head back and laughed—a fake sound. "This is why we love you, Einav."

"Captain Ben-Ari," she corrected him.

"Captain Ben-Ari, of course." Pike nodded, poured hot water into a mug—*her* mug—and blew on it. "We at Chrysopoeia have been most impressed with your career. Stories of your courage have traveled far and wide."

"I've heard." Still she kept her hand near her gun. "Back on Earth, the Never War movement wants to arrest me the day I land and charge me with war crimes. Supposedly, defeating a space bug hellbent on destroying humanity now constitutes alien genocide."

Pike took a sip of his tea and winced. "Needs more cream." He added a packet. "Yes, we at Chrysopoeia Corporation are well aware of your legal woes, Captain Ben-Ari. I'm familiar with the lawyer prosecuting you, one Ben Bradley. We studied together at Dartmouth, actually. How long has it been since you visited Earth?"

Five years. It had been five long years that she had served
here in space, her only shore leave on planets that made
Antarctica seem like a tropical paradise. With promises of arrest at
Earth's spaceports, she had never dared visit home. Not that
much awaited her on Earth these days. No family. No friends.
Her life was the military. Her life was here in the darkness.

And yet . . . Ben-Ari still longed to see the sea again. To
hear trees rustle. To breathe fresh air, not the recycled gases that
filtered through space stations. To walk along the beach, alone
with her thoughts. To paint in a sunlit garden. To read at a
lakeside, a campfire crackling. To be normal, if only for a day.

Someday to retire, she thought. *To leave the military. To meet a
man. Maybe to have a child. To live by water and trees.*

"Why are you here?" she said, voice stiff, hating that she
heard the twinge of sadness in it.

"I've come to make your legal troubles disappear," said
Pike. "At Chrysopoeia Corporation, we have the best legal defense
teams in the world. We hire only the best, Captain Ben-Ari. Most
of our managers were once officers in the Human Defense Force.
In fact, I personally insist on hiring only distinguished military
officers, men and women who have proved their leadership on
the battlefield. I value them far more than squeaky-clean
applicants with shiny MBAs and no dirt under their fingernails.
I'm here to offer you a job, Captain Ben-Ari. You've served in the
military for seven years now. Your term is up for renewal soon,
am I right? Consider retiring from the military, a distinguished

officer with a proud career. And consider a second career, one with Chrysopoeia. On Earth."

"On Earth," she whispered.

Pike nodded. "On beautiful, green Earth. We'd be happy to offer you a corner office with a view of the sea." He handed her a pamphlet. "I've written our compensation offer under a photo of our offices. I hope it's to your satisfaction, though it is negotiable."

Ben-Ari stood frozen for a moment. She thought of her conversation with Admiral Komagata. She thought of losing her friends in the war. She took the pamphlet.

The photos did make her heart melt a little. She had to confess that. Chrysopoeia Headquarters looked more like a spa resort than an office building. The pamphlet showed palm trees, seaside trails, a nursery for children, and a cafeteria brimming with the bounty of Earth. On the last page, she saw a view of a corner office facing the water. Beneath it, Pike had handwritten a number. Her suggested salary.

It was seven times what the military paid her.

She looked up at him. "What do you want me to do?"

"Are you sure you don't want some tea?" Pike said. "Perhaps to sit down? Or at least to move your hand away from your pistol?"

She sat on her bed, but she kept her hand near her gun. "Talk."

Pike placed down his mug and leaned closer to her, looming above her, a vulture over prey. "We understand that recently you experienced an . . . alien encounter."

She stared at him, eyes narrowed. "I can neither confirm nor deny that."

Pike nodded. "Ah, yes, militarily confidential, of course. But, see, classified information, even within the military, has a pesky way of spreading. To, say, an admiral. To a fellow officer, somebody you feel you can trust. To a lover, perhaps? And soon the news spreads. Only to a few close friends, mind you! Yet friends tell friends, and information inevitably leaks. And we certainly don't want to spread any panic, however limited. Fear is bad for stock prices."

She stared at this man, and Ben-Ari remembered. She remembered seeing the symbol of Chrysopoeia Corp, a snake eating its tail, on the prison uniforms. Deep in the demilitarized zone. A prison owned by Chrysopoeia. A prison overrun with aliens.

"You're buying my silence," she said.

"Not at all!" Pike leaned back. "We want you to function as a consultant. A liaison with the military. Our largest client, after all, is the Human Defense Force. But of course, silence is part of the job." He smiled thinly. "The military is so crude with sealing its information. Squeeze an orange hard enough and the juice leaks. When there's a corner office, a cushy salary, and a company car to lose, well . . . we find that leaks tend to be plugged." He licked his lips, reached out, and touched her shoulder. "Don't think of us as buying you, Einav. Think of us as . . . recruiting you to our team. Join us." A strange light filled his eyes, and his voice became breathy. "There are such terrors in the dark. There is such cruelty in space. And there is such profit."

What the hell did I stumble onto? Ben-Ari thought. *The admiral. Chrysopoeia Corp. Both trying to keep this hush.*

She shuddered to remember the dark world, a planet deep in no man's land, existing in shadow. The structure there, a pile of webs and tar overlaying a prison, still haunted her nightmares. The creatures within, monsters of claws and fangs, feasting upon human brains, still filled her nights. She would never forget seeing Malphas, lord of the beasts, staring at her from across the border. Grinning. His jaws full of fangs.

The nightmares are coming, he had said. *We will meet again.*

Ben-Ari stood up. Her bunk was so small her head nearly hit the ceiling, and Pike had to take a step back. She silently said goodbye to that airy office overlooking the ocean.

"No," she said.

Pike narrowed his eyes the slightest. "Does the salary not meet your expectations? Or is the office—"

"Mr. Pike," she said, "as you said, there are terrors in the dark. There is cruelty in space. My duty is to fight it. For generations, my family has served, has fought evil. So long as there is evil out there, I will remain on the frontier. I will be humanity's first line of defense."

The marauders lurk in the darkness. Creatures I'm not even allowed to speak of. Creatures they all want to keep hidden. Creatures I must fight.

Pike stared at her for a moment longer, then sighed. He sat down and sipped his tea. "Yes, I was afraid you might say something like that. Of course, we at Chrysopoeia prepare for all eventualities." He wrinkled his nose. "Too much sugar."

Movement caught the corner of her eye.

Ben-Ari spun around.

She leaped aside, hitting a cabinet.

A dart flew, pierced the wall, and quivered.

Ben-Ari drew her gun.

She ducked, and another dart sliced her hair.

Impossible. Impossible!

She saw nobody. Nobody there! But still she moved. She thrust her gun, swinging it like a club, and heard a grunt.

A man flickered into and out of existence like a crackling television set.

She heard Pike rise from his seat. Ben-Ari spun back toward him, knocking him down with a roundhouse kick. She reeled back toward the flickering man. He had taken form now, wearing a suit overlain with cables—some kind of invisibility suit.

The man raised his dart gun again, and Ben-Ari raised her own weapon, catching the dart against the muzzle. She thrust her pistol forward, hitting the assailant's nose, shattering it.

She spun back toward Pike, who was drawing a gun from under his jacket. She kicked, knocking the pistol out from his hand. Back toward the man in the electronic suit. She lashed her gun again, driving the muzzle into his throat. He grabbed his neck, choking. Still she dared not fire.

I can't attract more enemies. Silently!

Pike managed to grab his gun, to fire. There was no bang; he was using a silencer. A bullet whizzed, hitting Ben-Ari's arm. She bit down on a scream. The bullet emerged from her flesh and lodged itself into her mini-fridge.

Before Pike could fire again, Ben-Ari grabbed his head and snapped his neck.

She turned toward the second man, the one in the invisibility suit. He was gasping for air, clutching his throat. His nose gushed blood. Ben-Ari grabbed him, knocked him down, and twisted his collar.

"Why?" she said. "What are you hiding?"

He stared into her eyes. "I . . . have failed. They know."

Electricity crackled across his suit.

Ben-Ari bit down on another scream. The electricity slammed into her arms, and she stumbled back, trembling. The man thrashed on the floor, his invisibility suit crackling, awash with electricity, and smoke rose. The electricity died with a crackle. The man lay dead.

They know. They know.

Still trembling with shock, her arm bleeding, Ben-Ari looked around the room. Both men lay dead. Both had died quietly.

But had somebody been watching? Had somebody remotely activated the man's suit, electrocuting him?

Somebody is still after me, Ben-Ari thought.

Her head spun. She was losing blood. Her fingernails were burnt from the electrical shock. She still had her first aid kit in her bunk, the one from the war. She splashed antiseptic into the bullet wound on her arm, gritted her teeth, and began to bandage it.

She froze, the bandage halfway around her arm.

If I'm caught here with two dead bodies . . .

She stood for a moment. She should report the attack to the military police or her commanding officer. She knew this. And yet . . .

Ben-Ari didn't know how deep this ran. Admiral Komagata himself, commander of Nightwall, had insisted that she keep the marauders secret. Admiral Komagata—a man with a dwindling fleet, a man who depended on Chrysopoeia Corp building him more starships. Chrysopoeia had built this entire space station they all served on.

If I report this attack, will the military investigate the powerful Chrysopoeia, or will they make sure I—a mere junior officer—disappear?

She knew the answer.

She pressed her ear to the door, gun in hand.

She heard nothing.

She kicked the door open, pointed her gun, burst outside, aimed left and right.

A young private, a scrawny boy with freckles, squeaked and fled.

No Chrysopoeia agents. No military police. But there, on the wall . . .

A garbage chute. A chute leading to the incinerator.

Ben-Ari grimaced.

Come on, Einav, she told herself. *You did a lot worse in the war.*

The hour was late, and nobody else walked down the corridor, but she worked quickly. The bodies were heavier than she was, and she was wounded, but fear gave her strength. She dragged them into the corridor. She pulled them up against the wall. She shoved them through the garbage chute; they barely squeezed through.

Deep in the bowels of the space station, they would burn in the inferno, instantly cremated.

Ben-Ari stumbled back into her quarters, covered with sweat, her arm still bleeding. She didn't have time. They would send more men after her. She dared not turn to her commanders; she didn't know who was working for who.

"What the hell did we uncover out there?" she whispered.

Door locked and gun in hand, Ben-Ari stared out her porthole. The stars spread outside, and in the distance, she could see Achernar, the star marking the edge of the demilitarized zone. They were waiting there. The creatures. The monsters. Malphas, the one who had smiled.

The nightmares are coming.

CHAPTER SIX

After a night on Steve's couch, Marco brushed potato chips and cat hair off himself—which was odd, considering there were no pets in Steve's apartment. After guzzling down the black tar Steve called coffee, Addy and Marco headed back to the library, hoping to find a way back into their home.

They found more protesters than ever.

To make things worse, construction workers were also on the scene, trying to get by with some very big bulldozers.

"Fuck," Addy said.

Marco cringed. He didn't know if he could stand another night on Steve's couch, listening to Stooge snore and Addy scream to God with religious fervor. After the noises he had heard last night, he still had trouble meeting her eyes.

Both he and Addy wore scarves, toques, and sunglasses, hiding their features from the protesters, construction workers, media personnel, and human supremacists. Nobody seemed to recognize them. A handful of passersby paused to snap photos of the library, but most hurried along the police barricades.

A commotion at the edge of the crowd caught Marco's attention.

A young boy stood there, wrapped in a black coat, his back turned to Marco. He was arguing with a policeman.

"Let me through, damn it!"

A woman stood beside the boy, her hair curly and blond, and Marco couldn't help but notice that she was quite attractive.

"Yes, let her through!" the young blonde said, her accent Eastern European. "She lives there."

"Yeah, that's my goddamn home!" said the boy. "At least, that's what the knucklehead who lives there promised me."

Marco froze.

He recognized that voice.

That wasn't a boy.

He ran forward, and she turned toward him. Her eyes widened.

"Lailani!" Marco said.

She gasped, stood frozen for a moment, then ran through the snow toward him. She hugged him. She wore boots with thick soles, but standing only four-foot-ten, the top of her head didn't even reach his shoulders.

"No more buzz cut?" he said, touching her hair. It had grown into a boyish pixie cut, just long enough to fall across her ears and forehead. "Your hair is longer!"

"It's a fucking waste of time, washing and brushing it," Lailani said. "I'm going to chop it all off again."

"Don't!" he said. "Keep it. I like it."

When he had met Lailani five years ago, she had been an angry, haunted eighteen-year-old, a refugee from the slums of Manila. A recruit in the Human Defense Force, she had been all fire and ice. After cutting her wrists had failed, she had joined the army to die in battle.

Marco had fallen in love with her, had tried to reach the joy inside her. And over time, Lailani had softened. She had learned to release her anger, to find some love. Today, tattoos covered the scars on her wrists—roses on the left wrist, lilacs on the right, her favorite flowers. These joined the dragon and rainbow tattoos on her arms, both now hidden under her sleeves. Her longer hair softened the tougher look her shaved head had given her.

The longer hair also hid the scar on her head—the scar from her brain surgery. Marco had never forgotten. Lailani was only ninety-nine percent human. The rest was alien DNA, connecting her to the scums' old hives. Surgery had blocked the aliens' ability to control her mind. Today Lailani was as human as anyone—more than most, if you asked Marco.

"Oh, Marco." She embraced him again and laid her cheek against his chest. "What the hell is going on here?"

He kissed the top of her head. "A mess. A mess we'll solve."

Lailani blinked up at him, eyes damp. "I just got back this morning. Nice welcome home party, huh?"

"Welcome to civilian life!" Marco said. "Where instead of army bureaucracy and aliens, you get to deal with anti-war activists, fascists, and city hall."

"And snow." She shivered. "I could never get used to snow."

A high voice rose behind her, speaking with that Eastern European accent. "I've always liked snow. It reminds me of my home in the Ukraine."

Marco raised his eyes, and despite his love for Lailani—a love he was fully, deeply committed to—he couldn't help but notice this woman's beauty. Her blond tresses cascaded, her eyes were large and green, and her smile displayed teeth whiter than the snow. She wore an elegant black overcoat, a beret, and boots with high heels. She reached out her hand to him.

"Sofia Levchenko," she said. "Pleased to meet you. You are friends with Lailani, yes?"

"I'm Marco," he said.

"Nice to meet you, Marco," said Sofia, then pulled Lailani close to her and kissed her cheek. "You are very lucky to be friends with this one. She's a sweet flower." She played with Lailani's hair, then kissed her lips.

Lailani blushed. "Not in front of my friends," she whispered.

Sofia laughed and mussed her hair. "You're shy."

Marco blinked, for a moment confused. This was more than casual affection.

Addy hurried forward. "Sofia! Nice to meet you. Addy Linden." She spat into her palm, then held it out, ignoring Sofia's look of horror. "New to Canada? There's a coffee shop across the street owned by a Mountie, and he sells real, chocolate-coated moose droppings! Come, let me show you while these two old friends catch up."

Addy grabbed Sofia's arm and all but dragged her away. When the elegant Ukrainian tried to protest, Addy overpowered her with talk of deep fried beaver tails. As she passed him, Addy gave Marco a quick, concerned look, then vanished with Sofia around the block.

"We should get out of here too," Marco said to Lailani, glancing toward the protesters around the library.

It began to hail. Marco and Lailani hurried through the downpour, covering their heads, and stepped down into a subway station, seeking shelter. Graffiti covered the walls, and a tattered poster for *Space Galaxy III* hung nearby. Somebody had given Captain Carter, the movie's dashing hero, a Hitler mustache and breasts. The train tracks plunged into the dark tunnel, and several commuters huddled on the platform, breath fogging. A phone stood by Marco and Lailani, its single button blinking red, and a sign hung above it. *Thinking of jumping? You don't have to. Hit the red button now to speak to a counselor.*

"I missed you, Marco." Lailani embraced him again. "When I was out at the Oort Cloud, light-years away, I thought of you a lot. I love you."

Marco held her close. "I missed you too. I love you too."

"It's all such a fucking, goddamn shit-show," Lailani said. "The whole world is messed up."

Lights flared out in the tunnel, and a train rumbled, clattered, screeched along the tracks, showering sparks. It must have been a hundred years old, coated with rust, some ancient, hollowed-out caterpillar of iron and tattered plastic. For a moment they could not speak, and all the world was shaking metal and concrete, whooshing doors, and commuters huddled in coats flowing in and out past sliding doors. With belches and creaks and screaming metal, the train left the station.

"So," Marco said. "Sofia seems nice. Very . . . affectionate."

Lailani met his gaze. "Do you remember how, three Christmases ago, we talked? I was just about to leave to the Oort Cloud. We knew I'd be there for three years. You told me that if I got lonely, I could date others, even sleep with other people—so long as they were girls. You said that! So long as they were girls."

"Jesus, Lailani, I was fucking kidding." Marco's eyes stung, and his throat felt tight. "It was a joke."

"You seemed serious."

"Besides, even if I *was* serious, I didn't mean you could bring a girlfriend back home. Back here! To me."

Now some anger filled Lailani's eyes. "I don't need your permission to do anything, Marco."

"You do if you intend to live in my apartment," he said, allowing too much of his pain into his voice.

She snorted. "Last I checked, gangs of communists and Nazis were fighting World War Three in your apartment. Besides, Sofia isn't my girlfriend. She's my mentor."

"Oh, good to know she's a mentor. I would hate for a girlfriend to be kissing you in front of me. Did you even tell her who I am, Lailani? That I'm your boyfriend, your fiance?"

Lailani lowered her eyes, and her fists loosened. "Marco, what we were . . . that was years ago. We were kids. I've barely seen you in years."

He refused to cry in front of her. Refused to let his grief show. "Lailani . . ." He reached out to touch her cheek. "I love you."

A tear flowed down her cheek. "I'm only here for a day, Marco. I came to say goodbye."

"Goodbye?" Marco whispered. "But . . . you're out of the military now. You're a civilian. You can stay here."

More of her tears flowed. "I can't. I met Sofia in a church. Out in the Cloud. They're called Sisters of Earth. They do a lot of charity work in the Third World. Sofia and I are moving to the Philippines together." She raised her eyes, and some light filled them. "We're going to build schools. Mobile schools! Wagons with blackboards, chalk, books. We'll teach the children to read, to do their numbers, to find jobs when they're older. If I can save just a few orphans from the kind of childhood I had there . . . It's something I have to do."

Marco took a deep breath, blinking rapidly. Another train roared by, and for a moment they couldn't speak, and the world was shadows and headlights and sparking metal. The train vanished down the tunnel like a burrowing insect in an alien hive.

"Then I'll go with you," Marco said. "I'm not very religious. But I'll join your church. If Sofia will have me, it'll be the three of us. We can be together, Lailani. After all this time apart."

She placed a hand on his chest. "Marco, you'd hate it there. It's hot. It's muggy. The towns we'll stay in—there's no electricity, no running water, no internet, no sanitation—"

"As if the army had those things," Marco said. "And I survived."

"And you were miserable."

He bristled. "And Sofia can handle it?"

Lailani's eyes flashed. "Sofia grew up a hungry orphan, running from the Russian tanks, and eked out a living by selling matches to soldiers."

"Well, I'm very sorry that I don't have a miserable childhood story like you and Sofia, but that doesn't mean I can't help too, that—"

"Marco!" She gave a mirthless laugh. "Listen to yourself. You only want to help to be near me. Not to actually help the children, to actually serve the church. I know that you're not religious. You'd only go there to be with me, and you'd hate it, and I'd feel guilty, and . . ."

"And you want to be with Sofia," he said, voice strained. "Alone."

She sighed. "It's not like that. Not like you think. I still love you. But . . ." She looked at her feet. "I love Sofia too. We found something. A connection. An understanding. A shared experience." She touched his cheek. "I have to do this, Marco. I love you so much, but I have to do this. Without you." She smiled through her tears. "I'll come back every Christmas. Just like from the army."

Another train roared by, louder than the others, loud as bombs, as fleets, as collapsing worlds, and it ripped his heart from his chest, dragging it along the tracks, and he couldn't breathe, and again his ribs pressed inward, and his hands shook, and his head spun, and he couldn't take it, couldn't take it. This couldn't be real. This had to be a dream. Just another nightmare like those nightmares of the hives.

"Don't leave," Marco whispered, knowing she couldn't hear him.

A train, deafening, and the station rattled. A neon light shattered. Lailani glanced around, then stood on her tiptoes, embraced Marco, and spoke into his ear, her voice nearly drowning in the din.

"Marco, I can't tell you what I did in the Oort Cloud, what I learned. It's still classified. But there's something coming. Something bad. Something worse than the scum." Her fingers tightened around his shoulders. "They'll want you in the army again. If that happens, you say no. You injure yourself. You do whatever you must, but you don't serve again. You just run and you hide, Marco, all right?"

"Lailani." He frowned. "What's coming? Another attack?"

Lailani was weeping now. She squeezed him against her, kissed his cheek, then fled the station as the train roared down the tunnel. By the time the rumbling had died down, she was gone.

Marco stood alone on the platform by the blinking red phone and tattered poster. All the other commuters were gone. He stood lost in shadows. He did not know the way out.

CHAPTER SEVEN

"Good thing the doctors were here to give you a hand," Ben-Ari said.

Lying in the hospital bed, Kemi cringed and flexed her new prosthetic. "How long have you been waiting to tell that joke?"

Ben-Ari smiled. "Throughout your surgery. Can I shake it?"

"No!" Kemi pulled her prosthetic hand against her chest. "It's still tender and the nerve endings are still fusing into the circuitry. Right now, even bending the fingers feels tingly, almost painful. But they said that should go away in a few days."

Ben-Ari took a deep breath. They didn't have a few days. Chrysopoeia had tried to kill her. And she knew they would try again. She needed to find information—today. And she needed Kemi's help.

Ben-Ari stared at her lieutenant's new hand. Some amputees chose prosthetics that looked realistic, nearly indistinguishable from the real thing. Others chose futuristic, even artistic prosthetics—hooks, blades, snapping tools, sometimes painted with flames or tribal motifs. Kemi had chosen something in between. It was shaped like a regular hand but made of naked metal, the bolts and welding visible. The prosthetic looked like something out of an old steampunk comic.

Ben-Ari moved her gaze to Kemi's face. The pilot was still so young, only twenty-three, but her eyes were older. Both women had seen too much, had grown up too fast, had lost too many loved ones. Ben-Ari hesitated, then broke protocol and stroked Kemi's hair.

"You're not just my lieutenant, Kemi," she said. "You're not just an officer under my command. You're my friend. You're like a younger sister. I love you like I would love a true sister."

"Now don't get all sappy, ma'am," Kemi said, but her voice choked up. "I'm all right. It's just a hand." Her voice softened. "But thank you, ma'am. I never said it properly. Thank you. For saving my life. I would have been spider food without you."

"Part of you was." Ben-Ari smiled wryly.

Kemi winced and gazed at her prosthetic hand. "Don't remind me. I just hope I gave that space bug indigestion." She flexed her mechanical fingers, then winced. "Tickles."

Leaving the bedside, Ben-Ari walked toward the porthole. The hospital was located inside Space Station One, the largest space station humanity had ever built. From here, she could see the rest of Nightwall, this bastion of human ingenuity and power, its light in the darkness of space. A rocky planet below, orbiting no star, harbored military barracks. Dozens of satellites and vessels orbited this world, from enormous warships to single-pilot Firebirds.

Nightwall. Earth's shield. Only a few years ago, it had been so much larger. Since the war, Ben-Ari had seen ship after ship scrapped. Space station after space station torn down. Brigade after brigade dismantled, its soldiers flown home to Earth. The scum had been gone for four years, the survivors hiding in their holes, defeated so badly they would not rise again for centuries.

And so we moved from war to peace, from destroying to rebuilding, Ben-Ari thought. *No longer do we, soldiers in space, receive the lion's share of Earth's money, its resources, its brains.*

She winced at that last word. She had been thinking of scientists and engineers and strategists, but a different thought now rose. The memory floated before her: the marauders, great arachnid aliens, cracking open human skulls, lapping up the brains.

With a shaky breath, she stared at Achernar, the brightest star in the sky, so close to here. Just beyond that star, they lurked. They digested. She remembered staring into their leader's eyes. Remembered his mocking grin. Cold sweat trickled down Ben-Ari's back.

Wincing, Kemi rose from bed and walked toward her. They gazed together out into space.

"They're out there," Kemi said softly. "Those creatures. What were they? Why was a human prison out there in the DMZ?" She looked at Ben-Ari, eyes haunted. "And why can't we speak of this?"

"I don't know." Ben-Ari took a deep breath. "But I'm going to find out."

Kemi winced. "Captain." She glanced around and lowered her voice. "The admiral himself told us to keep this hush. We can't go snooping around now against orders. Whatever was out there . . ." She sighed. "We just have to hope those in charge know what they're doing."

"How well has that served us in the past?" Ben-Ari placed her hand on the viewport. With the tip of her finger, she could hide Achernar. "We trusted Admiral Bryan. We thought he was a hero. Then he betrayed us, betrayed millions of us. I no longer know if we can trust our generals, our admirals, our politicians, or just our own moral code."

"Sounds like a good way of ending up in the brig," Kemi said.

"Sounds like a good way of ending up on the bad end of a firing squad," Ben-Ari confessed. "But both those fates seem kind compared to what's out there. To what we saw."

Kemi shuddered. They were both silent for a moment, remembering. An alien structure on a dark world, deep in what had been the scum empire. Within it—a human prison, draped in webs. Prisoners, their skulls carved open, their brains removed. Aliens—large creatures the size of cows, with six clawed legs, with jaws that could swallow a man whole, with trophy skulls on their backs, with intelligent eyes.

"Spiders," Kemi said. "Spiders with crocodile mouths. Who crave brains. Spider-croco-zombies. From space."

Ben-Ari smiled wryly. "Just like monsters from a B movie. Except these ones destroyed our squad. And for some reason, the top brass wants them hidden. Kemi, I can't let this rest. You understand, don't you? I have to investigate. If we're in danger, if Earth is in danger, if Admiral Komagata is corrupt . . ." She held her lieutenant's good hand. "All of humanity might be at stake."

Kemi stared into her eyes. "So what do we do?" she whispered.

"I'm a captain," she said. "A higher ranking officer than you."

"Sure, rub it in, *ma'am*," Kemi said.

Ben-Ari gave a tight smile. "But my security clearance still doesn't go high enough. Not to find out what I need. But . . ." She bit her lip. She was developing a callus from biting her lip so often these days. She spoke in a whisper. "Before he died, my father, a colonel . . . gave me his codes."

Kemi frowned. "He gave you secret military codes?"

"Well . . ." Ben-Ari shifted her weight from foot to foot. "They were on his communicator."

"What, just typed in there?"

"Yeah," Ben-Ari said. "In code. Behind a few walls of encryption. Which, well, needed a black market hacker to crack. But otherwise, just written down. Totally irresponsible, if you ask me."

"Ma'am!" Kemi leaned in, eyes wide, and whispered urgently, "Are you telling me you stole security codes from an HDF colonel?"

"Shush!" Ben-Ari glanced around the room, then back at Kemi. "If I can get into the Augury, I can plug in the codes. I can dig deep. I can access information a captain can't but a colonel can."

"Ma'am, I don't know . . ." Kemi said. "Blasting aliens with guns is one thing. We're good at that. But defying the HDF?" Her voice dropped to a whisper. "It's *illegal*."

Ben-Ari stared out there. Into space. In the darkness, she could still see him. The marauder. Malphas. Waiting for her.

"Yes," Ben-Ari said. "I must."

That evening, Ben-Ari and Kemi walked through Space Station One, the carpeted floors muffling their steps. Many soldiers were retiring to their quarters or a lounge, their workday done. The two women passed by pilots, engineers, computer programmers, scientists, doctors, analysts, janitors, cooks, and a few guards, all wearing the navy blue of Space Territorial Command. A couple times, Ben-Ari and Kemi stood at attention as a general walked by, but mostly they passed NCOs and junior officers. They were all here to watch the darkness, to defend Earth from the terrors of space.

Yet how can we defend Earth if we hide what's in the shadows?

They reached the Augury door. A guard stood here, rifle in hands. Here was one of the few doorways in Space Station One that was constantly under guard. Ben-Ari handed over her own security codes. She didn't need to use her father's stolen codes yet. As a captain, she could enter this room, even if she couldn't get much from it. The guard nodded and the door slid open. Ben-Ari stepped inside, leaving Kemi in the corridor.

The Augury was small, not much larger than an elevator, with rounded walls. When Ben-Ari stood in the center, she felt like a child trapped in a well.

"Activate Augury," she said.

The lights shut off, leaving her in total blackness. Stars kindled around her. The walls were all holographic projectors. The illusion was complete. Ben-Ari felt as if she floated through space.

She reached toward some stars. With her hand gestures, she was able to grab some, to pull them toward her, to tap them and expand informational windows. When she grasped Achernar, it zoomed toward her, a crackling ball of bluish-white plasma, several planets orbiting it. A hovering text box offered information on the star: its physical properties and its political importance, a beacon denoting humanity's border in the Milky Way. Smaller stars, when pulled toward her, revealed their own planets and properties.

Ben-Ari tapped planets beyond Achernar, searching for information on their inhabitants. It was believed that millions of planets harbored life in the Milky Way. Over ten thousand species had been cataloged so far, most of them mere microorganisms, others as advanced as animal or plant life on Earth. A few hundred intelligent species had been discovered, most still in their stone age or iron age. Only a handful of star systems in the Orion Arm of the Milky Way, where Earth resided, harbored spacefaring civilizations. Most of those—the Guramis, the Silvans, the

Altairians—were peaceful, their reach extending to only a few nearby worlds.

Ben-Ari kept searching, but she could find no information on the marauders. How could a species so brutal, so intelligent, have been covered up this long?

"Show me all arachnids," she said, and she found information on hundreds of spiderlike aliens, but none with six legs, massive jaws, and an appetite for brains.

"Show me all predatory, newly formed civilizations," she said, and several star systems zoomed toward her, home to warlike aliens. She saw voracious blobs, malicious squids, intelligent clouds that communicated with lightning bolts, and beings formed from fire and stone, but no marauders. No threats that had ventured near humanity.

The dark world, the one with the prison planet, did not even appear in the Augury's charts.

Ben-Ari spoke into the communicator on her wrist. "Kemi?"

Her lieutenant answered, voice soft. "I'm here, ma'am, right in the hallway. All clear."

Ben-Ari took a deep breath. If this failed, it could mean her life. This was a criminal act that could get her the death penalty if she was lucky, life on a penal asteroid if she wasn't. She had faced death before, too many times, and survived. This was a different sort of battle, but it required the same courage.

"Computer," she said, "I'd like to input a new code." Her father's security code had been easy to memorize.

Einav_May_1_2124_Wilbur. Her name. Her birthday. Her childhood dog. After all the hacking to retrieve the code, it wasn't even particularly secure.

New stars shone in the Augury.

Thousands of new informational windows lit up, then faded to a dim glow, waiting to share their knowledge.

Yes, her lip was definitely developing a callus.

She had to hurry.

She pulled stars and planets toward her, shoved them aside, seeking them, the marauders, the—

There.

She froze.

There!

A star shone before her, and several planets orbited it. The system was swarming with clawed ships—like the marauders ships that had chased her, that had nearly destroyed the HDFS *Saint Brendan.*

"Kemi?" she whispered into her communicator.

"All clear but hurry," came the lieutenant's voice. "I don't like this."

Ben-Ari nodded. She tapped a clawed ship. A window popped up.

Type: Ravager-class alien warship. Propulsion: Warp drive. Armaments: Plasma cannon. Length: 50 meters (estimated). Complement: Unknown. Maximum velocity: Unknown. Hull construction: Unknown.

No new info here, aside from the name. *Ravager*. It seemed some senior intelligence officer had a good imagination for naming alien vessels.

Ben-Ari scrolled down. A new line of information appeared, this one more interesting.

Species: Magna Insecta.

"Here we go," Ben-Ari whispered, clicking the name.

A new informational bubble appeared, titled: *Magna Insecta, the Marauders.*

Below the title appeared a photograph of one of the aliens.

"You are an ugly bastard," Ben-Ari muttered.

Kemi had described them as zombie spiders with crocodile mouths, but they were worse. A lot worse than that. These beasts made the scum seem cuddly. Six serrated legs sprouted from their bodies, ending with clawed digits that looked flexible enough to manipulate tools and deadly enough to disembowel a brontosaurus. The alien's jaws thrust out, lined with teeth on the inside, horns on the outside. Ben-Ari had seen these creatures suck out the brains of their victims, leaving the flesh to rot. These jaws had not evolved to feast on meat but to devastate enemies. These jaws were *weapons*, and Ben-Ari wagered that they could rip through steel.

Most sickening was the creature's abdomen. She placed her finger on the three-dimensional image, spinning it around to another angle. Skulls covered the alien's body, glued on. Some were alien skulls, but others were human, staring with agony through empty eye sockets.

"How do they find human skulls?" Ben-Ari whispered.

She could not bear to look at the skulls anymore. She spun the creature's abdomen away, but that only brought its jaws back into view. Its four eyes stared at her. Here were not the empty, dead eyes of mere insects, creatures like the scum with only hive intelligence. No. These eyes were cunning. These eyes seemed to peel back Ben-Ari's uniform, her flesh, to stare into her soul. The words of Malphas, the marauder who had chased her to the border, would not stop haunting her. *We will meet again.*

The holographic marauder's jaw stretched into a grin.

Ben-Ari inhaled sharply and closed the file, and the marauder vanished. Her heart pounded. Cold sweat covered her. How could this photograph have moved? How could it have been looking straight at her? Her pulse pounded in her ears.

Hello, Einav . . .

The words sounded in the chamber. *His* voice. The guttural voice of the alien. Just a whisper, an echo. No. No, just her imagination. Malphas couldn't be speaking to her here, not truly.

We are waiting for you . . .

Just the hum of machinery, that was all. She was too tired, too scared, imagining voices in the darkness.

Across the Augury, the stars and planets moved. Solar systems zoomed in. Dozens, hundreds, thousands. Around them all—ravager ships. Millions of ravager ships.

We will meet soon . . .

"They're surrounding us," Ben-Ari whispered. "These are invasion formations. They're planning an invasion of—"

"Captain!" Kemi's voice emerged from the communicator on Ben-Ari's wrist. "Captain, you're about to have company!"

Damn.

Ben-Ari began to close star systems. But thousands were opened around her, and each one needed to be clicked. No time. No time!

"Computer, shut down!" she said.

"Too many open systems," intoned a robotic voice. "Do you want to save your configuration?"

"Shut down now!" Ben-Ari hissed.

"Shutting down now will close all open star systems. Do you wish to save your—"

"Close them all!"

"Initiating shu—" The computerized voice changed in tone. "System locked. System locked."

Ben-Ari cursed. She couldn't leave the Augury, not with the information on the marauders still displayed. But if she was caught here . . .

She made for the door. She couldn't see it in the darkness. She reached through holographic space, felt a wall, pawed for a door handle . . .

The door opened before she could reach it.

Light from the hallway flooded the Augury, washing over the holograms.

At the doorway stood three military policemen. Among them stood Admiral Komagata.

She met his gaze.

"They're all around us," Ben-Ari said. "An army. An army kept classified. In shadows. Admiral, this isn't just a typical species venturing to the stars. The marauders are—"

"Men, stun her," said Admiral Komagata.

The military policemen raised their guns.

Ben-Ari leaped aside.

Bolts of electricity flew into the room, narrowly missing her. They burned the floor where they hit. She had no weapon. She knew Krav Maga, but—

In the hallway, the air rippled. A funnel of air drove forward like animated sound waves. Once. Twice. Two military policemen fell.

"Lieutenant, stand down—" began an MP.

The air rippled again, and the third policeman crashed down. The admiral drew his pistol, aimed it down the hallway . . .

Ben-Ari leaped out from the Augury. She kicked, knocking the pistol from the admiral's hand. An instant later, another ripple of air slammed into Komagata. He crashed down among the three MPs, unconscious.

Kemi stood in the corridor, panting, her mechanical hand raised. An opening in her palm clattered shut.

"I had a stunner installed into the palm, Captain," she whispered. "I never thought that . . . Oh God." Kemi stared down. "I knocked out the admiral." She looked into Ben-Ari's eyes. "They'll hang us for this."

"If what I saw in the Augury is true, we're all going to hang," Ben-Ari said. "And it'll be by spiderwebs rather than ropes. Come, Lieutenant. Follow me."

They began running down the corridor, leaving the unconscious men behind.

"Where are we going, Captain?" Kemi said, panting as she ran, undoubtedly still woozy from losing her hand only days ago.

"To find more information. To fight like we've always fought." Ben-Ari flashed her lieutenant a smile. "Ever steal a starship, Lieutenant?"

Kemi groaned. "We already stole military secrets, resisted arrest, and knocked an admiral unconscious. Yeah, I think I can handle stealing a starship."

They raced through the space station, heading toward the docking bay. Her lieutenant perhaps was worried about military law, but Ben-Ari only thought about the fleet of ravagers, the marauder smiling at her, and those words that would not leave her mind.

The nightmares are coming.

CHAPTER EIGHT

They arrived at the library early in the morning to find police barricades, a small army of construction workers, and their apartment's contents dumped on the snowy street.

"At least the protesters are gone," Marco said, giving Addy an uneasy smile.

They ran toward the barricades. A couple policemen were guarding the place, sipping steaming coffee, their breath frosting. They turned toward Addy and Marco, who were busy climbing over the barricades.

"Sir, ma'am, halt!"

"That's our stuff!" Addy shouted. "We live here."

She and Marco leaped over the barricades and hurried toward their things. The apartment above the library had been emptied out. Mattresses, the couch, the television, tables and chairs, piles of clothes—all lay on the street, covered in snow and mud.

"My hockey trophies!" Addy said, pulling them out from the snow. "My favorite jeans!"

They began fishing items from the sludge. Marco found a bundle of papers with his old short stories and his *Loggerhead* manuscript; they were sopping wet, the ink washing away.

Cringing, he stuffed them into his jacket. His photographs were scattered across the sidewalk. He raced after them, collecting muddy photos of his parents, of himself as a baby, of Kemi. When he found a photo of himself and Lailani, posing with silly faces on an army base, he hesitated, then grabbed it and stuffed it into his jacket too.

"Addy, look for the old coffee tin," he said.

Addy stood a few feet away, holding their war trophies. In one hand, she held the can of Spam she had stolen from an army kitchen. In the other hand, she held a scum claw the size of a sword. Her eyes widened, and she nodded.

"Civilians, move back!" boomed a policeman's voice through a megaphone. "This building is being demolished. Move behind the barricade!"

"This is our home!" Addy shouted. "You'd know that if you waited six to eight weeks for our paperwork to process!"

Ignoring the voices calling them back, they finally found it: a dented tin can labeled *Colonel Coffee*, emblazoned with a cartoon of a smiling colonel drinking from a steaming mug. Marco peeked inside, nodded, and closed the lid again. He stuffed the can into his coat pocket, where it barely fit.

"All right, kids, you've had your fun." A policeman grabbed them. "Behind the barricades."

"We haven't had time to collect all our things," Marco said.

"We posted a notice on the front door months ago," the policeman said.

"We were off in the military!" Addy said. "Protecting Earth! We didn't see your fucking notice until a few days ago, and those fucking goddamn commies and Nazis were blocking us, and—"

"Watch your tongue, citizen," said the cop, "unless you want to spend the night in a jail cell."

Addy fell silent, but Marco wondered if a jail cell might be an upgrade from Steve's apartment.

Clutching whatever they had salvaged, they stepped back toward the barricade, but they did not climb back to the street. Construction crews were bustling around the library. A man in an armored suit emerged onto the sidewalk, then stepped back, reeling out a cable.

"Ten minutes to detonation!" somebody boomed through a megaphone.

"What about the books in the library?" Marco asked, turning toward the policeman, but the man only shrugged and kept sipping his coffee. Marco ran toward the construction crew. "There are still books in the library! Who's the foreman here?"

A potbellied, mustached man in a hardhat approached. "Look, kids, I know you're war heroes and all, but you're going to have to step back and let us do our work."

Marco found rare fury inside him. "There are books in there. Thousands of books. Tens of thousands. You'll just bury them?"

The man shrugged. "We tried, kid. We asked around. There are no other libraries in this city. We sold some of them on the street last month, if that makes you feel better. The romance, thrillers, the dragon stuff, that went fast. Got a few for my wife. Whatever's left inside is what nobody wants to read. Besides, barely anyone reads paper books anymore."

"I do," Marco said.

"Not anymore," said the foreman.

Addy fumed. "Fuck. This. Shit." She grabbed Marco's hand. "Come on, Poet. We faced the scum in battle. We can defeat a few construction workers. Let's save your stories."

She was about to pull him into the library when a voice rang out behind them.

"Marco Emery? Addy Linden?"

They spun around. A man wearing a suit, expensive shoes, and a woolen overcoat was approaching them, holding a bundle of papers. A Rolex shone on his wrist.

"Who the fuck are you?" Addy said. "Are you funding these goons?"

The man reached out his hand to shake. Neither Marco nor Addy took it. The man never lost his smile.

"Name's Ben Bradley, attorney at law. My clients, the nonprofit organization Never War, have raised some concerns about your involvement with human supremacist groups, as well as possible war crimes perpetrated against alien lifeforms." Smile sparkling, he handed Marco the bundle of papers. "Here is the summons for your trial. It's set to begin tomorrow morning, address and time on your papers. Please be on time."

"What the fuck?" Addy grabbed the papers, stared at them, then tossed them into the snow. "Fuck this! The trial is in Never War's headquarters, not a proper court. And you're just a goddamn lawyer, not some sheriff, and can't give us summons. This isn't how it works. I know! My dad was in jail enough times that I learned the stuff."

Bradley's smile never faltered. "Things have changed around here, Linden. The war changed everything. We must be a bit more . . . efficient these days. Never War is in the process of legitimizing all its courts, in accordance with the Civilian Duty laws passed last year. Rest assured that these documents are legally binding, as supervised by the Government of the North American Alliance, as well as Chrysopoeia Corporation, owners of all correctional facilities on the continent. If you cannot afford a lawyer of your own, you will have the opportunity to defend yourselves at your trial." He nodded. "See you tomorrow morning. Sir, ma'am."

"You'll see my foot in your ass!" Addy shouted as the lawyer walked away. "Fuck you and your kangaroo court! And—"

A rumble sounded behind them.

Marco and Addy spun back toward the library.

The building fell with clouds of dust, with crumbling stone, with dying memories. The jets screeched overhead. The landing craft stormed down toward the alien world. The missiles rained and the corpses of men and bugs flew. The starships fell like a thousand comets from the sky, burning, crashing into the desert, raising storms of sand and fire and smoke. Before him, as his home collapsed, the war flared, and the dust painted him, and his wounds howled with agony.

It only took a few moments. It lasted for years. The library fell and the apartment seemed to stand for an instant above it, resting on a cloud, until it too fell and vanished and all that remained was stone, dust, an old life. Gone.

"I never even took my mother's paintings," Marco said softly, staring.

Addy placed her arms around him. They stood together, embracing, staring at the debris for a long time.

"Fuck it," Addy finally said, voice choked. "Fuck them all. Let's go get drunk and watch *Robot Wrestling*. We'll fight them all tomorrow."

Yet as they walked away, eyes damp, Marco didn't know how to fight this, didn't know how to fight a war with legal forms, with lawyers, with words. He couldn't just raise his gun here, couldn't blast aliens away with a hailstorm of bullets.

Maybe that's all I am now, Marco thought. *A brainless killer. Maybe the only way I can fight is with a gun. But this too is a war. This too is a battle I must fight. But I don't know how. And I'm losing.*

The snow kept falling, scented of dust and burning metal.

CHAPTER NINE

There she stood in the hangar. The HDFS *Saint Brendan*.

My starship, Ben-Ari thought.

She paused, just for an instant, gazing at her. Across Nightwall, they would be hunting her. The admiral was probably waking up around now. The military police would be deployed, and soon the fleet. But for just that instant, Ben-Ari had to stop. She had to stare. She had to look at the ship that meant everything to her.

"Look what they did to my girl," she said.

Ben-Ari had worked hard since the war to earn this, a ship under her own command. After the Battle of Abaddon, she had left the infantry, had served on other ships—some massive warships with a crew of thousands, others smaller ships with a couple hundred soldiers aboard. And for four years, she had watched ship after ship decommissioned, too costly to maintain with a ravaged, crumbling Earth needing to be rebuilt. For four years, she had served loyally, relying on her skills of command rather than kissing the right asses, a route many of her fellow officers took. And finally, only months ago, she had earned this.

The *Saint Brendan*. A ship of her own.

She was a small ship, large enough for a crew of fifteen, no more. She was still only a captain, a junior officer; majors and colonels commanded the larger vessels, and only generals could command the mighty starfighter carriers with their complement of thousands. Ben-Ari was still young, only twenty-five, but she was smart, she was eager, and she had dedicated her life to the military.

The *Saint Brendan* was more than just a stealth ship. It was her new home, her house, her treasure.

And today, sitting here in a hangar aboard Space Station One, the *Saint Brendan* was hurt. Maybe badly. The ship looked like a beat-up tin can. A mechanic stood on a ladder, working on replacing an exhaust coil. He had already sealed the large crack exposing the crew quarters, and it looked like the exhaust was almost done, but the hull was still dented. That would hurt the ship's stealth capability, its most valuable asset. When Ben-Ari had taken command of the *Brendan* only a few months ago, she had been slick, beautiful, a black shard of night, as graceful as a midnight horse galloping under the moon. She was ugly now.

But you will still fly, Ben-Ari thought. *Because you're my ship. And we need you. We all need you.*

"Ma'am, we have to move," Kemi said, standing at her side. The lieutenant panted, still weak from her injury. She clenched her good hand, and her new prosthetic hung at her side. Only hours ago, she had lain in a hospital bed, recovering from the surgery to attach her new metal hand.

Ben-Ari nodded and turned toward the mechanic.

"Sergeant, we're taking her out," she said. "Now."

The mechanic stepped back from the ship. He wore a white jumpsuit, heavy boots, a hardhat, and a tool belt.

"Pardon, ma'am," he said, "but the ship isn't space-worthy. The exhaust still needs work. She—"

"We're flying *now*," Ben-Ari said. "Step back."

She stepped toward the ship and reached for the doors.

"Ma'am, I must object," said the mechanic, letting harshness fill his voice. "She won't be ready for days. I'm going to ask you to step back now." He moved to block the ship's airlock.

Ben-Ari glared at him. "I'm carrying out orders from high above. The information is above your security clearance. Stand aside and prepare to open the hangar doors. That is an order, Sergeant."

"Ma'am, with all due respect, I don't take my orders from you," the mechanic said. "I'm happy to ring my commanding officer, and you can discuss this with him, but right now, you're not stepping onto this ship, and—"

An alarm blared across the hangar. Voices emerged from speakers.

"Security alert. All hangar bays to shut down across Space Station One. Any soldier or officer with information on the whereabouts of Captain Einav Ben-Ari to report at once."

The mechanic reached for his communicator.

A funnel of air burst forward and slammed into the mechanic. He cried out, struggling to stay standing. A second blast from Kemi's metal hand hit his chest. The mechanic fell, banging his head against the exhaust pipe on his way to the floor.

"Looks like he's exhausted," Kemi said, pointing at the unconscious mechanic. "Get it? *Exhaust*ed?"

Ben-Ari sighed. "Hurry up, Lieutenant. Into the ship."

The alarms kept blaring. The hangar doors opened, and armed military policemen entered.

Kemi blasted out a funnel, knocking down a man, then leaped into the ship. Ben-Ari followed.

My military career is over, Ben-Ari knew as she ran through the ship. *All my years of work, my family legacy—over.* She clenched her fists. *But if the marauders invade, it's over for everyone.*

She raced onto the bridge and leaped into her captain's chair. Kemi sat down beside her at the controls.

"Officers, halt!" boomed a voice through a megaphone. "Halt now or we will fire!"

"Kemi, get us out of here!" Ben-Ari shouted.

The ship turned around, creaking, toward the hangar airlock. Kemi hit buttons madly, but the doors remained closed.

"It's locked!" she cried. "I can't open it by remote! I'll have to get out and open it manually, and—"

"Fire!" shouted a soldier outside, and bullets slammed into the *Saint Brendan*.

Ben-Ari hit her control panel. Photon bolts blasted out from the *Saint Brendan*'s front cannon, slamming into the airlock hatch.

The hatch shattered open, exposing the vacuum of space.

Kemi shoved down on the throttle.

As the fleeing air caught the military policemen, tugging them toward the breach, the *Saint Brendan* roared out into space.

Space Station One floated behind them. The dark planet of Nightwall spread below. Dozens of Space Territorial Command warships hovered ahead. For an instant, Ben-Ari was struck by the madness of it. She had dedicated her life to the military. For generations, her family had served. Now, like this, within an instant, she was tossing a military dynasty away. She was fleeing her post. She was a traitor to be captured and killed. And she had to do it. She had to reach Earth. If the high command of Nightwall was hiding the marauder threat, Ben-Ari had to make this threat public. Humanity had to know, had to prepare for the oncoming storm.

Or we're dead. All of us.

Ahead, a hangar bay opened on a massive warship. A squadron of Firebird starfighters emerged.

"Lieutenant—" Ben-Ari began.

"I see them," Kemi replied, tugging the joystick. The *Saint Brendan* veered upward, moving farther from the dark planet below. The Firebirds followed, splitting into two groups, seven starfighters in each.

Damn it. Damn it! They were still too close to the planet for warp speed; its gravity and radiation wouldn't let their azoth engine bend spacetime properly. Would they make it far enough?

"They're too fast!" Ben-Ari said.

"I know Firebirds," Kemi said. "I flew them for five years. And I know how to escape them."

Speakers crackled to life on the bridge. A voice emerged.

"HDFS *Saint Brendan*! Cease your flight now, or we will open fire. Do you copy, *Saint Brendan*?"

Kemi spun the ship around, facing the pursuing starfighters.

Ben-Ari cringed. "Lieutenant . . ."

"Trust me, ma'am."

The Firebirds stormed toward them. Behind them hovered several warships. Farther back loomed Space Station One, a massive structure, roughly shaped like a mushroom. Its rounded top supported a smaller bulb—the Dome where Ben-Ari had first met the admiral.

"*Saint Brendan*, you have five seconds to shut off your engines or we will open fire!" rose the voice from the Firebird squadron.

"Hold on, Captain!" Kemi said, yanking the joystick back.

Ben-Ari gripped her seat.

Missiles flew from the Firebirds.

The *Brendan* veered upward, and Kemi hit a button, releasing a hundred whizzing lures.

The missiles slammed into the lures, attracted by their heat. Explosions lit space, rocking the *Saint Brendan*.

"Add more lures to our shopping list!" Kemi said.

"And a new pair of underwear!" Ben-Ari said, clutching her armrests.

They flew back toward the space station. The starless planet spun ahead, its black surface dotted with military bases, all powered by nuclear reactors built deep within the rocky world. Behind the *Saint Brendan*, the Firebirds kept pursuing.

"They can't fire on us with the station ahead," Kemi said. "Just . . . need . . . to . . ."

Cannons blasted from the space station.

Wincing, Ben-Ari fired the *Brendan*'s guns, hitting the missiles flying their way. Plasma and shards of metal flew through space. Shrapnel scraped their hull.

Kemi shoved the throttle forward, and they plunged toward the world below, racing along the space station's stalk.

Missiles soared from the planet's surface, streaks of light in the darkness.

Kemi yanked sideways, and the *Brendan* barrel-rolled, dodging the blows. One missile flew between wing and hull, then slammed into a Firebird that swooped above them. Firelight filled the bridge.

An instant before they could hit the planet surface, Kemi pulled back, and they skimmed along the rocky plains. A few last military bases shone ahead, and the *Brendan* dodged their fire, then flew into darkness.

Kemi whooped. "All right! We're flying below the radar now. Captain, mind if I turn off the lights?" Not waiting for a reply, she flipped a few switches, and the bridge plunged into darkness. Only the control panels now glowed. "We'll be harder to detect like this. Our stealth engine is a bit wonky, but the planet's surface should disguise us well enough." She dipped down to fly within a canyon.

Ben-Ari checked the monitors. The enemy ships were still following, but they were lost in darkness.

Enemy ships? she thought. *So quickly I begin to see the Human Defense Force as my enemy!*

"Lieutenant," Ben-Ari said, struggling to hide the tremble in her voice. "What I saw in the Augury . . . we're not prepared for it. Myriads of marauder warships, surrounding our territory. At Nightwall, there's only the remnants of a once-proud fleet. Reports from Earth speak of no preparation. Humanity is being kept in the dark." She inhaled deeply. "I don't know if Admiral Komagata is a marauder agent or just horribly incompetent, but one thing I know. There can be no peace with those creatures we saw in the prison."

Kemi looked at her mechanical hand. "They tend to prefer pieces to peace."

"Do we have enough fuel to make it to Sol?"

"Back to our home star?" Kemi scrunched her lips. "If we coast through warped space, and we slingshot around a few stars, then coast some more . . . yes, we can make it back home. We'll be running on fumes and might have to get out and push the last few kilometers, but I think we can reach Earth."

Ben-Ari smiled wryly. "I said we're heading back to our solar system. Not to Earth. We're going to the asteroid belt."

Kemi raised an eyebrow. "What's on the asteroid belt?"

"The only person who can help us now," Ben-Ari said softly. She looked back at the rear viewport. "Looks like our Firebird friends are scattering. We're invisible." She patted the ship's control panel. "Good girl. Best ship in the fleet."

They kept flying through canyons and along valleys, picking up speed, until the lights of the fleet and space station faded behind them. There they dared leave the planet and plunge into the deep darkness, praying their stealth technology cloaked them from the fleet. Far behind them, they could still see Firebirds scanning the night, finding no trace of the escaped spy ship. The lights grew smaller and smaller, until the starless planet vanished in the distance.

"Ready, Captain?" Kemi said.

Ben-Ari nodded. "Take us out, Lieutenant."

Kemi typed on her control panel. Deep within the starship, a heavy engine rumbled. Spacetime itself flowed into the azoth crystal, then burst out like light through a diamond, taking new form. Around the *Saint Brendan*, spacetime—the very fabric of the universe—curved, forming a warped bubble. Light bent and the distant stars appeared as streaks.

They shot forward at many times the speed of light. Without azoth technology, using traditional engines, it would take millennia to travel from here to Sol. With their azoth engine, it would take three weeks.

"I just hope we're not too late," Ben-Ari said.

As they flew, she kept seeing it. The marauder in the prison. The one called Malphas. The claws, the fangs, the tongue lapping up the brain. How his eyes had stared into hers. How he had grinned. How thousands of his ravager ships surrounded this corner of the Milky Way, preparing to invade.

We will meet again, the creature had told her. *The nightmares are coming.*

"Yes," Ben-Ari whispered. "We will meet again. I'm waiting. I will be ready."

They flew on through the darkness, a single dented ship, hurtling toward hope.

CHAPTER TEN

The four of them sat on the filthy sofa, knees pressed together.
Marco. Addy. Her hulking boyfriend Steve. The bearded, silent
Stooge, his eyes hazy. On the television screen, two robots were
pounding at each other. One of the machines swung a hammer,
crushing the other robot. Gears and saw blades flew.

"Hell yeah!" Steve said, leaping from his seat and
pounding the air. "Hammerhead pounds again!"

"Fucking shit." Addy pulled a sweaty cigarette pack from
her back pocket and tossed it at him. "You win again. Someday
Switchblade will win."

"Switchblade is a loser." Steve gave a victory lap around
the couch, scattering empty beer cans and potato chip bags.
"Hammerhead kicked Switchblade's shiny metal a—"

"Shh, the news is coming on," Marco said.

Steve snorted and patted Marco's head. "Got to watch the
stock quotes, little dude?"

"Actually, they seem to have a story about Addy and me,"
Marco said, eyes widening.

"Whoa." Steve sat back down, cramming between them.
"No way."

"Whoa," Stooge opined, the most vocal Marco had ever heard him.

The television showed footage from outside the library yesterday, back when the library had still stood. The Never War peace protesters stood on one side, and the Earth Power supremacists marched toward them, circling around Marco and Addy to protect them.

"My ass is *not* that big," Addy said, frowning at the television.

"They do say the camera adds ten pounds," Steve said. "But judging by this footage, I'd say it's more like thirty."

Addy punched him.

The footage froze when Marco was trying to shove away a violent protester. The freeze frame caught him with his hand raised, looking to the world like a Nazi salute. A caption appeared beneath the frozen frame: *Marco Emery, Neo-Nazi?*

Addy gasped. "Marco! How could you?"

"Oh, shush."

A stern-looking broadcaster appeared. "The location of Marco Emery and Addy Linden, suspected war criminals and white supremacists, is still unknown. According to our sources, their trial is set to begin tomorrow morning. Both Emery and Linden served in the Second Galactic War and are suspected of carrying out atrocities against the aliens' homeworld, including the destruction of their central hive, resulting in the death of millions of sentient, intelligent alien beings. Sources tell us that Never War lawyers will seek police intervention if the two refuse to appear in court."

Addy rose to her feet and turned off the television.

"Down in front!" Steve said.

Addy turned toward them, hands on her hips.

"Now you listen to me, Marco Emery." She glared at him. "I know what you're thinking. You want to go to that court. You want to defend our honor. You want to fight with words, to show the world our innocence. Well, fuck you and your words. I'm a warrior. Maybe not a soldier anymore, but a warrior still. I'm staying right here, and if any of those goons show up to arrest us, I'll fight them. I don't have a gun anymore, but I have this hockey stick." She grabbed a stick from the wall. "And I have my fists. And I'm strong."

Steve rose to his feet. "I'm with you, Ads. We fight." He raised his fist. "Like Hammerhead!"

Addy patted his head. "Yes, Steve, just like Hammerhead."

"I can't believe I'm saying this," Marco said, "but I agree with you, Addy."

"Marco!" She grabbed his collar. "I told you to listen! We can't go to their stupid court. We—"

"Addy, I'm agreeing with you!" Marco pulled her fingers off his shirt. "For God's sake, calm down. I'm not going tomorrow either." He smoothed his shirt. "If we show up at their court, we're legitimizing it. You heard their lawyer. He's working on getting his court to be government-approved. That means they're still not legal. Not yet at least. If we step into their headquarters, it means we respect their authority. And we do not. We stay right here, and with any luck, the media will find some other scapegoat to harangue tomorrow."

Steve's brow furrowed. "Does that mean I don't hammer anyone?"

"I hope not," Marco said.

That night, Stooge slept on the floor again; Steve assured them that his bearded, laconic friend was most comfortable there, especially after several nights of falling off the couch. Marco lay on that couch, unable to sleep. Too much stress, too many nightmares. Too many dreams of that creature with his face. When Addy and Steve began having noisy sex again in the bedroom—she was shouting out to God like an enraptured nun, and he was grunting like an enraged warthog—Marco knew it was hopeless. He flipped on the television, restless, and cranked up the volume to mask the noise. Stooge kept snoring in the corner, peaceful as a babe in his mother's arms.

Marco paused on a random channel, which was screening an episode of *All Systems Go!*, a Japanese cartoon about a katana-wielding, cat-eared schoolgirl who fought crime. The bright, flashing colors were so jarring Marco was thankful when a commercial break interrupted the show. He sat on the tattered couch, staring, the light from the television washing over him. On the screen, children gave the thumbs up while munching on Scum Cereal, each piece shaped like a little centipede. A commercial for Chrysopoeia Corp appeared next, showing happy miners tipping their helmets; according to the narrator, they were paving our way to the stars. Marco winced when he remembered the mines of Corpus. On the screen, soldiers replaced the miners, marching across the desert, waving flags. Their drill sergeant pointed at Marco, wanting *him* to enlist today.

"Been there, done that," Marco muttered.

The desert vanished, replaced with a green suburban street. A family was playing ball in a yard, and a Golden Retriever wagged his tail. Trees rustled, a milkman waved from his truck, and a lovely woman in a flowery dress rose from the garden she was tending to. She smiled at Marco.

"Do you still dream the American dream?" she said. "Some on Earth say it has died. But not in the colonies!"

The camera zoomed out, showing street after suburban street, all lined with trees, then zoomed out some more, showing an entire city enclosed in a massive bubble. Still the shot zoomed out, showing a lush planet. Finally the camera pulled back even more, taking the viewer into a starship that orbited the planet. The same woman in the flowery dress somehow stood in the spaceship too, and she smiled at Marco.

"Book your ticket to Haven today. We seek settlers who dream!"

Smiling, tanned colonists stepped in front of the camera, waving. "Join us in Haven and we'll dream together!"

They vanished, and Godzilla was now fighting a giant scum in Tokyo. *Godzilla vs. King Scum!* Coming this winter to a theater near you.

As the giant scum reared on the television screen, as Addy screamed in the bedroom, Marco couldn't take it. He was back there again. He couldn't stand this stifling apartment, these sounds, these visions, these flashbacks. Not even pausing to grab his coat, he burst out of the apartment, raced downstairs, and ran out into the night.

He stood on the street, the snow rising around his feet. It was cold. It was so damn cold. His wounds ached as if claws still dug into him, and he looked up at the stars, a futile attempt to seek warmth from those distant suns. Their light was so cold. So far. His tears flowed down his cheeks, freezing.

"I miss you, Father," he whispered. "I don't know what will happen tomorrow. I don't know if I'm going to prison, if I'll end up homeless, if I can still find a life here. Lailani left me. Our home is gone. We're treated like war criminals. And I'm scared. I wish you were here. I don't know what to do."

A voice answered from behind.

"Well, first of all, put on a jacket, you fucking idiot. And then stop pitying yourself."

He turned to see Addy there, holding out his jacket. She wore her own coat. He accepted it gratefully.

"You should have been in military intelligence with all your eavesdropping," Marco said.

She rolled her eyes. "Please. You're the one who kept listening to Steve and me banging."

"The entire city was listening to Steve and you banging," Marco said.

"Well, it's nicer than hearing neo-Nazi chants at least." She elbowed him. "Come on, Poet. It's not that bad. We're still alive, right? And we're back in Canada. So long as those two things are true, it's not so bad."

He looked up at the stars, silent for long moments. "I miss it, Addy. Not the war. Not the army. Just . . . being up there. When I was in space, all I wanted to do was come home to Earth. But I don't know if this planet is my home anymore. We saved the Earth. We saved it for billions of people. But not for us. We don't belong here anymore."

She gazed up at the stars with him. Her breath frosted. "Fuck, I need an ice cream sundae. A giant one. There used to be an all-night place around here. Lots of drunk losers would go there after clubbing." She took his hand. "Come on, it's on me."

"You don't have any money, Ads."

"Can I borrow some? Just the price of two ice creams? My treat!"

She pulled him down the road. Two blocks away, they found the place, a rundown ice cream parlor squeezed between a tattoo shop and a psychic. The place only had four tables, and they sat by the window. Addy ordered a sundae large enough for a family, topping it with chocolate chips, sprinkles, and bacon bits. Why the place even offered bacon bits, Marco didn't know, but Addy tossed them onto her sundae like it was her job.

Marco wasn't hungry, especially after witnessing Addy's culinary butchery. He just ordered a coffee.

"I'm telling you, Poet," Addy said between spoonfuls. "I'm not sharing. Get something."

"Not hungry, and we need to save our cash."

"Ice cream is more important." She shoveled in another spoonful, swallowed, winced, and touched her forehead. "Ow, ow, ow. Brain freeze."

He gasped. "I didn't know you had a brain!"

"Funny, old man with his sad little coffee." She took a sip of his steaming drink. "There, my head is better already."

Marco checked the clock on the wall. "Ads, it'll be morning in four hours. They'll find us. They'll drag us to their kangaroo court. What do we do? We can't hide in Steve's apartment forever. He uses dish soap for shampoo, Addy. Dish soap. And that stick of butter I found in the fridge? It was a moldy cucumber."

Addy cringed. "And I put it on a sandwich." She stuck out her tongue. "Thank God for ice cream to freeze out the germs."

Marco stared into his coffee cup. "This is fucked. All of it. They take us as kids. Eighteen years old. Scared shitless. They have us fight aliens for five years. Then they toss us back out, like nothing ever happened. No money. No place to stay, at least for us. No jobs. No pension, not with the war debt. We're twenty-three years old, and we're helpless as babies on this planet. We know everything about cleaning a gun and killing space bugs, nothing about how to survive on the planet we saved."

Addy nodded. "Shit's fucked up."

A pile of newspapers and magazines topped a garbage bin. Marco approached. He pushed aside a tabloid, its headline announcing that Bat Boy had been named commander-in-chief of the HDF. He cringed to see a photo of himself, supposedly giving a Nazi salute, on the cover of the *Toronto Moon Gazette*. Finally he found what he was seeking, the week's real estate magazine. He returned with it to the table, where Addy was devouring the last few bites of sundae.

She belched and patted her belly with satisfaction. "Anyone for seconds?"

"God, I don't know where it all goes with you," Marco said.

"I burn all the energy with sex."

Marco cringed. "TMI, Addy. Too much information. Sheesh."

He opened the magazine, leafing through real estate editorials. He cringed to see a full-page ad for Midtown Skylight Condos, set to be built over the ruins of the library. He quickly flipped the page. Finally he found the section he sought: the chapter on Haven Colony.

Humanity had built several colonies within the so-called Human Commonwealth, called by some the Human Empire, the sphere of space and stars around Earth. The most famous of these colonies was Nightwall on the frontier, a massive military base, headquarters of Space Territorial Command, home to many of humanity's brightest scientists and bravest soldiers. Most other colonies were owned by corporations, homes to miners. But a handful of colonies were purely residential. There was a sizable colony on Mars, smaller ones on Europa and Titan. By far, the largest colony was Haven.

"Haven," Marco read from the magazine. "Your home among the stars since 2075."

Addy leaned closer, peering at the page. "Haven. Harboring losers who can't make it on Earth since 2075."

Marco pulled the magazine back. "You made that up."

"Did not! I'd never know a word like *harbor* by myself."

Haven colony took up thirty pages, the entire second half of the magazine. Marco flipped to a page showing an aerial view of the colony. Its planet was named New Earth, due to its size, temperature, and gravity, all of which were nearly identical to Earth. But Marco thought it looked more like Old Earth, like Earth before humanity had polluted and overbuilt it, before the aliens had ravaged it. The colony of Haven nestled between pristine mountains and a shiny blue sea. Silvery skyscrapers rose along the coast, but most of the colony was covered in trees, the roofs of houses peeking between them. Marco assumed that the photo had been taken inside the protective dome covering the city, holding in its air.

"It's pretty," Addy said. She moved her chair beside him, gazing with him at the photo.

"Nicer than this dump," Marco said. "Expensive, though."

"Good thing you're going to be a famous rich author someday."

Marco sighed. "If I can ever find a publisher for *Loggerhead*, then write another few books."

Addy flipped the page. Her eyes widened. "Ooh, I like this neighborhood. And look! Hockey!"

The page showed a watercolor painting of an idyllic neighborhood. Two children were playing street hockey while Mom and Dad waved from the patio. Page after page showed beautiful homes with catchy slogans.

Live among the stars!

Live the Human Dream!

Live on Earth as it was!

A fresh start for humanity!

Mommy, can my doll come with us to Haven too?

All veterans of Abaddon welcome!

"Kids, we're closing for an hour," said the shop owner. "Got to clean before the morning rush."

Addy frowned at the bald, pot-bellied man. "I thought this place was open twenty-four hours."

"Yeah, well, I thought Angelo was coming to my apartment to clean the carpets, not bang my wife." He gestured at the door. "Life ain't fair."

Marco and Addy stepped outside into the cold. They stood on the snowy street, hands stuffed under their armpits. They walked down the block toward Steve's building. Halfway there, Marco paused.

"Ads, wait."

She stopped beside him. "What, Poet? I'm freezing my ass off and I got to piss."

"Let's go."

"That's what I'm saying!"

Marco shook his head. "Not to your boyfriend's place. To hell with that." He looked at the stars. "Up there."

"What, onto the roof?"

Marco groaned. "Addy."

"To Haven?"

Marco nodded. "We're veterans of Abaddon, right? We fought on the scum's planet. We survived where millions fell. That means we get free green cards to Haven. So let's go." He took her hands. "Let's go now."

"Before I even pee?"

Marco nodded. "Hold it in!" He pulled the coffee tin from his pocket, the one he had fished out from the snow outside the library. He opened it, revealing the wads of cash within. "My dad's life savings."

Her eyes widened. "Fuck me! I never knew Carl squirreled away a fortune. How much is in there?"

"Not much," Marco said. "A couple million bucks, mostly in bills of fifty thousand. Not a fortune since the great inflation and the wars. But enough for two tickets to Haven. One-way tickets only, and we'll probably have to fly with the pets in cargo, but we might just have enough." He put the tin back in his pocket. "Like the magazine said. Our home among the stars."

Addy grew solemn. "I don't know, Marco . . . It's lovely up there. Almost too lovely. Can you imagine us living in a house like that? With a yard and everything, like a couple boring suburbanites?"

"Beats this place." Marco looked around him. He saw frozen sidewalks. Rusty balconies. Raw concrete apartment blocks. A homeless man was shuffling down the street, while another lay sleeping on a vent. "Addy, Earth is no longer our home. You know that."

She took a deep breath. "And Haven can be? We'd arrive there broke. You said the tickets would suck us dry. How will we survive there?"

"We'll find work," Marco said. "I learned some computer skills in the army. Remember, I spent my last three years there working with computers, gaining experience. And I can write more novels, maybe even sell one. And you're a great fighter. I bet you can teach martial arts, or even start your own security company. With a steady paycheck, we can get a mortgage, maybe rent a place until we save up some cash. Come on, Ads! We survived Abaddon. We can survive fucking *Haven*."

"Let me see that again." She snatched the magazine from him, and she stared long and hard at the watercolor painting of the children playing hockey on their driveway. When she looked back up at Marco, her eyes were damp. "Let's do this. Let's go. Just . . . I really *do* have to go back to Steve's place and pee first." She bit her lip. "I'll be careful not to wake him. I'll leave him a note." She grinned. "Maybe I'll even use the word *harbor*."

The rocket rumbled.

Fire filled the world.

Their seats rattled, and they gripped the armrests, and Addy hooted with joy.

They took off.

The rocket soared through the atmosphere, and within moments, they were in space. Through the viewport, Addy and Marco could see Toronto grow smaller, then all of North America, then a blue sphere floating in the blackness, limned with a thin band of azure sky.

Three hundred people filled the starship. Marco and Addy sat side by side, prepared for a week in space, then a lifetime on a new world. He wore old corduroy pants and a gray sweatshirt, both tattered and stained with mud and snow, and his sneakers were torn. Addy wore jean shorts, sandals, and a tank top, exposing the tattoos on her arms: a Maple Leaf for her favorite hockey team and a star for each scum she had killed.

Everyone around them was well dressed. Clean. Well spoken. Immigrants with money and dreams. Marco and Addy were just two weary, poor, homeless veterans and orphans. War heroes. Refugees. The most celebrated and hated people in the human empire. They were the highest of the high and the lowest of the low. They were dreamers and they were haunted with shattered dreams. Addy kept prattling and joking, but when Earth faded to a pale dot of light, she grew silent, and they sat together, gazing at it. From here, Earth seemed no larger than a star.

"How did you once say it?" Addy asked. "A dust ball?"

"A mote of dust suspended in a sunbeam," Marco said. "That's what Carl Sagan called this view of Earth. A long time ago."

"Must have been a smart dude." Addy yawned. "I'm going to sleep for a week. Wake me up when we reach Haven." She closed her eyes, then opened one and smiled at him. "I'm happy, Poet. I'm happy we're doing this. I'm happy you're with me."

She closed both eyes, leaned her head on his shoulder, and slept. Marco closed his eyes and slept too. By the time he woke up, Earth was gone from view.

CHAPTER ELEVEN

Marco had never sympathized so much with his hamburger.

Alpha Centauri, their destination, was the closest star system to Earth. Their ship's azoth engines were capable of warp drive, bending spacetime around them, enabling faster-than-light travel. Even so, it was a week's flight. A week to another star system, perhaps, was once the realm of science fiction, a miraculously speedy journey. But for Marco, crammed into this small starship with hundreds of other passengers, confined to a seat no larger than his body, it seemed to last an eternity.

"We're like cattle in here," he muttered. He shoved away his dry burger—not that there was much room to shove it before it hit the seat in front of him, but he gave that inch everything it was worth. "I've got no appetite. I feel for the poor cow."

Addy sat beside him, knees pulled to her chin. She grabbed his burger and added it to her plate. "You should talk. Imagine surviving this journey with long legs like mine."

"We're the same height," Marco said.

"Well, then you need to be flexible like me." Addy took a bite of burger. "Mmm, tastes like Spam!"

The kid behind Marco was still kicking his seat. Marco had tried all manner of glowers—both at the kid and his parents—but nothing seemed to help. He rose to his feet and stretched as much as room allowed. The rows of seats filled the fuselage. Through the portholes, he could see stars stretched into lines as the azoth engines bent spacetime. There wasn't an empty seat. Families with crying children. Veterans. Religious pilgrims clad in robes. Migrant workers. Retirees. Young dreamers. All manner of people had paid the price to leave Earth, to fly to Haven, to begin a new life or end a long one in the colony. The smell of sweat, cheap deodorant, and hundreds of dry burgers filled the hot, stale air. The cries of babies and the hum of engines filled the vessel. Several people kept coughing. Marco had hoped to walk up and down the aisle, but it was clogged with a dozen people waiting in line for the bathroom, a cart selling refreshments probably dating back to the Golden Age of Air Travel, and even somebody's therapy pig.

"Therapy pigs," Marco muttered. "For God's sake, *therapy pigs.*"

The animal's owner overheard and glared at him. Her pet pig gave a glare too, followed by a haughty oink.

I don't know if there's even a difference between us and the pig, Marco thought. *We're just animals here, crammed into a cattle car.*

He had flown to the stars before. In the military, he had traveled deeper into space than this. But the military was rich, and their ships offered bunks, actual cots, mess halls, relaxation lounges. Their engines were larger and faster too. Those trips had been pleasant. Here, Marco was already wishing a renegade scum pod would attack and end their misery.

"It'll be worth it when we reach Haven," Addy said. "Just one more day."

"Every day here lasts a year, I'm sure of it," Marco said. "Something to do with relativity and time dilation. That's science."

"That's just your whining," Addy said. "So sit your ass back down and let's look through the brochure again."

She pulled him back into his seat. His hip banged against the sidebar, and his elbows pressed painfully against his sides. He didn't even need Addy's elbows to poke him here; his own elbows were doing the work. He reached between his legs and pulled out the real estate magazine, the one they had picked up at the ice cream parlor back home.

Addy sighed. "It's beautiful."

The magazine had dedicated thirty pages to Haven, and Marco and Addy had examined them through and through countless times over the past few days. The images were already seared into Marco's mind, but still they flipped the pages, slowly, savoring each one.

There was an aerial view of the colony, showing tree-lined streets, charming houses with large yards and swimming pools, and natural paths coiling between forested hills toward lakes. There were watercolor paintings of serene brick homes, children playing in the driveways, Mother smiling in the garden, Father reading a newspaper on the porch. Ads appeared alongside the paintings, promising an easy start for colonists.

Cheap mortgages for brave colonists, no background checks!
Workers wanted! Free training course for all veterans!

Affordable kitchens for your new colony home! Choose from marble, granite, and so much more!

Live on the waterfront! Veterans come first!

Forested trails right outside your home! Live among Haven's pristine beauty! Native whistling birds right outside your window!

"Addy, you know, some of these houses are kind of expensive," Marco said. "And our asses are broke."

She poked the page. "Look! See? Cheap mortgages!"

"You need a job to get a cheap mortgage."

She poked another page. "Workers wanted! Done." She gripped his hand. "Look, Poet, I don't expect to land and live in a palace right away. We'll start small. We'll rent a place until we find work. We've seen some nice rental listings. We'll work hard. We'll save money. We're smart and tough. Within a year, we'll be living in this house." She pointed at a painting of a two-story home by a forest. "Native whistling birds!"

"Great," Marco said. "Whistling aliens who'll wake us up at five a.m."

"It'll be my fist in your face waking you up for being so grumpy."

Marco tried to keep his expectations low. He didn't want his optimism running wild like Addy's, leading to disappointment. But he had to admit, her enthusiasm was infectious, and their times perusing the magazine were his best hours since leaving the military.

I just wish you could be here with us, Lailani, he thought, sudden pain stabbing him.

Since she had gone to the Oort Cloud three years ago on a secret mission, Marco had survived in the military by dreaming of reuniting with her. A couple Christmases had not been enough. In his dreams, he married Lailani in Toronto, lived above the library with her, found joy, an end to war and pain. Every night, he had dreamed of holding Lailani in his arms, never letting her go.

And now you left again, he thought. *On another mission. With another lover.*

He lowered his head, his joy at the prospect of Haven fleeing. What would Haven be without the woman he loved?

You don't want to get close to me, Lailani had told him five years ago. *I'll just break your heart.*

Marco had known this. Known that Lailani was a wild flame, known that she preferred dating girls to boys, known that she could not be held down. He had not chosen to fall in love with her; his heart had chosen this path on its own. And now Marco felt like Lailani was taking a part of his heart with her, that it could never be healed again. Could he find new love in Haven? Or was he doomed to forever sleep on the proverbial couch, listening to Addy's lovemaking while he watched reruns of *Robot Wrestling?*

I won't end up like Stooge, he vowed, shuddering. *Whatever happens in Haven, let Stooge be a warning!*

He sighed. Right now, crammed into his starship seat, he actually missed that ratty old couch.

He closed the magazine. "Just a few more hours left. Let's get some sleep."

They lay across their seats in fetal positions, Marco crammed against the backrests, Addy pressed against the seats in front of them. Only his arms prevented her from falling. It was horridly uncomfortable but a welcome change from sitting upright. Addy snored but Marco only slept fitfully, his arm falling asleep under Addy.

In his dreams, he wasn't in a crammed starship but in an actual cattle car. Thousands of people filled the car with him, naked, bald, frightened, clawing at the walls, desperate for water, for air. The cars rattled down tracks, and through the windows Marco could see alien eyes, claws, great spiders moving on webs, licking their jaws. Ahead loomed a slaughterhouse, pumping out smoke, a place to butcher humans, to prepare the meat, and claws sawed open skulls, and people screamed, wrapped in webs.

"Arrival at the slaughterhouse!" boomed a voice, and deep laughter rumbled. Webs grabbed Marco, and he struggled against the aliens, struggled to escape the cattle car, but he was crammed in here, and they were rolling in, and—

"Arrival at the slaughterhouse!"

Claws shook him.

"Poet, we're here."

His eyes opened. He was back on the transport ship. The pilot's voice emerged from the speakers.

"Arrival at Alpha Centauri B! Azoth engines shutting off in one minute."

Marco groaned, the dream still clinging to him.

"Poet!" Addy was shaking him. "Wake up, sleepy."

"I'm up, I'm up." He tugged off her hands. "God, your fingers are like claws."

She snarled, fingernails pointing at him. "Hiss! Claw!"

He sat up and stretched as much as he could. The kid behind him was kicking his seat with new vigor. Marco peered out the window, and Addy leaned over him, staring out into space with him.

The azoth engines hummed down. After a week of their purring, the starship seemed eerily silent. The bubble of warped spacetime enveloping the ship smoothed out. The lines of starlight blurred, then slammed into points.

Marco grabbed his barf bag but thankfully managed to hold in his few bites of hamburger. Reality rearranged itself around him. His stomach seemed to float somewhere in the overhead compartment, then in his feet. His very soul seemed to hover a meter away before slamming back into his body. He covered his mouth, biting down hard, willing himself not to gag. Several passengers were less fortunate, losing their meals into paper bags.

Addy rubbed her temples. "Damn. Almost as nasty as brain freeze." She tapped her chin. "Now I want ice cream. With bacon bits."

"You always want ice cream," Marco said. "And bacon bits on ice cream is disgusting."

"Lobster is disgusting," Addy said. "Sea-aliens. And I've seen you eat those."

"Those were shrimp, Ads. I can't afford lobster."

"It's the same animal, genius!" She tapped his head. "Just baby ones."

Groaning, Marco turned back to the porthole. Outside he could see it now. Alpha Centauri B. The closest star to Sol, Earth's sun, only four light-years away. Now it shone nearby, filling the cabin with light. When Marco squinted, he could make out New Earth orbiting the star.

"Do you see, Ads?" he said. "New Earth. Twin to our world."

"It looks like a star from here," she said.

"It's a terrestrial planet. Similar to ours. It has the same size, mass, gravity, and atmospheric pressure as Earth. The air's composition is so similar to ours that, if you stepped outside the dome, you could even breathe it—for a while, at least, until your lungs started burning. A virgin world. That's where Haven is." Marco couldn't keep the excitement from his voice. "This is it, Ads. No more snow. No more protests. No more fascists. No more pollution or grime or Stooge's couch or any of that junk back on Earth. A new, pristine world. *Our* world."

Her brow furrowed. "What was wrong with Stooge's couch?"

"You'd like sleeping on it," Marco said. "I found a few bacon bits under the cushions."

Addy smacked her lips. "Mmm, couch-bacon! If they don't have bacon on Haven, I'm stealing that therapy pig. Bacon is *my* therapy."

"Get your elbow off my groin." He tried to shove her off, but she pressed down more forcefully, leaning across him to peer out the porthole.

New Earth grew closer, clouds covering its surface, revealing scraps of sea and soil. Soon the planet covered their field of vision, and flames roared as the starship dived into the atmosphere.

They emerged into a storm.

Gray, indigo, and charcoal clouds swirled. Rain fell in sheets. The ship shuddered and rattled, and Marco tightened his seatbelt. He kept peering outside, and Addy leaned across him, and there below—there they saw it! Lights. Roads. Buildings. The colony of Haven nestled in the rain, gleaming wet, gray and deep blue and startling yellow.

"I don't see the dome," Marco said. "In the magazine, there's a huge transparent dome around it."

"Well, duh, they pull the dome back when it rains," Addy said. "To water all the plants."

Marco wasn't so sure. He tried to get a better look at the colony, but it was hard to see much through the rain and clouds, and a thick haze lay over the city, obscuring most of it. It seemed to stretch for kilometers.

"Five million people live here," he said. "The second biggest colony, the one on Mars, has only fifty thousand settlers. Can you imagine it, Addy? Five million people living in space. Colonizing the galaxy."

"Six million once we land," Addy said. "I think there are about a million people crammed into this spaceship."

"Just the kid behind me is half a mil," Marco said. "At least he's kicked me that often."

The fog thickened. Marco could barely see a thing. The roads were only visible by the headlights of vehicles, moving forward like orderly fireflies through mist. The tops of several buildings and bridges appeared through the fog, soon vanishing. The miasma enveloped the starship, and then—with a thud so sudden Marco jumped—they landed.

The thruster engines hummed for a moment longer, then fell silent.

Scattered clapping sounded across the fuselage.

"Play Freebird!" Addy called.

They emerged into a bustling, indoor spaceport, muscles aching, joints creaking, eyes blurry. For a colony so far from Earth, the port was surprisingly busy. Families stood in coiling lines, waiting for their passports to be stamped. Several soldiers were listening to their platoon commander nearby. A group of Hasidic Jews were swaying as they prayed, while several Buddhist monks were meditating in a corner. A few farmers in overalls and straw hats were leading goats right through the airport, and chickens bustled in pens. In the middle of the spaceport rose a statue, larger than life, of Professor Ilana Teitelbaum, inventor of the azoth engine.

"See that, Addy?" Marco pointed at the statue. "It's thanks to that lady that we're here. She invented warp drives, opening up space to humanity. Thanks to her scientific discoveries, we can fly to new stars."

Addy snorted. "Oh yeah? Well, I invented using a rake to roast ten hot dogs at once, but you don't see me going around demanding statues."

"Addy, you spent that entire camping trip demanding we erect statues in your honor."

"And the statue you built was horribly inadequate!" Addy said.

Marco rolled his eyes. "That wasn't a statue. That was a straw effigy of you we were burning."

She gasped. "So that's why I got sunburned!"

With a sigh, Marco turned away from her. He kept glancing around, waiting for the local police to arrest him. He wasn't sure how powerful Never War's lawyers and lobbyists were, whether they could influence the police on Earth, let alone Haven. But he wasn't taking any chances.

"Remember, Ads, we fly under the radar," he said. "We suffered enough hostility on Earth. We should use fake names, try to keep a low profile, and—Addy? Addy!"

She stood by a kiosk, pounding on the counter, speaking loud enough for hundreds to hear. "What do you mean it rejected my debit card? I want that bag of bacon bits! Do you know who I am? I'm Addy Linden, war heroine! That's right, Addy Linden—that's A-D-D-Y—check the news sometime! And this is Marco Emery, bug killer! Look, we're on that newspaper over there, and—"

"Addy!" The blood draining from his face, Marco pulled her away from the kiosk. "For God's sake. Calm your belly. Ow! Stop biting me!" He tugged his arm free from her jaws.

"But I'm hungry!"

"You've been eating my lunch for a week," Marco said.

"Good. So go buy yourself a meal. So I can steal that too."

"First let's get out of this spaceport," he said. "After a week in space, I want to step outside into the open air, to feel some sunlight on my face, to see Haven. We'll get something better than stale snacks in a plastic bag."

Addy eyed the therapy pig walking by, tugging its owner on the leash. She licked her lips. "Something fresh does sound nice. All right. Agreed. Maybe ten hot dogs? Oh, and I'll also need a rake."

The wait through customs was long and exhausting, but at least they hadn't checked any baggage. All they had was in their backpacks: a few old clothes Steve had given them, a couple of toothbrushes, a handful of books Marco had managed to salvage, and several crumpled photographs. As for money, they had none. The coffee tin was empty, its cash spent on the tickets here. Marco just hoped his credit card would work in Haven until he could find a job. And, he hoped, Never War didn't have the authority to trace his transactions.

"All right," he said. "Here's the plan. We need two things at first. Temporary shelter and work. For shelter, we can check out hotels, hostels, and ideally an apartment we can rent month to month—hopefully using credit for the first month. For work, we'll scour wanted ads, knock on doors, and take whatever we can get. In a few months, once we've saved some money, we can buy nicer clothes, walk into a bank, apply for a mortgage, then move into a permanent place. Once my writing career takes off, we can—Addy. Addy! Are you listening?"

She was busy staring at the therapy pig, licking her lips. She looked back at Marco. "Where in all this do the rake and hot dogs fit in?"

"Those come after we buy a house. We'll get a fire pit for the yard. And we'll build a fire every night, if we want to." His voice cracked, and he was surprised to find tears in his eyes. "You'll roast your hot dogs on your rake, and we'll eat so many it hurts. And we'll just sit outside at night by the fire, looking at the stars, and point out Sol in the distance. We'll tell stories from home. From Earth. And we'll forget about all the bad things that happened. And we'll be happy."

She looked at him, and her eyes softened. She squeezed his shoulder. "We'll be happy." She mussed his hair and kissed his cheek. "I love you, little dude. You know that, right?"

He gave her a playful shove. "Love you too, you crazy Viking berserker."

Finally they reached the exit doors. They held hands, took deep breaths, and stepped outside onto the surface of a new world.

They rushed back inside.

"Fuck," Addy said.

Marco shivered, frost and grime clinging to him. "What the hell was that?"

They opened the doors again, peering outside. They could barely see a thing. The planet stormed. Clouds gurgled overhead and fog filled the streets. Muddy drops and ash rained from the sky. The air stank—hot, acidic, burning their nostrils.

"Move it," somebody said, shoving past them, and stepped outside. He wore a bulky suit and helmet. Through the doorway, Marco could see other settlers wearing similar garments. They looked more like hazmat suits than spacesuits.

Marco and Addy hurried away from the doorway, fleeing the malodorous fog and rain. A man leaned against a nearby storefront, broom in hand, chuckling.

"Uhm, excuse me, sir," Addy said. "But what happened to the dome?"

"What dome?" the shopkeep said.

Marco held out his magazine. It displayed a photo of Haven enclosed within a protective bubble, shielding it from the elements of a foreign planet. "This dome! 'The bubble lauded across the galaxy,' it says here."

The shopkeep snorted. "That thing? They've been talking about building that for years." He jutted his thumb. "Read the plaque if you like."

Marco and Addy approached a sign on a wall. It depicted the same graphic from the magazine—a huge dome enclosing a city like a snow globe. Words appeared beneath it.

Biodome (trademark of Chrysopoeia Corp): Coming soon to Haven!
Did you know? The Biodome (trademark) will ensure ideal weather for all
colonists. Call your member of parliament today! Insist on funding the
Biodome (trademark). Make sure your grandchildren enjoy weather from
home . . . among the stars.

Marco sighed. "So, Addy, you want to get busy making those grandkids? Right after we call our local politician, that is."

She stared dejectedly at the magazine. "It lied to us. I can't believe a magazine lied."

"I'm in shock," Marco said dryly. He fished his credit card from his pocket. "Let's just hope this baby works up here. We'll need a couple of those atmosuits."

She gasped. "That's my bacon money!"

"You can hunt the therapy pig instead." He led her back toward the shop. "Come on."

A few moments later, they stood in the shop, wearing the bulky suits. In the military, spacesuits had been slick like diving suits—embarrassingly form-fitting, Marco had often thought. There was no such problem here. These things were a cross between a parka and a garbage bag, as graceful as a potato. The hood zipped up at the neck, transparent in the front. A cheap, plastic air filtration system was connected to a bag simply labeled *Earth Air.*

"I thought the air on New Earth was breathable," Marco said to the shopkeep.

"Sure it is!" the man said. "I breathe it all the ti—" A coughing fit interrupted his words.

"I think we'll stick to Earth Air," Marco said. "Add another couple bags to our bill."

He paid with his credit card, praying it would work. It was an expensive bill, as costly as a month of rent above the library. Thankfully, the transaction seemed to work, but Marco already ached at the thought of interest piling up. It might be a while before he could pay it back.

They left the shop, and once more, they braved the surface of Haven.

It felt like walking through a hurricane.

Their atmosuits fluttered in the wind. Their hoods kept sticking to their faces. Raindrops were flying sideways, slamming into them, painful even through the suits, splattering them with mud.

"I wonder what the chemical composition of the atmosphere is here," Marco said. "Is this organic matter?"

"Whatever it is, it stinks," Addy said. "Where are the trees? The flowers? The puppies?"

"Probably waiting for that dome," Marco said.

Addy grabbed the magazine from him and tossed it into the trash. "This is the worst case of false advertisement since your dating profile claimed you're a good cook."

Marco felt his cheeks blush. "First of all, *you* set up that profile for me. Secondly, I'm sorry that I can't match the culinary genius of hot dogs on rakes or bacon bits on ice cream. Finally, you should never have used that photo of me from gym class."

"Why not? It's a great photo."

"I was buried under a pile of football players, Steve on top!"

"Exactly!" Addy said. "It shows you love sports."

"I was the towel boy!"

"Just say thanks I didn't use that photo of you as a toddler on the potty."

"You did!" he said. "That was the second photo!"

Addy patted his head. "And you looked adorable."

He groaned. "Let's focus on our task. Shelter. Work."

"And hot dogs," Addy said. "Never forget the hot dogs."

Marco wanted to reply, but the wind intensified, making speech impossible. They walked hunched over, breathing stale air from a bag, trudging through their new homeland.

CHAPTER TWELVE

The *Saint Brendan* streamed through space, dented, hobbled, a dozen military police ships in pursuit.

"Are you sure about this, Captain?" Kemi sat stiffly in the pilot's seat. Her hands—one real, one mechanical—hovered over the controls. "A penal asteroid swarming with guards and military police . . . After the shit we've pulled, it's the last place I want to visit."

Ben-Ari could sympathize. A prison was low on her list of vacation destinations, especially after witnessing the horrors in the demilitarized zone. More than anything, she wanted to keep flying. To head deep into the darkness. To find a distant, uninhabited world, ideally one with a tropical island and a bunch of Golden Retrievers, and spend the rest of her life hiding out there.

And yet, the dozen military police ships were chasing them, only a few astronomical units away. And countless marauder ships were gathering around the human sphere of space, a tightening noose just ready to squeeze them. Chrysopoeia Corporation and Admiral Komagata were involved in covering up the enemy threat.

And there was only one man who could help them now.

"We need him, Lieutenant," Ben-Ari said. "If anyone can give us the information we need, it's Noodles."

Kemi sighed. "Lovely. The hope of humanity rests on the shoulders of a man named Noodles." She glanced at Ben-Ari. "Remind me, Ramen or Shanghai?"

Ben-Ari was weary, scared, and it felt like a hungry honey badger was digging through her wounded arm for treats, and yet she cracked a smile. "He has a real name. Private David Min-jun Greene. I commanded him in Fort Djemila. For a while, at least."

She thought back to those days. Better days than this. It was five years ago. She had been only an ensign, a twenty-year-old girl fresh out of Officer Candidate School. A golden bar had shone on each of her shoulders, fresh and polished—a newly minted officer of the HDF, so afraid, so innocent of the horrors ahead. For her first mission, they had sent her to command a platoon undergoing basic training. There, in the safety of a training base, with an experienced sergeant mentoring her, Ben-Ari had learned leadership.

Many of those soldiers had become her friends. After their training, many had followed her to war. They had fought bravely. Some had never come home. She was proud of both those who had survived and those who had fallen.

But two soldiers Ben-Ari had failed. Those two still weighed heavily on her conscience.

One had been named Hope Harris, known as Jackass to her friends and enemies alike. The girl had bounced from one basic training base to another, spending most of her time in the brig. Finally she had come to Djemila's Dragons, Ben-Ari's platoon. Only a couple weeks later, Jackass had placed her rifle into her mouth and blown out her skull before Ben-Ari could stop her. Ben-Ari had never forgotten it. Jackass had been the first soldier she had lost, even before the Second Galactic War had begun.

The second soldier Ben-Ari had failed was Noodles.

She had commanded him for only a few weeks, and nothing she, the platoon sergeant, nor the squad leaders tried could help him. Noodles was weaker than the other recruits, even weaker than the diminutive Pinky and Lailani. After running for only a few steps, he needed his inhaler. He could barely see without his massive glasses. The other recruits mocked him, bullied him; only Marco, it seemed, had ever shown him some kindness. Noodles ate apart from the others, stood apart from them, and shied away if approached. On Sundays, when the recruits played football, Noodles stayed in his tent, reading *The Lord of the Rings* or *The Wheel of Time* or *A Song of Ice and Fire*. He was always last to finish the obstacle course, and he struggled to do a single push up.

Ben-Ari had hoped to toughen him up. A minority herself, she had perhaps sympathized with Greene, the son of a Jewish father and a Korean mother. But after a few weeks, she had realized that Noodles had different strengths. His body was weak, but his mind was brilliant. When she spoke with him privately about his trials, he revealed a startling intellect, a vast knowledge of technology, computing, science, and literature.

And so Ben-Ari had dismissed him from boot camp. She sent him straight to Military Intelligence. There, behind a computer screen, he had thrived, a rising star. He helped analyze the scum's networks, finding patterns in the signals the aliens blasted across space. He even coded the computer chip that went into Lailani's skull, blocking the signals from the scum, enabling Lailani to delve into the hive while blocking the enemy's attempts to control her.

I felt like I redeemed myself for Jackass, Ben-Ari remembered. *I lost one soldier but saved another.*

Then, a year later, the military police had barged into Noodles' room.

The young, scrawny corporal was busted for hacking into Nightwall's computers. He was caught after confessing the crime to a beautiful, adoring young woman—a military police detective in disguise.

Since then, Noodles had languished in an asteroid prison.

"Today we break him free," Ben-Ari said. "We need more information about the marauders. We need to know why Chrysopoeia and HDF top brass are covering this up. If anyone can hack into their computers, can find us this information, it's dear old Noodles."

Kemi cringed. "That, or we end up languishing on the same penal asteroid with him. At least you two can spend eternity reminiscing about Fort Djemila." She sighed. "Ma'am, we're wanted refugees now. The MP is following us. By now, the galaxy must know we're wanted women. And we're going to fly into a *military prison?* Isn't that like fleeing the cat by hiding in the litter box?"

"It's also a good way to end up in deep shit." Ben-Ari smiled thinly. "But there's a reason they chose this asteroid for Noodles' imprisonment. There's no wormhole nearby. Communications are slow. No information channels to hack. It'll be a while before anyone there hears about our own crimes. By then, we'll be flying off with our very own genius hacker."

Controls beeped. A monitor displayed an image of this sector of space: the *Saint Brendan* in the center, several pursuing vessels only a few Astronomical Units away, and ahead—the penal asteroid.

"We won't have long, Captain," Kemi said. "A couple hours before the military police catches up with us."

Ben-Ari took a deep breath and nodded. "It'll be enough."

After another half hour of flight, they could see the asteroid with the naked eye. It hovered ahead, the size of Delaware. It was large enough to have a moon of its own, a boulder the size of a town.

"Fort Blackwell Disciplinary Barracks," Ben-Ari said. "The most infamous prison of the HDF."

Kemi shuddered. "I knew a guy who spent time here. He came back saying his week clearing out a scum hive was easier."

Ben-Ari nodded. "They don't call it Hell's Hilton for nothing."

Two structures rose here, their lights dim. On the main asteroid rose concrete buildings and guard towers—a maximum security prison for serial killers, rapists, and other galactic lowlifes. On the asteroid's moon rose a simpler structure, a massive box of metal: a supermax prison for those deemed too dangerous to mingle with the other prisoners.

In that metal box on that moon languished Noodles.

"Ma'am, are you sure?" Kemi winced, pointing at several MP ships orbiting the asteroid. "They've got some serious firepower here. I see five battleships. Maybe twenty gun turrets on the asteroid. All Military Police, the same guys who are hunting us. This is basically the last place in the cosmos I want to be."

"No, I'm not sure," Ben-Ari said. "It's likely that we won't rescue Noodles but join him. But we will take this chance." She turned toward Kemi and smiled. "Remember, Lieutenant. It'll be two hours before they know we're wanted women. Within two hours, we'll be a million AUs away from this place."

Kemi gulped. "Several prison ships are approaching us, ma'am."

Ben-Ari produced the Military Police pins and armbands she had stolen from the men on Space Station One. She handed a set to Kemi. "Put these on. And let me take the lead. As we planned. We faced the scum, Lieutenant Abasi. We can certainly face a few prison guards."

Within moments, the MP ships—armored battle boxes—were escorting them down toward the asteroid. As they approached, Ben-Ari was struck by the sheer *size* of this rock.

Lumpy and misshapen, it was a hundred kilometers long, all dark rock, canyons, cliffs, and mountains. Its moon, a chunk of stone the size of a warship, shadowed the *Saint Brendan* as it passed overhead on its way around its larger brother.

They thumped down on the main asteroid. The prison rose before them, a complex of concrete buildings topped with guard towers. Fort Blackwell Military Disciplinary Barracks, unofficially known as Hell's Hilton, was the most secure prison in the galaxy with a history of zero escapes. Many of its prisoners were famous: Corporal Leighton Redmond, who had gone berserk on Earth, firing a machine gun in his son's kindergarten; Colonel Wilfrid "The Strangler" Temperley, once a commander of an entire space port, revealed to be the serial killer who had raped, strangled, and stolen the underwear of six female soldiers under his command; Sergeant Brooklyn Ann, who had stolen scum eggs during the war, then released them in a crowded shopping mall, letting the hatchlings kill thirteen people.

And one scrawny computer hacker I once commanded, Ben-Ari thought. *One little genius I now need more than an army.*

She and Kemi donned their helmets. Their stolen Military Police armbands shone for all to see, the letters *MP* large and red on a white background. With deep breaths, they stepped off the ship onto the surface of the asteroid.

A dozen armed guards awaited them there, and more guards stared from the towers, submachine guns in hand.

"Good morning, men!" Ben-Ari spoke into the communicator in her helmet. "I'm Captain Einav Ben-Ari,

Military Police. I've come to speak to your warden. Take me to him at once."

The guards glanced at one another. Ben-Ari's insides shook. She was famous across the military, perhaps across all the Human Commonwealth. She had led the platoon that killed the scum emperor. She had given only one media interview after the war, but it had been viewed by millions. Everyone, from general to guard, knew of Captain Ben-Ari, heroine of Earth.

I just pray they don't know I'm now a wanted woman, she thought.

"Ma'am!" A guard saluted. "We didn't realize you served in the MP, no longer the infan—"

"Officers move between corps, soldier," Ben-Ari said. "Take me to your warden. *Now.*"

They led her through several layers of doors, each built of fortified metal, each guarded by guards with big guns. Finally they walked down a cell block. Cages—they looked too cramped to even be called cells—lined the corridor, row after row of them, stacked together. Prisoners languished inside like human hens. The stench of sweat and human waste hung in the air. As Ben-Ari and Kemi walked by, prisoners catcalled, hooted, pulled down their pants to flaunt their genitals, then screamed as guards hit buttons, sending electricity pulsing through their cages. Some of the prisoners showed signs of repeated electrocution, their bodies charred, their faces sallow.

No wonder they call this place Hell's Hilton, Ben-Ari thought, suppressing a shudder. Yet as horrifying as this prison was, it was a five-star hotel compared to the prison she had seen in the DMZ, the one the marauders had overrun.

Only minutes after they had landed, Ben-Ari and Kemi entered the warden's office.

We have maybe another hour, she thought. *Ninety minutes at most before the ships chasing us arrive, before we join Hell's Hilton as permanent guests.*

"So. Captain Ben-Ari. Lieutenant Abasi. You're here about one of my inmates."

Colonel Caleb Smith, warden of Fort Blackwell, was a stodgy man in his fifties with a thin white mustache.

The two women stood before his desk. His office held framed photographs of famous prisons from Earth, from the Bastille to Alcatraz.

"Yes, sir," Ben-Ari said. "We're here to interrogate Corporal David Min-jun Greene, currently serving a life term for cybercrimes. He still withholds information about his many crimes. We will extract it from him."

"Private," said Colonel Smith.

Ben-Ari frowned. "Sir?"

"*Private* David Greene," the warden said. "Not corporal. We demoted the boy, of course."

Ben-Ari nodded, cursing herself for her mistake. "Yes, sir. Of course."

Smith leaned back in his seat. "Captain, I appreciate your service in the war. You served honorably. You are a heroine of humanity." His voice betrayed just a tinge of bitterness—envy perhaps? Wounded pride that a mere girl should become a heroine while he, a respected colonel, languished on an asteroid?

"Thank you, si—" she began.

"But this is highly unusual," Smith continued. "I interrogate all my inmates personally here at Fort Blackwell. Inmate Greene has surrendered all the information he has. Trust me, Captain, when I waterboard a man, he talks. I spill water. They spill secrets. Greene now rots in his cell. I cannot allow anyone to see him, not without approval from high above."

Ben-Ari stiffened. "I told you, sir. Approval is incoming. If you had a wormhole here—"

"I do not allow wormholes near my prison, Captain. Not with some of the galaxy's most notorious cybercriminals in my possession." The warden leaned forward in his seat, and now a flash of anger filled his eyes. "Inmates like Greene could use a fucking toaster to hack into the HDF's most secure computer systems. I will not allow wormholes within a light-year of the bastards I hold here."

Ben-Ari nodded. "Understandable, sir. I appreciate your concern for our security and your passion for your profession. But my lieutenant and I are on a highly classified mission, serving alongside Military Intelligence, and require immediate interrogation of—"

"You served in the infantry, didn't you?" the warden said. "During the war."

She froze. "Yes, sir, but—"

"You fought on Abaddon, did you not?"

Ben-Ari inhaled sharply. "Sir, I fail to see how—"

"I know what the other corps say of us." The colonel rose from his seat. He was an imposing man, tall and broad. "They look down on the Military Police. They call us the traffic cops of the galaxy, handing out parking tickets while better men fight." Smith narrowed his eyes, staring at Ben-Ari. "Tell me, Ben-Ari. Why would a decorated war heroine, a captain in the infantry, a warrior who won many honors, join the Military Police, the most scorned of all corps?"

He knows, Ben-Ari thought. *Damn, he knows, he knows.*

At her side, Kemi squirmed but remained silent.

Stay calm, Kemi. Let me talk.

Ben-Ari met the colonel's eyes, staring steadily, refusing to evince her fear.

"Yes, I fought the scum in the war, sir," she said. "I defeated them. And yes, I won many honors. But the true enemy of the military, sir, comes not from external forces. It comes from weakness within. The Roman Empire did not fall because some barbarians were gathering outside the gates. She fell because rot spread within her walls. I joined the Military Police to fight the true enemy: criminals within our ranks. Let the others sneer." She raised her chin. "This is where we find honor."

The colonel's stance loosened. He nodded. A thin smile touched his lips. "Well said, Captain. Well said. It's why I myself joined the MP. We're a misunderstood lot, but we understand our own code of honor." He pulled a box of cigars from his desk and held it out. "Cubans. Actual Cubans from Earth. Technically illegal here in Fort Blackwell but . . . even wardens bend the laws sometimes." He winked.

Ben-Ari had never smoked a cigar, but she and Kemi accepted them, and soon smoke filled the office.

"Sir," Ben-Ari said after a few puffs, "we have reason to believe that Private Greene still withholds sensitive information. I commanded him myself at one point. He coded the microchip implanted into Staff Sergeant de la Rosa, the soldier who led me to the scum emperor. Greene still holds many secrets. I can get him to talk, but I need him alone. I need him on my ship. We have devised . . . new ways of making prisoners speak."

For the first time, Kemi spoke. "We have ways." She flexed her metal hand.

The colonel puffed on his cigar, feet on his desk. "I assure you, Captain, Lieutenant, I've interrogated Inmate Greene. Thoroughly. I've used enhanced interrogation techniques, over and over. Whatever information he has of his criminal activities, he revealed."

"You mean the waterboarding, sir," Ben-Ari said.

He nodded. "Repeated waterboarding. I broke him."

Ben-Ari turned toward the framed photo of the Bastille. She studied it, then turned toward the colonel. "There are . . . older, more intense methods of interrogation. Methods that have worked for thousands of years."

Kemi nodded, opening and closing her metal fist. "That can still work."

"Methods that are illegal in military installations," Ben-Ari continued. "Methods that involve a hell of a lot worse than waterboarding. Aboard my ship, we've built a special chamber. A chamber full of special tools. We'll take the prisoner only ten thousand kilometers away from your prison. Legally, we'll be outside military jurisdiction. And we can . . . test our new tools."

"We'll test them well," Kemi said. "And it'll be nice and legal."

Colonel Smith licked his lips. "So you mean . . . torture? *Real* torture?" He inhaled, a tremble to his breath, and his pupils dilated.

"I mean," Ben-Ari said, narrowing her eyes, "that on our ship, he will speak."

"And scream," Kemi said. "They say there's no sound in space. But I bet they'll hear his screams for light-years away."

We have maybe half an hour, Ben-Ari thought. *Half an hour until the MPs chasing us arrive. And then we'll be the ones screaming.*

Colonel Smith tamped out his cigar and walked around his desk. "I'll go with you. I'll witness this. I'll do my part to help. Me. Two guards. The inmate. We'll board your vessel together. Two of my ships will escort us the appropriate distance away. And we'll test your methods, Captain."

A colonel. Two guards. Two ships. They were the best odds Ben-Ari could hope for.

She nodded. "Very well. But we must move at once. Now. This information cannot wait."

"Agreed," said the colonel. He stepped out of his office. "Guards!"

They flew toward the asteroid's moon—the *Saint Brendan* and two prison ships. Here was no moon like Luna, round and fair, but a second asteroid orbiting the larger rock. The supermax prison clung to the moon, and the ships landed beside it. Guards stepped into the windowless building, then emerged wheeling a chained, masked prisoner strapped to a vertical gurney.

"God damn," Kemi muttered, watching from the *Saint Brendan*'s bridge. "They got him trussed up like Hannibal Lecter."

Ben-Ari stood at her side, staring through the viewport as they wheeled Noodles across the rocky surface. "Hannibal? Like with the elephants?"

"Never mind, Captain. Twentieth century buff here. Even Marco never understood half my references, and I spent years regaling him with them."

The airlock opened. Warden Smith entered the *Saint Brendan* first, followed by his two guards who wheeled the chained Noodles.

"Take him to the interrogation room," Ben-Ari told the guards. "I'll lead the way."

She walked through the ship, heart pounding, breathing between her teeth.

Calm yourself. You can do this.

She led them down the corridor, opened the door to the bridge, and stepped inside.

"In here," she said.

The guards wheeled the gurney, Noodles strapped onto it, into the room. The warden followed. The stocky colonel narrowed his eyes.

"This is your interrogation room, Captain?" he said. "This is your bridge. What—"

Kemi raised her metal hand. A bolt of energy blasted out, rippling the air, and hit one guard. A second bolt flew. A second guard fell.

The colonel spun toward Kemi, cursing, and reached for his gun.

Ben-Ari swung her own weapon, pistol-whipping the colonel. He hit the floor with a thud.

"Lieutenant, take us out," Ben-Ari said. "Now. Fly!"

Kemi nodded, her knees shaking. She leaped into the pilot's seat and hit buttons. The *Saint Brendan* began to rise from the asteroid. The two guard ships, unaware that their colonel was lying unconscious on the bridge floor, rose with them.

They traveled slowly. Still too close. They had to be distant from any heavy world, even a large asteroid, to engage their azoth engine, bend spacetime, and blast forward faster than light. For an object as small as an asteroid, ten thousand kilometers should do it. Ben-Ari watched the distance on the HUD. A thousand kilometers. Two thousand. Three thousand . . .

She glanced back at the three unconscious men.

The colonel was stirring and reaching for the communicator on his wrist. Ben-Ari slammed her pistol down again, hitting his head. He collapsed again against the floor.

She looked back at the controls. Six thousand kilometers from the asteroid. Seven thousand . . .

Alarms blared across the bridge.

"Damn it!" Kemi blurted out. "Our friends are here."

Ben-Ari didn't need to check the beeping dots of light on the monitors. She could see them herself through the viewport, emerging from warp drive.

A dozen MP ships. The dozen who had followed the *Saint Brendan* here all the way from Nightwall.

"Go to warp drive!" Ben-Ari shouted. "Now!"

"But we're too close—"

"Do it!"

"The azoth engine needs time to prime, Captain!"

"How long?"

"It's still warm, but we'll need another few minutes, and—" Kemi bit down on her words, grabbed the controls, and yanked hard to the left. "They're firing, Captain! They—"

The *Saint Brendan* shook. Blasts slammed into them. Walls creaked. Sparks flew from the controls.

Ben-Ari hailed the enemy ships. "Hold your fire! We have Colonel Smith aboard, and—"

"They're firing again!" Kemi pulled up hard. Photon bolts streamed beneath them.

Ben-Ari leaped toward a control board. Half the circuits were fried. She hit buttons, managed to activate a starboard cannon, and a missile flew toward the enemy ships. An instant later, a vessel exploded.

"More ships rising from the asteroid!" Kemi said. "Too many!"

Ships swooped from above. More plasma rained, and the *Brendan* jolted. Other ships flew from their starboard side, and bullets rang out, slamming into the hull, denting it.

"Lieutenant, I need you to activate the azoth engine—*now*."

"Yes, ma'am." Kemi was still tugging madly at the joystick, trying to dodge the assaulting ships. Missiles and plasma flew everywhere. The *Brendan* spun, careened, dipped down toward the asteroid and its moon.

"Lieutenant?"

"Azoth engine priming. In five . . . four . . . three . . ."

"Get us farther from that asteroid!" Ben-Ari said.

"Too late!" Kemi cried. "Hold on!"

The stars stretched into streaks around them.

Spacetime bent.

Below them, Ben-Ari saw the prison towers bend, curve inward, then shatter.

The hull creaked and dented.

Their engine roared, and they blasted out.

They shot forward, a bubble of warped spacetime around them, moving at many times the speed of light. Each second of travel they crossed millions of kilometers. Before Ben-Ari could exhale, the prison was as distant as Earth from the sun.

But they were not in the clear yet.

"Captain, the vessels have entered warped space behind us," Kemi said. "Our stealth engine is down. Damaged when we warped spacetime; the asteroid exerted too much gravity. The enemy ships know exactly where we are."

Ben-Ari looked at the three unconscious MPs on her floor, at the chained and gagged Noodles, and at the dots on the monitor, showing the enemy ships following.

She took a deep, shaky breath.

Damn.

CHAPTER THIRTEEN

The buildings of Haven soared at their sides, their tops vanishing in the murk. Asphalt blanketed the colony, hiding the original surface of New Earth. The wind shrieked. Ashy rain fell. A gangly bird flew overhead, screeching like fingernails on a chalkboard.

"Is that one of your whistling birds?" Addy shouted.

"I changed my mind!" Marco cried back. Both had to shout to be heard over the storm. "I don't want one near my house."

He hoped that sometimes, at least, Haven enjoyed better weather. But it was hard to be optimistic. From space, the storm had seemed to cover the planet. If this was the best planet the colonists had found, he hated to see their rejected options.

Cars rumbled down the streets, spraying Addy and Marco with mud. Not that it mattered; the rain drenched them with filth anyway. A few beggars lay on the sidewalks, asleep or maybe dead, mud staining their cardboard signs. A mouse-like alien scurried by and a stray cat hissed, fast in pursuit. Nobody else seemed crazy enough to be outside. Marco and Addy stopped at a few buildings, hoping to step into the lobby, to breathe the air, to rest, to warm up, but the doors were all locked. At a few doors, guards gave them stern looks. They carried big guns.

"Poet, can we go home now?" Addy said, the wind yanking her atmosuit.

"We're broke, so we're stuck here," Marco said. "Come on. It can't be all bad. We'll find the nice neighborhoods soon. You know, the ones with the houses from the magazine."

"Oh, those houses under the dome, right?" Addy said, her sarcasm as thick as the mud. "Great idea, Poet. Real genius thinking! 'Come to Haven, Addy! We'll eat hot dogs all day long. We'll be rich and famous and play bridge with the ghost of Queen Victoria.'" She groaned. "I'd rather be watching *Robot Wrestling* with Steve and Stooge."

Marco shuddered. As bad as Haven was, he still wasn't convinced it was worse than Steve, Stooge, and two robots smashing each other.

It's not that bad here, he told himself. *Really! Five million people wouldn't live here if it were bad.*

A bearded man lurched toward them, not even wearing an atmosuit. His face was coated with mud. "Spare a few bucks?" he rasped, revealing a mouth full of rotten gums and no teeth. "Kicked out of Earth for panhandling! Spare a coin, sir, ma—" He collapsed into a fit of coughing.

They had no coins to give the man, but Addy had plenty of glares for Marco.

"You brought us to a damn leper colony!" she said. "It's where they banish you for panhandling!"

Marco wanted to be optimistic, to cheer up Addy, to speak of finding those homes and trees and peaceful life. But the fear ate at him. This was not the military. There was no starship waiting to bring him home at the end of his mission, and the flight here had cost his father's life savings. It could take years to save enough money to fly home. This was where they made their stand, like it or not.

And we'll have to survive here.

His eyes stung.

I came here to find a better life. Now I'm thinking of just surviving.

He was about to try and comfort Addy, mostly to comfort himself, when he saw the figure in the alleyway.

Marco froze, frowning.

A girl stood in the alleyway. Instead of an atmosuit, she wore a tattered dress that seemed woven of ash. Her long black hair flowed in the wind, its tips burnt. She wore a white kabuki mask, its expression blank, the eyes and mouth mere slits. Her arms were long, bony, and flared out to pale hands with three clawed fingers. As Marco stared, brow furrowed, the girl turned her head toward him. The kabuki mask stared right at him. She raised one hand, its three fingers inhumanly large, the claws like daggers, and—

"Poet, come on!" Addy shoved him. "What are you gawking at?"

Marco blinked, looked at Addy, then back at the alleyway. The girl was gone.

"Did you see her?" Marco said. "A girl. With a kabuki mask." He shuddered. "Strange hands."

Addy peered at the alleyway. A poster hung there, displaying an anime girl in a schoolgirl uniform, cat ears sticking out from her hair. She held a katana, surrounded by Japanese icons. English letters appeared beneath her: *All Systems Go!*

"That?" Addy said. "Marco, that's just a poster for a cartoon. Come on."

Marco rubbed his eyes, peering into the shadows again. The strange girl was gone. Had he just seen the poster? Was his mind playing tricks on him?

"Yeah, all right," he said, a chill still tingling his spine. He kept walking with Addy.

They trudged down a few more streets, only finding more guards, more locked doors. Those damn birds kept circling above, screeching, and Marco became convinced they were alien vultures, waiting for Marco to collapse dead.

"Poet, remember how you said we have to find the good neighborhood?" Addy said. "I think this *is* the good neighborhood. Guards at every doorway. How do you call those fancy guards? Congee airs? Con Sea Urgs? Anyway, through the windows, some of those apartments seem nice. I think—hey! Watch it, asshole!" She shook her fist at a car that sprayed them with mud, then turned back toward Marco. "I think we might have to expand our search a bit. Come on. I see a subway station. Let's see where it'll take us."

She took his hand and pulled him along the sidewalk. Gray sludge—a mix of mud, snow, and ash—was piling up to their knees now. They made it to concrete stairs that delved into a tunnel. They walked downstairs, moving slowly to avoid slipping, and found themselves on a subway platform. Tracks ran to one side, and kiosks and eateries lined the other side.

Finally they removed their hoods. Marco inhaled deeply. The air bag he had purchased at the spaceport was nearly empty. The air here in the subway was hot and rank, but he breathed it gratefully.

"One problem," Marco said. "We're out of money. No way to buy subway tokens."

"Your credit card," Addy said.

He shook his head. "No can do. They don't accept it." He pointed at a box selling tokens. "See the sign? Cash only."

Addy stared, then cursed. She spat. She pounded the wall. "Fuck, fuck, fuck!" She let out a loud groan. "Fine." She reached into her pocket, then pulled out an embroidered coin purse.

Marco's eyes widened. "Addy! You carry a coin purse? Like a little old lady?" He gasped. "And look! It's embroidered with little flowers!"

"Your face is going to be embroidered with my fist!" Addy growled. "This coin purse belonged to my grandmother." She clicked it open, stared inside, and sighed. "And these coins, they . . ." She sighed and wiped her eyes, which were suddenly red. "Ah, fuck it." She walked toward the token machine, shoved the coins in, and subway tokens spilled out. "There, now we can ride."

A train trundled down the tracks, the same kind of subway train Marco remembered from his childhood on Earth—an old, clunky design, more rust than metal. Its cars displayed the symbol of Chrysopoeia, a snake eating its tail. The doors creaked, jammed, and Marco had to tug them open. He and Addy stepped into the cabin.

Two tattered seats were still free. Marco and Addy sat, knees pressed together. Paper cups, old newspapers, candy wrappers, an old sock, and other junk covered the floor, half-buried in muck the commuters dredged in. A bearded, skeletal man sat across from them, wrapped in a tattered blanket that barely hid his naked, wrinkled body. Nearby sat a careworn woman in a long coat, holding a wilted rose, only two blackened petals remaining. She raised the flower to her nose, inhaled, and smiled wistfully. A man sat by her, arguing with an invisible presence, pounding his fists against his knees. An obese woman, so large Marco was surprised she had squeezed through the doors, occupied two seats, wearing a tattered dress, her belly spilling out and dangling between her knees.

Marco and Addy sat silently.

Exiled from Earth for panhandling, the man with no teeth had said.

Marco looked around him, and he saw the poorest members of humanity. The mentally ill. The hungry. The homeless. A cadaverous woman with needle marks on her arms. A man whose clothes were held by tape. A man holding a paper bag full of empty booze bottles. A naked man wrapped in a tattered blanket, his eyes sunken, his beard long. Beggars, junkies, alcoholics. The wretched, the miserable.

Exiles? Marco thought. *Earth's unwanted? Or refugees who had come here with dreams, like Addy and me, who withered away?*

Still he did not dare speak. Addy sat at his side, silent, staring at her knees. This subway cabin was, Marco thought, the saddest place he had ever seen.

The train screeched to a halt, and the doors opened, jammed again. Marco and Addy stepped out onto another platform.

They stood for a moment under flickering neon light.

"Addy," Marco said, needing to talk about something else, to stop thinking of the poor souls he had seen on the subway. "Those coins. The ones in your mother's purse. You started to say something about them. Before the train arrived."

"Forget it, Emery," she said. She almost never called him that; it was strange to hear her speak his surname. "Come on. Let's go back aboveground. Maybe this neighborhood will be better. And maybe the storm is dying down."

They grabbed a folding map from a stand, showing many subway stops scattered across Haven, this colony of five million people. Marco also grabbed a tourist brochure. It proudly announced that Haven was turning one hundred Earth years old, and that celebrations would be held across the colony. Judging by the brochure's date, Marco and Addy had missed the festivities by three years.

"A hundred and three years," Marco said as they climbed a staircase, heading back toward the surface.

"And I don't think they updated a damn thing since year one," Addy said. She cringed as a rat the size of the late Sergeant Stumpy scuttled by, then vanished into the shadows. "Ugh, space rats."

They emerged back onto the surface. The rain had died down, but clouds still hid the sky, and ash coated the ground. The air still stank, burning Marco's throat, and he felt lightheaded until he placed his hood back on.

He looked around and cringed.

"Well, at least there are no guards outside the buildings here," he said.

Addy nodded. "Of course not. They'd get shot."

If before they had walked through an expensive area of the colony, here was decay such as Marco had rarely seen on Earth. Rust coated the buildings. Graffiti covered walls. Gangs of youths sat on fences and stairwells, breathing through thin plastic masks, their skin exposed to the harsh elements, withered and covered with boils. Marco couldn't see a single person without a gun, knife, or leashed pit bull.

"Uhm . . . how about we try the next stop?" Marco said, suddenly missing his assault rifle.

Addy nodded. "I like the way you think."

They headed back down into the tunnel. They inserted another token, crossing the barrier to the tracks. They climbed into another subway and rode on.

Posters hung from the subway car's walls, coated with graffiti. One poster asked for donations for a homeless shelter.

Another gave the address of the shelter, offering a bed for the night. A third poster advertised a strip club, while a fourth showed passengers what drugs did to their teeth. Below the posters sat dozens of commuters, staring ahead blankly. A hefty, elderly woman held plastic bags full of clothes. A massive, burly man—his steroids must have been on steroids—stroked his yellow handlebar mustache, his bare arms covered with tattoos. Two children, brother and sister by the looks of them, huddled in a corner, dressed in rags. Both children were missing their arms. A man was swaying down the car, broken bottle in one hand, shouting about how he was going to stab his wife. A handful of passengers were well dressed—a couple men in jackets and ties, three women in high heels and power suits—but they stood apart from the others, not seeming to notice them.

"What happened to this place?" Addy said softly. "These are the colonies. The best of humanity should be here, but most of these people seem . . . not just poor, but hopeless. Their eyes are dead."

"I don't know," Marco said. "Maybe the war against the scum impoverished the colonies. Maybe this was a penal colony, and all the unwanted from Earth were sent here to rot. Or maybe it's a big city, and we can still find those green places, those streets with puppies and trees and hockey on the driveways."

Addy sucked her teeth. "I miss home. Marco, were we idiots?"

"No. Addy, what did we have back on Earth? Our library was demolished. We had no jobs, no home—and don't say

Stooge's couch! Never War wanted to toss us into prison for war crimes, the media portrayed us as Nazis, and the actual Nazis were worshiping us. Look, Ads. We're immigrants here. Immigrants have it rough at first. We'll work our way up. With a little elbow grease, a little can-do attitude, we'll find those watercolor homes from the magazines."

"What if they don't exist?" Addy whispered.

"Then we'll build them," Marco said.

For a moment they were silent, waiting for a drum player to walk by, collecting coins.

"Marco, what if there's no more place for us in civilian life?" Addy said. "They took us into the army as kids. We were eighteen. Just fucking kids. For five years, we were soldiers. What if that's all we know how to be? What if we just can't be civilians anymore? What if we . . . just go back to the army? Maybe they'll let us back in."

"You're talking like a prisoner who can't survive on the outside anymore," said Marco.

"That's how I feel. Poet, for a year I fought the scum. Then for four years, I trained recruits to be soldiers. And it sucked. It sucked sweaty scum balls. But it was better than this." She swept her arm across the decaying subway car.

Marco looked at his fellow passengers. The poor, the ill, the refugees, the hopeless. Old. Weary. Some without masks or hoods, consumed with disease, the toxic air of this world eating away at their lungs. And among them . . .

Marco's heart burst into a gallop.

It's her.

The girl from the alleyway. She sat at the end of the subway car, wreathed in shadows. A girl in a tattered, ashy dress. With long black hair. With three fingers on each hand, tipped with claws, resting on her lap. She raised her head and looked at him. A girl in a kabuki mask, barely there at all. As the subway raced forward, the dim lights of the tunnel streamed across her, until with a screech the train reached another station. Fluorescent lights bathed the car, banishing the shadows.

The girl vanished.

Marco rubbed his eyes.

He was going crazy, had to be. He wanted to tell Addy what he had seen, but she would only mock him, say he was missing Lailani or seeing anime girls move in posters again.

"Come on, Poet, another stop." Addy grabbed his hand and pulled him off the subway.

They kept traveling, stop by stop, exploring each neighborhood. They found a square where neon lights advertised strip clubs, where prostitutes prowled the street like stray cats, hissing through oxygen masks. At another stop, they found a closed mental institution, its windows boarded up and its walls splattered with graffiti, and along the sidewalk paced a hundred bewildered, sniffing, weeping, shouting, laughing, mumbling people. A third stop took them to chimneys pumping out smoke, hammers clanging, drills drilling, and the stench and sound of industry. At another stop—a hundred people lining the street, clad in rags, waiting for a soup kitchen to open.

Finally they could bear their hunger no longer. At a rundown stop, they walked down a tunnel that branched off into several subterranean roads. Local businesses crowded the tunnels: second-hand electronic shops, stalls selling pirated movies, spice shops offering everything from cardamom to cocaine, and local eateries. They stepped into several restaurants, only to flee from owners shouting, "Cash only!" Finally Marco and Addy found a Chinese place that accepted credit. The menu was in Cantonese, and the staff could not speak a word of English, but Marco pointed at a roast duck in the window. "This."

"It's hopeless," Addy said as they ate. "Whatever neighborhood we explore, it's either a slum or a guarded community."

Marco swallowed a bite of duck. It was mostly fat, skin, and bone, but it was heavenly. Finally a bit of joy here in these tunnels of despair. As he ate, he examined the massive, folding map of Haven he had picked up at the spaceport. There were two parts to this city. One side of the map showed Haven aboveground. The other side showed the network of tunnels, some for subways, others for businesses, that sprawled below. Both cities were of equal size, one rising into the storm, the other delving underground.

"Look, Addy." He trailed his finger along the map toward its edge. "See these roads? They lead beyond the map. To the suburbs." He nodded. "That's where the nice stuff is, where we'll find those houses with the yards and puppies."

"And hockey in the driveway?" Addy said.

"Presumably." Marco took another bite of duck. He wiped sauce off his chin. "But the subways don't go there. I bet that's where the rich people of Haven live. Here, the inner city—this is where the refugees, the outcasts, the ill, the unwanted, this is where they end up. Some were banished from Earth. Others fled, nothing left for them at home. Maybe a handful of rich people live here, but they live high in their ivory towers, hidden behind guards. Most people with money don't live where we are now. They live beyond the map."

"Or maybe there's nothing beyond the map but giant alien slugs," Addy said.

"Then they wouldn't build highways there." Marco gestured back at the map. "See? Highways leave this city."

"I think," Addy said, "that it's time to get hitchhiking."

For hours, they stood on the roadside, wearing their atmosuits, thumbs sticking out. The storm lashed them with hot ash, with sticky rain, with wind that cut through their suits.

Cars raced by, splashing them with mud.

A few taxis rolled to a stop.

"The burbs?" one driver said, then barked a laugh. "We ain't allowed in there. Private property. I can take ya as far as the potash quarry, if you like."

"Fuck!" Addy said as they stood on the roadside, sopping with mud and ash and putrid water. "Fuck, fuck, fuck. The burbs may as well be another planet."

"We could try walking," Marco said.

"For what?" Addy shook her head. "What do you think they'll do up there, if they see two miserable, homeless bums show up on their nice streets? Call the cops, that's what. And we'll end up in the same trouble. Nothing's waiting for us in the burbs, Poet. Private property. And we own nothing." She stomped off the roadside, dragging him with her, into a cluttered alleyway filled with the homeless. "Look around you, Poet. Look at them. Drug addicts. Traumatized veterans. The lowest of the low. That's us. That's all we are now."

"That's *not* what we are." Marco glared at her through the raining ash. "Addy, we fought the scum on Abaddon. We won the war. We're worth something."

Behind her visor, her tears were falling. "We were worth something in the army. Not here. We don't know how to be civilians." She sat down in the sludge.

Marco growled. He grabbed her. He yanked her up. "No, Addy. No!" He pulled her away from the alley, past the rolling bottles of booze, the needles, the human waste. "No. You will not give up. Not so soon. We are fighters. This is just another war. A war we will win. We beat worse than this. Does Haven have aliens with claws? Scum queens birthing alien warriors? Plasma cannons? Come on. We've faced worse than this."

"What do we do, Marco?" They walked down a street lined with ten-story buildings. The sun was setting, and only a few scattered street lamps turned on, barely visible through the haze. "How do we survive this?"

"First we find shelter for the night. Tomorrow we'll find an apartment to rent. Just short term. Then we'll find work. Then I'll publish my books. Then we'll be rich. Then we'll move up to those burbs, Ads. I promise you." He cursed his tears. "I promise."

They explored the streets, seeking shelter, until they found a staircase leading into a tunnel. The subway platform was silent, the trains shut down for the night. Somewhere in these shadows, a man was laughing, cursing, then snoring.

Marco and Addy sat on a bench, shivering. A gunshot sounded somewhere above, or maybe just a breaking bottle, followed by screams, then finally silence. Marco and Addy could not sleep. They sat in silence, holding each other, until the trains rumbled again at dawn.

CHAPTER FOURTEEN

"Stealth mode . . . fixed." Noodles leaned back in his seat, placed his feet on the dashboard, and wove his fingers together behind his head. "Am I good? I'm good."

"Get your feet off my control panel," Kemi said. "This is the bridge of the HDFS *Saint Brendan*, not your mother's basement."

"What's the matter, sweetheart?" Noodles blew her a kiss. "You need to dust?"

Kemi raised her metal fist. "I'll need to punch my metal fist through your mouth if you don't shut it."

"Soldiers, silent!" Ben-Ari said. She leaned forward, examining the monitors. Noodles seemed to be right. Once more, they were flying in stealth mode. Behind them, only a few million kilometers away, the enemy ships were still following, displayed as green dots on their screens. "Lieutenant, adjust our course. Let's see if they follow."

Noodles gasped. He peered at her through his thick glasses. "You don't trust me, Captain?"

"I wouldn't trust you if I were falling off a cliff and you had wings," Ben-Ari said. "Lieutenant, adjust."

Kemi flashed Noodles a smug grin, then turned to her controls and changed the ship's course through warped space. Behind them, the enemy vessels continued along their old path, blind to the *Brendan*'s change of course. Meanwhile, the warden and his guards were now too far to see; Ben-Ari had jettisoned them a while back, enclosing them in spacesuits and giving them communicators to call for aid.

"It's working," Ben-Ari said.

"Of course it's working!" Noodles stiffened. "It was fixed by yours truly, InfectedNoodle1337."

Ben-Ari looked at the wispy private. He wore a new uniform, a spare found on the ship, which hung loosely across his scrawny frame. Too poor to afford laser surgery, his eyes blinked from behind Coke-bottle glasses. She remembered commanding a timid, trembling soldier five years ago, a boy too frightened to speak to other recruits, who skulked apart from his comrades, reading *The Lord of the Rings* while the others laughed or played ball. Noodles had not grown any larger or stronger, but he had certainly grown cockier. Life as a famous hacker, it seemed, had boosted his confidence more than Ben-Ari's training ever could have.

"Well, InfectedNoodle337—" Ben-Ari began.

"InfectedNoodle1337," he corrected her. "The number means *leet*. Which means elite. Which means I'm the best."

"If you were the best, you'd have never been caught," Kemi said.

Noodle leaned back farther in his seat. A sigh rolled through him. "Ah, but I was not caught due to any intellectual neglect, only a mistake of the heart. I spilled my beans to a comely lass, an MP agent in disguise." He glanced at Kemi. "She looked a little like you. Beautiful, big hair, kissable lips . . ."

"That's enough!" Ben-Ari barked before Kemi could pound him. "Private, I'll be more than happy to blast you out of the airlock like I did to your guards. I didn't bring you here to hear your bragging or quips. I brought you here because—"

"Because you need me." Noodles nodded. "Like you needed me to code the chip that went into sweet Lailani's head. Like you needed me to fix your stealth engine." He placed his feet on the floor, leaned toward Ben-Ari, and narrowed his eyes. "But any engineer worth his salt can fix a stealth engine. A *child* could fix it. If you needed me, the absolute best, you surely have more of a challenge for me. So what is it, Einav?"

"You will call her ma'am!" said Kemi.

Noodles looked over his shoulder at her. "Calm your tits, toots."

This time Kemi had heard enough. She leaped toward the scrawny hacker, knocked him onto the floor, and wrapped her metal fingers around his throat. Her knee shoved into his chest. Noodles gasped beneath her, struggling to free himself. He looked at Ben-Ari and just managed to whisper hoarsely.

"Call her off! Call off your beast!"

Ben-Ari shrugged. "I thought you're the best, Noodles. Why would you need my help?"

He tried to speak again, was turning purple. Kemi was not a large woman, no stronger than average, but Noodles was weak as a child. He was growing limp.

"All right, Lieutenant, that's enough," Ben-Ari said.

With a grunt, Kemi released the private and stepped away. Noodles gasped for air, rose to his feet, and glared at Kemi.

"We have ways of making you miss your prison cell," Ben-Ari said. "So play nice. Help us. And life will be good." Her voice softened, and she tossed in some honey along with the vinegar. "I know that you're the best, Noodles. And I need your help. Only you can help us."

The combination of threat and flattery seemed to mollify him. He leaned back in his seat. "Very well. But first I require some sustenance. Frozen lasagna if you have it, steak and taters otherwise. A few bottles of Mountain Dew—every starship comes with them. A tablet with a library, ideally one with a wide collection of fantasy and comic books. And a date with Kemi. Kidding, kidding!" He inched away from the furious lieutenant. "Just the food, drink, and reading material should suffice. Oh, and a full pardon for all my crimes."

Ben-Ari sighed. "I'll see what I can do about the pardon after we save the galaxy."

This would be a long, tedious flight. She should have just brought a marauder aboard for interrogation; the creature would have been more pleasant.

While Noodles sat in the kitchen, feasting on lasagna and drinking wine, Ben-Ari told the private everything she knew. About the marauders taking over a prison in the demilitarized zone. About seeing their battle formations circling human space. About the high command and Chrysopoeia Corp keeping the information hushed.

"What I need you to do," Ben-Ari said, "is to hack into Chrysopoeia Corp's mainframe. I need you to find information on their dealings with the marauders. I need to know what the enemy plans and why this is being kept secret."

"Piece of cake," said Noodles.

"So you think it'll be easy, huh?" Ben-Ari said.

"No, I think it'll be exceedingly hard, much like my manhood during Slave Leia's immortal scene. Piece of cake, please." Noodles swallowed his last bite of lasagna and pointed at the pantry. "Chocolate."

"You'll have all the cake you want once you start working," Ben-Ari said.

He sighed. "Don't I even get a day off? I just got out of prison, you know."

She shook her head. "Get to work."

He stood up and brushed crumbs off his uniform. "All right. Here's what I'll need. The highest security access codes you have into military and civilian databases. Three computers, separate from the ship's mainframe—one for me to rebuild, another to function as a code test harness, a third to stream *The Lord of the Rings* while I work. Access to every terminal on the *Saint*

Brendan with admin passwords. And I'll need us in the solar system as soon as possible and out of warped space; I can't reach Earth's networks from here. Coffee. Lots of coffee. And finally, a straw and some duct tape."

Ben-Ari frowned. "Why a straw and duct tape?"

"Because I'm going to need to stream that caffeine directly into my veins. Chop chop! Bring me what I need." He rubbed his hands together. "Let's get to work."

Hours passed, and Noodles worked.

Hour after hour, he typed, hummed, cursed, sipped his coffee, broke apart computers, and put them together again.

The hobbits had left the Shire by the time Noodles cracked his first smile. "Aha! Access codes are working fine."

By the time the beacons of Gondor were lit, his smile had widened. "Here we go, baby."

Frodo was sailing to the Undying Lands when Noodles yawned and took his first nap. He was up three hours later, typing away again.

They were floating around Neptune, back in regular spacetime, when Noodles' smile faded.

"Oh boy," he mumbled. "This is bad."

He had taken over the empty berth that had once housed the ship's squad of marines. The fifteen cots had been moved down to cargo, making room for an array of computers, cables, keyboards, monitors, and a handful of anime posters (which Noodles claimed he needed for inspiration) featuring the cat-eared heroine from *All Systems Go!*. The hodgepodge reminded Ben-Ari of a marauder's web. Noodles sat in the center like a spider, typing on two keyboards at once.

"What is it?" Ben-Ari said.

He leaned toward a monitor, squinting. "Oh, this is very bad. I have to dig deeper." He clapped once—a loud sound. "Kemi, fetch me more coffee!"

Kemi's head popped around the doorframe. "I'll fetch you a fist to the teeth."

"I'll get your coffee," Ben-Ari said. "Keep working."

"Remember, five lumps of sugar this time!" Noodles said. "I'll know if you skimp out and only use four again."

As he kept working, Noodles' frown deepened. "Unbelievable," he muttered. "This is some nefarious Sauron shit right here. Evil as the dark overlord of Mordor himself." He pushed a keyboard away and shuddered. "We're onto something. We're really onto something here."

Ben-Ari sat beside him. "Tell me what you found."

Noodles looked green, and it wasn't just from all the Mountain Dew. "I reached the Chrysopoeia mainframe. That was easy. But I found layers upon layers of encryption and protection. It was as hard as breaking into the Iron Bank of Braavos, I can tell you. But finally I made my way in. I explored their little chamber of secrets. And what I found . . ." He gulped. "Let's just say that Voldemort himself would cringe."

Ben-Ari couldn't understand half of that, but that was normal with Noodles.

"Tell me," Ben-Ari said softly. "Whatever it is, we'll fight it."

"You told me that you found a prison in the demilitarized zone," Noodles said. "That the marauders had overrun it, had captured the prisoners. But you were wrong. The marauders were *given* those prisoners. Chrysopoeia, which owns all civilian prisons in the Human Commonwealth, invited the marauders there. A gift for the aliens."

Ben-Ari winced. "Why?"

"Because the marauders crave this." Noodles tapped his head. "The juicy brains inside our skulls. The smarter the brain, the tastier the meal. As you can imagine, an inmate with my sizable cranium would be especially vulnerable. Luckily, I was in a military prison rather than a civilian one. That probably saved my noggin. Let me pull up this report on the marauders, written by Chrysopoeia's exobiologists. There. Brain-eaters."

"Like zombies," Ben-Ari said. "Lieutenant Abasi called them zombie croco-spiders."

"But zombies, crocodiles, and spiders are dumb," Noodles said. "These beasts are smart. They're at least as smart as humans, maybe smarter. And here's the kicker. Their favorite food is *sentient* brains. Mere animals won't do. Offer them a cow's brain and they'll raise their noses at it. They'll eat animal brains only in a pinch. If a brain can't figure out language and basic arithmetic, it's flavorless." He cringed. "Mine must taste like filet mignon."

"And they collect the skulls as trophies," Ben-Ari said. "I saw the skulls on their backs."

"Probably how they built armor before they discovered metal," Noodles said. "Today the armor is ceremonial, a way to boast of their hunts. The smarter the victim, the more valuable the skull. Again, as you can imagine, I'm particularly vulnerable. Want to hear the weird thing, though? Nobody knows their homeworld. Nobody knows how they evolved. I can't find any record of them more than a few years old. It's as if they just popped into existence." Noodles shuddered. "Maybe aliens from another dimension? Another universe? The buggers came out of nowhere, hungry for conquest and brains."

"And Chrysopoeia has been feeding them," Ben-Ari said.

Noodles nodded. "I have the shipment logs right here. They're written with a lot of euphemisms. Where it says *clients*? That's the marauders. Where it says *meals*? That's prisoners."

Ben-Ari stared and felt the blood drain from her face. "Five hundred meals a day. Five hundred prisoners."

"Quite a few brains," Noodles said. "Enough to keep the marauder elite happily fed. Of course, there are millions of marauder warriors—mere commoners—who still just eat flesh or animal brains. The possibility of tasting human brains, just like their masters, could probably motivate the marauder grunts to attack Earth. We have billions of delicious brains, enough to feed their entire horde."

Ben-Ari rubbed her temples as if she could feel her own brain being sucked out of her skull. The sight of the prisoner in the DMZ, his skull sawed open, begging as his brain quivered, still haunted her. She felt queasy.

"Why is Chrysopoeia doing this?" she said. "What are the marauders paying them?"

"Technology," said Noodles. "The marauders are quite intelligent. Admirable, really. According to one Chrysopoeia exobiologist, the average marauder intelligence is analogous to a human IQ of 130, quite bright by human standards. And many among them have IQs well into the 200s. That's as smart as a Von Neumann, a Gandalf, a Yoda. Must be all the brains they eat. They're brilliant scientists; even I don't understand all their tech. They're nasty buggers, but I'm impressed."

"And they're giving Chrysopoeia some of that technology in exchange for prisoners," said Ben-Ari.

"Specifically, regenerative technology. Used in the medical field. See, the marauders have the ability to cocoon themselves during times of drought, famine, or other hardship. Possibly an ability they naturally evolved years ago, maybe refined with genetic engineering. When they're near death, they can simply cocoon themselves. In times of peace and plenty, they can emerge from their cocoons, healed, and continue their search for brains."

Ben-Ari nodded. "It sounds like stasis. Before humanity developed warp drive, scientists experimented with the idea. You freeze the passengers. You send them into space at sub-light speeds. A thousand years later, you wake them up among the stars. Before the technology could be widely used, we discovered warp drive and it became obsolete."

Noodles grinned. "Here's where it gets interesting. Stasis is still used—in the medical field. It's not common. Only a few hundred patients use it. Their illnesses were too great to cure. They were near death. So their doctors froze them. Some are centuries old already, still on ice. There's an urban legend that even Walt Disney's severed head is frozen in a jar somewhere. The problem is—we don't know how to *unfreeze* the patients without killing them. But with marauder technology, we can. We can cure these poor souls, have them emerge healed from stasis like marauders from their cocoons. And boom—Bambi sequels all over the place. And guess who's one of those frozen patients? Besides Disney, that is."

Ben-Ari thought.

Somebody important, she knew. Or rather—somebody related to somebody important. Somebody with family high up— who would make sure this deal happened, make sure the prisoners reached the marauders, made sure the regenerative technology reached human hands.

A memory flashed through her.

An aging, grieving admiral.

Words echoed in Ben-Ari's mind: *My eldest daughter is dying of cancer.*

"Admiral Komagata's daughter," she whispered.

"Bingo!" said Noodles. "Give that woman a cookie! Admiral Komagata himself, commander of Nightwall, one of the highest ranking generals in the Human Defense Force. His daughter has horrible cancer. She's still alive—frozen, only moments away from death. Chrysopoeia's doctors believe that they can heal and revive her using marauder technology."

"Chrysopoeia and the Human Defense Force have long been in bed together," Ben-Ari said. "They build our weapons. We fight with them. Now these two bedfellows have invited the marauders into their bed."

Noodles nodded. "Why fight the aliens? Too dangerous. And the marauders are good business partners. Stupid human brains for smart alien tech. It's a good deal for the shareholders. And Admiral Komagata certainly doesn't want to jeopardize any chance to cure his daughter."

"Except these marauders are building massive armies," Ben-Ari said. "I've seen them in the Augury. Fleets. Fleets of warships, surrounding us. I didn't see business partners. I saw an army that's planning an invasion." She shook her head. "Why is Admiral Komagata allowing this? Is he willing to sacrifice the entire species just to save his daughter?"

Noodles' grin widened. "Oh, he's a wily bastard. I dug up the dirt on him too. Guess who just bought himself a deserted, habitable moon in the Gurami sector, far from any potential war between marauders and humans? That's right. Our dear friend Admiral Komagata. He plans to be far, far away from the bloodshed before the invasion begins—with his little daughter spending her days splashing around in their new swimming pool. As I said, Sauron-level evil shit."

"There's only one thing to do now," Ben-Ari said.

"Get the world's biggest can of bug spray and pray that the Rohirrim show up to help?"

"The next best thing," said Ben-Ari. "We go to the only authority higher than the military and Chrysopoeia Corporation. We go to the woman who once pinned a medal to my chest. The president of the Alliance of Nations—the leader of humanity. We fly to Earth and we land right on her front yard."

CHAPTER FIFTEEN

"I promise you, ma'am," Marco said. "We're smart. We're educated. We're good workers. We'll find a job. We'll be good for our rent. We—"

"No job, no rent!" The woman pointed at the door. "Out. Out! Out or I call cops."

Marco and Addy hurried out of the building, pulling on their hoods. They stood on the street. The cursed rain had stopped, but a foul, unbreathable haze filled Haven today, and ash still wafted.

"It was an ugly building anyway," Addy said.

They turned back to look at the building. A *Vacancy Available* sign stood in a dirt yard. Tiers of concrete balconies rose into the clouds.

"We'll find another place," Marco said.

They walked onward. Cars raced down the road, spraying them with mud. A helicopter buzzed above, scattering whistling birds—or screaming vultures, as Marco had come to think of them. It was a neighborhood a few kilometers away from the subway stations but still crowded. Thousands of people clogged these streets. Some seemed well off, wearing business suits under their atmosuits; they emerged from expensive cars and stepped into office buildings, commuters from the burbs. Others were the locals, wearing only rags, and Marco even saw two naked men sleeping on a concrete slab, their beards long, their bodies covered with sores.

"Look, another one." Addy pointed.

A brown building rose ahead, and a sign outside announced: *Apartment for Rent.*

They stepped into the lobby, thankful for a respite from the shrieking wind and screaming birds, and rang the superintendent.

"No job, no rent!" The old man glowered. "Go, go. Go sleep on street! Employed tenants only!"

Again, Marco and Addy fled back outside.

Addy screamed.

"Fuck!" She punched a wall. "Fuck. That's ten apartment buildings that rejected us today, Marco. Fuck. Fuck! I'm not spending another night on a bench. I'm not!"

It had been weeks since Marco had slept in a proper bed. The thought of another sleepless night on a subway platform, shuddering as screams and groans sounded in the darkness, seemed worse than anything he had faced at boot camp.

"One more," he said wearily. "Maybe a bit farther from the subways. Less competitive."

"There's no point."

Marco was inclined to agree, but he only said, "We have no other choice. We have to keep trying."

They walked onward.

"No job? Sorry."

"Sorry, sir, only with pay stubs."

"Go, go! No rent!"

As the sun was setting, they sat on a bench in a park. A few withered trees grew in glass tubes, barely visible through the grime. Dark buildings rose all around them, and cars raced by in the shadows. They sat in silence for a long time.

Finally Marco spoke softly. "I can almost understand her."

Addy was too weary to lift her head. "What the fuck are you talking about, Poet?"

"About Lailani." He stared at an alien beetle the size of a cat scurrying by. "How she used to live before the army. She was homeless until boot camp. When we talked about how tough boot camp was—the food, the tents, everything—Lailani once got mad at us. She said we knew nothing. But I know now. At least, I got a small taste of it. Of what she survived for eighteen years until the army. And I think I understand why she left me. Why she went back to the Philippines after the army. To help the children there."

Addy leaned against him and placed her hand on his thigh. "Dude, I'm sorry she dumped you."

He smiled thinly. "And I'm sorry you broke up with Steve to come here. Actually, no I'm not. I hated him."

Addy laughed. "He's not that bad."

"Addy, he thought Plato was a form of putty. He asked me if Berlin was an outlet mall. He had never heard of Vikings. We played Trivial Pursuit. It scared me."

She laughed harder. "All right, so he's not the brightest. We can't all be geniuses like you."

He sighed. "Some genius I am. I got us into this mess. I must be dumber than Stooge."

She stared at him, suddenly serious. "Marco, you do realize that Stooge has a doctorate in physics, right? That he suffered a trauma in the war, that Steve has been helping him recover?"

"Oh." Marco lowered his head, suddenly ashamed. "I had no idea. I'm sorry. I—"

Addy burst out laughing again. "Got you." She elbowed him hard. "Stooge—a scientist! And I'm the Queen of England." She affected a high-pitched British accent. "Heavens, you naughty boy, you are quite the gullible chap."

"Ha ha, very funny." Marco rose from the bench. "Making fun of a poor couch potato. Not nice!" Street lamps were turning on, revealing more apartment buildings in the distance. "Come on, Addy. One more attempt before we call this bench our bed. Maybe those buildings over there."

"I don't see any vacancy signs."

"Worth a try anyway. Big buildings. Come on, Ads. Move your royal ass."

Exhausted, filthy, stinking and sweaty inside their atmosuits, they trudged across a concrete courtyard toward the complex. Three buildings rose here like three walls, ugly Brutalist structures, the metal balconies leaking rust. A statue of Admiral Evan Bryan, hero of Earth, rose between them, splotched with bird droppings. Evidently, the landlord had never heard of—or didn't care about—Bryan's corruption. Marco shuddered as they passed by the statue. He remembered the lair of the scum emperor, remembered shooting the admiral there. Even here on Haven, he couldn't escape that war.

"Hello, friend!" A short, slender man approached Marco, wearing no atmosuit but breathing through an oxygen mask. Well groomed, he wore dress pants and a pink button-down shirt. "You look like you could use some company. Here, here, have a look!"

A second man approached, this one burly and ugly, his face covered with warts. He wore torn jeans and a grimy denim jacket. With sausage fingers, he held out a photo album. It contained photos of timid Asian women, perhaps Thai or Filipino, some of them young, most of them well into their forties or fifties.

"Which one?" the slick, shorter man asked. "Choose any one you like!"

When Marco glanced behind the men, he could see the women huddling in the shadows under a balcony. They wore oxygen masks, but Marco could see that one had a bashed, bandaged nose. Another had a black eye. They were covered in filth, aging, rotting away.

"Cheapest girls in town!" said the man.

"No thank you," Marco said, hurrying by, ignoring the men's disappointed noises. Addy glanced back at them, then hurried after Marco toward the three concrete buildings.

A bearded man, wearing no mask, was digging through a garbage bin outside the central building. He fished out a needle, gave Marco and Addy a frightened look, then vanished into the shadows. Another one of the cat-sized rats scuttled by.

"Nice place you found us, Poet," Addy said.

"Come on. It's better than a park bench."

They stepped into the central building. Thankfully, despite the late hour, the superintendent answered the buzzer. He was a one-eyed, middle-aged man with stubbly cheeks. He wore a tool belt, military dog tags, and a stained wife beater. Several stars were tattooed onto his arm, denoting several scum killed.

"Come on in," he rasped, the hint of rye on his breath. "You two look more miserable than the dead monk-rat I fished out of the water cooler this morning. Smell worse too. Name's Grant. Come."

He led them down a carpeted corridor and into his office.

Marco's breath died.

"Holy fuck," Addy whispered.

The super's office was a shrine to the war. A framed poster above the desk displayed a squad of soldiers, all raising their guns, above a dead scum. A young Grant, still with both eyes, grinned from the photograph. A rifle hung on another wall in a glass casing, a plaque beneath it proudly announcing: *Three scum killed.* Several scum claws hung on racks, and an actual scum head—antennae and all—was mounted above a beaten leather chair. The flags and symbols of platoons, companies, and battalions covered every space of wall that remained. The only non-military decoration was a poster of *All Systems Go!*, displaying the same anime schoolgirl Marco had seen in the subways, a katana in her hand. But even that poster hung in a frame decorated with empty bullet casings.

"So, Grant," Addy said, "let me take a wild guess. You're a veteran."

Grant barked a laugh. "What gave it away? Yeah, twenty-five years in the army. Retired master sergeant here. Fought in the big one. Fought on Abaddon itself. Served under Admiral Bryan, and I don't care what the papers say, the man was a damn fine soldier. He shook my hand once. Yep. Killed me three scum in the war. That bastard hanging over the chair?" Grant snorted. "He's the bugger that took my eye. So I took his goddamn head."

"Impressive work," Addy said, looking at the mounted head. "That's a terrestrial scum too. A male soldier, yes? Thirty-six legger?"

"You're goddamn right it is," Grant said. "Meanest sons of bitches that ever came out of space. You know your aliens. What about you two? You fought in the war? You look like you might be old enough, but hard to tell with the grime covering your faces."

"We fought," Marco said softly. He didn't like talking about the army. He didn't like seeing this scum head. Too many memories. Too much pain.

"You're goddamn right we fought!" Addy said, already picking up Grant's mannerisms. "We fought on Abaddon itself. Went deep into the hive. Blasted the scum emperor to bits."

Grant barked a laugh. "Now now, young lady, no need to exaggerate. Serving on Abaddon is an honor in itself."

"We *did* kill the scum emperor!" Addy said. "Tell him, Marco."

"Addy, please," Marco said, squirming. "We don't want to bore him with war stories."

Grant stared at them, his one eye narrowed. "Hang on a goddamn minute. You said your names are . . . Marco? Marco Emery? And Addy Linden?" He gasped, reached to his desk, and grabbed a framed photograph. "Goddamn. Didn't recognize you with the grime on your faces. It *is* you!"

Marco looked at the photograph. It showed him and Addy back during the war, wearing battle fatigues, still with corporal insignia on their sleeves.

"Fucking hell," Addy said. "Seriously, my ass is *not* that big. The camera adds ten pounds, you know."

Grant's eye teared up. "By God. You'll excuse me if I shake your hands." He grabbed Addy's hand first, then Marco's, shaking them firmly. "You two are personal heroes of mine. Never in all my days did I think I'd get to meet you. I don't care what the papers say. I don't care what some pampered broadcasters say on the videos. You two are heroes through and through. It's my deepest honor to have you here, in my office, two of the soldiers who killed the scum emperor himself."

"It's all right," Marco said softly. The man looked ready to weep.

"Please, please, sit down," Grant said. "Excuse my rudeness. Let me get you some coffee. Or something stronger? And how about some food?"

"Actually, we just came to ask if you have an apartment to rent," Marco said. "I know there's no sign outside, but—"

"Do you have any bacon bits?" Addy interjected. "How about hot dogs? We'll also require a rake."

Grant didn't have any hot dogs or bacon, but he did pour them both whiskey—the good stuff, he said, not from his cheap bottles—and gave them each some beef jerky to chew. Real meat, imported all the way from Earth, he bragged, not the synthetic crap they made in test tubes.

"We don't have any pay stubs," Marco said, holding his cup. "We don't have jobs. But once we have shelter, a place to shower, some dry clothes, we'll go looking for work. We're smart and hard workers, and we'll find a way to pay you. We might be late the first month, but—"

"Any war hero is welcome to stay here," Grant said, cutting him off. "Say no more. My wife's pa owns the building. I'll make sure the old man doesn't cause any trouble. We have only one apartment left, and I'll be honest, it ain't the best one. But I'd be honored to have Sergeant Emery and Sergeant Linden staying with us."

"Just Marco and Addy is fine," Marco said. "That's all we are now."

"No." Grant shook his head. "You're more than you know. You're worth so much to so many. I pray that someday you realize that." He wiped his eye. "Come now. I'll show you the place. You'll have a warm shower and a roof over your heads tonight."

He took them to the tenth floor, where they entered an apartment. The wooden floors were scratched. There were no curtains and the windows faced brick walls. The bathroom was old, the sink loose, the kitchen rusty. Empty bottles of pop still stood on a counter. But there were two small bedrooms. There was no mold. And Marco knew this was home.

"You'll have to sleep on the floor tonight," Grant said. "But I'll grab you a couple spare blankets from my place, and a couple pillows from my couch, if you want them. And I'll order you guys a pizza. On me. Least I can do."

"Make sure there's bacon on the pizza!" Addy said, hands on hips, then stepped forward and hugged the one-eyed veteran. "Thank you."

They sat cross-legged on the living room floor that night, devouring the greasy pizza Grant had ordered them. Marco left his crusts for Addy, who scarfed them down, then tilted the empty box over her mouth, letting the crumbs slide in.

"You're going to turn into Stooge one of these days you know," Marco said.

"What are you talking about?" Addy belched. "I'm a petite, beautiful girl. Not some mindless animal who lives for food."

"A piece of bacon is stuck to your cheek," Marco said.

She gasped. "Face-meat!" She gobbled it down.

Marco looked around him at the apartment. "Well, it's not a palace. And there's no furniture. And the windows face brick walls. But it sure beats last night, doesn't it? This will be home for a while. Maybe a few months. Maybe even a few years. But we'll get our house eventually. Someplace that's green. Like the old song."

Addy bit her lip, looked down at her knees, then into his eyes. "Marco," she said softly.

"Uh oh. What? You almost never call me Marco."

She thought for a moment, then blurted out, "I'm never going to sleep with you again. You know that, right?"

"What?" He frowned and rose to his feet. "What are you talking about?"

Her cheeks flushed. She stared at her feet. "Remember? A few years ago?"

He sighed and sat back down. Of course he remembered. He had never forgotten. How could he? Even to this day, sometimes in his sleep, the memory resurfaced as a dream: he and Addy, trapped on a distant space station, having scared, lonely, urgent sex.

"Addy, we were young," he said. "We were afraid. We didn't know if we'd live another day."

"I know." She twisted her fingers. "It's just . . . sometimes when we talk about buying a house together, it's like we're husband and wife or something. Or boyfriend and girlfriend. And . . . you know I can't be that to you, right? Even with Lailani gone." She finally dared meet his gaze. "You're like a little brother to me."

"I'm a few days older," Marco said.

"That's not what I mean. I know we're not really siblings. But we've been living together for so many years—since we were kids—that you *feel* like a little brother. And I loved that night. I loved having sex with you. It was the best sex I ever had. Really. Better than with Steve or anyone else. But I can't do it ever again. Even if we live here together. Even if we buy a house. I just wanted you to know."

"I know," he said, throat suddenly hoarse.

She scooched toward him and leaned against him. "I still love you a ton, though. More than anyone in the world. Always. Always." She mussed his hair and grinned. "My silly little brave hero."

He brushed crumbs off her shoulder. "Love you too, you Stoogette."

"Remember the coins?" she said. "The ones I bought the subway tokens with? From the coin purse you laughed at?"

He nodded. "I remember."

"Well, you mocked me for having a coin purse. But those coins were special to me. Remember the one time you came with me to a hockey game?"

"Yes, I only went with you because I lost a bet," Marco said.

"You were miserable there. I know." Addy nodded. "But I think you had fun at the end. I bought us hot dogs and chips and ice cream. And you didn't understand the game at all, but you laughed at my jokes, and you blushed so much when the kiss cam turned toward us, when I kissed you with everyone watching."

He cringed. "I still haven't gotten over that."

"The Leafs lost, but I had so much fun, Marco. It was the best game I ever went to, because it was with you. Because I was able to share something I love with you. To show you why I love it. To see you have some fun, even if it was just a bit. The coins in that purse were change from that day, from the hot dog and ice cream I bought you."

His eyes widened. "You saved the coins? All that time?"

"And others too. A few coins were from the poker game we once played with your dad. Other coins were change from the vending machine at boot camp. Remember how we found a vending machine in the desert? How we bought snacks, sat on the sand, and remembered home? That was my coin collection, my collection of memories with you."

Marco placed a hand on her knee. He spoke softly. "And you spent them."

She wiped her tears. "I had to. So we could find a home. So we could make new memories. And that's what we're going to do here in Haven. Make new memories. Not bad ones, not like the ones from the war. But good memories, like that hockey game. Like the vending machine. Like this, right here, right now."

"Well, we're out of coins, but you can still save these crumbs." He pointed at the floor.

Her eyes lit up. "Floor pizza!"

Macro cringed as she ate them.

They slept in the living room that night, using Grant's sofa cushions and two spare blankets—one which they placed below them, the other above them.

Addy fell asleep first, and Marco looked at her for a moment. During the day, she was all poking elbows, groans, loud laughter, eyes that could switch from love to fury and back again in an instant. In her sleep tonight, she was peaceful, not twitching with nightmares as they sometimes did. He pulled her blanket up to her shoulders.

Good memories, he thought. *Let's make a lot of them.*

He slept a deep, dreamless sleep for twelve hours.

CHAPTER SIXTEEN

Earth floated ahead, a blue marble, growing closer.

Home, Ben-Ari thought. *So small. So fragile. So close to falling.*

Flying on the *Saint Brendan,* she saw so few defenses around Earth. Only five years ago, at the height of the war, the Iron Sphere system had surrounded the planet—a massive network of military satellites. Among them had flown thousands of warships, patrolling Earth's orbits.

Today, most of that was gone.

Ben-Ari saw a handful of warships. A few Firebirds. Half a dozen military satellites. The Scum War had cost more than all previous wars combined, going back to the first battles fought with sticks and stones. More lives, more dollars, more resources had been spent on defeating the scum than on any project, military or civilian, in human history. Today Earth languished in poverty, half its colonies dismantled, most of its ships and satellites grounded, millions of its children orphaned.

Today Earth is vulnerable, Ben-Ari thought. *And today the marauders muster a fleet greater than any the scum had ever flown against us.*

"Captain, the stealth engine won't keep us hidden forever," Kemi said, sitting beside her in the pilot's seat. "Not this close to the planet. By now, Earth will know that we're wanted. They'll see us. They'll blast us apart."

Ben-Ari nodded. "The time for secrecy has ended. Now it's time to see if an old friend is still loyal."

She thought back to that day four years ago. Earth had been reeling from victory . . . and its cost. The scum had been defeated but cities lay in ruin, millions lay dead. In its anguish, Earth had sought heroes. They had found them among Ben-Ari and her platoon, the warriors who had plunged into the imperial scum hive, who had slain its emperor. In a ceremony broadcast across Earth and her colonies, the president of the Alliance of Nations—the most powerful person on Earth—had pinned a medal to Ben-Ari's chest. Ben-Ari had spent a weekend with the president on her ranch, but under the shade of willows, by the soothing lake, she had only seen the fire and blood, had found no peace, and the medal had felt heavy on her breast.

Welcome me to your ranch again, Ben-Ari thought. *Today I need you more than ever.*

She had kept the president's personal communicator signature. She wrote to her now, broadcasting the message down to Earth.

Dear Madam President. It's Einav. I need your help.

For long moments—silence.

Ben-Ari waited, checking her communicator. No reply.

Then—*message seen.*

Her breath caught.

More silence.

"Captain!" Kemi said. "They've spotted us. Earth Guard ships flying our way!"

Ben-Ari cringed. "Get ready to blast our azoth engine. We might have to escape in a hurry."

"No can do, ma'am," Kemi said. "We're too close to Earth. This isn't a tiny asteroid. If we make the jump here, the gravity field might crush us like a tin can."

Alarms blared across the ship. Voices boomed out of the speakers.

"HDFS *Saint Brendan*! Disarm your weapons at once and prepare to be boarded."

"Ma'am, they're aiming weapons at us," Kemi said.

Noodles rushed onto the bridge. "What the hell is going on?"

"Should I disarm, ma'am?" Kemi said.

"Wait," she whispered.

"Captain, their cannons are heating up!" Kemi said.

"Wait!" Ben-Ari said. Her communicator beeped on her wrist. She checked the small screen. A message appeared from the president.

See me at once. My ships will escort you.

"Ma'am, the Earth Guard ships have lowered their canons," Kemi said, voice shaky. "That was a close one."

"I almost wet my pants," Noodles said. "But that's mostly thanks to the abysmal coffee on this ship."

The Earth Guard ships, emblazoned with the blue and green colors of the Alliance of Nations, surrounded the *Brendan*.

Soon they were all flying in formation, entering the atmosphere with roars of fire.

They descended toward a green valley in Switzerland, shaded by the Alps. They landed by a glistening lake. Snowcapped mountains soared, pines spread across the foothills, and deer grazed in meadows. An ancient church rose on a hill. Here was a place of Old Earth, the planet as it had been, still untouched by the wars. Ben-Ari had grown up on military bases, raised by soldiers, playing with guns and riding in tanks instead of on tricycles. To her, this place seemed unreal, a hologram, a place so beautiful it could not truly exist on this planet of dust and grime and broken stones.

President Katson met them on the porch of her lakeside chalet. She was a stately woman in her sixties, didn't dye her hair, and still showed a scar on her cheek—a scar from the Cataclysm fifty-five years ago.

This woman has been fighting for Earth for more than half a century, Ben-Ari thought. *First as a teenager, serving in the resistance to the scum. Then as an intelligence officer in the HDF. Today as president of the Alliance of Nations.*

"Einav!" The president reached out her arms, stepped forward, and embraced Ben-Ari. "It's so good to see you." She still carried a slight Georgia drawl, a remnant of her childhood in America. Her blue eyes softened with concern. "When I heard about all your troubles, what happened . . . I couldn't believe it. But you're safe here, Einav. You're safe."

Kemi and Noodles were back on the *Brendan* half a kilometer away. A man was rowing in the water, undoubtedly a security guard, and no doubt security filled the chalet as well. But here on the front porch, overlooking the water, the two women were alone: an elderly president and a young officer, two leaders in a place of peace, two women in a galaxy that threatened to collapse.

"Madam President," Ben-Ari said, finding tears in her eyes. Her legs shook. Finally all her emotions were coming out, all the fear, the loneliness, the terror of the past few weeks. "I didn't know where else to turn. I need your help. We all do."

For an instant, it seemed that President Katson would cry. Her eyes reddened, but then she sniffed and stepped back from Ben-Ari.

"Luka!" she barked. "Luka, some sweet tea please!" She turned back toward Ben-Ari. "I taught him to make sweet tea like back home in Georgia. The boy's a bit dense, but he's pretty enough to look out."

A handsome blond man emerged from the chalet, carrying a tray with two tall glasses. He placed them down on a low table.

"Should I bring out biscuits and gravy, Madam President?" His Swiss accent was thick.

"Heavens, no, it's far too early for that. Be a dear and go vacuum the cat."

"Madam?"

"Get, get!" She waved him away. "See, Einav? Dumb as a doorknob and prettier than this lake."

The two women sat by the lake, but Ben-Ari did not sip
her tea. She had no time for pleasantries, no time to discuss
handsome servants.

"Ma'am," she said, "a new enemy has arisen. They've
infiltrated the DMZ. They surround humanity's sphere of
influence in space. A race of vicious, predatory aliens, larger and
smarter than the scum. The military is covering it up. Chrysopoeia
is providing them with live human flesh from their prisons. We're
in grave danger. An invasion of Earth is imminent, and we have
no proper defenses in space. I've gone AWOL from the military,
ma'am, because I could not remain silent. I had to warn you. We
must prepare!"

President Katson leaned back in her seat, sipped her tea,
and watched the lake. "Einav, I knew your father. We served
together in the military."

"I know," Ben-Ari said. "But right now, ma'am, we—"

"He was a wise man, your father." Katson continued as if
she hadn't heard Ben-Ari. "I admired him. He was a good soldier.
Do you know why?"

"Because he dedicated his life to the military," Ben-Ari
said. "I know this more than anyone. I was raised on army bases.
Even I, his child, was just a future soldier to him. Sometimes I
think he made me just to make another warrior."

And now, even with the marauders' threat, even with the
Military Police after her, with the cosmos tearing at the seams,
that old grief filled Einav. The grief of a motherless child. A girl
who played with bullets instead of dolls. A girl raised by gruff

sergeants instead of loving parents or even dedicated nannies. Yes, her father had been a good soldier. And he had made sure that everything in her childhood would lead to her following in his footsteps.

"He was a good soldier," said President Katson, "because he knew when *not* to fight. He knew how to forge alliances."

Ben-Ari nodded. "I remember. So often in my childhood, he'd fly off the planet. He'd fly to distant worlds. He'd meet alien species, negotiate, forge peace treaties, find allies. He never took me with him, of course. I remained behind with this or that sergeant. While he, the famous colonel, the great statesman, wove the galaxy together. Other soldiers destroyed. He built."

President Katson nodded. "And that is what we must do now, Einav. We must build alliances. We must not rush into war but seek to forge lasting peace. And the greatest peace is forged with the greatest enemy." The president placed down her cup of tea. "Einav, I know about the marauders. Admiral Komagata and I speak about them daily."

Ben-Ari leaped from her seat. She trembled. When she blinked, she saw the marauders, laughing, scuttling over the pristine mountains and vales, then vanishing in a flash.

"Ma'am!" she said. "If you knew, why is Earth not defended? Where is the Iron Sphere? Where are the fleets? Why . . ." She shook her head in disbelief, and her voice dropped to a whisper. "And the prisoners fed to the marauders . . . I saw them, ma'am. I saw it happen."

Katson paled. "You saw one . . ."

"I saw more than one." Ben-Ari stared into her eyes, refusing to flinch. "I saw an army of them. I saw them stack the bodies of their victims—human bodies. I saw them carve open the skull of a living prisoner and feast upon his brain. And in the Augury, I saw a fleet of those creatures. I saw them surrounding us. How could you know and do nothing?"

Red flashed across Katson's cheeks. She took a deep breath, forcing herself to calm down. She sipped her tea, but her hand trembled. The ice clinked. "Einav, this new enemy . . . They're not like the scum. They're stronger, smarter, beyond anything we could defeat, even during the glory days of our fleet. What would you have me do? Fight them? No. That is a fight we would lose. The best we can do is . . . appease them." She twisted her lips, as if the tea had gone bitter. "It's not a word I favor, *appeasement*, and its historical connotations are clear to me. But it's the only choice, Einav. We made a decision. Myself. My ministers. My generals. The shareholders of Chrysopoeia Corp. We face a hungry tiger. All we can do is feed him scraps and hope to sate his appetite."

Ben-Ari stared at her president in disgust. "And you think prisoners are the scraps. They're humans, ma'am. Human beings. Five hundred of them a day. More if the enemy's appetite grows. And what if they're not sated? What if they demand more and your prisons run empty? What then—the poor? Cargo ships full of people from the Third World, fed to the enemy to keep you, your ministers, your generals, and your shareholders comfortable in your chalets, while—"

"To save Earth, yes." Katson rose to her feet, cheeks red. A strand of her white hair came free and fluttered in the breeze. "To save billions of us, yes, I would gladly sacrifice thousands, even millions. I would feed them to the marauders, because the alternative is our extinction."

"The alternative is to fight!" said Ben-Ari. "To win! To rebuild the fleet back into its glory. To face this new enemy with the same grit and courage as when we faced the scum."

"I will not doom millions of soldiers to death!" Katson was shouting now. "I will not watch billions perish on Earth, food for the marauders. Enough have died, soldier! We watched millions die only years ago. I will not condone more violence. And I will not hear more of your warmongering."

"Warmongering?" Ben-Ari barked a bitter laugh. "I call for defense, not assault! It's you who are sending hundreds daily into the slaughterhouses. And you dare invoke my father's memory to justify it! Tell me, President. Do you do this truly for humanity? Or only for winning the next election?"

President Katson gazed at the lake. The man in the boat was rowing toward the shore. Birds fled from his advance.

"This has always been a beautiful place," Katson said softly. "This has always been a beautiful planet. Someday, Einav, maybe you will learn this lesson. That to save the many, we must sacrifice the few. That to protect something we love, we must take actions we hate." She turned toward Ben-Ari, and her eyes were damp. "All this beauty. But you will never see it again, child. Five years ago, you saved Earth. I will not let you destroy it now."

The rower reached the shore.

Men with suits and guns emerged from the chalet.

Ben-Ari had no weapon; they had disarmed her before meeting the president. She turned to run, hoping to make a beeline to the *Saint Brendan*, but the ship was too far. More agents emerged from behind a shed and trees.

They raised stun guns.

Ben-Ari cursed. She ran, zigzagging, dodging several shots.

"Kemi!" she shouted, but she already saw the agents race toward the *Brendan*, saw them fire their guns toward the engines. The ship was trying to rise, fell back down.

An agent emerged from behind a tree. The blast hit Ben-Ari's chest before she felt it.

She froze.

She couldn't breathe.

She tried to inhale. Her lungs would not obey.

She took another step. She kept running.

A blast hit her shoulder, knocking her back. She fell.

Up. Run. Run, Einav!

Her father's voice. They were laughing in the park, a stretch of greenery on some military base, and he chased her, pretending to be an alien, and she squealed as she fled him.

Run! Run, Einav!

A monster, a monster!

She managed to rise again. She dodged an agent. She ran.

She was running from the scum. She was running across Fort Djemila as her soldiers died around her. She was running through the hive.

A third blast hit her, this one to her head. She could barely even feel hitting the ground. A man grabbed her arms, tugged them behind her back, and the last thing Einav Ben-Ari felt before losing consciousness was the handcuffs close.

CHAPTER SEVENTEEN

They sat on the apartment floor. A single light bulb hummed above. On their old pizza box—it was a month old by now—sat two bowls.

"I never thought I'd say this." Marco stared dejectedly at the meal. "But I miss Spam."

"I miss Spam all the time." Addy reached for her bowl. "Just close your eyes and scarf it down, buddy boy."

For several days now, they had been eating the same dinner. Soppy, sticky rice, bought from the bargain bin at a wholesale shop an hour's walk away. The rice was grown locally in underground farms here on Haven, and once boiled in water, individual grains vanished, leaving a sticky, tasteless mush. A few corn nibblets floated in the porridge, golden treasures from the single can they allowed themselves to open each day, to share, to spread across three meals.

"Is there anything else we can sell?" Marco said. "Maybe buy some cheap meat? Some vegetables? Anything other than fucking soppy rice porridge."

"We already sold our atmosuits," Addy said. "And the scum claw you captured in the war. And your watch."

"Maybe if you sold your hair to make wigs," Marco suggested.

She glared at him. "Maybe if you sold a book."

Marco winced. That one hurt. "You know I've been trying to sell *Loggerhead*. You know publishers aren't buying literary fiction now."

"So write something better!" Addy said. "Write a fucking fantasy quest story with dragons and shit. Fuck me, write smut about Fabio banging vampires, just make some money from your goddamn writing."

Marco forced down a bite of gruel. "Why don't you open the can of Spam you carry around everywhere if you're so desperate for protein?"

"That's my souvenir from the army. You know that."

"Well, you sold *my* souvenir!" Marco rose to his feet. "You sold my scum claw."

Addy snorted. "Big deal. It barely fetched enough to buy a bag of milk. Which, by the way, you drank more of than I did."

"We shared it, Addy."

"Yeah, we shared it by you drinking three cups and me only two!" She leaped to her feet, teeth bared. "The way I see it, you can go pimp yourself on the street and let the junkies fuck you for money, but you owe me a glass of milk, and . . ." She let her words die, then lowered her head. "Fuck, Poet. I'm sorry. I don't know what came over me. I'm being a bitch."

He sighed. "It's the hunger. I feel it too. It's making us antsy." He looked around him. "And it's this damn place. This damn prison cell, and no work, and we're out of cash again."

He looked around the apartment. After a month of searching for work and finding nothing, their new home on Haven was still bare. Their only furniture was the pizza box, which served as their rug/tabletop, and the sofa cushions Grant had let them keep, which served as pillows or seats. Sometimes the storm faded, and the intense radiation of Alpha Centauri blasted through the windows, heating the apartment to intolerable levels. They still had no curtains, no blinds, and certainly no air conditioning on those scorching days when it must have soared to fifty degrees Celsius. They slept on the floor. They ate on the floor. When the storms outside raged in a fury, with their atmosuits sold, they stayed indoors. Trapped. A stained wooden floor. Concrete walls. Glass windows that showed either murk or blinding sunlight between them and the next brick wall. This was their world on Haven.

"We'll try again tomorrow," Marco said. "There's that new office building we found. We'll knock on doors."

Addy nodded. "All the other buildings loved seeing a pair of disheveled refugees in rags knocking on their doors. I'm sure it'll work this time too."

"With that attitude, it won't," Marco said.

She slammed her bowl onto the floor. Sticky rice oozed out. "Fuck you, Marco Emery. Fuck you with a scum claw."

Leaving the mess, she grabbed a pillow, marched into her bedroom, and slammed the door shut.

Marco sighed. With no paper towels to clean the mess, he had to scoop up the rice with his fingers and deposit it in the sink, handful by handful. For the first few days here, they had slept together in the living room. They had two blankets. With one on the floor, another pulled above them, it had seemed almost like a real bed. And Addy's presence at his side had helped keep the nightmares at bay. But for two weeks now, Addy had been snapping at him, then sleeping in her own bedroom, the door closed. And often, when she closed that door, Marco felt a sense of relief, free for a few hours from her sharp tongue and angry eyes. He missed her poking elbows. They had been kind compared to the Addy he knew now.

It's the stress, he knew. *It's the poverty. It's the cabin fever. Once we find work, she'll be the same old Addy, all goofy grins and jokes and hugs.*

But Marco knew, deep inside, that it was more than that. She had been happy on Earth, living at Steve's place. Marco had taken her to Haven with dreams of a house in the suburbs, a friendly dog, a peaceful garden. All lies. A scam he had fallen for. If such a place did exist on this planet, it lay far beyond the reach of the subways, and walking far through this hellish atmosphere—even if they still had their suits—was impossible. Perhaps the suburbs of Haven were only a few kilometers away, but they might as well have existed in another galaxy.

He pulled his blanket and sofa cushion into his small bedroom. The storm was back on outside, slamming at his small window. He lay on the floor, blanket beneath him, and hugged his pillow.

I miss you, Addy, he thought. *I miss you, Lailani. I miss you, Father. I miss home, and I don't even know where home is anymore. I don't know if it was the library, the army, or this place. I'm lost. I'm lost and I don't know what to do.*

They had a handful of other items to sell. His watch, worth maybe a meal or three. The medals from the war he kept stuffed at the bottom of his backpack; they perhaps could buy another few meals. But sooner or later, Grant's patience would run out. The man perhaps admired them, but he didn't own the building. He could not let them live here rent free forever, and it had been a month already. After that, it was homelessness. It was the soup kitchen for their meals. It was hunting the dog-sized rats of Haven. It was a slow decay. It was death worse than any the scum had promised.

He looked at the wall. Beyond it, Addy was in her own bedroom, and Marco ached to go to her, to hug her, just to feel her warmth, to let her presence comfort him. But he dared not. He feared the rage that had been growing in her. He closed his eyes and he slept.

In his dreams, as always, he was back there. In the hives. Sometimes it was the mines of Corpus, other times the sprawling labyrinth of Abaddon, but most times Marco couldn't tell the difference. He was racing through the tunnels, as he did every night, desperate to find a way out, the scum pursuing him.

There were always monstrosities in the tunnels. Human and scum hybrids. His undead friends, risen to haunt him, deformed into terrors with centipede bodies. But tonight he saw a different creature in the hives. She stood in shadows, watching him, clad in a wispy gray dress. Her long black hair framed a kabuki mask, and she stared at him through the eye holes. Her arms were long, too long, gray and knobby, and they ended with hands the size of her mask, three clawed fingers growing from each palm.

"Who are you?" the girl whispered.

Marco's eyes snapped open. He was back on the floor of his bedroom, drenched in cold sweat. He couldn't breathe. He still felt trapped. Every breath was a struggle, and he was so hot, dying of heat, suffocating. It was so dark.

Morning dawned hard, foul, and full of hot, stinking wind. The storms of New Earth painted the world umber and mustard today, and stinging ash flew everywhere. They stepped outside. In the courtyard, the junkie was sleeping by the garbage bin. The two pimps—the thin slender one and the ugly brute—were already at work, showing off their photo album to passersby. Marco cringed to see a man park his car and hold out a wad of cash. One of the prostitutes, a middle-aged woman with a bandaged nose, entered the back seat. The car drove away. Marco walked on.

Without their atmosuits, it was a miserable slog to the subway station. For two kilometers they ran. They stuck the nozzles of their air bags straight into their mouths, able to breathe during the journey—just stale air they had collected from their apartment—but couldn't save their skin. They arrived at the station covered in grime, panting. Inevitably, some of the foul air entered their nostrils, entered their lungs, burning. Marco wondered what diseases he was allowing into his body, what rotting death would someday bloom inside him. For now, he had no choice. It had been sell the suits or starve.

For a miserable eight hours, they walked through the underworld, trudging through the tunnels that spread below the city. Many of these tunnels were used for the subways, but others were for foot traffic, clogged with Havenites, lined with shops and eateries. Below each high rise, a staircase led to the lobby. Marco and Addy climbed into every office building, knocked on doors, asked for work, were turned away.

A receptionist wrinkled her nose, staring at Marco and Addy's shabby clothes.

"Next time wear business suits," she said.

In another office, a security guard reached for his gun. "Go, get lost! No soliciting."

At one company that manufactured medical supplies, a kind old Indian chemist sat them down, listened to their story, nodded sympathetically, and promised to be in touch should a position become available. They had no phone numbers for him to jot down. They left, still unemployed, but each holding a tin of curry from the chemist's wife.

"Maybe some of the mom and pop shops in the tunnels need somebody," Addy said. They sat on a subway platform, eating the curry chicken. "Somebody to man the cash register, or sweep, or stock shelves."

Marco looked at the shops. One sold a thousand kinds of dried mushrooms. Another sold dirty movies and sex toys. In a third shop, an old woman sold pancakes she was frying up on a greasy griddle. In a fourth shop, women in lingerie stood on pedestals. A blond man in a pinstripe suit walked up, examined the women, pointed at one, and escorted her into the shadows.

"I don't know about this," Marco said, but still they tried a few shops—giving the brothel a wide berth. They were beyond pride, would gladly have taken minimum wage, part time, anything that could stave off homelessness and hunger. Again they were turned away from shop after shop.

"Well, at least we got curry," Marco said when they returned home that evening.

"I'm still hungry," Addy said. "Fuck it, maybe we should panhandle. I'm not too proud to beg."

Marco's stomach growled. "Let's cook more rice."

That evening, Addy finally opened her can of Spam, the one she had carried with her all the way from Fort Djemila five years ago, her souvenir from boot camp. They fried it up and ate it with the rice. They finished their last can of corn. Tomorrow, unless they begged or found work, it would be just plain sticky rice and tap water.

"Marco, I have an idea," Addy said when their meal was done. "Why don't you write an intergalactic bestselling novel that makes us millionaires? I mean it. I'm not mocking you this time. You need to write again. How long has it been since *Loggerhead*?"

"Four years," Marco said. "I've written many short stories since then. Novellas too. No other novels."

Addy grabbed his backpack and pulled out his notebooks. Some of them, years old, contained his original manuscript for *Loggerhead*. The other notebooks were still empty.

"Well, either sell this one or write a new one!" Addy said. "A more commercial one. There are still empty notebooks and you have a few more pens."

Marco looked at the notebooks, at the ones with *Loggerhead* and the ones still empty.

"I've tried to sell *Loggerhead*," he said. "You know that. It's not like the old days before the Cataclysm. Back then, you could just upload your book to the internet. Anyone could. And you'd find readers, make a few bucks. But now . . ." He sighed. "The golden age of ebooks is over. You have to sell it to a publisher these days. There are only five publishers, all of them on Earth, and they've all turned down *Loggerhead*." He pulled his rejection letters out from one notebook. "See? They all say the same thing. Thank you, but we receive hundreds of submissions a day, and we can only publish one or two new novelists a year. It's hopeless."

Addy grabbed the rejection letters from him. Before he could stop her, she tore them up.

"Well, fuck them," she said. "And fuck *Loggerhead*. Come on, Poet. I love you, but a book about a turtle? You need to write something people want to read. Not about fucking sea turtles.

Write about . . . swords. Guns. Shit like that. Add some sex. Some hockey."

"People don't want to read about hockey," Marco said.

"Sure they do! You can make me a character. I can defeat evil monsters by whacking them to death with my hockey stick. Maybe your villains can be mutant turtles."

"Ninjas?" Marco said.

Her eyes widened. "Yes! I like the way you think."

Marco sighed. Obviously, Addy was not a twentieth century buff like he was.

That night, as Addy retired to her room, Marco sat on the living room floor with his notebooks. He took a pen, an empty notebook, and sat for a long time.

No words came.

After an hour of staring at the blank page, he began to draw.

He scribbled aimlessly. He drew himself in a towering prison cell, arms over his head, a single ray of light falling on him from a window high above. Serpents coiled in the shadows, threatening to constrict him. He flipped the page, drew another drawing, this one of tunnels delving deep, a network, a small figure lost within it. On a third page, he drew an anguished face, claws reaching out to grab it.

On a fourth page, he found himself drawing the feline schoolgirl from *All Systems Go!*, the anime show he had seen posters of. She stood ready for battle, holding her katana, her black hair flowing in the wind, ready to fight the evil agents who sought to capture her, to study her superhuman powers. Except as Marco kept sketching, he found that instead of giving her a Japanese schoolgirl outfit, he was drawing the girl with a long, wispy, tattered dress. Instead of cat ears, he gave her a kabuki mask, its expression blank.

The drawing seemed to stare at him.

A whisper filled the apartment.

Who are you?

Marco dropped his pen, and his heart burst into a gallop. Eyes. Eyes were staring at him from the kitchen! He spun around, stared at the shadows. Nothing. Nothing there.

It was just the humming air filtration system. Had to be. The damn vents were probably a century old, dating back to Haven's founding, and rumbled and moaned when the storms outside swelled. Or perhaps it was the junkie speaking outside, the one who rummaged through the garbage bin for needles; that bin was directly below the kitchen window.

But Marco had seen this girl in the kabuki mask before. And not just in his dreams. Not just in his notebook. He had seen her in an alleyway, standing under a poster of *All Systems Go!* He had seen her on the subway.

"Or am I going completely crazy?" he said. "And now I'm talking to myself too."

He returned to his notebook. He stared at the girl. She was part *All Systems Go!*—the katana, the fighting stance. But she had the ashy dress and kabuki mask of the shadowy figure he had seen. Around her, he began to drawn her enemies, creating claws, fangs, webs, until spiders appeared. Spiders with huge jaws. With skulls on their backs. Skyscrapers rose around them, and a neon sign hung in the background, proclaiming: *Girls! Girls! Girls!*

Marco paused for a moment. He scratched out the sign. He added a new sign above it. *Kill! Kill! Kill!*

"Kill 'em, girlie," Marco said. "Kill or be killed."

He wrote words beneath her: *Le Kill.*

He paused again. Then he added: *A novel by Marco Emery.*

He flipped the page and began to write the first chapter.

* * * * *

He sat at the breakfast table, meaning the pizza box on the floor, eating sticky rice. His eyes were bleary, his stomach rumbling.

"God, I wish we had coffee." He rubbed his eyes and yawned. "I've been up late writing your damn book."

Addy gasped. "Did you add hockey?"

"No hockey."

"Turtles? *Ninja* turtles?"

"No turtles this time, Ads."

She leaped toward the corner, grabbed his notebook, and flipped to the first page. She read the title out loud. "*Le Kill.*" She frowned and looked up at him. "*Le Kill?* What does that mean?"

"It's French," Marco said. "It means the. *The Kill.*"

Addy placed her hands on her hips. "So why didn't you just write *The Kill*?"

"Because it doesn't sound as good."

She flipped another page. "Hey, the rest is in English! I thought you said it's French."

"Addy! For God's sake. I don't speak French. Just a few words. Just half the title is in French. For literary effect."

She scrunched her lips. "I think hockey has more of an effect than French. What's it about, anyway?"

"It's cyberpunk," Marco said. "About a futuristic, crumbling metropolis, full of urban decay, neon lights, graffiti, drugs, and gangs. A girl named Tomiko is the heroine. She wields a katana, and she hides her identity behind a kabuki mask. She fights mutant spiders created underground by an evil corporation—the same corporation that gave her super senses, that now tries to capture her, to experiment on her. It's an urban noir tour de force full of hailing gunfire, social breakdown, dark technology, and the seedy underbelly of a high-tech world. It's— Addy. Addy! Stop writing in my notebook!" He snatched it from her.

"What? I was just adding hockey turtles!"

"No hockey turtles!" Marco said.

"What if they're low-life cyberpunk junkie turtles with tattoos?"

"No! Now get ready, Ads. Put on your best clothes and your best smile and a-hunting we will go."

They left the apartment. They ran for two kilometers, breathing from their air bags. They delved into the tunnels. They kept searching for work.

Every day—a run. Burning nostrils. No money for trains, so they walked, crawling through these tunnels, these hives of man, as stifling as the hives of insects. Receptionist after receptionist. Frown after frown. A shameful trip to the soup kitchen, where they picked up more canned corn, more sticky rice. And more anxious looks from Grant. And another threatening letter from Grant's father-in-law, warning of eviction.

"Wear a suit next time."

"Is this how you show up looking for work?"

"We're just not hiring right now."

"You mean you have *no* experience in this field?"

Day after day. Days of grime and hunger. Nights of writing *Le Kill*, of vanishing into the nightmarish, decaying world of neon lights, of mutant spiders, of girls with kabuki masks and katanas fighting the agents of an evil corporation. Days of pimps and prostitutes. Of junkies digging through garbage bins. Nights of spiders, nights of sirens and gunfire and flashing blades, of Tomiko leaping between skyscrapers, cutting down nefarious agents. Nights of men outside his apartment, handing over money, buying women for an hour. Day after day, and the two worlds—the world of Haven and the world of *Le Kill*—blended in Marco's mind. His existence had become one of dark fantasy, and when he saw the kabuki girl again one day, eating noodles in an eatery by a subway platform, then vanishing when he approached, he didn't know reality from fiction.

Every day, Grant seemed more uncomfortable when he saw them, his "good morning!" less enthusiastic. Soon he began to mumble about his father-in-law running out of patience, the bastard. Then he warned, eyes dour, that the firm was preparing eviction papers, "but I'll fight them off as hard as I can, same as we fought the scum together on Abaddon." And Marco knew it was a losing fight.

"Look," Addy said the morning the first warning letter appeared posted to their door. "Here's the plan. We find the next spaceship heading to Earth. We hide ourselves in suitcases. And we sneak on board."

"Yes, because spaceport security will never suspect two suitcases with legs hopping into the cargo bay," Marco said. "Especially one that keeps talking about hot dogs."

Addy scrunched her lips and tapped her chin. "All right. New plan. We find a junkyard. We build a spaceship out of old vacuum cleaners and popcorn machines, and—"

"Addy!"

"—and when the engine runs, it'll make us fresh popcorn, and—"

"Addy!" Marco waved the notice at her. "This says we have only a week to find a job. This is no time for joking."

Addy turned away from him. She faced the apartment window. The storm had finally died down, revealing the brick wall of the neighboring building. Her fists tightened, and she was silent for a long moment.

Finally she blurted out, "I got a job offer."

Marco frowned. "Addy, what—when—?"

"A few days ago," she said, still staring at the window.

"What—?" Marco laughed. "Addy! That's great. Isn't it? You're not smiling. It's not something . . . demeaning, is it?"

She spun around and punched him—hard. "It's not being a stripper, if that's what you mean. Though I'm sure you'd love to see that." She sighed. "It's to be a security guard. On the subway. For the rougher stops, some that had assaults and burglaries."

Marco thought for a moment, not sure how he felt. Finally he said, "That's not bad. That's a good start."

"Poet, I came to Haven to get away from fighting in tunnels," Addy said. "And it wouldn't even be as a soldier! It would be just me and a baton and a fucking Taser. Standing there all day. In the dark tunnel. With all the nightmares of Corpus and . . ." She bit down on her words. "And I don't know. But I have no choice. So tomorrow I'll show up and see if they'll still have me." She raised her fist. "But you better finish that killer turtles book of yours and make a fortune!"

Along with his relief—by God, soon they'd be able to buy more than rice—he felt guilt. He wanted to contribute too. It felt unfair that Addy should support them both. The next morning, as Addy went to her new security firm, Marco continued his search, finding no more leads, only more raised noses.

That evening, he returned home, dejected, to find Addy in a security uniform. The uniform was navy blue, and a baton, a flashlight, and handcuffs hung from her belt. A bruise spread across her cheek, and her knuckles were cut.

"Addy!" he rushed toward her. "What happened?"

She looked at him, eyes damp. "You should see the other guy." She sniffed. "I can't have a gun yet. I'll get one in a month, they said." She pointed at a plastic bag in the corner. "I bought you a gift."

"Let me take care of your knuckles," he said. "Addy, what—"

"Forget it!" she roared, clenching her lacerated fists. "Go open your present."

Inside the plastic bag were clothes. Black dress pants. A button-down white shirt. A blue tie. A poncho to ward off the ash that forever fell here.

"They paid me my salary in advance," Addy said. "Benefit for veterans of Abaddon. I got some canned goods too, and there's meat in the fridge, and—Poet. Poet! Enough with your sappy hugging!"

But he kept hugging her. His eyes dampened. "Thank you, Addy. Thank you."

"Get off!" She squirmed free. "You're getting my uniform dirty." But soon she was smiling. "Now you won't look like a stinky pig when you go job hunting. Just like a sweet smelling therapy pig."

On his first day job hunting with his new shirt and tie, Marco found a job.

It was in a cluttered call center, a warehouse crammed full of desks. It paid minimum wage and offered no benefits. It was ninety minutes away from their apartment. But it was a paying job and he took it and that evening, he used his first paycheck to buy Addy a rake and hot dogs. They stood in their kitchen, holding the rake, roasting ten hot dogs over the stove while laughing like idiots. After two months of privation and hunger, it was one of their best nights, and they spilled the rice out the window and let the storm claim the grains. The rice flew in the wind like a million snowflakes and vanished into the night.

CHAPTER EIGHTEEN

Ben-Ari sat, chained to the chair, head lowered.

Above her, the judge loomed like a vulture over a carcass.

"Captain Einav Ben-Ari." His voice boomed through the shadowy courthouse. "You have been accused of the following." He listed her crimes. Theft of military property. Assaulting a superior officer. Resisting arrest. Hacking into secure military databases. Orchestrating a prison break. With each crime listed, the crowd murmured. Ben-Ari did not look up.

"Einav Ben-Ari!" The judge's voice boomed again. "I find you guilty on all counts. I hereby demote you to private, strip you of all your medals and honors, and sentence you to death." The crowd roared its approval. "Before your execution, Private Ben-Ari, you will spend thirty years in a maximum security prison cell, where I urge you to reflect upon your crimes and seek peace with whatever god you worship. May he have mercy on your soul."

The gavel fell.

They dragged her outside the courthouse into the searing sunlight. A crowd awaited. Cameras flashed. Protesters chanted or cheered.

"Warmonger!" somebody shouted.

"Alien killer!"

"Free the heroine!"

"Fascist!"

"Free Ben-Ari! Free Ben-Ari!"

Signs. Lights. Colors. People tossed their shoes at her. Scuffles broke out. An MP shoved Ben-Ari into a van, chained her to the seat, and they drove.

Time passed in a haze.

Something inside her felt dead.

They took her past towering walls. They strip searched her. They deloused and decontaminated her. They dressed her in an orange jumpsuit. They shoved her into a rocket. They blasted her into the darkness. They took her to an asteroid with its own moon. They marched her down a cell block as men jeered and tossed excrement at her.

They shoved her into a cell. She saw a concrete slab topped with a thin mattress, a smaller concrete slab for a stool, a metal toilet, concrete walls.

The door slammed shut, sealing her in shadows.

Ben-Ari lay down on her cot. For the first time since her trial, she wept.

CHAPTER NINETEEN

Marco sat at his desk.

His ears pounded. His head spun.

"Good morning, sir," he said. "Would you care to hear about our new credit card insurance premium pla—"

A dialtone hummed. A thousand voices clattered around him.

"Good afternoon, ma'am!" he said. "I'd like to offer you a free sample of Happy Joy Bubbles, a brand new ash-cleaning detergent, straight from Japan, that—"

A ring tone like an air raid siren in his ear. A thousand phones, rising, falling from a thousand desks, and fluorescent lights hummed, a thousand insects overhead.

"Children, please, is your father home? I have a special offer for him, two toolboxes for five easy payments of—"

Around him the other salespeople all chattered like insects. A heavyset man with a turban was selling toasters, and Sergeant Singh died in the tunnels. A young Asian girl giggled as she sold a mutual fund, and Lailani ripped out Elvis's heart. A light died overhead and the flashlights died in the tunnels and the centipedes moved in.

"Yes, sir," Marco said into his phone, "or your money back guaranteed, but I assure you, these are quality steak knives capable of cutting through a shoe. A shoe, sir! And—please, sir, don't hang up."

The siren again. A flat sound. All clear. All clear.

"Emery, if you don't start selling some products, your ass is on the street."

Marco stood in the boss's office, head lowered, hands behind his back. The man pounded his desk, snorted, pointed at the door, gave Marco one more chance. He left, the soldier who had killed the scum emperor, a scolded boy. He returned to his desk, one in a thousand in this warehouse of human cattle and buzzing lights.

"Yes, ma'am, just like on the television! A vacuum that can suck up marbles. I guarantee it."

He shuffled away from his desk. A coworker pointed at him, whispered something to his friends. They laughed. A man pounded Marco on the back. "Good job, war hero!" A few people snickered.

Marco stepped outside into the storm. Another day at the call center ended. Was it his second month now? His third? He no longer knew. It felt like years.

He plunged into the subway station. Countless commuters crowded around him, shoving forward, a great sea of humanity, shoulder to shoulder, crotch to ass, sweat to sweat, coughing, sneezing, and a train slammed its doors shut. "No more room, wait for the next one!" And they shoved, and another train rolled by, then a third, and Marco squeezed onto the fourth, shoved his way in. He stood in the sardine can, the other commuters pressing against him.

The train died in the darkness. For long moments, they stood still on the tracks, and Marco was in the mine again. His legs shook. He had to get out. He had to! When the train moved again, he exited at the next stop, still far from home. He sat on a bench, and he trembled. His legs wouldn't stop shaking and he couldn't stop thinking of the mines. He waited an hour for the crowds to die down. He took another train, tried to ignore the shouting drunk man at the back. Tried to ignore the woman laughing as she pissed her pants. Finally he made it to his stop, belly roiling with hunger.

He shuffled by the pimps and the prostitutes.

"Hey, Marco!" the thin pimp cried. "You going to buy a lady tonight?"

The burly pimp held out his photo album. "Choose. Choose!"

The prostitutes, imported all the way from Thailand and Indonesia, stood in the shadows. Meek. Afraid. Aging. Bandaged, bruised. Marco shook his head and walked on. Past the man rifling through the garbage, he made it indoors. The elevator was dead. He climbed ten stories and returned to his apartment, and he felt dead.

Addy was already home. She still wore her security uniform. She had a new black eye, and again her fists were lacerated. Marco wanted to ask her what happened, but her look silenced him.

Don't, her eyes said.

So he didn't.

They sat at their new table. A cheap piece of plastic, made for lawns, not kitchens. They still could not afford chairs. They sat on flimsy plastic stools. They ate silently. Some pasta. Some tomato sauce. They had no money for meat tonight, not while paying back two months of rent. Not after buying the table.

They lay down on air mattresses for the night, and cardboard covered the windows, makeshift curtains. It was all the furniture they had.

Before he drifted off to sleep, Marco pulled out his notebook. He wrote another chapter in *Le Kill.* Tomiko, his masked heroine, was trapped in a factory farm, a great slaughterhouse for humans. Rows and rows of cages filled the building, crammed together like desks in a call center. Using the magic of her ancient kabuki mask, she summoned her katana from the demons of the underworld who had captured it, and she sliced the bars, escaping her cage. She freed all the captive humans, and they fled into the night, forming an army to fight the corporation and its evil president.

The train screeched along the tracks. It broke down again. For long moments, they languished in the hot tunnel, and Marco's chest constricted, and his belly ached, and his skull felt too tight, and he couldn't take it, couldn't take being in this tunnel, crammed here in this sea of flesh, with the scum scratching at the subway, and he knew it was them. He could smell them. He was ready to scream, to pass out, by the time the train moved again.

He was late to work.

"Damn it, Emery, I don't care what you did in the war!" His boss pounded the tabletop. "I'm docking you an entire day of pay. And don't tell me you were only an hour late. I don't give a fuck. You sell something today, or I'll kick your ass onto the street. Don't think you'll get special treatment here because you were some hot shot in the army. You're worth less than my shit here."

As Marco walked back to his desk, he felt the eyes on him. Hundreds of eyes. Everyone was staring. He heard them whispering, laughing. When he finally reached his desk, he found a picture of himself there, right by his phone. Somebody had drawn him in a crude cartoon, the words 'Ass-kissing Emery' written beneath it. He heard them laughing. He felt their eyes.

He sat down.

"Good morning, ma'am! As seen on TV, the new super iron can smooth out any wrinkle in—"

"Yes, sir! Our new six-shooter hunting rifle can hit a whistling bird from two kilometers away, and that's no exaggeration. Buy now, and we'll toss in a free—that's right, *free*—bottle of Hearty Haven BBQ sauce."

He sold a rifle.

The trains screeched.

He made his way home.

His head spun when he finally stepped off the train, and his legs trembled.

He shook his head at the photo album.

He crashed onto the air mattress.

The trains screeched.

"Yes, sir, we—"

His boss yelled.

The commuters crammed against him.

The train died.

"Choose a girl! Choose!"

"We're experiencing delays in service."

"Damn it, Emery!"

More drawings on his desk. More jeers. Somebody printed a photograph of him, hung it in the kitchen, scribbled on his face. A toothless smile from the junkie. More bruises on Addy's face.

"Ma'am, we—"

The train horns.

He slept.

Was it month seven? Eight? He no longer knew. He was dead. He had died on Corpus. He was trapped in the mines, forever lost in the darkness, forever in his nightmare. Repeating. Repeating. Lost.

He slept.

CHAPTER TWENTY

It was reading and writing that saved Ben-Ari's sanity.

All she had in her prison cell was time, the boundaries of her mind, and words to explore those boundaries.

A cell of concrete. Two by two meters large. Not even large enough to pace. Barely wider than she was tall. A slab of concrete topped with a thin mattress. Two more slabs of concrete, forming a crude desk and stool. A toilet by the bed. No window. Twenty-three hours a day here in isolation. A few days down. Thirty years to go.

Once a day, they escorted her outside of her cell. She showered with child abusers and serial killers. They sat her by a barred window and let her stare outside at a concrete wall and a narrow view of the stars, just a strip of darkness with one or two dots of lights. Then back into her cell for another twenty-three hours of creeping madness and desperate efforts to stave it off.

Thirty years, Ben-Ari thought, sitting in her cell under the flickering fluorescent light. *Thirty years of this hell until they execute me.*

She would be in her fifties when they finally hanged her. Would any shred of her sanity remain by then?

She would join no prison gang. With a single hour outside their cells a day, prisoners formed only loosely organized gangs.

With Noodles still on the lam, she was the only Jewish prisoner, hated by the Aryans, shunned by the other gangs. Showering quickly. Keeping to herself. Beaten when cornered. Thankful when she returned to the safety of her cell. One time they jumped her. She fought back, hard. They gave her bruises. She broke their bones. They left her alone after that, but she was always cautious, always relieved to return to her cell.

Her cell. The boundaries of her mind. Words to explore them.

They gave each prisoner a choice of a single holy book, the only reading material allowed. Ben-Ari chose the Old Testament. She had never been overly religious. Her father had been a staunch atheist, railing against the evils of faith. As a child, as a form of rebellion, Ben-Ari had dabbled with religion, had secretly read the Bible, worn a Star of David, prayed at night. As a soldier, she had lost her faith. She had seen too much horror, too many friends killed, to still believe. She had explored much of the galaxy, and she had seen no sign of God. And yet here in the darkness, the old rituals comforted her. Her faith was still shattered, but the comforts of words, of memories, of older times—they warmed her in the cold.

For hours a day, she read the book, savoring every word. She let herself escape into those old stories. She traveled with her ancestors, the Israelites, out of captivity in Egypt. She fought with King David against the Philistines. She lived in an ancient land of sunlight, of palm trees and rustling vineyards, and she heard the song of turtle doves and of maidens dancing over grapes, crushing

them for wine. She walked through the streets of Jerusalem in the
desert, hearing the words of prophets. She was trapped in a
concrete cell, but in her mind, she lived in an ancient kingdom of
sand and sunlight. Here was her escape: if not through prayer then
through ritual, through words, through imagination and collective
memory.

When she wasn't reading, she wrote.

At first, they had refused to give her more than her bible.
It was months before a guard walked in, grunted, and handed her
a stack of notebooks and a box of pencils.

"Thank your friends on Earth." He snickered. "They
protested for you. You get paper and pencils now."

"What protests?" Ben-Ari asked. "Who? What are they
saying? Is Kemi Abasi in prison too? And what of—"

But he slammed shut the door to her cell. Her mind went
wild, imagining thousands of people marching down the streets
on Earth, calling her a heroine, demanding her freedom. Freedom
she still didn't have. But perhaps they had alleviated her
conditions here in prison. The guards would not move her to a
minimum security installation. They would not give her more
books or a television. But they gave her paper. They gave her
pencils. And Ben-Ari was grateful.

And she wrote.

She started at the beginning.

She wrote about her birth, six weeks premature, struggling
for life—the stories her mother had told her. She wrote about her
mother's death, stung by a bee, a death so mundane for a family

of warriors. She wrote about her father, the famous colonel who had traveled the galaxy, forging alliances with alien races.

But mostly, she wrote about her war.

They brought her more notebooks, more pencils, and her wrist ached every day, but still she wrote. About entering Officer Candidate School at eighteen, a path laid out for her at birth, and graduating at the top of her class. About her first assignment at Fort Djemila, training boys and girls who would grow into heroes, into legends. About leading those heroes to Corpus, to fight the scum in the mines. About leading them into the hives of Abaddon, finding the emperor in his pit, and crumbling that alien empire.

And she wrote about the marauders, this new threat for humanity. About leaders weary of war, bankrupt, afraid, feeding prisoners to this enemy, this beast whose hunger could never be sated.

You may feed the wolf scraps for a while, she wrote. *But sooner or later, he will bite off your arm.*

One day, when they gave Ben-Ari her ten minutes at the small barred window, Earth came into view in the narrow strip of sky. A pale blue dot, barely visible in the distance. The world she had fought so hard to defend, the world that might now fall.

She did not know the lifespan of marauders, the length of their patience. She did not know if they would pounce tomorrow or next century. But one thing she knew. They were preparing for war.

"All my life, I fought for you, Earth," she said to that distant light. "But now you're in great danger, and now I cannot help you."

And so, she knew, there was only one thing she could do. One way she could still save her planet.

She was trapped in the most secure prison in human history, marooned on an asteroid in the depths of space. And she would have to escape.

CHAPTER TWENTY-ONE

He stood by the window, staring at the brick wall.

He paced the apartment.

He felt trapped in a cell.

He stood outside in the storm, letting the ash hit him.

He lay on the floor of his apartment. He stared at the ceiling.

I can't, he thought. *I can't.*

It was the weekend. It was two days in this prison cell. Two days before he returned to the inferno of the subways, the boss, the phones, the desks.

I can't. I can't. I want to die. I can't.

Addy came home from work that evening. She worked Saturdays too. She walked straight to the bathroom, favoring the right leg, and a cut bled on her fist. Marco knew better than to challenge her, knew she wouldn't speak of her job underground. But he saw the haunting pain in her eyes.

I can't.

He paced. He stepped outside into the storm, back again. Addy locked herself in her room.

I can't. I want to die. Please let me die. I can't.

"We need to splurge," he said the next morning.

Addy sat in the corner, staring at the blank wall. Her day off. She wore gray sweatpants, a white tank top, white bandages on her knuckles. Her eyes were sunken, her hair limp. She looked older than her twenty-four years. A cigarette dangled from her lips, the only luxury she allowed herself. Their only furniture was still the flimsy plastic stools. They were too poor to afford more than rent and cheap food.

"We're broke." Her voice was cracked. "And we need to save to buy a house in the suburbs. Or to fly home to Earth."

"Fuck that," Marco said. "Fuck the suburbs. Fuck Earth. Fuck them both for today. Today we need to splurge. I have to get out of here, Addy. From this apartment. I have cabin fever."

And I have PTSD. And I have depression. And I want to die. And I can't. And I have to get out of here.

They left the apartment.

They walked through the storm.

They sat in a small Chinese place, eating greasy noodles. A *Robot Wrestling* match mumbled on the TV. They did not speak. They had no words. They kept glancing up from their noodles, meeting each other's eyes, then looking down again. They ate, silent.

"Not as good as hot dogs on a rake," Marco finally said. And finally Addy cracked a smile.

"That was pretty funny, when we did that," she said. The rain streamed outside the windows.

Marco nodded. "I liked that night." He sighed and looked down into his bowl. "There haven't been many good times lately, have there?" Suddenly his throat felt tight. "Boot camp was worse. Less sleep. Harder on the body. But . . . we had fun there. We had our friends. I feel alone here." Suddenly his words were spilling out, and he struggled not to shed tears. "I miss my dad. And Lailani. And our friends. I hate my job. I hate going there every day. I'm already dreading the next time I have to get on that subway. I see people on the subway, Addy, and their eyes are dead. They just stare ahead, eyes blank. Some of them have gone mad. They talk to invisible friends, and . . . sometimes I think I see a figure. A girl in a kabuki mask. And I think I'm going crazy, and I'm scared, and I'm trapped here, and I'm depressed, and . . ." He exhaled slowly. "I'm sorry. That was a lot. I know it's hard for you too."

Addy thought for a moment, chewing her lip. Then she pointed at Marco with her chopsticks. "You need to get laid."

Marco snorted and rolled his eyes. "Addy, I just spilled my heart out. And that's your reply?"

"I mean it! You need to get laid. Writing isn't enough for you. Your *Le Kill* book is too scary anyway. You need some wild, crazy sex, and you need a girl to love you. To look after you. To treat you good. To bring back the old Marco."

Marco gave her a sidelong glance. "You're not saying that . . . That you . . ."

"Not me! For fuck's sake, Marco." It was her turn to roll her eyes. "You *wish* it were me. And I don't mean those ladies who hang out outside our apartment either. You need a proper girl. A girlfriend."

He slapped cash down onto the table. "Well, after these noodles, I'm too broke for breakfast tomorrow, let alone a girlfriend."

"Then you need a sugar mama!" Addy said. "From the burbs! Where the rich ladies live, looking for a young boy toy like you."

Boy toy? Marco didn't feel like a boy. He was only twenty-four, but he felt old. He felt like he had lived too many lifetimes. Like he had no business still being alive. If once he had been a boy, that had been another lifetime. He was twenty-four and ancient and dying inside.

Grant had given them his old computer a few months ago—a clunky tablet that hummed and clicked. Marco mostly used it to read; he could not afford to buy new books, but the tablet came loaded with the classics, good company for sleepless nights. Addy used the tablet to watch hockey games; not the new games from Earth, which cost money to watch, but old reruns from years ago. This Sunday, however, Addy sat cross-legged on the floor, tongue sticking out, typing away at the tablet.

"Ads, what are you doing?" Marco looked up from his notebook, where he was working on *Le Kill*. He had just finished revising the twelfth chapter, the one where Tomiko found her father, a missing scientist whose discoveries the corporation had stolen to mutate the spiders.

"Shh!" Addy said, typing vigorously with two fingers. "Almost done . . . there!" She hopped toward him and showed him the tablet. "Look. Nice, right?"

Marco stared in indignation.

"Addy! Not again!"

She grinned. "Hands off!" She pulled the tablet away before he could snatch it. "You need this, Marco."

He groaned. He managed to grab the tablet and yanked it toward him. He looked away, his stomach curdled, and his cheeks flushed.

The tablet was open to Colonial Love, a dating website for the colonists of Haven. Addy had created a profile—for *him*.

"*This* is the photo you chose?" Marco said. "The photo of me with half a cow in my mouth?"

"Girls appreciate a man who enjoys a good cheeseburger!" Addy said. "Shows you're not some refined dandy."

"Addy, I'm blinking in the photo!"

"Well, it was either this photo, or the one I snapped of you peeing in the field. Those are the only two I have."

Marco sighed. "Cheeseburger was better." He looked back at the tablet and cringed to see the profile name she had chosen. "Cuddles143? Really? *Cuddles143*? This is supposed to make me seem manly?"

"Girls love cuddles!" Addy said. "I'm a girl. I know. Cuddles are the way to a girl's heart." She grinned. "I'm having fun with this. I'll teach you. I'll turn you into a regular Casanova."

He read out loud the profile Addy had created for him, his incredulity increasing every moment. "Male, 24, seeking female. Successful author. War hero. Hardy colonist. I enjoy long walks on the beach. Never judge a book by its cover. I play hard and party harder. I love dogs, cuddles, and treating a woman like a princess. I enjoy both going out and staying indoors. Looking for my partner in crime. Is it you? Don't worry, we'll tell people we met at a bar!"

Addy grinned at him. "Good, huh?"

Marco groaned. "Addy, this is horrible. First of all, I'm not a successful author. I'm not even published. Second, I don't want to advertise to Haven what I did in the war; you saw how well that worked out on Earth. Third, you used a million clichés here, and clichés are the death of good writing."

"See? Successful author! You know all about using words. But I know about love. And trust me, this will find you love."

"I'm deleting this," Marco said.

"No!" She snatched the tablet away. "You are not. Marco, you're a dude. And dudes have dicks. And dicks need to stick into places. If you don't get laid soon, you're going to just become a huge, whiny pain in the ass." She touched his knee. "Marco, you need to get laid. And if possible, you need somebody to love you. To look after you in ways I can't. To make you happy again. So please. Do this."

He flopped down onto his back. "I'm going to regret this."

Addy whooped with joy. "All right! Now let's browse for your future wife!"

"Addy!"

"All right, all right, just a date at first." She bit her lip. "And I get to choose your date clothes."

"I'll just wear the work clothes you bought me."

She sighed. "Dear oh dear. I've got a lot of work to do with you."

* * * * *

The message popped onto his tablet.

Meet me tonite, bitch.

Marco sat in his bedroom, door closed. He stared at the girl's profile.

Katya. 19 years old. A pretty girl with long brown hair.

He glanced up at his bedroom door. He wondered if he should show Katya to Addy, ask her opinion, discuss the prospect of meeting the girl. But Marco suddenly felt embarrassed. Somehow this felt private, awkward, not something he wanted to share with Addy. Not yet.

Yo, bitch, you there? ;)

Her message popped up. Marco answered. *Yeah.*

10 pm. These coords. L8r, bitch. Haha.

Her profile went offline.

Marco put down the tablet. He sat still for long moments. He had only contacted Katya because she listed creative writing on her profile. He had introduced himself as a fellow writer. They had exchanged ten, maybe fifteen messages, and she had shared some of her poems with him, before she invited him to meet.

I shouldn't go, Marco thought. *This is stupid.*

He should stay home. Of course he should stay home. What kind of girl sent such messages? She looked sweet in her photo. Smooth hair, big brown eyes, pale skin. A beautiful girl. But . . . No. He didn't know her. He should stay here. He had his foam mattress, newly acquired, and he had saved for months to buy it. He could lie down, reread chapters from *David Copperfield* on his tablet. He could work on *Le Kill*; he was almost done writing it, almost ready to submit it to publishers. Of course he should stay home.

He picked up the tablet. He looked at Katya again. She looked shy in her photo, her hair hiding her cheeks, her eyes peering out, a nervous smile on her lips. She sat in a shadowy room, vulnerable. A fellow author, scribbling in the shadows.

Addy would tell him to go. Addy would tell him he needed this.

He stood up. He stared around his bedroom. A small room. A cell. A single mattress on the floor. A tablet with a few old movies. A few notebooks in the corner. A window facing a brick wall.

He got dressed quickly before he could lose his resolve. A pair of black jeans. A gray hoodie. Sneakers.

He stepped into the living room, saw that Addy's door was closed. He sneaked outside without saying goodbye.

He trudged for two kilometers. After several months of work, he had bought the mattress, bought a new atmosuit, but still the journey to the subway station was hellish. The atmosphere of Haven lashed him, sludge rose to his knees, and his breath rattled as he sucked on his oxygen bag.

He rode the subway, traveling farther than he ever had. An old man sat across from him, wearing short shorts and a tank top, revealing a wrinkled belly. A woman lay on a bench nearby, covered in newspapers. A group of teenagers were laughing, poking a dead rat with a stick. After an hour, the train rolled into its last stop. Marco stepped out. He stood on the southern edge of Haven.

He checked his tablet. There was no mistaking it. The coordinates Katya had given him lay beyond the city. She waited in the wilderness of New Earth, this stormy planet orbiting a strange star.

He stood at the subway stop, staring into the storm. Gray, deep purple, and indigo clouds rose toward white mist, and acidic rain swayed in sheets. The planet's moon was a faded smudge of yellow through the roiling gases. A highway stretched ahead, vanishing into the clouds of ash, soil, and storm.

I should never have come here, Marco thought, throat tight. *Not to this last station. Not to this planet.*

He pulled out his wallet. He had a few bills. If he worked hard, saved every last coin, it would be five years before he could afford a flight back to Earth. But he could still go back to his apartment here. He could work on his book, and—

No.

He tightened his lips.

His nightmares had been growing worse. Many nights he only slept an hour, maybe two, arrived at work bleary-eyed. Feeling dead. He would not survive another five months of that, let alone five years. He needed someone. He missed holding Kemi, laughing with her, feeling safe, feeling strong. He missed Lailani, kissing her, blessed with her love. Those two lights had always guided him through darkness, but now he had no beacon. Now he was truly lost.

And so in the abyss, he sought a new light. He spent his last few dollars. He rented a car. He had not driven a car in years, not since high school. But he had fought from starships; what was driving a car? He drove that car along the highway, leaving Haven behind, heading into the storm.

Clouds rose around him, taking the forms of beasts, great leviathans and behemoths and creatures of ancient myth. Rain slammed against the roof of his car. A gust of wind nearly shoved him off-road, and ash pelted the windshield. He could barely see more than a few meters ahead, but he drove faster, climbing up to a hundred kilometers per hour, two hundred, racing forward.

The highway was empty. The colors swirled around him. Above, he saw shadows swooping—great birds, larger than the screaming pests in the city, large as his car, alien life diving through the roiling atmosphere.

I have to turn back, he thought. This was a prank, that was all. Just a damn prank! There was no girl here. She had given him fake coordinates.

"You're an idiot, Marco Emery," he told himself. "You're a fucking idiot. What are you doing here?"

He tightened his hands on his steering wheel. He kept driving. Because he could not turn back. His friends were in the darkness ahead. Trapped in the mines. Kemi was there. She needed him. So he drove the train onward, ferrying the soldiers through the tunnel, and they were everywhere. The scum emerged from the walls, the ceiling, rose along the tracks, and gunfire blazed, and he couldn't turn back. He couldn't. And Corporal Diaz died. And Beast died. And Singh died. And Elvis died. They all died around him, but he couldn't go back. He couldn't go back. He had to find the azoth crystal. He had to find light. He kept driving.

He drove for an hour, maybe more. The highway split in several places. He tried to choose the right route, to seek the coordinates the girl had given him, but soon he was lost. He must have taken a wrong turn. He was a hundred kilometers away from Haven now, deep in the wilderness, a single car lost in a storm the size of a world. He didn't know if he'd find his way back. He was lost in the mines. He was lost in his nightmares. This had to just be a nightmare. He would soon wake up. He would soon die here. A fool. A fool. A—

He slammed down on the brakes.

Fuck!

The car skidded. He yanked the steering wheel. The tires screeched. The car spun a full one-eighty degrees. Marco winced and finally managed to face forward again and roll to a stop.

His heart pounded and sweat trickled down his back.

A metal wall loomed before him, only meters away. He had nearly hit it. The wall soared so tall it split the storm; he could not see its top. The clouds lashed against it like ghostly hosts trying to break it down. A gate rose in the wall, closed tight.

Marco pulled out his tablet. A message was waiting for him.

Yo, bitch, where r u?

He typed his reply. *Gate.*

He waited.

A minute passed. Five minutes. Nothing. He wanted to turn around, to drive home, when the gate creaked open.

He drove through.

The storm was weaker behind the wall. Only a few swirls of dust danced alongside the road. The sky gurgled above, a watercolor painting all in umber and deep angry black. A few low buildings rose here, filling a compound. Marco stopped his car, looking around, seeing nobody. What was this place? He gripped the steering wheel. A clang sounded behind him, and he spun around to see the gate slam shut. His heartbeat increased.

Where are you? he typed.

No reply came. Marco looked from side to side, but it was so dark here. A few scattered lanterns lit the compound. And there, in the mist . . .

His heart pounded against his ribs. It was her. The girl in the kabuki mask! The girl with claws! She swept closer. She reached for the car door. She pulled the door open, and Marco needed a weapon, and—

A girl slipped into the seat beside him. Her brown hair dangled across her face. He could see only the tip of her nose and a peering eye. No kabuki mask. No claws. She wore a long coat, and she giggled.

"Katya?" Marco said, voice shaky.

She nodded. Then she burst out laughing. "Katya, Katya. Yes!" She giggled. "Yes. I'm Kat. I'm a cat. Meow! Now drive. Go on!" She punched his arm, laughing uncontrollably. "Drive!"

He drove. The road was gravelly. He looked around him, seeing greenhouses. Just barely visible through their windows, he saw plants growing in darkness. He smelled livestock. Fertilizer.

A farm, he realized. *Just a farm.*

A massive shadow swooped from above. A shrill cry pierced the air. Wings beat, scattering smoke, and he caught sight of burning red eyes, a beak lined with teeth, and—

Katya laughed hysterically. "Drive! Just a bird. Drive."

His heart wouldn't slow down. Cold sweat dampened his palms. He drove.

"Where do I go?"

She giggled. She fell over, hit the doorway, laughed again. She yanked her seat back and placed her feet on the dashboard. "I don't know! Silly!"

He tried to speak to her again, but he could coax out no more words. He drove. Finally she pointed.

"Stop. Stop!" She laughed, shouting. "*Stop!*" She rolled around on her seat, as if she had just told the world's funniest joke.

He stopped by a squat concrete building. Katya stepped out of the car. She danced toward the building, spinning, laughing. Marco followed. They stepped inside.

It was a barn. Along one wall, chickens sat stuffed into cages, squawking, laying eggs into tubes. Across the room, cows lazily flicked their tails. The place was hot, filled with the odor of animals. Katya pulled him between the cows and chickens, taking him to a back room. An old mattress lay on the floor. A television stood on a concrete slab, showing an old movie from the twentieth century, back from when the world had been good. Katya stared at the movie for a moment, laughing.

"So . . . you like to write too?" Marco asked.

She turned toward him. Her hair still dangled across her face. He could barely see her. She doffed her coat, letting it fall around her feet. She was naked beneath it. Her body was slender, pale, her hips narrow, her breasts small. She wore nothing but a dog collar around her neck, attached to a leash.

"Take me for a walk," she said. She handed him the leash, then got down on her hands and knees. She laughed.

Marco knelt before her. He tried to part the hair covering her eyes. She squealed, scurried back, and hissed at him.

"No," she whispered, then barked. She laughed hysterically, rolled on the ground. "Take me for a walk."

He saw the holes on her forearms. The telltale signs of her addiction.

"Katya," he said. Gently, he reached forward and detached the leash from her collar. "Sit down. Let's talk. Let's watch the movie."

She crawled onto the mattress, still on hands and knees. He sat beside her, and she rubbed herself against him. She moaned.

"Take me," she whispered. "Now. Now. Don't wait." She closed her eyes. "I'm yours. Take me. I'm yours."

She took his hand and guided it between her legs, and he felt the wetness there, and she moaned, eyes still shut.

Gently, he pulled his hand back. "Katya, let's talk for a while first. I want to get to know you."

She glared at him. Her eyes filled with anger. "What the fuck is wrong with you?" She stood up. "Are you gay? Are you a chick?"

"No." He stood up too. "I just . . . I'm used to talking to girls before I sleep with them."

She stared at him for a moment longer, then burst out laughing. She laughed and laughed, laughed so hard she fell, rolled around. "You're so silly!"

The storm rattled the windows and the alien birds screamed. He lay down beside Katya. She tugged off his shirt, his pants, and he lay beside her in his boxers. And he held her, tried to speak to her, to hear about her stories, but she kept burying her face in the mattress, giggling, moaning, pushing herself against him. And Marco thought of Lailani, thought of how he had held her back at Fort Djemila, and he wanted that feeling here too. He wanted to make love to Katya, to love her, but this felt wrong. When he tried to kiss her, she turned her head away. And he felt trapped. He rose from the mattress and pulled on his clothes.

Katya lay, naked, looking up at him.

"I'll sing for you," she said. She rose to her feet, and she sang, a beautiful song of old Earth. And as she sang, her hair fell back, and he could see her pale face, her brown eyes. He sat, listening, until she giggled and fell silent.

"It's beautiful," Marco said.

"It's opera," she said. "Classical music. From Earth. Before my dad took us here, I was going to be a singer." She lowered her head, smiling, her hair covering her face again. "Drive me to the gate, silly. It's near my house."

They left the barn. He drove back to the gate. Katya hugged him, giggled, then ran off into the clouds of dust and vanished into the night. Marco drove back home.

Addy was already asleep, and Marco climbed into his bed. He lay staring up at the dark ceiling. In only three hours, he had to wake up for work. But no sleep would find him. He thought of Lailani. He wanted to hold her, to say goodbye one last time. He thought of her until dawn rose, and the train rattled, and he sat in the warehouse at his desk, a thousand desks around him. A farm animal. A chicken trapped in a cage. They all clucked around him, thousands of them, phones ringing, chirping, mooing, animals trapped in pens, slowly going mad.

CHAPTER TWENTY-TWO

"Doc, I can't sleep. I lie awake at night for hours. I'm lucky if I get two hours a night. During the days, I can barely focus, barely think." Marco sat on the exam table on the sheet of paper, feeling like a sandwich about to be wrapped. "Is there nothing you can give me?"

He had waited for hours in the cluttered waiting room, surrounded by coughing, sneezing, moaning people, most of them with some respiratory disease brought on by New Earth's ashy atmosphere. Marco hadn't developed the famous Haven Huff yet, what they called the cough you developed here after a couple years, but his insomnia had turned his days into stretches of agony, his eyes burning, his head pounding, his muscles aching, his stomach roiling, his nights dark and eternal.

The doctor peered at him over his half-moon glasses. He was a lanky man, white-haired, wearing a lab coat.

"Son, are you eating? You look too thin."

Marco nodded. "I'm eating. The problem is I'm not sleeping. I tried over-the-counter sleeping pills, but—"

"Those don't work." The doc scribbled something unintelligible onto a piece of paper. "Here. Buy this outside. You'll sleep."

"What—" Marco began.

The doctor groaned. "Sorry, son, I only get two minutes per patient. Come back another day if you still have questions."

The old man left the room.

Marco went home, the pills rattling in his pocket. When he entered the apartment, he found the bathroom door open, Addy standing inside in front of a mirror. She wore only underwear and a tank top, and she was wrapping bandages around her knuckles. The bandages were already turning red.

"Addy!"

She turned toward him. She began to close the door. Marco rushed forward and stopped the door with his foot.

"Addy, what happened this time?" he said.

"Marco!" She glared at him, eyes bugging out. "I'm in my underwear."

"Addy, I've seen you in your underwear a million times." Marco shoved his way into the bathroom with her. "Blood on your fists again. A new bruise on your cheek. Every week, there's some injury."

He reached toward the bruise. She shoved his hand away. "Marco, I realize you're just worried about me, but you're being a pest, and you're not respecting my privacy."

"I want to know what's going on!"

"Work!" Addy said. "Work, okay? I don't work in a nice, air-conditioned office like you. I'm down there. In the tunnels. Where the creeps live." She stared at her reflection in the mirror, eyes hard. "It's another war down there. But I'm fighting it. I'm winning it."

"This is another war for both of us," Marco said softly. "But I'm not sure either one of us is winning." He touched her arm, gentle. "I just want to know what's going on, how I can help you."

Addy stared at him, brow furrowed. Then her hand lashed down. She reached into his coat pocket. She pulled out the rattling bottle of pills.

"And what's this?" she said.

"Ads—" he began.

"Oh, you don't like me snooping? You like privacy, do you? Well too bad!" She pulled the bottle out of his reach, then read the label. Her eyes widened. "Marco! Do you know what this is?"

"Sleeping pills," he said. "I've been having trouble sleeping."

She barked a laugh. "Dude, I see these pills in the tunnels. The crazies take them—or *should* be taking them. Marco! Whatever doctor gave you these needs to be fired. These are heavy-duty antipsychotic meds. They give them to schizos, Marco. Not for fucking insomnia."

He reached for the bottle, but she pulled it away.

"You're not a doctor," he said.

"Neither is whatever quack gave you these!" She opened the bottle, and before Marco could stop her, she dumped the pills into the toilet and flushed.

"Addy!" he shouted. "Those cost money. I need those!"

"No you don't."

"I do—"

"You're not listening!"

"I needed that medicine. You don't understand—"

"You're not crazy, Marco—"

"Maybe I am!" His shout filled the bathroom, too loud. Tears streamed down his cheeks. "Maybe I *am* crazy, Addy. Maybe the war made me crazy. Maybe this place made me crazy. Maybe I need to be like those people who live in the tunnels. Like those junkies who rummage through the trash outside. Maybe that's all I am now." He was shaking, weeping. "I keep seeing it, Addy."

She was crying too. She could barely whisper. "Seeing what?"

"The hive." He sobbed. "The hive on Corpus. The hive on Abaddon. The scum. I see them everywhere. I dream I'm still in the hive. I can barely take the subways, because I'm back there. I can barely walk between the desks at work, because I'm trapped again. I can barely listen to people talking, because I just hear the bugs. I don't know what to do. I don't know what to do . . ."

They fell to their knees in the bathroom, and Addy held him, crushing him, weeping against him.

"I'm with you, Marco," she whispered. "I'm with you. I'm with you. I love you. Don't get lost, Marco. Don't get lost in that mine. I'm with you. Always hold my hand."

He held her bandaged, bloody hand. "Always," he whispered.

The trains rattled.

The phones rang.

His boss shouted.

His coworkers snickered.

He checked his Colony Love messages, and he went out again.

Paris was a girl from the suburbs. She drove her car to his apartment. As they walked down the street, she looked around, nose wrinkled in disgust.

"It's so *ghetto* here." She made a gagging noise.

"It must be nice up in the burbs," Marco said.

Paris stared in disgust at a homeless man. "My dad would *die* if he saw me here. Die! He's a manager at a big company, you know. He makes seven-and-a-half-times the average salary. Seven-and-a-half! He doesn't just drive a Chrysopoeia car either. He drives a Lexus. That's a very expensive car." She looked at the old cars driving down the street. "He would *die* if he saw these cars. Die!"

Marco took her to a nearby restaurant. It served Middle Eastern food. She sniffed at the meal.

"This isn't real meat," Paris said. "My dad only buys real meat. He goes to the store every day to bring us real meat, real vegetables, fresh from the farm. This is lab-grown shit. He would *die* if he ate this." She nibbled her shawarma, then laughed. "It's so ghetto."

"Food must be real nice up in the burbs," Marco said.

She tugged her sleeves lower for the thousandth time. "People are looking at my bracelets." She glanced around at the other diners. "Do you think many of them are thieves?"

"Most, probably," Marco said.

Paris cringed, pulled her ring off her finger, and hid it in her pocket. "My dad bought me this ring. He got it from Buccellati. Do you know that store? Of course you don't. They don't have it here. You need to book a visit in advance, and they close the whole store for you. My dad always says that a true lady must wear true jewels. These stones came from underground. From the ground! Not some lab. You can buy me one someday. If you can afford it." She pushed her plate away. "I'm done. You can pay for me now."

Marco paid for her. They walked back to her car, which was parked outside his apartment. She kissed him then. A long, warm kiss.

"You can invite me upstairs now," Paris said.

He took her upstairs, and she looked around his apartment. Her eyes were wide.

"Let me guess," Marco said. "Your dad would die if he saw you here."

"Die!" Paris said. She sat down on his bed. "I'll suck your cock now if you like."

Marco closed his eyes. As they slept together, he tried to ignore the memories. To ignore those visions that always rose behind his eyelids. He focused on her warm body, and she moaned beneath him, and it was good. And for a few moments, there was no pain. For a few moments, there were no memories. For a few moments, everything was warm, beautiful, and good. And he lay beside her, holding her, and he was Marco again, and he was healed.

She stood up and got dressed. He walked her to her car.

"Would you like to meet again sometime?" Marco said.

Paris laughed. She patted his cheek. "Marco, sweetie. You're far too poor."

She drove off.

The trains rattled.

Phones rang.

"Sir, might I interest you in our newest vegetable peeler? It can peel a potato in three seconds flat, yes, sir—"

"Marco, my friend! Marco, will you hire a girl tonight? Choose one! Any one from the album!"

He lay on his bed, staring at the ceiling.

The junkie rummaged through the trash.

He went out again.

He met Brook in her apartment, only half an hour away by subway. She was a bubbly woman, pretty and gloriously overweight, easily twice Marco's size, all laughter and squeals and pats on his arm. Her apartment was a single room, cluttered with her abstract artwork on the walls, her couch serving as her bed, and she baked him cookies and cupcakes and chattered on and on as he ate.

"See that one?" She pointed at one painting. "I've named him Andre. That's the ghost I saw last year. Oh, and that one?" She pointed at another painting. "Henry. An old ghost who lives in the laundry room."

"You see ghosts?" he said.

"All the time! They live all over Haven, you know."

"They look like blobs," Marco said, looking at the artwork.

She laughed and playfully slapped him. "They're alien ghosts, silly! They don't look like humans. I know a whole bunch of them." She frowned, and a touch of anger filled her eyes. "You don't believe me." Her voice rose louder. "You think I'm some kind of crazy person?"

"No, no," Marco said, suddenly worried she'd burst into tears or explode with fury.

She scrutinized him, then laughed. She pointed at another drawing. "And that one is Bella. She was my friend for years."

Marco hesitated. "Have you ever . . . seen a ghost with a kabuki mask?"

She raised her eyebrow, then poked his chest. "You're crazy, Marco." She leaned against him and slung a leg across his lap. "I like you."

He wanted to leave. He wanted to go home. He didn't know if this girl was crazy, if she was mocking him, if she had truly seen ghosts. He didn't know what to believe anymore in this cosmos with shadowy girls in masks, with aliens that haunted your dreams, with storms along the highways, with empty nights.

"Sleep over," Brook whispered, and she lowered the couch into a bed, and she kissed him deeply, hungrily, and she took off his clothes, and they made love, and it was good. And for a few moments, there were no nightmares. And for a few moments, there was no pain. For a few moments, he was happy.

In the morning, Brook made him pancakes, and when he didn't eat enough she yelled. She sobbed. She dropped the plate and shattered it. She talked about her ghosts, and they always ate her food, and Marco could never see them now. He left.

The train rattled.

"Yes, ma'am, it will peel that potato in three seconds!"

He reread *David Copperfield* on his tablet. Another sleepless night.

"Any girl you want, Marco!" The brute with the photo album held it out. "Choose one."

He shook his head.

He went out again.

Terri took him dancing. Marco had never gone dancing before. The club lights spun around him. The beat sounded like the guns. He began to shake. The shadows and faces whirled around him, and he thought he heard them screaming.

"Loosen up!" Terri laughed. "Have a drink!"

He drank a beer.

He drank another one.

He drank a shot of vodka.

He drank eight more.

He fucked Terri in the bathroom.

He threw up into the toilet.

He stumbled home.

He lay awake at night, staring at the ceiling.

He went out again.

She was a sweet girl. He didn't know her name. They sat in the restaurant, and he ordered a drink. Another drink. After the fourth drink, he began to talk. He told her about the mines of Corpus, and how the scum had experimented on humans, sewing them to alien flesh. And he told her about the ball of skin with his face. And he drank again. The sweet girl with no name said a friend called her, that she had to go. Marco remained at the table, and he ordered another drink, and he threw up in the alleyway.

He took a girl home. He knew her name. He drank and he fucked her in the living room, even with Addy at home, hiding behind her door. And after she left, he slept on the living room floor, the empty bottle beside him. He called the girl the next day, but he could not remember her name, and she did not answer.

He met a girl in her car. On his walk over, he had emptied a bottle of whiskey. She wrinkled her nose at his smell, but she slept with him in her apartment full of cats, and he forgot to use a condom, but she didn't care, and he promised to call her again. But he lost her number.

He went out again.

Another girl laughed.

Another bottle of booze rolled away.

He had sex with Ria in his bed. Then with Liz the next day. Then with Ria the day after that, and he couldn't find his condom, and he didn't care, and he held her all night, and he felt safe.

He went out to the club. Alone. The beat sounded like gunfire. The dancers were aliens. He bought a bottle of whiskey and drank the whole thing, and two girls helped him stumble home, leaving him outside his building.

He threw up in the lobby. He managed to make it upstairs, and he threw up in the toilet, and all night he moaned in pain. His belly was melting. His head pounded. He struggled to the bathroom, tried to reach the toilet, threw up in the sink. He crashed down, moaning, shivering.

He finally passed out on the living room floor, vomit trickling out of his mouth.

For a few hours, he slept, and strange dreams filled him. He was flying in a small starship, moving beyond explored space, the stars streaming around them. Captain Ben-Ari was there, commanding the vessel, and Kemi too, and Lailani, and Addy, and they were together again like in the old days. They wore uniforms. Soldiers, back in the war. But there were different enemy ships ahead of them now, ships like claws, and inside them flew arachnid creatures, claws long, fangs wet, weaving webs.

"Who are you?" asked the girl with the kabuki mask.

"Who are *you*?" Marco said.

She leaped toward him, and her mask split open, revealing a massive jaw. The jaw grew larger, larger, soon taking up most of her body, lined with teeth, and she was about to swallow him whole. He raised his arms, felt her breath against him. Cold.

Shockingly cold. Ice. Ice washing across him, and his eyes opened, and he was on the floor. He was dripping wet.

He blinked, shivering, and sat up. Water drenched him and ice cubes floated on the floor.

"You fucking idiot," Addy said. She stood before him, holding an empty bucket.

Marco rubbed his eyes. "Did you just spill ice water over me?"

"You're too heavy to drag into the bath," she said. "And you stink. You stink of puke and booze and sex."

He was on the living room floor. He hadn't even made it into his bedroom last night. Dawn rose outside. It was a rare day when the storms were low, and only a thin veil of ash fell outside the windows. Alpha Centauri B shone behind the haze, a yellow blob.

"I'm late for work," he said.

"I called in sick for you," Addy said. "You almost died last night."

His head pounded and he rubbed his temples. "I was just a little tipsy. All right, drunk. Fine. Busted. Hardly dying, though." His head throbbed.

She tossed her empty bucket on him. It hurt.

"You had alcohol poisoning!" she said. "You were choking on your vomit in your sleep. I had to tilt your head over, and I had to reach into your mouth to pull out your tongue. It was *disgusting*."

Marco had nothing to say. His cheeks burned.

"What are you doing, Marco?" Addy whispered.

"Trying to stop the pain," he said.

"By developing addictions to sex and alcohol?"

"God, Ads. I'm not addicted to anything."

"Yes you are!" She stared down at him, hands on her hips. "You bring another girl here every other day. How many has it been now? Thirty? Forty girls you fucked in our apartment?"

"*You* wanted me to sign up to that dating site!" Marco struggled to his feet.

"So you could meet a nice girl!" Addy said. "Not . . . not these hood rats you bring home."

He snorted. "And what are we then? We're no better than they are."

"We're war heroes!" she said. "We fought on Abaddon! We—"

"We are nothing now!" Marco roared, voice so loud he knew the neighbors could hear. "Nothing! You're just a security guard, and I don't even know what kind of fights you're getting into down there. And I sell fucking potato peelers for minimum wage, and I probably lost my job today when I didn't show up. We're poor. We're miserable. We're trapped here. And we can never go home, Addy. Do you hear? We can never go home! Even if I ever sold a book, even if we ever had the money, what's on Earth? They'll arrest us there for war crimes. I'm just trying to sell a novel, but nobody will buy it, and I'm just trying to meet a nice girl, but I can't, Addy, and I can't find a better job, and I can't stop drinking, and I can't stop the nightmares. All right? I can't stop the memories. Do you want to know why I have sex and drink? Because when I'm drunk, or when I'm fucking a girl, that's the only time I'm not remembering. All right? That's the *only time* I'm not remembering the war."

Addy was crying. "I can't see you like this," she whispered, reaching out to touch his cheek. "I can't. This isn't you."

"This is who I am now," Marco said. "Whoever I was on Earth—that person is dead. This is all we are now, all we'll ever be."

She shook her head. "No." She was sobbing. "We can escape this. We . . . we can still save money. Buy that house in the suburbs. With the hockey. With the trees. With—"

"It was a dream, Addy. Just a dream."

He left the apartment.

Late in the morning, most people in Haven had already gone to work, and the subways had seats to spare. Marco took a rattling train, then another, then a third, just moving randomly, not choosing a route, until he stepped out at a distant stop. It was one of the city's rich neighborhoods, a place with guards outside the buildings, keeping the riffraff out. Marco walked through the tunnels, passing by jewelry stores, cinnamon bun bakeries, and clothing shops. He took an escalator into a shopping plaza, a place where he could never afford to shop, and found a sprawling bookstore, two stories tall.

He was still hungover, probably stinking. A rat from the slums. The bookshop was well lit, filled with rich patrons, and they moved away from him. One girl gave him a sneering look. Marco ignored them.

I used to be a librarian, he thought. *I used to work among books. Now you look at me like I don't belong here.*

He wandered between the shelves, inhaling, savoring the smell of the books. A librarian? Yes. He had been once, but he could barely remember that person. It was a different lifetime. How old was he now? Twenty-four? Twenty-five? No. He was ancient. He had lived a thousand lives. He had died a thousand times.

He passed his fingers along the spines of books. Hardcovers with glossy dust jackets. The authors' names written in gold. Fantasy novels. Science fiction. Thrillers. Mysteries. Romances. Literary fiction, award winning, profound.

He thought of *Loggerhead,* languishing at home, rejected by every publisher in the cosmos. He thought of *Le Kill,* already collecting rejections.

This is what I wanted to be, he thought. *A novelist. This is what I thought I could become after the war.*

"Excuse me, sir." A bookshop employee. "This is a bookshop. If you're looking for the center for addiction down the street, I—"

"I know it's a bookshop." Marco glared at the young man. "Do you think I'm an idiot?"

"Sir, there's no need to raise your voice. I would be happy to—"

"I want this book." He grabbed one off the shelf, not even knowing which one it was. "And this one. And this one." He bought them on his credit card. He could not afford them. He stepped down the street, found a bench under a tree in a tube, and he read. He read until night. His eyes kept blurring, his mind kept racing, but he forced himself to keep reading. Just to move his eyeballs, line by line, to try to be the person he had been. To try to remember Marco Emery.

When he returned home, Addy was waiting for him, sitting at the table. A pizza lay before her, uneaten, misshapen. Several hot dogs topped it, not even sliced into pieces.

She looked up at Marco. Her eyes were damp, and wet napkins lay on the floor around her.

"I made us a pizza," she said. "I made the dough myself." She gave him a shaky smile. "Hot dog pizza. I tried to serve it on the rake, but it kept falling off. I brushed off the dirt, though, don't worry."

He knelt before her, and he laid his head on her lap. "I'm sorry, Addy."

She stroked his hair. "I know, you idiot." Her voice was barely audible.

He laughed. "Hot dog pizza. Perfect."

She laughed too. "Help me slice it."

The pizza was cold. Half the dough was burnt, the other half soggy. But it was the best damn pizza Marco had ever eaten, and Addy and he stayed up late, watching B movies on their tablet, and she slept in his bed that night. They did not make love.

They did not sleep holding each other. But it felt better than a thousand nights of sex with a thousand other girls.

I love you, Addy, he thought before drifting to sleep. *I don't know who I am. I don't know what I can still become. But I'm glad you're with me.*

CHAPTER TWENTY-THREE

He had been in Haven for twenty months when he realized he was dying.

He walked into work, legs shaky. The subway had broken down again, crammed with commuters, stuck in the tunnels. Another suicide on the tracks. Another hour trapped underground. Another hour back in the scum hive. As Marco walked between the desks in the call center, his head spun. His breath ached in his lungs. His hands shook, and he spilled his coffee, and people laughed and pointed and somebody clapped.

"You look worried," somebody called his way. "Who'd you kill today?"

A girl gasped and giggled. "You can't ask him who he killed. He'll probably shoot you too." Her voice dropped. "I heard he killed his own friends in the war."

"I heard he fucked an alien," somebody whispered. "Real horror story stuff."

Marco reached his desk. He sat down, shaky, struggling to collect himself. Late. Late to work again. More money docked from his paycheck. An email waited on his computer. His boss wanted to speak with him. Urgent. Urgent. A red flag over the email. Urgent.

Sirens.

Sirens wailed.

Scum attacking!

The pods rained. The aliens attacked. The aliens swarmed over Fort Djemila, and Caveman died on the tarmac. The aliens slammed into the HDFS *Miyari*, and they plunged down toward the moon. Lost. Lost in the hive.

His chest ached.

He rose to his feet.

"Emery!" his boss shouted.

He rushed between the desks, made it outside, and stumbled into the stairwell. He sat, breathing heavily, head between his knees. His skull was constricting, crushing his brain, and his ribs were digging into his heart.

A heart attack, Marco thought. *I'm having a heart attack.*

It was an hour before he could walk again.

He sat for hours in the clinic's waiting room. It was as crowded as anywhere in Haven. A hundred people, maybe more, sat here on plastic chairs, coughing, sneezing, some looking barely alive. Some wore masks; others coughed in the open. Every cough sounded to Marco like the croak of a dying soldier.

Finally they ushered Marco into an examination room, where a silver-haired doctor saw him, where a nurse slapped EKG probes onto his chest, where they told him, "Nothing's wrong. Just stress. Go home."

"But—"

"Time's up. You're fine. Go home."

That night, Marco only slept for two hours.

He sat in the crowded waiting room.

He saw another doctor.

"It's my head," he said. "My skull feels too tight. It keeps hurting."

X-rays clattered.

Needles poked.

"Nothing wrong with you, kid. Go home. Get some sleep."

Another doctor, a woman with curly hair.

"My heart won't slow down. Sometimes I can't breathe."

"Your lungs look fine, Marco. Here, try these vitamins."

Another waiting room. Another doctor, an old man with wispy hair.

"I think I have cancer, doc," Marco said. "I've lost weight. I can't sleep. I can't eat. My hair is falling out. I threw up yesterday."

"Take these for anxiety," said the doc.

"I'm not crazy, doc. I think I might have cancer. Everything hurts."

The doc nodded. "You're suffering from shell shock, son. Post-traumatic stress disorder. I've seen it a thousand times. You're a veteran, right? Most think that wars wound only the body. But the human mind can only take so much punishment before it too scars. Take the pills. They'll take the edge off. Go home. Sleep. And eat something."

"But it's my body too, doc. My chest hurts, and—"

"I'm sorry, son. Your time is up. I've got a lot of patients to see."

Marco hid these pills in his pocket, not letting Addy see them, fearful she would flush these too down the toilet, would call him crazy.

He let the pills languish in his drawer for two weeks. One night, when his chest kept aching, when his head kept spinning, he took a pill.

He didn't sleep at all that night. Not even an hour. The next day, he could keep nothing down. He spilled the pills into the toilet and flushed.

He drank.

He hid the bottles under his mattress where Addy wouldn't see them, and he drank, and he went out to pounding bars where music blared, and he drank again because it was too loud.

He woke up in his bed. A woman lay beside him, naked. He could not remember her name. He could not remember meeting her, bringing her home. He could not remember putting on a condom. He could not remember if he had slept with her.

"You'll call me tomorrow, right?" she said. But he didn't know who she was.

He waited in the cluttered waiting room, because he was dying, he knew he was dying. He could see it in the mirror—a dying wretch. But all he got was a doctor rolling his eyes, a placebo of some vitamins, and a bad cough caught from another patient. For a week, Marco lay in his bed, coughing, vomiting, trembling, his fever blazing. For a week, he felt close to death.

"You better come back to work tomorrow, Emery, or you're fired."

He walked between the desks, lightheaded.

"Marco, talk to me!" Addy said. "You look like shit. Have you seen yourself in the mirror? You look like fucking Gollum."

"I'm fine."

"You need to eat!"

"I'm eating, Addy. For fuck's sake, leave me alone!"

He rushed out of the house. He sat outside in his atmosuit, the storm swirling around him. With gloved hands, he held his pen, and he wrote. He wrote another chapter in *Le Kill*, a chapter about Tomiko fighting the spiders, but the ash stained every page, effacing his words.

He went back home late at night, and he sat on his bed, and he wrote Lailani a letter.

Please, Lailani. Take me back. I'm sorry.

His tears splashed the words.

I want us to be together. Like we used to be. I can't live without you.

Foolish. The words of a foolish boy! He tore up the letter, loathing himself.

He stared out the window, hoping to see the stars, but could see only the brick wall and the storm above. And like everywhere on this world, he felt trapped.

CHAPTER TWENTY-FOUR

Anisha Morgan was twenty years old, a pretty girl with curly black hair, brown skin, and large green eyes. Those eyes were soft as she gazed at Marco.

"You did all that on your own?" She leaned over her plate of sushi. "You moved here after the war, penniless, found work, and you're writing a novel?"

"It's not that much," Marco said, sitting across from her.

It was a small restaurant, not even in the tunnels—a nice place on the thirtieth floor of a glass tower. Through the windows, they could see the storm of Haven, but from up here, it seemed like a Van Gogh, all swirling colors and beads of light. Inside the sushi bar, paper lanterns glowed like a thousand stars across the ceiling.

"And after everything you did in the war, what you saw . . ." Anisha reached across the table and touched his arm. "You're very brave."

"I was scared most of the time."

"I missed the war. It had just ended by the time I turned eighteen. I didn't serve. I just can't imagine . . ." Anisha stared into the distance, reflective, then back at him. She smiled and bit her lip. "I'm buying you ice cream after dinner. My treat for the brave war hero."

Anisha paid for the sushi. She insisted on paying. She took him to the top floor of the building, and they stood on the observation deck, surrounded by a glass dome. It seemed like they floated in the atmosphere of this distant world. She bought them ice cream—vanilla and strawberries, actual fresh strawberries, grown in the greenhouses outside the city.

"My dad used to take me here when I was little," Anisha said, watching the roiling colors with him. "I used to love watching the clouds. We don't come into the city much anymore. My dad hates leaving the burbs now. He said the city has gotten so bad since the war, since refugees came here. But he doesn't know. He doesn't understand how bad it became on Earth. How much you fought." She leaned against Marco. "Tell me about Earth."

"You've never been?" Marco said.

Anisha shook her head. "My parents were born in Haven. My grandparents too. We've been here since the beginning a hundred-and-five years ago. What's Earth like? What does the sky look like? Is it really blue like they say?"

"Sometimes," Marco said. "But it can be a thousand colors more. Golden and red and orange in the sunset, pink at sunrise, gray and indigo and deep purple in a storm."

"And trees really grow in the open, not just in bulbs or domes?"

"Millions of trees," Marco said, "all rustling in the wind."

She slipped her hand into his. "You've seen so much. The farthest I've gone from the burbs is this tower in the city."

They kissed on the observation deck. They caught a subway to his apartment, and she handed out coins to every beggar on the way. At home, they lay on his bed, watching old B movies, and she laughed. She laughed truly, fully, her eyes sparkling, her teeth white, the most honest laugh Marco had ever heard.

The next weekend, Anisha took him to see the latest *Star Trek* movie, and she dressed up in a *Star Trek* uniform and gave him the Vulcan salute, and she laughed and slapped a Starfleet insignia she made onto his shirt. She insisted on paying, and the next week, when Marco was sick with the flu, she drove to his apartment with homemade soup.

"My poor hero." She stroked his hair. "I'll nurse you back to health."

She became good friends with Addy. When Addy turned twenty-five that fall, Anisha gave her a signed hockey puck she had ordered from Earth. Addy displayed it proudly on the shelf, declaring it the best gift she had ever received.

"This one's a keeper, Marco," Addy told him. "You better marry this one." She mussed his hair. "Happy for you, little bro."

And for the first time since being drafted into the army years ago, Marco was happy. Truly happy, and it seemed to him that despite his dead-end job, despite his poverty, despite his failure as an author, he was finding joy in this world, finding a relief from the pain. He slept well, and he was no longer too thin, and he laughed every day.

"Come meet my parents," Anisha said on their six-month anniversary. "You really need to meet them already! We're cooking crab legs for you. Do you like crab legs?"

"I've only had it once. I think I liked it."

"You'll love the way we make it! My dad gets it fresh from Earth, delivered in an actual tank." She grinned. "And my mom is baking you a cake with strawberries. I told her all about how you love strawberries."

The day before meeting her parents, Marco stood in his apartment bathroom. He stared at his reflection. His reflection stared back, and Marco saw a stranger.

He saw the librarian's son, the studious writer.

He saw the soldier at war, lost in darkness.

He saw the veteran, poor, hungry, shell shocked.

And he saw somebody new, somebody he didn't recognize. Somebody he was afraid of. Somebody he didn't know if he could become. If he deserved to become.

He lifted his bottle of whiskey from the cupboard. Another bottle. One of countless bottles he had stashed away these past few months. His hand shook.

I'll go to her house, and I'll get nervous, he thought. *I'll remember the war. I'll have a flashback. I'll mess up. I need to drink. No. No, I can't. I promised Addy.*

His eyes dampened. He shut them. He unscrewed the bottle, took a sip. Sipped more. Drank too much. He ripped the bottle away, heart pounding, and poured the rest down the sink. It had cost him a full day's pay, and he watched the precious, costly liquid swirl away. He brushed his teeth. Again. Again. He washed his hands until they bled. He got dressed and he stepped downstairs, and Anisha was waiting there in her car, smiling.

She drove, playing The Rolling Stones, singing along and teasing Marco for not joining her.

For the second time since arriving in Haven, Marco left the inner city. The first time, he had rented a car, had driven south along the highways to the farms. This time, they drove north. The road was wider, smoother, and enclosed in a silica roof, a transparent tunnel through the storm.

After an hour of driving, Marco saw giant turbines ahead—large as buildings. They hummed, blowing back the storm, raising clouds of gray, umber, and dusty gold. One by one they loomed, an army of them, great machines rumbling on the surface.

"Fans," he whispered in awe.

Anisha nodded. "Airdome, they call them. They help keep most of the storm out. They were just meant to be temporary, until they built a proper dome over Haven." She sighed. "They were supposed to build that silly dome fifty-something years ago. Then the Cataclysm hit Earth. Then just five years ago, when they were about to build it again, the Second Scum War happened. I don't think they'll ever build our dome. So century-old fans it is."

"At least the dome still exists in the real estate magazines," Marco said.

"They should be sued for false advertisement, but I think all the lawyers must have died in the scum wars."

"Not all of them," Marco said, remembering the lawyer who had threatened him on Earth. "But we can always hope for a third war."

Anisha looked at him, frowned, then laughed and shook her head.

They drove between two of the towering fans, entering the burbs. Indeed, the storm was lighter here. A few flurries rose along the streets, but the atmosphere here seemed almost Earthlike, eerily calm. Marco gazed through the car window, clasping his fingers in his lap. He struggled for breath.

The burbs were beautiful.

Oaks, elms, and maples grew in airy glass tubes, glittering with lights. Mansions—he could not think of them as mere houses—rose alongside the quiet streets, each one unique, built in the old style of Earth's glory days. Domes enclosed them and their yards, and they shone like snow globes, their lights warm. A few children were playing outside, wearing expensive helmets like space heroes, flying a drone. Down one road, a huge dome rose over forested paths and a glittering lake, and residents played ball on the beach.

"It's heaven," Marco said softly. "It's like Earth before the Cataclysm. It's like the magazines said. It's real. It's only an hour away from Haven's inner city. It's a different universe."

Driving down the peaceful streets, Anisha squeezed his knee. "It's luck, Marco. It's just luck. My great-grandparents moved here at the right time. Everyone got these nice houses then. I'm just lucky." She looked at him, eyes soft. "Don't ever think otherwise. You're stronger, braver, and smarter than anyone who lives here. Just less lucky." A grin split her face. "And when we get married, and you're a famous author, we'll live here together." She laughed. "I'm kidding. Don't jump out of the car and bolt!"

Her house, while humble for the burbs, was larger than any house Marco had ever been in, three stories tall and glowing with lights. Within its enclosing dome, trees and flowers bloomed. Once they stepped into the dome, Marco was surprised to see that the sky turned blue and pristine, no longer the dusty, swirling orange and gray.

"It refracts the light like Earth's atmosphere," Anisha said. "That's what they told us when we got it installed. Blue Earth skies, they said. You could also buy a Mars dome, but who wants that? Does it look realistic to you? I've never seen the real thing."

He looked up at the shimmering blue glass. "It looks perfect."

A Golden Retriever ran out to meet them, tail wagging, and jumped onto Marco, licking him.

"Wilson, leave him alone!" Anisha said, laughing. "I'm sorry. He's the worst guard dog ever. He loves strangers."

Her father, a balding man of Old English ancestry, wore a sweater vest and smoked a pipe at the dinner table. Her mother, a beautiful woman of Indian descent, wore a purple sari and looked barely older than her daughter. Their maid served dinner: crab legs, fresh garden salad, steak, and mashed potatoes, all real, nothing lab made.

Marco sat stiffly, eating little, feeling self-conscious. On his plate, the crab legs looked like the claws of aliens. When he tried to crack one, to reach the meat inside, his hands shook, and he ended up spilling butter onto his lap. He quickly lowered his hands, cheeks flushing, trying to hide the stains.

"So, Marco," Mr. Morgan said. "What do you do for a living?"

Marco clasped his hands under the table, fearful of dropping more food.

Marco and Anisha spoke over each other.

"I work in a call center."

"He works in sales."

For a moment, silence.

"He's an excellent salesman," Anisha said.

Mr. Morgan took a bite of steak and chewed thoughtfully. He swallowed. "So where did you go to school, Marco?"

"Actually, sir, I trained in the military with computer systems. I'm thinking of taking some night classes too." That last sentence was a lie; he could not afford an education beyond what the military had paid for.

"He's also an excellent writer," Anisha said. "He wrote two novels. They're wonderful."

"Mmm." Mr. Morgan sipped his wine. "Who's your publisher? Is it Magpie? I know the CEO of Magpie. We play golf every summer."

"Actually, sir, I'm still looking for a publisher," Marco said. He was beginning to feel dizzy. He didn't want to talk about his pile of rejection letters at home, about how *Loggerhead* or *Le Kill* never sold, about how he was a failure of a writer, about how he wasn't a real salesman but just sold potato peelers on the phone, about any of it. He felt under the spotlight. Beneath the table, his fists clenched, and his pulse quickened. He felt trapped. He felt like an ape placed among humans. He didn't belong here.

For a moment, they all ate in silence. Insects began to hiss, and Marco almost jumped, and his pulse pounded in his ears, but it was only the sprinklers coming on outside.

"So, Marco!" Mrs. Morgan said. "Are you enjoying your crab legs?"

"Oh, yes, ma'am, they're very good," he said, hoping nobody was staring too closely at how he had mangled the shell. "Thank you so much for preparing this meal. It's nice to finally have a homemade meal. My roommate's idea of cooking is roasting hot dogs on a rake."

They stared at him, silent. Under the table, Marco dug his fingernails into his palm.

The dog barked. Marco winced. Gunfire. Gunfire in the deep. He stared at his plate, and he saw the meal Sergeant Singh had cooked in the tunnels of Corpus. He saw his sergeant torn apart.

He raised his eyes, forcing himself to breathe deeply, to calm his shaking legs. Sweat soaked him. A painting hung on the wall, abstract, and in it Marco saw spiders. Spiders scurrying.

"Is that a Kandinsky?" Marco asked.

Mr. Morgan turned toward the painting, then back toward his plate. "Pollock, I think. Is that Pollock, dear?"

"Definitely Pollock," said Mrs. Morgan.

"Oh." Marco reached for his knife, dropped it onto his plate. It clanged. "Excuse me, please."

He went into the bathroom, trembling. Sweat soaked the new shirt Anisha had bought him. And it seemed to him like the button-down shirt was a costume. Like his fresh haircut was a disguise. This wasn't him. He was an impostor. He didn't know how to eat this food. How to talk about these things. An alien. An alien invader. An insect at the dinner table. He washed his face.

Anisha drove him home, and they sat in silence, the storm whipping the tunnel around them.

"Did you enjoy dinner?" she finally asked, glancing at him hesitantly.

He nodded. "It was very good, thank you."

They drove the rest of the way, an entire hour, in silence. She parked outside his apartment.

"Do you . . . want me to come up for a bit?" Anisha said.

His hands kept shaking. He looked at the pimp leaning against the wall. The junkie in the alley. The shadows of shrieking birds outside. He thought of the glittering, snow globe houses in the north, and art by famous artists, and crab legs that cut his hand, and stock prices and CEOs and golf and all the other things Mr. Morgan had talked about, and the sprinkles hissed like insects, and spiders were in the painting, and—

"Anisha," he whispered. "I don't think this is working out. I'm sorry."

She frowned. "What do you mean?"

"I . . ." His throat felt too tight. "I need time alone. I can't . . . I can't do this."

Her eyes dampened. "Are you breaking up with me?"

"I'm sorry, Anisha. I'm sorry. I just . . ."

"I love you, Marco." A tear fled her eye. "I love you. Don't you love me?"

"I need time," he whispered.

"Is this because I asked you to get married? I was joking, Marco!" Anisha touched his arm. "It was a joke!" Her tears flowed. Her voice dropped to a whisper. "Don't do this. Please."

But she had not been joking. Marco knew this. Knew she would never live with him here in the slums. Knew he could never belong with her there in the burbs. And he was shaking. And he had to run. He was trapped here in the car. He was trapped in the mines. He had to go. He had to run. They were after him.

"I'm sorry," he whispered and fled the car.

"Marco!" she cried after him.

He walked through the darkness, legs shaky. He ignored her cries.

"Hey, Marco buddy, you want a girl tonight, huh?" The thin, short pimp approached. "Choose, choose a girl!"

The burly, ugly pimp in the jeans jacket approached. He held out the album. "Choose?"

Daniel Arenson

Marco couldn't see the album. His eyes were burning. He couldn't breathe. Blindly, he tapped one photo, then shuffled on toward the building.

"Excellent choice!" said the thin pimp in the dress shirt. "I'll send her up to your place in moments."

He stumbled on. Tears burned in his eyes. He couldn't breathe. His legs shook, his chest constricted, and he was having a heart attack, and he was scared, and he didn't know who he was, where he was. A soldier. Just a soldier without a gun. He made it into his apartment, and Addy wasn't home, and his bottle of whiskey was empty. He had another. Damn it, he had another bottle somewhere. He needed it. Needed the drink. He emptied drawers, yowling, scattering his possessions until he found it. His fingers shook so badly he could barely unscrew it. He drank. He guzzled it down like water.

A knock sounded on the door. He opened it, blurry-eyed, to see the woman there. One of the prostitutes from downstairs. She was a petite Asian woman in her forties, haggard, dressed in a ragged frock. She could have passed for a struggling cleaning lady, a poor soul coughed out from the dregs of the inner city, barely alive, cancerous and cadaverous. A wretched soul.

Like me. Like me. This is all we are.

He took her into his bedroom, and she pulled off her clothes. Her breasts sagged, and her belly showed the stretch marks of past pregnancies. And he held her. He held her and he wanted some comfort. He wanted sex. He wanted to forget. But he could only kneel by her, shaking, head spinning.

The apartment door opened.

"Marco!" Addy's voice boomed. "Marco, what the fuck did you do?"

He tried to rise to his feet. He fell to the floor, head spinning with booze. The naked prostitute knelt beside him. Before Marco could close his bedroom door, Addy burst into the room. Anisha, her eyes full of tears, stood behind her.

Both women stared.

For a moment they were all silent.

Then Anisha let out a sob and turned to flee. Addy gave Marco a shocked, furious stare, then turned and followed Anisha.

Marco lay on the floor.

"I think you should leave," he said quietly.

"You need pay." The prostitute pulled on her clothes. "You pay half hour."

He paid her. He paid with the last money he had. She left, and Marco lay on his bed, trembling. He needed more booze.

Hours passed, maybe only moments, and Addy returned, this time alone. She stood over his bed. She stared down at him, silent.

Marco closed his eyes. "I'm not feeling good."

She punched him. Hard. On his jaw.

He rolled on the bed, fell to the floor, and touched his jaw. Pain flared.

Addy kicked him hard in ribs.

"Addy, stop!"

She grabbed his shoulders, shook him. "What the fuck is wrong with you!" Her eyes burned. "You get drunk? You bring whores into this house? I found Anisha crying outside. She said you left her for no reason. Why, Marco? She was good for you. Why?"

"I want to sleep."

She shook him, shouting. "Why?"

"Because this is who I am now!" he shouted back. He stood up. "Because I saw her house. I saw how she lives. And I can't be that man. I can't live there. I can't make it to the burbs. We're never going to belong there, Addy, we'll never be like them."

"We can—"

"We can't! I can sell a book, and I can make a million dollars, and I can marry Anisha, but I can't be like them."

"You don't have to." Addy wept. "You don't have to be this person. You're addicted to sex. To alcohol. To doctors. To . . . to hurting yourself. That's all you do now. Hurt yourself. Until there will be nothing left. Marco . . . it doesn't have to be like this. You can still find a good life. We both can."

He stared at the wall, blinking too much. He spoke softly. "They died. Elvis. Beast. Caveman. Sheriff. Our corporals and sergeant. Our friends. They died in the war. And Addy . . ." He turned toward her. "I died there too. I died somewhere in the mines of Abaddon. Whoever left that place, whoever made it to Haven . . . he wasn't Marco. He was never truly alive. Just a ghost. Just a ghost."

Addy shook her head, tears on her cheeks. Her voice was a cracked whisper. "I never should have flushed your pills away. I was wrong. You *are* crazy. You need help, help that I can't give you."

He met her eyes. "I'm not the one who comes home with bloody fists. Tell me, Addy. Are you really fighting criminals down there, or are you just punching friends in the jaw?"

She sniffed. She rubbed her eyes. She left the room.

The next day, Addy moved out.

She packed all her things in a cardboard box, and a friend from the security firm helped her move, and she was gone. She said nothing to Marco. Not even goodbye. She gave him one last look, eyes haunted, shook her head, and left.

Marco slept in the living room that night.

"Good," he said. "Good. I have the place to myself. Good!" He rose to his feet, and he shouted. "Good!"

He lay on his back. He stared at the ceiling. He trembled. And he prayed.

Please, God. Please. Let me die. Please. Please. Please.

Yet the heavens remained silent, for there were no gods in space, only endless, lingering darkness.

CHAPTER TWENTY-FIVE

He lay on the floor, alone.

The sun set. It rose. It set. He lay on the floor. He paced his apartment. He lay down again. The sun rose and set. He was alone.

The trains rattled.

He shuffled between the desks at work.

A snort. "There goes the weirdo."

"I heard he went crazy in the army."

"I heard he exterminated like an entire species."

"Hey, weirdo!"

He lay alone in bed.

He paced his apartment.

The trains rattled.

He called Addy. He called her again, again, again, again. She never answered.

The sun rose. The sun set.

He stood on the observation deck on the thirtieth floor. He ordered vanilla ice cream with real strawberries, but he had no appetite. He stood where he had first kissed Anisha. The storm was thin up here, swirling gently against the glass walls, abstract paintings, always changing. Marco found a service door in the back, and he stepped outside onto a rail, and a ladder led him to the roof.

He stood in the open, the world of New Earth around him. The tops of skyscrapers rose from the mist. Below the atmosphere was thicker, but as the clouds swirled and moved, they revealed the lights of roads and low buildings, a painting of darkness and light, ever-changing like the sea. The haze danced around Marco, whirled around his feet, and rose to coat the sky with indigo and black.

He approached the edge of the roof.

He stretched out his arms.

Standing here, Marco could imagine that he floated in the sky, and he wondered if he could float forever, if in death his soul would dance in the storm, free, rising higher and higher, vanishing over the clouds and the pain and the dreams. That was all he wanted. To fly forever. To never come down.

He took a half step. His toes no longer touched the roof. Only his heels kept him grounded.

He did not look down. It would spin his head. All he had to do was take another step. No—to leap. To fly.

Marco.

It was Addy's voice, echoing in his mind.

"There's too much pain," he whispered.

You need to live.

"It's too painful. It's too painful. I can't take this pain."

Don't, Marco.

"You don't know how much it hurts."

I hurt too.

"You're stronger than I am. It's too much to carry. It's too heavy."

We'll carry the weight together.

"You left, Addy. You left. I'm alone."

You need to be strong alone. I can't help you.

"I'm weak."

You can fight.

"It hurts too much."

You don't want to die. I know this. You just can't handle the pain. But you don't want to die.

"I do. I do. I can't stop thinking it. I want it so much. Too much pain. Too much . . ."

His tears flowed, and he stared down at the storm. He could fall through those clouds. There would be no pain. Before the end, there would be freedom. Relief. His soul had died long ago; let his body join it. All the world was the clouds. There was no bottom. There was no sky.

Marco raised his eyes, and the clouds shimmered, a glittering veil. Wind flowed and the clouds parted above, pulling back, wisps of white trimmed with gold. And above, for the first time since landing on Haven, Marco saw them. The stars.

The stars where he had fought.

Where he had met Lailani.

Where he had served under Lieutenant Ben-Ari.

Where he had seen horror, lost friends, shattered into a million shards of light.

And among them—a bright star, brightest in Haven's sky. A star only four light-years away. Sol. Earth's star.

He stood on the roof in an alien world, and he gazed up, and there—it seemed so close he could reach out and grab it—Sol. A small light. The sun.

From here, he couldn't see Earth. That pale blue dot was too far. But he could imagine Earth as he had seen her from space long ago, back when he had sat in the spaceship with Addy, with Lailani, with Ben-Ari, with his friends. A blue marble swirling with white, beautiful and fragile. A world he had fought to protect. A world out there—just above him.

The light reaching him now from Sol was four years old. On this light from Earth, he was a younger man. He was hurt, he was broken, but he still had hope. He still saw a future. He still felt joy.

A star fell above like a wink from the heavens. Marco stepped away from the ledge.

He lay on his back, and for long hours, he watched a thousand stars fall above. And it was beautiful.

"Marco."

The voice came from behind him, soft, feminine.

"Marco."

He stood up, turned around, and saw her there. The girl in the kabuki mask. His muse. Her tattered dress and long black hair flowed in the wind.

"Who are you?" Marco said.

"One who has been watching you," said the girl.

"Why?" Marco took a step toward her.

She took a step back. When her dress billowed in the wind, he saw that her legs were inhuman. Animal legs. Her hands were too large, each with three fingers tipped with heavy claws.

"It is not yet time," she said.

"For what?"

"For shadows. For despair." She held out one hand. On it rested a silvery conch that gleamed in the starlight. "A gift from the cosmic ocean. May it shine in your deepest darkness. Take it."

He took the conch and turned it over and over in his hands. It was beautiful, smooth and cool to the touch.

"Who are—" he began to ask again, but when he raised his eyes, the girl was gone.

He looked at the conch. A gift from the cosmic ocean. He raised his eyes back up to the stars, these mementos of ancient light.

He placed the conch in his pocket, and he pulled out his tablet instead. Long ago, when they had parted, Ben-Ari had given him her messaging address. She had been his commanding officer. But she had also been his friend. Marco hadn't spoken to her in years. He had seen the reports about her coming from Earth. He knew she was imprisoned for various crimes—assaulting an admiral, accessing forbidden information, leaking military secrets. He didn't know if she would receive his message. He didn't know if they'd ever speak again. But still he wrote to her. Because he needed to write this. For himself.

Captain Ben-Ari,

Seven years ago, I was a frightened recruit, eighteen years old, meek, studious. You saw something in me. You gave me strength. You took me with you to war.

For a long time, I was angry at you. Angry that you led me into darkness. But I followed you because I believed in your strength, in your courage. It is your strength and courage that I've often longed to emulate.

I live in the colony of Haven. I live in a world of peace. I live in a world that is good. But the shadows are darker than ever.

We served humanity. We fought. We killed. We saw our friends die. We thought we would return home heroes. But we returned to a world that rejected us. That spat on us. That imprisoned you and drove me out. We returned home with scars on our bodies and our souls. We returned home needing help, needing care, but we found only scorn.

I'm afraid. I'm hurt. I find myself again trapped in a maze, one deeper than the hives of aliens. I was a librarian. I was a writer. I was a soldier. And now I am lost.

And so now, in my darkest hour, I think of you. I remember the lessons you taught me. I fight another battle, but I don't fight alone. I fight with a million other veterans. And I fight with all the courage that you gave me.

You saved my life many times in the war. And tonight, Captain Ben-Ari, six years after that war ended, you saved my life again. And tonight I make the same promise I made you years ago. To fight. To win. To march forth and fear no darkness, for beyond the shadows there is light.

I don't know where our paths lead. I don't know if they'll ever cross again. But if they do, know this: I am, and always will be, your soldier.

Marco

He sent her the message. It was likely, he knew, that she would never read it. But after sending that message, Marco felt a weight lift off his shoulders. He inhaled deeply.

Above, he imagined that he could see it. The thin wormhole, barely larger than a thread, used for sending messages back and forth between Haven and Earth, the electrons traveling faster than light through the tunnel. Somewhere in the darkness, Ben-Ari was in a prison cell. Somewhere in that distance, Lailani was fighting her new war. Marco wondered if they were thinking about him, watching the sky, seeing the distant light of Alpha Centauri.

I will live. For you. For Earth. I will fight like I fought before. I will be brave.

The storm was returning above, obscuring the stars. Sol flickered, vanished, reappeared, faded again. The brief moment of beauty was ending, swallowed up again by the clouds, but to Marco it highlighted the rarity of what he had witnessed, its holiness. He felt like the sky had given him a sign.

He frowned.

He narrowed his eyes.

Dark shards were moving above. It was not the clouds obscuring the stars but black shapes, moving fast.

Asteroids, Marco thought. *No. Starships. Thousands of starships.*

They stormed down toward Haven, leaving wakes of smoke and fire. As they drew closer, he saw that they were shaped like claws. Great iron claws with many fingers. In the sky, they bloomed open, revealing red, pulsing hearts.

Fire streamed down.

And across the colony of Haven, Marco heard that old, familiar song. Air raid sirens. The call of war.

CHAPTER TWENTY-SIX

He stood in the Dome, this transparent observatory above Nightwall, and beheld the terrors of the abyss swarm toward him.

"*Oni*," whispered Admiral Komagata, the word he had feared more than any as a child. "Demons."

Standing here, enclosed in the transparent bulb atop Space Station One, space spread all around him. And in the shadows— the creatures. The monsters he had fed, had tried to keep at bay. The terrors that now swarmed.

The marauders.

The ravagers, the clawed ships of the enemy, flew everywhere. Thousands. Tens of thousands. So many they filled the darkness. They bloomed like thorny flowers, like the ravenous mouths of lampreys, and flames blazed in their gullets. They spewed forth their wrath in a storm of fire.

Humanity's warships flew out to meet them.

Hundreds of Firebirds, single-pilot starfighters, streamed toward the enemy, leaving trails of light, firing missiles and bullets. They were like bees attacking tanks. Missiles hit the metal claws, doing them no harm. Bullets ricocheted off the enemy hulls in showers of light.

The marauder plasma streamed forth.

The inferno washed over Firebirds, melting them, sending them careening through space as balls of molten metal, pilots still screaming inside as their flesh blazed. Another squadron of Firebirds streamed toward the enemy. More missiles flew. More Firebirds fell, streaming down like flaming comets, then crashing against the dark planet below.

"Our end," said Admiral Komagata, watching from the Dome. "The demons risen into the world. The end of all life."

A starfighter carrier, a massive starship the size of a skyscraper, flew toward the enemies. Here flew the fabled HDFS *Terra*, the warship that had led the fleet to Abaddon five years ago, that had won the war against the scum. Its massive cannons, large enough to level cities, fired with all their fury.

A single enemy ravager, one ship among countless, crashed down to the rogue planet. Thousands of others stormed toward the starfighter carrier, a pack of wolves attacking a lumbering bison. Their plasma blazed. Their claws dug into the warship.

And the legendary carrier fell. The ship that had defeated the scum pitched down toward the planet. A ship the size of the Empire State Building, it crashed into the military bases that sprawled across the dark world. Fire blazed. Thousands perished.

One by one, like collapsing stars, the starships of the Human Defense Force fell. Starfighter carriers. Cargo hulls. Firebirds. Warships and medical ships and engineering barges. The lights flashed as they crashed onto the planet, burying barracks beneath them.

Cannons fired from below. The ravagers swooped, raining plasma upon them. Their claws, jagged monstrosities of metal, tore through the cables that lifted space elevators from below. The capsules hailed like shards of glass, people still caught inside them. Satellites careened, slammed into one another, and shattered. Shuttles tried to flee the battle, but the marauder swarm caught them, cracked them open, tossed the people within into the darkness.

Shards of metal. Severed cables. Torn seats. Human corpses. All floated around the admiral. The ruins of Nightwall—of a proud, fallen fleet.

In the center of the devastation, it floated—Space Station One.

During the war against the scum, several space stations had hovered here at Nightwall. They had been decommissioned, along with most of the fleet, to rebuild the ravaged world. Today Space Station One orbited here alone. Below burned the dark planet, explosions rocking its barracks, the nuclear reactors buried underground already leaking. All around floated the wreckage of the fleet, this mighty armada that had fallen to the enemy within moments. Cannons were still firing from the space station, but standing here above in the transparent dome, Admiral Komagata knew: *We lost. We lost Nightwall. We lost the earth. This is our extinction.*

All around him, the ravagers flew closer, a tightening noose.

Komagata stepped toward a table. He pulled back a silken scarf, revealing his most prized possession: an ancient katana. Its hilt was wrapped with silk over ray skin. Upon its handguard snarled a filigreed likeness of the thunder god. He passed his fingers against the lacquered wooden scabbard, tracing the engravings of waves and stars and ancient spirits.

The door to the Dome burst open.

A man in a business suit rushed in, face red, hair disheveled.

"What is the meaning of this?" the man shouted. "You're a man of the HDF! How did you let this happen?"

Admiral Komagata turned to look at the younger man, this agent of Chrysopoeia. He looked at the pricey suit. The gold watch. The shoes that cost as much as an officer's yearly salary.

"We have awoken a hungry beast," the admiral said softly.

"We've been feeding that beast!" the man shouted. "Damn it, you idiot. We've been feeding it our prisoners!"

Around the space station, the countless ravagers paused. The clawed starships hovered, a swarm, facing Space Station One, examining their prey. Slowly, they began to bloom open. From here, the admiral could see them. They lurked within their ships, gazing through portholes. Creatures with six legs. With long claws. With waiting jaws.

"Our morsels have awakened a deeper hunger in our enemy's belly," said the admiral. "Now the beast shall satisfy its needs with our flesh."

"Fuck you and your Godzilla shit!" The man pointed a shaky finger at the admiral. "This is your fault. You weakened the fleet. They smelled your weakness. My bosses will hear of this!

You fucking tanked our stock price, you son of a bitch! I'll have your hide. I'll—"

The ravager ships flew.

They thrust forward and slammed into the space station.

Claws dug through metal. The walls shook. The dome cracked. Alarms blared and smoke rose and cracking steel screamed, howled, a sound of agony, of a dying species. More of the ravagers flew. More slammed into the space station, attaching themselves like ticks, digging into the metal skin, carving their way in. The agent fell, still shouting. His briefcase opened, spilling out lists—the lists of prisoners fed to the aliens, the meals that had only whet their appetite.

Admiral Komagata stood in the center of the room, the cracks racing across the dome around him. He drew his katana. The rippled steel, hand-forged by the best master in Japan, reflected the enemy ships.

The floor cracked open.

From the pit it emerged.

Legs thrust out, each tipped with claws like daggers, claws that dug into the metal floor, that gleamed like the steel katana. The jaws of the beast followed, large enough to swallow men, filled with fangs like the mouth of an anglerfish. The marauder's saliva dripped and sizzled, and its breath was like rotten meat. Four black eyes shone above the beast's narrow nostrils, eyes full of intelligence, of malice. The marauder pulled itself into the Dome, and finally its torso emerged from the pit, bloated, dangling, sprouting a stinger. Upon the alien's back rattled a macabre armor, the skulls of its vanquished enemies.

"Humans . . ." the creature hissed. "Your . . . reign . . . ends . . ."

Another marauder emerged, then a third, then several more. They advanced on clawed legs, saliva dripping, breath steaming and foul.

"Stand back!" shouted Chrysopoeia's agent. The man drew a handgun. "Back, beasts! Back! This is against the terms of our contract!"

The marauders whipped their heads toward him. They grinned. They advanced, claws clattering.

The agent fired his pistol.

Bullet after bullet rang out, slamming harmlessly into the aliens. The marauders' nostrils flared as the agent wet himself, staining his costly business suit.

The marauders pounced.

One alien closed its jaws around the agent's legs, tugging flesh off the bones. Another marauder tore open the belly, pulled out the entrails, and devoured them. The agent screamed. His blood spurted across his lists of prisoners.

"Mama!" he screamed. "Mama, please! Help me!"

But there is no help, thought Admiral Komagata, watching the grisly scene. His legs felt wooden, frozen in terror. *No help from our mothers. Not from our leaders. Not from our soldiers. Humanity will fall.*

One of the marauders, larger than the others, walked toward the screaming, dying agent. The alien had a red scar across its face, and horns formed a crest atop its head. The creature licked its chops, staring down at the legless, disemboweled agent. The feasting marauders, seeing this towering alien, paused from their meal and bowed before it.

"Lord Malphas," they said, heads lowered, awe in their voices.

"So weak, the human body," Malphas said, voice like cracking boulders. "Among the weakest on their planet, yet risen so high. Their brains so large. So . . . delectable."

"Please." The agent wept. "Mercy. Mercy. I'll give you more prisoners. However many you want. Please . . ."

Malphas stepped closer. It reached down a claw and caressed the agent's head. Its saliva dripped, sizzling across the man's skin, burning through.

"We want you all," the marauder said, then thrust its claws deep.

The agent screamed.

Malphas dug, sawed, pulled off the top of the skull. The brain glistened within. The agent was still alive as Malphas scooped out his brain and swallowed.

Admiral Komagata lowered his head.

"I have done this," he whispered. "I have failed."

The aliens spun toward him, flesh dangling from their jaws. They hissed, moving closer. Outside, more of the ravagers slammed into Space Station One, digging in their claws. The entire space station tilted, began to fall toward the planet below.

"Their blood is upon you," said Malphas, advancing across the sloping floor.

A tear ran down the admiral's cheek.

"Then let me die in honor."

He raised his katana.

The marauders screeched and closed in.

Admiral Komagata thrust his weapon.

The blade sliced into the side of his belly, shocking with its pain.

The marauders leaped toward him.

Komagata yanked the blade sideways, carving open his abdomen. His entrails spilled.

As the aliens tore into him, ripping off his limbs, sawing open his skull, Komagata saw the stars stream outside, saw fire blaze. The space station was crashing down to the planet, and in the smoke and fire and blood, he saw the underworld. He saw his shame.

Fire washed across him, endless waves, as he traveled through the darkness, seeking his old gods, seeking forgiveness for his sins.

CHAPTER TWENTY-SEVEN

Brigadier-General James Petty, much like his starship, was old, creaky, and under immense pressure to retire.

Both he and the HDFS *Minotaur* had their birthdays today; he was turning sixty-five, she a spry fifty-five.

Both had reached retirement age. And both were being tossed aside.

"Sir, the decommissioning ceremony begins in thirty minutes, sir!" Osiris barged into his quarters and saluted. "Would you like some help preparing your speech? I'm happy to supply many jokes from a database full of cracking one-liners, sir."

Petty was staring out his porthole at Earth. With a grunt, he turned toward the android. "Don't you robots ever learn to knock before entering?"

Osiris tilted her head, staring at him. They had built her to look like a young woman—tall, slender, with a platinum bob cut. They had even given the damn machine a uniform—an actual uniform of Space Territorial Command!—as if she were anything more than a glorified toaster.

"Sir, you requested that I give you a thirty minute warning, sir, and—"

"President Katson requested that." Petty grumbled under his breath. "You're dismissed, android. Return to your duties. I'll be there on time."

The android smiled prettily. Something about that smile was unnerving. Something about the whole damn machine was unnerving, a terror risen from the depths of Uncanny Valley.

"Happy to comply, sir!" Osiris turned to leave, then looked back. "Oh, sir, and did you know how you throw a good party in space? You planet. It's funny because this is a ceremony and not a party."

He pointed at the door. "Out."

After she had left his chamber, Petty shook his head. Ridiculous. When he had been a young officer, they didn't need damn androids on their ships. They had proper computers then—confined to boxes—not ones that walked around and cracked jokes.

He looked across his quarters. They were austere. Raw metal flooring. A simple cot to sleep on. A desk—metal again. The *Minotaur* was the oldest ship in the human fleet, the first starfighter carrier ever built. She had been forged in the fires of the Cataclysm, rising from the ruin of the world. After the scum had butchered billions, as cities lay in ruins, the nations of the world had built her. The HDFS *Minotaur*. A great beast to protect humanity. To ferry two hundred starfighters and five thousand marines in her hangars. To defend Earth and smite her enemies.

She wasn't like the newer ships. She had no carpets on the floors, none of those fancy plastics and woods, none of the bells and whistles. No. The *Minotaur* was a bulky beast of steel and raw power, built not for comfort but for war. For victory.

Petty placed his hand on a bulkhead, caressing her.

"And now they're going to tear you apart, girl. And it won't be enemy fire that does it. You withstood a hundred enemy assaults. It'll be the bureaucrats. Those who call you too expensive to maintain. Those who say the wars are over. That you're good for nothing but scrap metal." He scoffed. "Those bastards don't know you like I do. You're more alive than any damn android will ever be."

Many other ships—newer ships—were gone already. The HDFS *Sagan*. The HDFS *Requiem*. A thousand others. After the scum war, Earth lay in ruin. The planet was broke. For fifty years, Space Territorial Command had used the bulk of Earth's resources, building humanity's might in space—might that had finally defeated the enemy.

Now Earth wanted its resources back.

Over the past few years, since the Scum War had ended, Petty had watched as ship by ship was scrapped, its materials used to rebuild Earth.

"But they don't know like we do, girl. That there is still terror in the darkness. That there are still enemies out there. That those creatures—the marauders—will cover our world. And that Earth needs us. Both of us."

As he passed his hand over the bulkhead, it came to rest on a framed photograph of his daughter.

Of Colleen.

A lump filled Petty's throat.

He gazed at her. In the photograph, she was so young, so joyous. Twenty-one years old, graduating from Julius Military Academy, grinning as she tossed her cap into the air. What a day that had been! God, it was sixteen years now. Yet it felt like yesterday. He had gone to the ceremony, had stood with Admiral Evan Bryan himself. He had been so proud of Colleen, this girl who had lost her mother at such a young age, who had become a cadet, then an officer.

"Until the darkness took you." Tears filled Petty's eyes. "Until in the mines of Corpus, you fell. Defending humanity."

He looked away. It was too painful.

Lieutenant Ben-Ari had come to him that day. She had brought him his daughter's tags. She had spoken of Captain Colleen Petty's courage. He still carried the identification tags in his pocket, his last memory of his daughter. And now Ben-Ari was in prison, locked up for daring to speak the truth about the marauders.

Nobody believed her. Nobody but James Petty.

"There is still evil in the darkness," he whispered. "How can I lose this ship? How can I lose the first, the greatest defender of humanity?"

He returned to the porthole. Not a fancy, flat viewscreen like the modern ships had, displaying a video feed full of augmentation features. Here was a simple porthole like those in an old submarine. Petty gazed out upon Earth. The planet was like a blue marble from here. Fragile. Beautiful. So alone in the vastness of space. For so long, James Petty had fought to defend her. For forty-eight years, he had served in the HDF, rising from ensign to brigadier-general. And now they would toss him aside like another bit of scrap metal.

He was not ready to retire. Not even after the heart attack two years ago that had left him bedridden for weeks. Not after hearing Ben-Ari's warning.

"Sir!" On his lapel, his communicator beeped to life. "Sir, only a few minutes to go, sir." Osiris's voice. "Will you still make it to the ceremony, sir?"

Petty grunted. "I'll be there." He turned off the communicator.

He looked at the porthole, and now his eyes refocused, and he gazed at his reflection.

He wore his mess dress today, the military's version of a tuxedo. He felt ridiculous in the thing. What kind of military uniform had a bowtie, for chrissake? The damn thing displayed his medals. Medals for defeating the scum. For fighting in a hundred battles. They had even given him a goddamn medal for suffering a heart attack on duty, as if a scum claw had torn through his heart instead of a blood clot brought on by too much booze. Damn it, he needed some of that booze now. He couldn't wait for the ceremony to end to crack open the bottle he had been saving. Maybe they'd let him drink it on the *Minotaur*, one last drink in space. Maybe he'd just huddle in the apartment they'd toss him into on Earth, a place to ditch the relics. They might as well toss him directly into a shallow grave.

He grumbled, looking up from that uniform to the face reflected above it.

He looked old.

His hair had always been pitch black, but the heart attack had strewn it with white strands. His face was lined now. Dark sacks hung under his eyes.

But those eyes were still strong. Still fierce. Still chips of dark iron. Goddamn it, he was still a soldier. Maybe, like the *Minotaur*, he was a relic from an older time. But not yet useless. Earth still needed him. If the Alliance of Nations, if President Katson, if all the rest of them objected, well—let them! He would fight them. He had defeated the scum. He could—

He sighed.

No.

He was a soldier, yes. A good soldier. And he would obey his orders, like them or not.

"I've already lost my wife and daughter," he rasped. "It hurts to lose my ship too." The *Minotaur* was the only family he had left.

He left his quarters.

He walked through his ship one last time.

The corridors were narrow, the bulkheads thick, built to withstand bullets, fire, and alien claws. Fluorescent lights shone overhead, but the ship was still dim, labyrinthine. As Petty walked by, young soldiers stood at attention. He gave them brief nods. He'd miss these men and women. They were fine warriors. He had lost his only child, but these soldiers were like children to him. They were all his sons and daughters. And damn it, Petty was proud to have served with them. Even if the Alliance of Nations didn't share his pride.

He passed by the engineering stations. The torpedo bays. The armories. By hangars full of Firebird squadrons, jets that could fight in both air and space. By the bunks of marines who filled the ship, an entire brigade, ready to deploy to any world necessary. The *Minotaur*. Last of the great carriers. The first, and still the greatest, defender of Earth.

Goodbye, girl.

He reached the mess hall.

He paused for a moment outside the double doors.

He closed his eyes and inhaled deeply.

I'm sorry, Colleen. I wanted to keep fighting for you. I defeated the scum, ship after ship of the aliens. But this is one war I cannot win.

He reached into his pocket, and he felt his daughter's identification tags there. The cold metal felt familiar, comforting.

He opened his eyes and stepped into the mess hall.

Hundreds of people were already here, dressed in their finest. Most were the officers regularly serving aboard the *Minotaur*, everyone from young ensigns and lieutenants—marine platoon commanders, Firebird pilots, engineers, navigators—to the senior officers who served with Petty on the bridge. But others were dignitaries from Earth, both officers and civilians.

The Minister of Defense had boycotted the ceremony—Petty was good friends with the man, knew he objected to the decommissioning, had tried to fight it and was preparing his resignation.

Maria Katson, president of the Alliance of Nations, had come aboard too. She was a steely woman in her sixties. Like Petty, she was all hardness but of a different sort. He was craggy iron. Katson was smooth steel. Her power suit was the bluish-gray of a blade, matching her eyes, while her hair was silvery-gold. She had fought hard for this, Petty knew—to decommission the fleet, to turn their ships into great projects on Earth. To use scrap metal for buildings. To spend the tax dollars—and maintaining a carrier did cost a fortune—to rebuild roads and bridges. A worthy cause, perhaps.

But there will be no Earth if we cannot defend it, he thought. *There will be nobody to live in the buildings you raise or drive on the roads you pave. The marauders are out there. You've muzzled me, but I know the truth.*

Across the crowd, the president gave Petty a thin smile and small nod. There was no kindness to it.

You tossed Captain Ben-Ari into a prison cell because she spoke of the enemy, Petty thought. *But I will not be silent. Not anymore.*

He walked through the mess hall. The hundreds stood at attention as he walked by. Petty approached a podium at the back, and he faced the crowd. The android had placed his speech on the lectern. Petty looked at the papers blankly. Platitudes. Slogans. He didn't need words somebody else had written.

He looked at the crowd. White-haired colonels. Civilian dignitaries. Cameramen, broadcasting the ceremony across the fleet and down to Earth. Young, eager lieutenants. Petty's eyes lingered on the rows of younger officers, the new generation of leaders. Brave men and women, barely into their twenties, who flew starfighters, who led platoons in battle, who had chosen military careers, had chosen to dedicate their lives to the Human Defense Force.

Lieutenants who'd now be going home.

Young officers who would never bloom into leaders.

Petty raised his head and gazed beyond them. At the portholes on the wall. At space outside. At the darkness that gathered, a noose tightening around humanity.

You feed them prisoners, Petty thought. *You seek to appease them with morsels. But their hunger will not be satisfied. It took a young captain to speak the truth, so you silenced her. But I will not be silenced.*

He pushed aside his prepared speech.

He stared at the crowd.

"Fifty-seven years ago," he said, "when I was but a child, the scum first attacked Earth. Billions died. Our cities burned. Our species hurtled toward extinction. But from those ashes, strength emerged. The *Minotaur* emerged. We forged her from the steel of toppled skyscrapers. We forged her with blood, sweat, and tears. She was the first of the mighty carriers and always the greatest among them. Her cannons could tear apart worlds. From her hangars, she could launch two hundred Firebirds to tear through the ranks of the enemy. She fought in every major battle of the Galactic War for five decades, and at the end, she fought at Abaddon and pounded the enemy's homeworld. We were victorious! We ushered in an era of peace."

He paused, looking over the crowd. They all stared at him. President Katson gave him a small nod. The cameras were rolling, broadcasting his words across humanity.

Petty reached into his pocket and wrapped his fingers around his daughter's dog tags. He continued speaking, voice louder.

"But there can only be peace when warriors with shields defend it." He raised his chin. "Civilization can only thrive when we resist those who would topple it. There is still evil in the darkness. There are still those in space who would see our species crumble. You've all heard the rumors. Perhaps you've watched the leaked broadcasts. Perhaps you've heard the words of Captain Ben-Ari, who now languishes in prison for speaking them. The marauders, a predatory species, gather their fleet. They gaze upon Earth, and they hunger. If allowed passage here, they would destroy everything we have built, everything we have fought to defend."

In the mess hall, they mumbled, gasped. A cheer rose from the back. President Katson rose to her feet, eyes flaming. She began to walk toward him.

Petty raised his voice. "I will obey my orders! I will obey my president. I will step down. I will not overthrow my government. But I will not go silently!" He formed a fist and pounded the lectern. "We need our ships, damn it. We need our warriors. We need to defend our world. You can tear down the *Minotaur*, but hear me, Earth. Hear me, humanity! Raise a great cry! Demand that your leaders defend you! We cannot appease the marauders with human sacrifice. Every human we feed to their jaws only whets their appetite, and soon they will come to devour us all. We must fight!"

Across the hall, they all rose to their feet. Many cried out in approval, others in dismay. President Katson stared with cold fury. At her sides, civilian agents took a step forward.

"Hell yeah!" shouted Captain Julian Bryan, grandson of Admiral Evan Bryan and now a fighter pilot himself.

President Katson stepped onto the dais by Petty. She gave him a withering glare, then turned toward the crowd, a tight smile on her lips. She raised her hands.

"All right, all right, settle down, everyone! The general is right of course. We need to—and shall!—defend our world. While this ship is antiquated, I assure you that we have ways of staving off the enemy. Not with guns. Not with war. With trade! With a boisterous economy. With—"

"Free Ben-Ari!" shouted someone at the back; Petty could not see who.

"Free Ben-Ari!" rose another voice.

"Sit down, soldiers!" Katson said, then spun toward Petty. "Is this what you were planning, General? A military coup?"

"No coup, Madam President," he said. "Only words of truth. When I joined the military, I took a vow. To defend Earth. To defend her colonies. To fight with determination until my last breath. No one can ask me to break that vow. Put me in a prison cell like Ben-Ari if you must, but I will not be silenced while the enemy encircles us."

Katson's eyes blazed with fury. "It is not your job, soldier, to speak of your politics. I can have you tried for this. I can have you stripped of your uniform and honors. I—"

An alarm blared.

Red lights flashed.

A robotic voice spoke through the speakers. "Enemy incoming! Enemy incoming!"

Katson reeled toward Petty, baring her teeth. "Is this one of your games, Petty? Is this—"

He ignored the president. He lifted his communicator. "Bridge, report."

His security officer, Major Hennessy, answered through the communicator. "We're under attack, sir! Thousands of ravagers just leaped out of warped space, and—"

The *Minotaur* jolted madly.

People fell.

Fire blazed outside the portholes.

The walls dented.

Outside Petty saw them—thousands of them—emerging from warped spacetime.

Ravagers.

The warships of the marauders.

"Full battle alert!" Petty said. "All Firebird pilots, to your hangars! All pilots, launch into battle formations and engage the enemy! Go!"

They ran. Hundreds of pilots. They raced down the corridors, and the *Minotaur* jolted again. For a second, artificial gravity was lost, and they floated before the system came back online.

Petty ran as the corridors swayed, barking orders into his communicator.

"All gun stations—fire your shells! Hit the enemy with full artillery fire!"

The warship rocked as the cannons fired. Through portholes, Petty saw the shells stream through space and slam into enemy ships.

They were everywhere.

By God, they were everywhere.

Petty reached the bridge, a semicircular room covered with screens, affording a full view of space.

For an instant—just an instant—Petty paused.

His chest constricted.

His old, wounded heart twisted.

He could not breathe.

He stared out into the darkness, and the terror gripped him.

By God.

He had never seen an assault of this magnitude. Not even during the Scum War. The marauder ships filled space, as numerous as the stars.

And they were heading toward Earth.

CHAPTER TWENTY-EIGHT

Kemi stood on the bridge of the *Saint Brendan*, watching the swarm flow toward Earth. Tears filled her eyes.

"It's here," she whispered. "The marauder invasion. Earth's fall."

Noodles stood beside her, gazing through the viewport. "Amazing! Look at how they move, hundreds of thousands of them, all synchronized! Similar to a school of fish, a swarm of bees, or a Dothraki horde. I bet I could write an algorithm to analyze the video, detect their flight patterns, then perhaps use the information to code faster data retrieval procedures, and—" He gulped and adjusted his glasses. "I mean, it's horrible. Horrible. Earth's destruction and all." He tilted his head. "Still, fascinating."

"Fascinating?" Rage flowed through Kemi, and her tears fell. "My parents are down there. Oh God, my parents are on Earth."

Kemi placed her hands on the viewport, gazing at the planet. The marauder ships—the ravagers—were streaming toward the blue planet, as numerous as the stars. The *Saint Brendan* had its stealth engines activated, and it reflected no light and hid all radiation. Kemi felt like a ghost watching the death of all those it loved, all those it had stayed behind to guard.

"For two years we hid here," she whispered. "For two years, we hid in the darkness, trapped in this invisible can, wishing, praying, dreaming to go home. Now that home will fall."

Hang in there, Mom and Dad, she thought, trembling. *Be strong.*

The past two years had been among the worst in Kemi's life. Two years since she had lost her hand, since the president's agents had arrested Ben-Ari. Two years since Kemi's mentor, commanding officer, and best friend had been sent to prison to await execution. Since then, Kemi had lived on the *Saint Brendan,* buying food and supplies from black market smugglers, buying fuel from outlaws, living on the fringes of the solar system. A refugee. Lost in darkness.

And tolerating Noodles.

"This is just like *Space Galaxy XII,*" the young hacker said. "You know, only the best entry in the franchise? The one where the aliens finally attack Earth? No? Nothing?" He rolled his eyes. "We have it saved in the entertainment system, Kemi. If only you'd expand your education to the classics, you'd—"

"Noodles, this is the real world!" Kemi snapped. "Not now with your nonsense."

She should have blasted him out of the airlock a million times. Several times, she had come close. And yet Kemi had kept Noodles aboard the *Saint Brendan,* because she needed him. He knew how to fix the computer systems. He knew how to hack into Earth's radio signals to find the best smuggling ships. And . . . as much as Kemi loathed the boy, as much as she missed her friends, perhaps Noodles had alleviated the loneliness, the cabin fever of having been trapped here for so long, her only shore leave spent in asteroid markets, sleazy space stations, and rundown lunar bars where she hid her face in a hood.

She had not stepped on Earth for two years. Now she doubted she ever would again.

They were still far from the planet; Earth was a blue marble from here. She hit controls, zooming in. She could see the ravagers more clearly on the viewport now, ships shaped like claws, streaming toward the planet. Only a handful of armed satellites protected the Earth these days, the remnants of the vast Iron Sphere system that had once held off the scum. Kemi watched as the satellites' cannons fired, as shells slammed into the ravagers, but the alien ships kept flying. It was like shooting pebbles at a charging army of armored knights.

Kemi zoomed in closer, and she gasped.

"They're rising to fight!" Fresh tears budded. "The Human Defense Force. Our fleet. Earth rises!"

Out from the atmosphere they soared: squadron after squadron of Firebirds. From behind the horizon charged several warships, cannons blazing. Only a few hundred spaceships flew here. It was a fraction of what they had flown against the scum. It was a drop by the sea of enemies. But the sight of fellow humans fighting raised hope in Kemi's breast.

She sat at the controls. She grabbed her joystick, and she fired up her engines.

"We're going to fight too."

At her side, Noodles cringed. "I don't know, Kems. We're not part of the HDF anymore, remember? I'm an escaped inmate, and you're a refugee. If they catch us, they'll sentence us to death, like they did to Ben-Ari. Why should we fight for them? Why— whoa!"

The *Saint Brendan* charged forward so fast Noodles almost fell.

"Everything that happened is now irrelevant," Kemi said. "Everything that has ever happened to humankind—our troubles, conflicts, hopes, all that we built, all that we destroyed, all that we dreamed—all is yesterday. Now there is only this. Now there is only our greatest hour."

I'm coming, Mom and Dad.

For the first time in two years, she switched off the stealth cloak, allowing her to prime the cannons.

She roared toward Earth, the ship thrumming, the controls shaking, countless ravagers before her.

They streamed across the distance, among the fastest ships humanity had ever built, so fast the hull rattled and she thought the ship would break.

The ravagers ahead saw her. Many spun toward the *Saint Brendan*, claws opening to expose the flaming innards.

Kemi howled wordlessly—the cry of a haunted woman, of a warrior, of a human who refused to fall—and fired her guns.

Two missiles flew out from the *Brendan*, leaving trails of fire, and slammed into two ravagers.

One missile barely left a dent. The second chipped a claw off the ravager, but the ship kept charging, a new claw uncurling to replace the lost one. Those claws opened to reveal swirling plasma, and fiery red bolts flew.

Kemi inhaled deeply.

I trained for this. I was born for this.

Noodles screamed.

She yanked her joystick sideways.

A fireball rolled over one wing.

She banked sharply in the opposite direction.

The second plasma bolt roared beneath their other wing.

She stormed forth, and she fired a hailstorm of bullets.

The bullets slammed into one ravager, ricocheting off claws, and a few made it into the flaming innards of the ship. Fire roared within. Kemi clenched her teeth and fired a heat-seeking missile.

She yanked back on the joystick with all her strength. The *Saint Brendan* shot upward, and the missile entered the fiery mouth of the ravager.

The marauder ship exploded.

Metal claws, each the size of a bus, shot out from the devastation. One claw slammed into a swooping Firebird, destroying the starfighter. Other claws hit ravagers, knocking them back. Kemi yanked on the controls, dodging more of the shrapnel, and rose higher.

She felt the blood drain from her face.

"So many," she whispered.

Earth was still far. The swarm covered the distance like locusts over fields.

And the human fleet was collapsing.

Thousands of Firebirds were flying ahead, falling fast, crashing toward Earth like comets. Each fallen ship stabbed Kemi like a marauder claw. She had flown a Firebird against the scum. She had flown these starfighters for five years, as a warrior, a guardian of humanity. She knew many of those pilots ahead. They were her friends.

And they were dying.

Here were no scum pods, weak ships made of fleshy, organic walls. The ravagers were terrors, and their spiky hulls withstood bullets and missiles. Only direct hits to their fiery mouths seemed to shatter them, but Kemi saw only a handful collapse, and even in their destruction, they blasted out claws, tearing down nearby human vessels. Human warships the size of office buildings were firing cannons, but the ravagers latched onto them like leeches, tearing their hulls, filling them with fire. A starfighter carrier was lumbering around the planet, only for thousands of ravagers to slam into it, to rip it apart. The massive ship, larger than the Statue of Liberty, tilted and plunged toward Earth, tearing apart in the atmosphere and streaming down toward the ocean.

Kemi kept flying, whipping around ravagers, dodging their attacks. Plasma blazed across the hull, heating, denting the metal, but she pulled left hard, rose higher, flew onward. Earth was close now, filling her field of vision. All around the *Saint Brendan*,

Firebirds kept crashing down toward the planet. Warships crashed onto Earth's surface. Cities burned. Already several ravagers were making their way down toward the planet, spewing fire. Forests blazed and tidal waves washed over the shores.

"Kemi, we have to get out of here!" Noodles shouted. "This world is lost!"

"Then we'll die with it!" Kemi shouted back.

"We can't defeat them!" Noodles said. "We only have a few missiles left. We have to run!"

Kemi checked the armory. Noodles was right. They were low on ammo, and there were hundreds of thousands of ravagers here.

"Noodles, sit down and hold onto something."

"Kemi, what—"

"Hold on!" she said, reaching for the azoth engine controls

Noodles paled. "Kemi, what—are you—don't!"

But Kemi flipped the switch. She winced and grabbed her armrests.

"Kemi!" Noodles shouted.

Large warships had massive azoth engines, and they required hours to prime up. The *Saint Brendan*, built for speed and spying, had a smaller, faster, state-of-the-art warp engine, able to prime within only moments and create a bubble of warped spacetime around the vessel. Flight instructors always taught to avoid flying near large objects when bending spacetime, and Earth was pretty damn large.

I'm already a refugee, Kemi thought. *Here's to breaking every damn rule in the book.*

Ravagers flew toward the *Brendan* from every direction, blasting out plasma.

With blue fire, the azoth engine kicked into life.

Spacetime warped around the ship.

The curve of the universe caught the charging ravagers. Claws bent, then snapped off. Plasma flowed across the bubble. A dozen ravagers shattered.

The *Saint Brendan* shot outward.

Kemi switched off the azoth engine.

She had flown in warped space for only a second, maybe two.

They had destroyed a dozen ravagers. The *Saint Brendan* now hovered well beyond the moon, millions of kilometers from Earth.

"Kemi, damn it!" Noodles shouted, looking green. "You could have torn us apart. Bending spacetime next to Earth's gravitational pull! Really! Is that how your mother raised you?"

"I destroyed a dozen ravagers, maybe even twenty," she said. She gazed back toward the distant Earth. From here, it was just a blue dot. But when she zoomed in her viewport, she could see the lights of battle, the human fleet overwhelmed.

Earth falls, she thought.

Kemi lowered her head. During her exile, she had tried to warn Earth of this menace. She had leaked all the information she had—the information Ben-Ari had retrieved, had gone to prison for—only to be dismissed as a kook, to be smeared in the media as a conspiracy theorist. She had secretly approached old comrades, fellow pilots, had urged them to listen, had tried to enlist them, only to flee when they threatened to call the military police. Kemi had tried to fight. She had failed.

And now humanity fell.

She winced, remembering the prison she had seen in the demilitarized zone. The webbings covering the walls. The marauders in the shadows. The piles of corpses. The man screaming as the alien sawed open his skull. Now this terror had reached Earth, right here before her, and she could not stop it.

But I can still fight, Kemi thought. *I can go down with Earth. I'm done hiding.*

She prepared to reactivate the azoth engine, to fly back into battle, to take down as many ravagers as she could before they shot her down.

"Wait," Noodles said, catching her wrist.

She looked at him. A scrawny young man, his glasses thick, his frame small. A cocky man, a genius, a narcissist, yet now he was pale. Now his hand trembled as he held her wrist.

"We have to go back," Kemi said. "We cannot abandon Earth, not while we can still fight, still fire our last missiles, still take down a few enemies."

Noodles stared at the distant planet and cringed. "Look, I agree about sacrifice, victory, saving the world, all that stuff. I've read Tolkien, and I'm all Team Frodo here. But we won't do any good charging into a suicide mission."

"So you'd have us linger in this ship forever?" Kemi said, eyes burning. "The last two humans, floating for all eternity in darkness?"

He managed to crack a shaky grin. "While I'm indeed tempted to remain trapped here with you forever, the last human man and woman forced to procreate—repeatedly, one would assume, and with much vigor—there's a better way. Well, no, not a *better* way, because nothing is better than that, but . . . Oh damn my honor! There might still be a way to win this war."

Kemi shook her head. "How could you joke at a time like this?" She looked back at Earth. Through the magnified viewport, she saw more marauder ships invading the atmosphere, making their way down to the surface. Barely any human ships still fought. Her tears splashed the controls. "Oh, God . . . Our home. Our home is falling. My parents . . ."

Noodles gave her an awkward pat on the shoulder. "Don't worry, Kemi. The marauders don't want to exterminate us like the scum did. They just want to eat our brains! They'll probably just farm us like cattle."

She reeled toward him. "Is that supposed to make me feel better?"

"No, but it does give us time," Noodles said. "Time to find help. Remember how I said I'm Team Frodo? Well, maybe right now, we need to be Team Aragorn. We just need some help from the undead."

"I have no idea what you're talking about," Kemi said. "Is this *Space Galaxy* again?"

Noodles groaned. "*Space Galaxy*? Damn it, woman, have I taught you nothing? *Space Galaxy* is the classic science fiction show that, tragically, only ran for three seasons between 2053 and 2056 before those geniuses at Red Fox Entertainment decided to cancel it. Cancel it! Can you imagine? Canceling *Space Galaxy*! This all happened because bean-counting execs don't appreciate creative integrity. Thank *goodness* they're still making the movies, but—"

"Noodles!" Kemi said. "For chrissake, you seem more upset about a century-old program being canceled than Earth falling. Get to the point!"

He heaved a sigh. "Right. Back to *The Lord of the Rings*. When the orcs were ready to destroy Minas Tirith, the noble Aragorn took the paths of the dead. There he summoned an army of ghosts to fight on his behalf. With their help, he vanquished the forces of the dark lord, and—"

"Noodles, enough!" Kemi said. "Speak English."

"I found something," he said. "It was a year ago. Back when Ben-Ari had me hacking into the military and Chrysopoeia Corp mainframes. At the time, I laughed about it. I thought it just an urban legend. A myth. But over the past couple yearse, between binging on *All Systems Go!* episodes, I've been doing more research, and I might be onto something here." His eyes lit up. "A legendary, ancient fleet. A *ghost* fleet. Ghosts, Kemi! Just like Arag—"

"Noodles!" Kemi reached back to the controls. "Enough ghost stories. We have to fight. We—"

He grabbed her wrist again. "No! Listen to me, Kemi. The military has been studying this. They've been taking it very seriously. The HDF has—or had, if the marauders already destroyed it—a secret base in the Oort Cloud. From there, two light-years away from Earth, they've been scanning the skies for this legendary ghost fleet. And some sources say they've already pinpointed its location."

It was Kemi's turn to groan. "A ghost fleet, Noodles? This isn't time for your stories."

"This is real, Kemi!" He wouldn't release her arm. "Okay, I don't know if a bunch of floating sheets with eye holes are hovering out there. But according to the data I collected, there is an ancient, derelict fleet thousands of light-years away, farther than humanity has ever flown. They say it's over a million years old, that this fleet was built when Homo Erectus was struggling to figure out how to bang two stones together. And they say that for a million years, that fleet has hovered in space, lost, waiting to fight again. They call it the Ghost Fleet, just a story soldiers tell, a story of alien spirits haunting the halls of those ancient vessels. But the HDF took this very, very seriously. The top scientists in charge of the project believed the fleet contained terrible weapons—weapons far more powerful than humans, scum, or even marauders possess. If we can find this fleet, we'll have the power to destroy the marauders' armada."

"Sure, no problem," Kemi said, hearing the weariness in her voice. "We'll zip across the galaxy, find an ancient ghost army, and save the world." She grabbed Noodles and shook him. "Are you even listening to yourself? You sound like some conspiracy theory nut!"

He shook himself free. "Well, if I'm a nut, so are a thousand alien civilizations. For years, aliens from across the galaxy struggled to find the Ghost Fleet, to gain its power. They all failed. It's a vast galaxy, and nobody could pinpoint the Ghost Fleet's location."

Kemi leaned back in her seat, feeling deflated. "And I suppose you'll tell me you have the coordinates."

Noodles shook his head. "No. But I know somebody who does. Somebody who worked in the Oort Cloud. Somebody who studied the Ghost Fleet with the best researchers of humanity. Kemi, darling, we need to find the only person who can help us now." He hopped into his seat and placed his feet on the dashboard. "Do you know the way to Manila?"

CHAPTER TWENTY-NINE

Lailani had parked her mobile school in the shantytown, ready to distribute books to the children, when death rained from the sky.

For a year now, she had been coming here, bringing hope to the most hopeless. For a year now, she had relived her childhood, living in the filth, the despair, the wretched disease, living among the lowest on Earth. But now, a woman, a veteran, a teacher, she lived here not to suffer but to alleviate suffering. To build. To heal.

The day had begun like any other. Lailani loaded books into her wagon; a new shipment had just arrived from her church overseas. Some days she loaded books into her rowboat, for many streets here were flooded, had become rivers clogged with debris. Other roads were alleyways, labyrinths that snaked through the hovels. She wore sandals, shorts, and a sleeveless shirt that revealed the tattoos on her arms: a dragon, denoting her strength; a rainbow, symbol of her heart; several stars, counting the scum she had killed in the war; and finally, flowers around the wrists, hiding the scars of her suicide attempt at age sixteen. The flowers were the most dear to her, for they symbolized beauty from despair, a rebirth of life, and that was her mission here. To bring such rebirth to those who suffered like she had.

Sofia walked at her side, a rosary hanging around her neck. Her blond hair was tied into a ponytail, and weariness filled her blue eyes. She had grown up in poverty too, hiding from the Russian tanks in the rubble of Ukraine, orphaned and hungry. For the past year, Sofia had marched steadfastly at Lailani's side, a fellow soldier in this new war, as much a sister-in-arms as those troops who had fought with Lailani against the scum.

"We'll head east today," Sofia said, helping Lailani wheel the wagon of books.

Lailani caressed Sofia's cheek and kissed her lips. "Hope into despair."

Sofia smiled, and for a moment, all her weariness and heartache faded, and true light filled her eyes. She repeated their mantra. "Hope into despair."

They rolled the wagon into the shantytowns. Visible from here, only a few kilometers away, rose the skyscrapers of Central Manila, a hive of concrete and glass and industry. But all around that glistening center, spreading for many kilometers, rotted the slums, a hell where millions of souls withered away.

There were no true houses here. The millions of poor collected slats of wood, sheets of corrugated aluminum, and scraps of tarpaulin, erecting them into crude shelters two or three stories tall. The wood rotted. The metal rusted. The scraps of cloth fluttered. Through slits in these sheds peered the eyes of children—eyes too large in their gaunt faces. Children. Children everywhere, millions of them, peering from behind wood and metal, running naked on the streets, splashing in muddy puddles.

With no birth control here in the shantytowns, the children filled the alleyways, crowding the slums, often dying from hunger or disease, ending up in the brothels, or sold to foreigners.

The stench of human waste filled the air, and trash piled up on the streets. Jumbles of electrical wires crackled overhead, thick as tangled spiderwebs, bringing intermediate power to the shelters, enough to heat the scraps of food collected from the trash heaps, to try and kill the bacteria, to boil the water collected from the dirty rivers. The garbage piled up everywhere, mounds, hills of it—wrappers, human waste, dead animals, all filling the hot, humid air with its fumes. One could barely see a shred of road, just water and mud filled with the waste of this place.

And everywhere—the millions, crammed in, covering the streets, dressed in rags, hungering, praying, begging. Here was the densest place on Earth, sixty thousand people crammed into every square kilometer—a density beyond what human sanity could endure. There was no privacy. No place to hide from the searing sunlight, the stench, the crowds, the agony. They sat on the mounds of trash. They stood pushed against crude, crumbling structures of rusted metal and scraps of wood cobbled together. Babies, millions of babies, squealed in the squalor, doomed to grow old in this labyrinth, to live and die and rot here. Lailani knew. She had lived this life herself.

These people have no hope, she thought, walking among them. *They are alive but they are in Hell.*

And into this hell, Lailani and Sofia came. They brought no prayers. They brought no charity. They would hand out no crosses, no food, no coin.

They brought books.

"*Tita* Lailani!" the children cried, running toward her, barefoot and hungry but grinning. "*Tita* Sofia!"

Lailani smiled and patted their heads. Sofia handed out pencils and notebooks. The children gathered around. Lailani set up the chairs, and the children sat, eager to learn.

And Lailani taught them their letters, taught them to read simple words, to write, gifted them books to practice with. There were no schools here in the slums. These children would never be allowed into the city center, never have the funds to pay for education. But as Lailani taught them to read, she dared to hope, to dream—that someday these children could leave the slums. Could find work in the city center or abroad. Could come back here like she had, could continue the cycle.

There are millions of children here, she knew. *And thousands more are born every day. I cannot save them all. But if I can save a few, then my life is worthwhile. Every child I save is worth more than a hundred scum I could have killed. Here is my true battle, my true nobility.*

She was practicing writing letters with a young girl, a tiny little thing in a blue dress, when the skies cracked open and the fire rained.

Lailani looked up, and her heart shattered.

Her eyes watered.

No, she thought. *No. Please, God. Not again.*

"A hurricane!" a child cried.

"Asteroids!" shouted the girl in the blue dress.

But Lailani knew what this was. She had seen it before.

"War," she whispered.

Starships. Thousands of starships. They descended from the sky, shrieking, spinning, spewing out fire. Ships of dark metal, shaped like claws. Alien ships.

The marauders.

Lailani recognized them at once. With much interest, she had been following the story of Ben-Ari's discovery in the DMZ, her trial and imprisonment, and the hunt for Lieutenant Kemi Abasi. She had read the reports Kemi had been leaking online— reports of vicious aliens mustering for war, of a military cover-up, reports dismissed as mere conspiracy theories, as the ramblings of a madwoman. But Lailani had served with Ben-Ari and Kemi. They were her friends, her mentors. She trusted them. She had always believed.

And now she saw this truth rain down with fire and death.

The ravager ships uncurled their claws. From their swirling centers, plasma rained. Like comets, bolts of fiery torment slammed into the shantytown. Huts blazed. People screamed. Farther west, on the hazy horizon, ships were slamming into skyscrapers, knocking them down, and dust and smoke filled the air, rolling over the city like tidal waves.

"Children!" Lailani shouted. "Run! Hide!"

The ships were slowing their descent. They came to hover above the shantytown, their fire dying down. On their hulls, doorways dilated.

"Run!" Lailani shouted.

The girl in the blue dress grabbed her. "But *Tita* Lailani, I'm scared!"

Lailani knelt by the girl. "You have to run now. Hide in your home. Help the other children hide."

Weeping, the girl ran, collecting her siblings. In the sky, webs unspooled from the ships, and clawed legs emerged.

Lailani turned to look at Sofia. Her beloved, her soulmate, stood behind the cart of books. Their eyes met.

"I'm ready," Sofia whispered, face pale.

Lailani nodded. She opened the secret compartment on the cart, then pulled out the forbidden book—a copy of *Loggerhead* by Marco Emery, a copy she had printed herself. But when she opened the book, she revealed not Marco's story but a box. A box containing two handguns.

She took one and handed the other to Sofia. Above them rose clattering, grumbling, and inhuman screeches.

"For Earth," Lailani said.

Sofia nodded. "For humanity."

They shared a quick kiss, then raised their guns.

From the thousands of ships above, the aliens emerged.

Lailani had heard stories of these creatures, but she had never imagined anything so vile. They were as large as cattle, all jagged horns and claws, moving on six legs down their webs, as nimble as spiders. Already they salivated for human flesh, baring rows of teeth as long as human arms. Their ceremonial armor of skulls clattered on their backs, and Lailani knew they would add many skulls to those bony suits today. All over Manila, they were descending, their ships filling the sky, their webs like sheets of rain coating the city.

Lailani waited, gun raised.

"Remember, Sofia," she said, thinking back to Kemi's leaked videos. "Aim for their eyes. The rest is bulletproof. Don't shoot until you're close enough to hit their eyes."

Fighter jets soared over the city, firing missiles. Flames exploded overhead. Armored vehicles rolled down the streets, and soldiers shouted and fired shells into the sky. A few marauders fell, burning, but thousands were still descending on their webs. A hailstorm of bullets rose from below, slamming into the aliens, shattering their ceremonial skulls but unable to harm the bodies beneath. A Firebird crashed down, pierced with ravager claws, and slammed into the shantytown only meters away from Lailani.

"Wait," she whispered. Children raced around her, screaming, burning. "Wait . . ."

She was a civilian now. She wore shorts and sandals, not a uniform and boots. But she still wore her old dog tags around her neck; she had kept them, never removed them. She was still a staff sergeant in the reserves. She was still a decorated war heroine. And she was still a fighter.

The aliens landed.

Screeching, they scurried through the city.

Their claws tore into fleeing children. Their jaws ripped flesh off bones. Several adults leaped from roofs, wielding knives and clubs, only to be ripped apart. Their corpses thudded onto the ground. The crude shelters collapsed.

"Wait," Lailani whispered.

At her side, Sofia raised her gun with one hand, held Lailani's hand with the other.

Fangs bloodied, the marauders scuttled down the alleyways toward them. One of the creatures made eye contact with Lailani. It grinned, a child's severed leg in its jaws. It leaped toward the two women.

Lailani fired her gun.

Her bullet slammed into one of the marauder's four eyes.

The creature squealed and fell.

Lailani stepped closer, firing again, hitting another eye. When the creature opened its jaws to roar, Sofia fired bullet after bullet into its maw. It screamed, thrashing.

A bullet to the third eye finished the job.

Shrieks rose behind them.

Lailani and Sofia turned to see a dozen more marauders racing toward them, ripping into children.

"We're going to run out of bullets before they run out of aliens!" Sofia said.

"Then we'll fight with knives," Lailani said. "And then with sticks. Then with tooth and nail."

She fired another bullet, missed an eye. Sofia fired and hit the mark, and the creature before them squealed. More howls came from behind, and Lailani turned, saw marauders ripping through the shanties, racing toward her. She fired another bullet, loaded another magazine. The two women stood back to back, the creatures surrounding them.

And so here is where I die, Lailani thought. *Here in my hometown. With the woman I love. With—*

Pain blazed through her skull.

She grimaced and touched the back of her head.

A buzzing thrummed across her skull. The chip! The chip in her brain!

A marauder leaped. Lailani fired, missed an eye, rolled aside, fired again. Sofia screamed beside her, firing more bullets. People fought around them with whatever makeshift weapons they could grab, falling fast.

Lailani fired another bullet. The pain subsided, blazed again, faded once more.

It had been years since she had felt the chip. Not since the war against the scum. In that war, Lailani had learned that her father hadn't been an American GI like she had thought. She had no true father. The scum had planted her into the womb of her mother—a homeless, thirteen-year-old prostitute from here in the slums. They had altered Lailani's DNA, giving her a touch of the scum, turning her into a drone. At their command, Lailani had killed, had betrayed her fellow soldiers, unable to stop the scum from tugging her strings, from controlling her from afar.

The HDF scientists had placed a chip inside her skull. Noodles himself, a boy Lailani had gone through boot camp with, had written the code. The chip disabled the scum from controlling her, from awakening that one percent of alien DNA. Whenever the scum had tried to control her, the chip had hurt, blocking them.

But the scum were dead. Here was a different alien species. Who was trying to access her mind now? Why was her chip heating up?

A marauder leaped toward her. An armored vehicle rumbled forward, fired a grenade, and knocked the alien back. Lailani fired into its eyes. She loaded her third and last magazine. A marauder leaped onto Sofia, and claws grabbed her leg, and she screamed. The Ukrainian fired bullet after bullet, emptying her magazine into the creature's mouth, but couldn't stop it.

"Sofia!" Lailani ran, leaped onto the armored vehicle, then vaulted onto the marauder's back. She landed among the skulls glued onto its back. Sofia screamed below, the claws tearing at her legs.

Die, fucker, Lailani thought, placing her gun against an eye. She fired.

The bullet entered the marauder's brain and it fell, burying Sofia beneath it.

Lailani slid off the dead alien, fear pounding through her, as marauders and soldiers fought around her, as the last few fighter jets burned above. She strained, shouting, using all her strength to shove the marauder off Sofia.

The young woman lay, legs bloody, but still alive. She managed to rise, wincing.

"I'm fine," Sofia whispered, trembling.

Another Firebird crashed. In the distance, a skyscraper collapsed. The city crumbled. And more ravagers kept emerging. More marauders kept descending from the clawed ships. The bullets of the human resistance died down to sporadic fire.

We resisted the scum for years, Lailani thought. *Do we fall to these new enemies within moments?*

She clasped Sofia's hand. They stood together as more marauders—hundreds, thousands—crept toward them from all sides. Human limbs crunched in their jaws. In a nearby puddle, a marauder cracked open a girl's skull and lapped up the brain. Blood drenched the corpse's blue dress.

"I love you, Sofia," Lailani whispered, down to her last few bullets. "Always."

"We go down together," Sofia said. "Fighting."

They fired their guns.

A *boom* shook the sky.

The heavens seemed to crack open.

A new ship emerged.

It was somewhat smaller than a ravager, perhaps the size of a truck. Its black hull was dented, burnt, but still showing its original slick design. A golden phoenix still reared on its starboard, clutching letters beneath it: *HDFS Saint Brendan.*

"The ship that was missing," Lailani whispered, tears in her eyes. "Kemi's ship."

The *Saint Brendan* lowered itself to hover above the shantytown roofs. The airlock opened, and Kemi stood there, a machine gun in hand. She fired, knocking back marauders. With her other hand—a metal prosthetic—she tossed down a rope.

"Lailani, come on!" Kemi cried.

A marauder leaped.

Sofia screamed.

Blood spurted, and the young Ukrainian fell.

"Lailani!" Kemi cried above.

Lailani fired another bullet, perhaps her last, killing the marauder who had sliced through Sofia's side. She knelt above her beloved.

"Sofia!" she cried.

Her face was so pale. Her blood kept flowing.

"Fight them," Sofia whispered. "Fight them always."

Lailani sneered. "We'll fight them together."

Marauders pounced. More gunfire sounded from above, knocking back the beasts, but thousands still swarmed. The *Saint Brendan* fired a missile, and a ravager exploded, crashed down, and buried huts beneath it. Fire blazed, and more ravagers swooped in.

"Lailani, hurry!" Kemi shouted. "Now!"

Lailani wrapped one arm around Sofia, and she grabbed the rope with her other hand.

The *Saint Brendan* began to rise at once, pulling them up from the ruin.

Marauders leaped from below, jaws snapping, like crocodiles leaping at a dangling morsel of meat. Lailani fired another bullet, missed the eye. Ravagers flew all around, and the

Brendan fired another missile, hitting one ship between the claws. The ravager shattered, and shrapnel blazed, narrowly missing Lailani. She dangled on the rope, holding Sofia, as the *Brendan* kept rising. She couldn't climb with one hand. Kemi was busy firing her machine gun, knocking back the leaping beasts. The sound of screaming bullets rang in Lailani's ears.

As they rose higher, the devastation became more clear.

Within only moments, Manila had fallen.

Skyscrapers lay strewn like fallen toys. Shantytowns burned. Ravagers covered the city sky, lowering more and more marauders into the devastation. The aliens were everywhere, killing, feeding, rounding up prisoners.

We are a feast to them, Lailani thought. *They didn't come to destroy like the scum did. They came to feed.*

They were hundreds of feet above the city, and Kemi began reeling up the rope, when the ravager flew directly beneath them.

The alien vessel was twice the *Brendan*'s size. With its claws closed, it looked like a black seed, spiky, metallic. It turned its pointed prow upward, facing the ascending *Brendan*, and bloomed open. Its claws pulled back like petals, revealing the fiery cannon in the middle, a pit of plasma like a cauldron of molten metal. It gurgled and smoldered beneath them, a gaping gate to Hell.

Lailani shouted, fired her gun into the blazing pit, emptied the magazine. She was out of bullets. The plasma roiled, brightened, about to shoot upward.

"Kemi, fire on it!" Lailani shouted.

"Noodles, aim our cannons downward!" Kemi shouted into the ship.

But there was no time. Lailani stared at the flaming pit below, at her death.

Like a volcano, the inferno blazed skyward toward them.

"Hope into despair," Sofia whispered, tears in her eyes. "I love you."

As the fire rose below, Sofia let go of Lailani.

She fell.

"Sofia!" Lailani screamed.

As the woman fell, she met Lailani's eyes, and she smiled.

The plasma washed over Sofia, and her burning body fell into the flaming pit in the heart of the ravager.

Flames roared out.

The alien ship exploded like a shattering Christmas ornament.

Metal claws flew in all directions, tearing through nearby ships. A scrap of metal sliced across Lailani's thigh, and she screamed. Another piece hit the *Brendan*, and the ship shook. Fire and metal rained onto the city.

Sofia was gone.

Lailani wept as Kemi pulled her into the airlock, wept as she stumbled into the hull, wept as the *Saint Brendan* shot into space. Below, she could see her city, her country, her planet burning. The blue planet seemed red. All of Earth wept.

The azoth engine hummed, and the stars stretched into lines, and they streamed through warped spacetime, moving millions of kilometers per second, leaving Earth behind.

Lailani stood at the porthole, tears on her cheeks, as Kemi stroked her hair.

Goodbye, Sofia, she thought. *Goodbye, Earth. Goodbye.*

Then Lailani fell to her knees, embraced Kemi, and softly sobbed.

CHAPTER THIRTY

Flying the *Saint Brendan*, Kemi saw it ahead, floating through space.

"Fort Blackwell Disciplinary Barracks," she said. "Otherwise known as Hell's Hilton. And the buggers got here first."

Sitting at her side on the bridge, Noodles cringed. "There are about a thousand ravagers around that asteroid. Kems, are you sure we need to save Ben-Ari?"

Kemi glared at him. "For God's sake, Noodles. She busted you out of this exact prison!"

"I know, I know!" He clutched his head. "But . . . Damn it. The *Saint Brendan* is already busted up. She can barely fly as it is. And you want us to blast through a hundred enemy ships, then infiltrate the most secure prison in the galaxy? And . . ." He winced. "You won't like hearing this. But you girls needed to save me. You needed my considerable hacker skills. But do we need Ben-Ari?"

Kemi gasped. "She's the commander of this ship!"

"*Was* the commander," Noodles said. "She's only a private now. She was demoted, remember? Look, Kems. We saved Lailani. She studied the Ghost Fleet while stationed at Oort, and she'll help us find it. But Ben-Ari is useless to us. I know she's your friend. I know I owe her a huge favor. But she's useless, and that's the hard truth. Maybe once the war is over, we can pick her up, and—"

Lailani walked onto the bridge and slapped Noodles' head.

"I'm not telling you a goddamn thing about the Ghost Fleet unless Ben-Ari is here," Lailani said. "We rescue Ben-Ari, or my lips are sealed."

Noodles glowered at her. "I have ways of making you talk. I can torture you. I can show you the *Star Wars Holiday Special.* I can code the ship's speakers to play Yowling Cat Perkins's Greatest Hits on an infinite loop. I—Ow, ow! Let go of my glasses! Okay, okay!" He snatched his glasses back from Lailani. "Fine! We'll rescue Ben-Ari, then save the galaxy. Happy?"

Kemi ignored him. She flew closer, the stealth cloak still on. The asteroid lazily rolled ahead, a hundred kilometers long. Its small moon, the size of a city park, orbited it. Ravagers flew around the twin asteroids, and more clung to the rocky surfaces. Already webs coated the prisons built here.

Kemi's heart sank. She had never forgotten the overrun prison in the DMZ. That place still haunted her nightmares.

Please be alive, Ben-Ari, she thought. *I can't do this without you. I need my friend, my mentor, my captain.*

They were getting close now. Soon they would be in visible range. The *Brendan*'s stealth technology did not offer complete invisibility. It protected them at a distance, scattering reflective light and cloaking emitted heat and radiation, making the ship difficult for sensors to detect. But at close range, the ship could still be seen by the naked eye.

They'll see us soon, Kemi knew. *We can't beat so many with strength of arms. But we have speed.*

"Noodles, are you sure she'll be held on the moon?" Kemi said. "Not in the main prison on the larger asteroid?"

"I'd bet on it," he said. "The installation on the moon is harsher, reserved for only the most notorious prisoners. They call it the Seventh Circle." He shuddered. "I don't miss that place. After the shit she pulled, Ben-Ari will be there."

Kemi nodded. "Here's the plan. We fly in, activate our azoth engine, and scatter the ravagers. We'll also knock the little moon out of orbit. We then fly back and blast the prison roof open. We climb down. We grab Ben-Ari. We climb back out. We fly like the wind."

"If she's still alive," Lailani said. She hit a few controls, and the viewport zoomed in on the prison. Lailani cringed. "Those bastard marauders covered the entire prison with their webs. Every prisoner inside might be dead already."

"Then we'll explore every cell until we find her body," Kemi said. "If there's even a tiny chance Captain Ben-Ari is alive—and to me, she's still a captain—I'm going to fight for her. She would do the same for us. She saved our lives more times than I can count. Whatever it takes, we're finding her. And if all we find is her body, we'll give her a proper burial. We—"

She bit down on her words.

"They saw us," Lailani whispered.

One of the ravagers was flying straight at them.

"Damn," Kemi muttered. "We're still far. They shouldn't have seen us yet."

"It's coming right at us!" Lailani said.

The ravager was heading their way, yet its flight was erratic. It rose, fell, swerved from side to side.

"Is there a drunk marauder flying that thing?" Noodles said.

"It seems to be malfunctioning," Kemi said. "Maybe it was damaged in the battle. We'll go around it. We need to conserve our missiles. We reach the asteroid, then engage the azoth engine and knock off all those ravagers. Hold on!"

She shoved down on the throttle and gripped her joystick. The *Saint Brendan* streamed forward, racing toward the asteroid. The rogue ravager kept careening toward them. In the distance, the other ravagers—those hovering around the asteroid—came flying toward them too. Plasma blasted out.

Kemi tugged the controls. They dodged one plasma bolt. She swerved sideways and barrel-rolled, dodging more of the assault.

Ahead of them, the rogue ravager took a blast to its back. It careened, righted itself, and kept flying forward. Smoke rose from its tail.

"They're firing on their own ship!" Lailani said.

"We're being hailed," said Noodles, sitting at the communication controls. "The rogue ship is hailing us. Kems?"

"Put them on screen!" she said, then winced and yanked sideways, trying to dodge more blows. "God damn it!"

Dozens of ravagers were now flying toward them. Kemi wanted to turn on the azoth engine, to bend spacetime, to knock those bastards back.

But let us talk first.

"Putting them through," Noodles said. "Central viewport."

On a screen ahead, a view of the ravager's bridge appeared. It was a dank, cavernous place covered in cobwebs. A marauder sat there, half its legs severed. Its three remaining legs were tugging on strands of web, piloting the ship. Blood dripped from its jaws, and it sneered at the *Saint Brendan*, malice blazing in its eyes.

"Who are you?" Kemi said. "What do you want?"

The marauder squealed, a cry of agony, and its head tilted.

Kemi, Lailani, and Noodles gasped as one.

The marauder had a blade embedded in its head. Ben-Ari stood behind the alien, holding the hilt.

"Captain!" Kemi cried.

Ben-Ari wore a bloodstained prison jumpsuit. More blood covered her face and stained her blond hair. She twisted the blade in the marauder's head.

"Keep flying, buddy," she told it. "And I might just let you live."

The marauder whimpered and kept tugging the webbings, piloting the ship onward. The ravager lurched forward.

Kemi wanted to say more, wanted to laugh, to cry, to speak to her captain after a year apart. But the other ravagers were flying in fast, and more plasma blazed forth. Both the *Saint Brendan* and the commandeered ravager lurched to the side, dodging the fiery bolts. A stream of plasma grazed the *Brendan*'s hull, and the ship trembled.

"Lieutenant Abasi!" Ben-Ari shouted through the controls. "I don't trust this ravager flying faster than light; we're likely to end up inside a black hole. Make the jump into warped space! I'll fly close. Suck us into your warp!"

"Captain, you'll have to fly *really* close!" Noodles cried. "As close as two coats of paint."

Ben-Ari nodded and drove the dagger deeper. "You heard them, buddy. Fly us right up to their ship, and I might let you keep the rest of your legs."

Kemi soared higher, moving farther from the asteroid. The ravagers pursued. Plasma blazed forth. She nudged forward, dodging one blow, then pulled back. More plasma streamed ahead of them. The commandeered ravager flew toward them, inching down, closer, closer—five hundred meters away, then fifty, then alarms blared as it moved within five meters of the *Saint Brendan*.

The enemy ravagers moved in from all directions.

A ring of plasma blasted out, storming toward the *Brendan*.

Kemi grimaced, praying Ben-Ari was close enough.

She activated the azoth engine.

Spacetime curved.

They blasted forth.

Strings of starlight smeared around them. The asteroid vanished behind; within seconds, it was millions of kilometers away. Kemi checked the viewport, heart pounding, and breathed in relief.

The commandeered ravager, Ben-Ari inside it, was still with them, flying a mere three meters above them, caught in their bubble of warped spacetime.

Kemi laughed. "We did it! We goddamn did it! We— whoa." She cringed as the ravager dipped too far down, banging the top of the *Saint Brendan*.

"Watch it, bubs!" Ben-Ari said, voice emerging from a viewport's speakers. Kemi glimpsed her captain tugging the blade sunken into the ravager's mutilated pilot.

"You all right, ma'am?" Kemi said.

"Damn it." Ben-Ari spat. "My pilot is losing blood fast. I might not have a pilot much longer. Lieutenant, are you reading any terrestrial planets nearby? Anywhere we can land?"

"Scanning," Kemi said, checking the logs. "Nothing but empty space or asteroids too small to land on nearby. Mars isn't far, but I'm detecting ravagers there too. Otherwise, the closest worlds are at Alpha Centauri, but it's still a bit of a distance. We'd need to fly for another few hours. Can you keep your copilot alive that long?"

"I'm not sure," Ben-Ari said. "But I'll try. If he passes out on me, try to catch me, will you?"

"I can open the airlock right now, Captain," Kemi said. "I'll extend a jet bridge for you."

"Negative." Ben-Ari shook her head. "I'm not leaving this ravager. We need this enemy ship. It might be our only chance to study one." She grabbed the bleeding marauder and yanked up its head. "Keep flying, buster! I don't allow you to die. If you make it to Alpha Centauri, I'll feed you a few nice cattle brains for a snack. Now keep flying!"

The marauder groaned, Ben-Ari's dagger still in its head, three of its legs severed. But with its remaining three legs, it kept tugging the webs, propelling the ravager onward. Kemi wondered how a human might fly that ship; she doubted it would be possible.

They flew on.

Kemi kept checking the controls for pursuing enemies. The ravagers from the asteroid were indeed following, but the *Saint Brendan* had a few seconds' head start. That meant there were millions of kilometers between them and the pursuing vessels. For now, they were safe.

But when we emerge from warp, we'll have a battle on our hands, she thought.

They flew in nervous silence. Several times the commandeered ravager began to veer, and Kemi flew closer to it, keeping it in their bubble of warped spacetime. All the while, the enemy pursued—a hundred alien ships, maybe more. The *Saint Brendan* perhaps had a stealth cloak, but their ravager companion did not.

Civilian starships, even with warp engines, would need a week to travel to Alpha Centauri, the nearest star to Sol. The *Saint*

Brendan, built for speed, made the trip within hours. Around the star orbited New Earth. Upon this planet rose humanity's largest colony in space, larger even than Nightwall: Haven, home to millions.

"I'll take us out of warped spacetime as close to New Earth as I can," Kemi said. "The atmosphere is thick. The planet is engulfed by a storm. We'll hide in there. Can you make it that far, ma'am?"

In the viewport, Ben-Ari nodded. The captain looked ragged, thin, her eyes sunken. Blood still covered her. She still held the knife embedded into the marauder, who looked even worse; the creature seemed barely alive, barely able to keep flying its ship.

"All right, Lieutenant," Ben-Ari said. "Lead the way. I'm right on your tail. Bring us down on the outskirts of Haven. We might want supplies from the colony."

Kemi nodded and flipped switches. "Deactivating azoth drive in three . . . two . . . one . . ."

The azoth engine shut down. Spacetime smoothed out around them.

Kemi grimaced.

"Fuck!" Lailani shouted at her side.

The marauders were here too. Thousands of their ships, the clawed ravagers, were flying around New Earth. A battle was raging. Firebirds, emblazoned with the colors of New Earth, were fighting the invaders. Here too, like back on Earth, the human force was falling fast. Firebirds burned, falling into the smoky atmosphere.

Behind the *Saint Brendan*, dozens of ravagers—those that had pursued them from the asteroid—emerged from warped space.

"Hold onto your butts!" Kemi said, diving toward the planet.

Ben-Ari's ravager followed only meters behind.

Kemi flew toward the battle, zigzagging between the Firebirds, and pointed her nose straight down. She plunged toward New Earth's atmosphere. Ben-Ari followed on her heel. All around them, Firebirds fired missiles and ravagers belched out plasma. Metal and flames filled space. Starships shattered all around. Shrapnel pummeled the *Brendan*.

"Here we go!" Kemi shouted, praying that the damaged hull would withstand entry.

They plunged into the storm.

Fire and smoke roared around them.

Kemi couldn't even see Ben-Ari's ravager anymore, could barely see more than a few meters ahead.

They dived straight down, sinking through clouds of indigo, blazing red, and swirling black and blue.

For a hundred kilometers, they plunged down, and the alarms blared.

Impact warning! warned a robotic voice. *Impact warning!*

Kemi grimaced, tugging on her joystick, leveling off. She couldn't see anything but clouds. They kept diving. She struggled to right the ship. Still only clouds, only—

There! She saw a mountain range ahead, rising from the storm. She sent out a blast of sonar, scanning the landform. Caves peppered the mountainsides, most too small. But one cave was just large enough for both ships to enter, if they squeezed side by side. It would hide them from the elements and prying eyes.

Kemi skirted a mountain peak, nearly shattering a wing. She kept diving, struggling to slow down, but they kept flying at terrifying speed. Through the storm, Kemi could see it now: Ben-Ari flying beside her.

"Down we go!" Kemi said, lowering the ship. She tugged up the nose. The mountains rose below, their peaks threatening to pierce the *Saint Brendan*, and she struggled to slow down, blasting out her forward thrusters. She was approaching the cave too quickly. Another peak rose, and she dodged, rose higher, and looped around the mountaintop. She spiraled down, slower now, heart pounding.

She glided into the cave and thumped down with a thud that shook the ship.

A second later, Ben-Ari's ravager landed beside them.

Both vessels shut down their engines inside the cave.

For long moments, the crew sat still, just breathing.

The scanners showed no enemies nearby. They were hidden here beneath the storm.

"Well," Noodles said, green in the face. "Does anyone have a change of underwear?"

Lailani slumped in her seat. "Put me down for a pair too."

Ben-Ari's voice emerged through the communicator. "Well, damn. My copilot just died on me. Good timing." She smiled wearily on the viewport. "Hang tight. The atmosphere here isn't too pleasant, but I'm making a run for it. Mind opening the airlock for me?"

Kemi raced into the airlock, opened the double doors, and saluted. Tears filled her eyes.

"Welcome aboard, Captain."

Ben-Ari's lips were tight, her eyes damp. Wearing a bloody, orange jumpsuit, she returned the salute. Broken handcuffs still dangled from her right wrist.

"It's good to be home, Lieutenant."

Then Kemi could help it no longer. She broke protocol and pulled her captain into an embrace. For a long moment, the two officers stood together, embracing, eyes closed.

"Someday you'll have to tell me how the hell you broke out of prison and stole a ravager ship," Kemi whispered, tears on her lips.

Ben-Ari laughed. "A massive alien invasion creates a terrific diversion." She swayed. "Dizzy."

Kemi led her captain onto the bridge, where Noodles and Lailani stood at attention. For the first time in over a year, Einav Ben-Ari sat in her captain's seat. Outside the cave, the eternal storm of New Earth raged on, obscuring the grotto and the two ships within.

"Tell me what you know," Ben-Ari said.

"We must tend to your wounds, Captain. You need rest, healing, food, and—"

"First I need briefing," Ben-Ari said. "Brief me, Lieutenant. I've been locked up for almost two years. Tell me everything."

For a long time, Kemi spoke, briefing her captain. She spoke of the ravagers destroying Nightwall and conquering Earth. She spoke of humanity's fleet collapsing. Of the marauders rounding people up across the planet. And finally, Kemi spoke of the mythical Ghost Fleet, perhaps only a legend.

"An ancient fleet," Kemi said. "A fleet built when Earth's apes were just starting to walk upright. For a million years, it floated through space, its alien pilots long extinct. Some claim that ghosts still haunt those hulls."

Ben-Ari nodded. "We studied the legend at Officer School. They say it's the greatest fleet ever built in the Milky Way galaxy, perhaps the greatest ever built in the cosmos. But a million years ago, the civilization that built the fleet vanished. According to myth, their ships are still out there, waiting for brave pilots to find them." She gave a tired smile. "It's a legend. A ghost story for children. Just a myth about haunted ships in the unexplored darkness. Maybe just a story created to give hope to species threatened by the scum . . . and now by the marauders."

For the first time since Ben-Ari had climbed aboard, Lailani spoke. She gazed out the viewport, seeming lost in thought. "And yet this story is told across the galaxy. Every culture has a version of it." Lailani turned to look at the crew. "For three years after the Scum War, I served at the Oort Cloud, several light-years away from Earth. And there, in the deep darkness, on a secret base, we studied this fleet, this supposed legend." She inhaled deeply. "It's more than just a myth. The Ghost Fleet is real. It can help us defeat the marauders. And I know where it is." Her eyes shone. "We picked up ancient signals. From many ships. Alien signals. They came from behind the Cat's Eye Nebula, thousands of light-years away. Farther than any human has ever traveled. But we will travel there."

They were all silent for a long moment, staring at Lailani.

Then Ben-Ari laughed.

"Guys! It's just a bedtime story. You can't be serious." The captain shook her head. "No. We have two capable ships here. We'll lie low just long enough to patch up the *Saint Brendan* and the ravager we captured. We can put together a harness, allowing a human pilot to control the ravager's webs. And we return to the fight. We might have only two ships, but we will do our part to win this war."

Lailani glanced at Noodles, biting her lip. Kemi shifted her weight from foot to foot.

"Ma'am," Kemi finally said, "the tribunal might have demoted you, might see me as an outlaw, but as far as I'm concerned, you're still my captain, and I'm still your lieutenant.

And I'll follow you to whatever battle you choose to fight. But with all due respect, ma'am . . . the war against the marauders is over. They won." She shook her head, her mane of curls swaying. "We cannot defeat thousands of ravagers with only two ships. Our only chance of saving Earth—of saving my parents, of saving everyone who's dear to us, of saving our species—is to find the Ghost Fleet. It might only be a faint hope. Maybe only a legend. But if Lailani says it's real, I'm willing to go chase that hope, the only hope we still have."

Ben-Ari narrowed her eyes. "You're serious." She looked at Noodles and Lailani. "You're all serious, aren't you?"

Noodles nodded. "Yes, ma'am. I looked into the data. I see a reasonable likelihood that the Ghost Fleet is a goal worthy of pursuing. In fact, it was my idea to pick up Tiny." He grinned at Lailani. "Never thought I'd see this little one after boot camp, but it's a small galaxy."

Ben-Ari sighed. "If only that were true. The galaxy is large and full of horrors, and the Ghost Fleet is thousands of light-years away. Even with the best azoth engine in the world, traveling at full speed, it would take months to get there and back. Maybe even a year."

"I'm up for a long quest," Noodles said. "Frodo-into-Mordor style."

"I've been living with this for a year already," Kemi said with sigh.

Ben-Ari swiveled her seat around, switched on a control panel, and spent a moment reading the updates coming from

Haven, the colony a few kilometers away on the surface of this stormy world. A few reporters were still covering the battles, streaming images of marauders toppling buildings, rounding people up, and loading them into ravagers.

"Haven is lost," Kemi whispered, looking over her captain's shoulder.

"Not yet." Ben-Ari turned toward her crew. "Looks like, during my captivity, I received a message from a friend. It appears we have another volunteer for our mission. We still have a soldier to enlist. He's here on this planet. We'll find him, if he still lives. And then we will chase light in darkness."

CHAPTER THIRTY-ONE

Brigadier-General James Petty stood on the bridge of the *Minotaur*, watching the human fleet collapse.

Around Earth, the last human warships were scrambling into defensive positions. Once thousands of warships had flown in humanity's fleet. Today only a couple hundred remained. Petty saw a few old Hydra-class warships nearby: the *Chimera*, the *Medusa*, the *Sphinx*. All three were sending out their starfighters. Farther out, the bulky *Cyclops* and *Nymph* were firing their cannons, desperate to repel the ravagers. The last few Iron Sphere satellites were firing their missiles, and Firebirds flew everywhere.

And within just that one instant, just that one stare, Petty saw that humanity was losing.

He saw dozens of Firebirds burn.

He saw a great warship with a thousand marines aboard— the mighty HDFS *Cerberus*—crack and sink toward the planet.

He saw human corpses floating through space.

He saw countless ravagers charging through exploding shells and photon blasts, barely dented in the assault, and fill space with their plasma.

He saw marauders already swarming through cities below. Manila. New York. Beijing. Toronto. They and hundreds of other cities were burning. Reports were coming in from the colonies. Mars. Nightwall. Haven. All were falling.

But we're still flying.

Petty stepped closer to the viewports that wrapped around the bridge.

The enemy was tough. But so was the *Minotaur.*

"Orders, sir?" Osiris said. The android sat at the helm.

"Full speed ahead," Petty said. "Tear through their lines. Get us closer to Earth and fire our torpedoes!"

To her credit, the android was quick to respond. "Full speed ahead, sir!"

The *Minotaur*—old, creaky, heaviest in the fleet—charged forth like a bull roused from slumber, gathering speed and bellowing in fury.

As they flew, the ravagers—each was several times the size of a Firebird—slammed into the *Minotaur.*

The ship shook. The ravager claws slammed into the carrier, digging, denting the hull.

"Deck C-a breached!" Osiris cried.

"Seal it off and fire those torpedoes!" Petty roared.

The ship's cannons fired.

More ravagers streamed toward them.

Torpedoes flew, massive missiles larger than men.

The ravagers roared out their fire.

The torpedoes tore through them. One of the missiles slammed into a ravager's side and exploded, and claws flew out, hitting ravagers alongside it, slicing across the *Minotaur.* Alarms blared and the ship jolted. Another torpedo flew between extended claws into the flaming center of a ravager, and the ship exploded, showering shrapnel.

"Keep flying forward!" Petty said. "Fire all guns! Firebirds, stay near us and tear down those ravagers. We're heading into Earth's orbit."

They kept barreling forth. Thousands of ravagers flew all around. Fire washed across them. Another deck shattered, and Petty saw soldiers—his own crew—spilling out into space. A ravager slammed into a hangar bay, burrowing into the ship. Explosions rocked the *Minotaur*, and the artificial gravity petered out again before coming back and knocking them down.

"We're breached!" rose a cry through the speakers. "Marauders aboard!"

Petty clutched a control panel with both hands. The ship jolted. Through the viewports ahead he still saw the thousands of ravagers flying in, their cannons blasting. Earth swayed in the distance.

"Marine Company Talos!" Petty barked into his communicator. "Head to Hangar 17. Kill the invaders."

The ship rocked as they kept barreling forward, ripping through clouds of ravagers, a bull tearing through a swarm of hornets. And the enemy stung them. Cracks, scars, and dents flowed across their hull. Around them, ships shattered. The mighty HDFS *Argos*, a warship nearly as large as the *Minotaur*, tore apart, its shards flying everywhere, slamming into Firebirds. Starfighter after starfighter collapsed. Debris filled space, peppering the *Minotaur*, tearing into smaller vessels, and raining toward Earth.

They finally reached orbit. Around them, the defensive satellites were firing—and falling fast. Swarm after swarm of ravagers spun around Earth, slamming into satellites, shattering them. More of the enemy ships kept emerging from warped space. Tens of thousands. *Hundreds* of thousands. Two human warships, all guns blazing, slammed into each other. The ravagers tore through a starfighter carrier, splitting the mighty vessel in half. It plunged toward the planet, breaking apart in the atmosphere, raining onto the world. Below on the surface, fires blazed. Cities burned. Firebirds were falling like sparks from a campfire.

Petty stared in horror as his ship shook.

It's over. We can't defeat them.

He sneered.

But I'm not dead yet.

"Keep plowing through them, Osiris," he said. "Our armor can withstand them a little longer. Divert more power to our shields." He spoke into his communicator. "Marine Company Talos? How is that hangar doing?"

Only screams came through the communicator.

Then the screams rose from behind in the corridors.

Human screams . . . and alien shrieks.

"Marauders in the corridors!" rose a voice. "Marauders aboard!"

Gunfire. Gunfire was rattling through his ship.

Petty gritted his teeth. He spun away from the viewports. He took a single step toward the corridor . . . and he saw it there.

A marauder.

The creature was the size of a horse. It moved on six clawed legs, insect-like. Its jaws opened in a howl, large enough to rip through trees, lined with teeth like swords, human flesh dangling between them. Skulls topped its back like a suit of armor. Marines stood behind the alien, firing, but the bullets glanced off, barely denting the creature.

And then the marauder spoke.

Its voice was impossibly deep. Demonic. Echoing.

"Who . . . leads . . . this ship?"

The bridge crew stared in horror.

Petty raised his pistol.

"I am Brigadier-General James Petty, and I want your corpse off my ship."

The marauder shrieked and leaped toward him.

Petty never flinched. He fired his gun four times as the creature vaulted.

Three bullets hit three eyes.

The fourth missed.

The creature slammed into him, squealing, blood gushing from its dead eyes. Its teeth sliced Petty's shoulder. He growled and fired another bullet, hitting the last eye.

He shoved the creature off, rose to his feet, and spat onto its carcass. It stank.

He turned back to the viewport. His officers—pale and trembling but still performing their duty—were flying the ship and firing all cannons. But every second the *Minotaur* shook as another ravager slammed into it. Another deck fell, cracked open by the claws.

And worse—everywhere the other human ships were falling.

Petty had never seen such carnage. Thousands of Firebirds—burning, falling. Hundreds of warships—collapsing. And still more ravagers were emerging, spinning madly around the planet like insects, tearing through the last defenses. Another warship crashed. A hundred more starfighters winked out.

"Sir, more ravagers are landing on Earth, sir!" Osiris said. "Thousands of them are landing, mostly in the large cities, sir. Chicago, Mexico City, Lagos, Rome, New Delhi, Saint Petersburg . . . they're all falling, sir."

Another warship blew apart.

More Firebirds crashed into the wilderness and oceans.

The *Minotaur* shook, and the lights died, then blinked back on, dimmer than before, as the backup generators kicked in. Monitors flashed scenes from across the ship: burning hangars, dying marines, another marauder on board. The ship jolted as a ravager slammed into her starboard, and another deck cracked open. Another warship exploded below them and its shrapnel plunged toward Eurasia.

Earth is lost, Petty knew. *All that we fought for. All that we built. Wiped out within an hour.*

"Petty." The voice came from behind him, soft. "General Petty."

He turned to see Katson there. The president had entered the bridge. Her navy blue suit was splattered with black marauder blood. A gash bled on her arm. She gazed out the viewports as more ships collapsed, as the swarm of ravagers tore through them, as the aliens landed on the planet.

"You should be in the ship's bunker, Madam President," he said.

"Petty," she whispered. "We have to leave. We have to leave now."

The ship rocked again. The cannons kept firing.

"We've just fired our last torpedo, sir!" Osiris cried.

"Sir, another deck is breached!"

The ship trembled. Smoke flared. More gunfire rang from deeper in the *Minotaur*.

"Sir, we're tearing apart!" an officer shouted.

Katson stared at him. "We must flee."

He clenched his fists. "No. I will not leave Earth. We keep fighting. We will go down with the planet if we must." He turned toward his officers. "Fire everything we still have. Keep tearing through them, damn it, full speed ahead!"

Katson placed a hand on his shoulder. "James. We have to go. Earth is lost. We have to flee now. To survive now. To regroup—all the ships that still fly. We must live to fight another · day."

Outside, only a handful of warships remained. Petty watched as a hundred ravagers moved as one, slammed into a warship, and the vessel exploded over Africa. The lands below burned. Thousands of ravagers kept swooping toward the surface.

"We can't help Earth by dying now, James," the president said. "Order the fleet away. You are the most senior general still alive. You command our fleet now. Order a full retreat."

He stared at her. "Madam President, we have a duty to defend Earth, to—"

"I am the president of Earth," she said. "I am your commander-in-chief. And that is my command. All ships. A full retreat. Now, James. Now."

He stared at her.

He stared at the battle outside.

He stared at his battered, cracking bridge.

How can I leave? How can I betray my duty? How can I run from battle?

He stared at his president. He knew that he could disobey. He could overthrow her—here as the world burned. He could ignore his commander-in-chief, seize control, keep fighting . . .

Yet how could I live with myself as a usurper, a tyrant?

"Now, James." Katson's voice was soft, sad . . . but determined. "Now."

Duty to Earth. Obedience to his chain of command. The terrors battled inside him as the ship shook, as more ships fell outside, as the enemy regrouped for another assault on the *Minotaur*—an assault that would likely destroy it.

Petty lowered his head. He clenched his fists. His voice shook as he spoke into his communicator.

"All Firebirds. This is Brigadier-General Petty. All Firebirds, back into your hangars. If your warship is lost, make your way to the *Minotaur*. We have a hangar for you."

Guns blazing, they fled.

The last ships of humanity—they blasted away from Earth, battered, cracked, limping through space.

The HDFS *Minotaur*. Five other warships. A handful of cargo vessels. That was all. From a vast fleet—a handful.

Behind them, Earth burned.

They flew through space. They flew to the edge of the solar system. And as they flew, Petty's shame grew.

"You did well, James." President Katson touched his arm. "You did the right thing."

"I should have died there," he said. "I should have gone down with them. What did you make me do?"

Past the orbit of Pluto, they emerged from warped space to lick their wounds, to tend to their wounded, to bury their dead in the cosmic sea. The screams of the dying filled the *Minotaur*, and engineers bustled across the ships, welding cracked hulls, and smoke rose and debris floated.

"Sir, three hundred and seventeen are dead aboard the *Minotaur*," Osiris said. "Three decks were lost and eighty-seven Firebirds never came home. Should I tell a joke to ease the tension, sir?"

He stared at the android. A machine. Devoid of emotion. Feeling no terror. No unbearable shame. He envied her.

"You have the bridge, Osiris."

He walked away.

He walked through the ravaged ship, past men who lay wounded, who screamed, burnt, sliced open with marauder claws. He walked past the twitching corpse of one of the aliens. He walked by what might have been a man, now a pile of rags and flesh and shattered bones.

He returned to his chambers.

Once inside, Petty fell to his knees and clutched his chest. The old ache returned. The old dead spot in his heart.

I'm having another heart attack, he thought. *I'm dying. I'm dying a coward.*

He took a deep breath.

No.

He gripped his table.

Stand up.

He pulled himself to his feet.

The battle is lost. The war—not yet.

He stared at the framed photograph of his daughter on her graduation day. Bright-eyed. Smiling. A day of light and life.

I will not abandon Earth to shadow. You did not die in vain, Colleen.

"Sir!" Osiris raced into his quarters, holding an envelope. "Sir, I forgot!"

He spun toward her, growling. "Damn it, Osiris, I told you not to barge in here without knocking."

The android nodded. "Yes, sir! But my memory threads were temporarily demoted to a lower-priority processing thread, sir, what with the battle." He frowned. "It's all coming back to me now." She raced back to the door and knocked. "Osiris here, repor—"

"Damn it, Osiris, what do you want?" Petty's hands trembled. He desperately needed a touch of the booze—just a sip.

She rushed back toward him. "A letter, sir! It came over the highest priority security channel—during the battle. I printed it and permanently deleted its records. According to protocol, sir, I must incinerate this letter as soon as you read it. Would you like me to fetch a lighter or perhaps build a small fire? Maybe we can roast marshmallows, and I can tell jokes. I heard a cracker of a joke just yesterday, and—"

He took the envelope from her. "That'll be all, Osiris."

She smoothed her uniform, squared her shoulders, and cleared her throat. "What did one hat say to the other hat? You stay here. I'll go on a head. It's funny because hats can't talk."

Petty pointed at the door. "Out."

When she left, Petty stood alone by the porthole. The remains of the human fleet—five other warships and a few cargo hulls—hovered outside, badly scarred. Petty opened the envelope and pulled out the letter.

To Brigadier-General James Petty, it began.

His eyes scanned down to the bottom.

Yours, with hope and prayer, Captain Einav Ben-Ari.

He returned his eyes to the top. He read the letter. He reread it.

He folded it and placed it into his pocket beside his daughter's tags.

He looked back out the porthole.

"Hope," he whispered.

He left his quarters. He returned to the bridge. There was a lot of work to do.

CHAPTER THIRTY-TWO

Around Marco, the colony of Haven crumbled.

War. Invasion. Another Cataclysm.

Through the storm and fire and blood, he ran.

"Addy!" he shouted. "Addy, where are you?"

He didn't know her address. She had left their apartment in anger, renting a place of her own. He only knew her neighborhood, no more. He ran through it, shouting her name. And everywhere, down every alley and along every road, the war raged.

The monsters descended from the sky, crawling down webs. They leaped from rooftops. They scuttled down roads. Beasts the size of horses, moving on six legs, skulls clattering on their backs. Their jaws tore into people, severing limbs, ripping flesh apart. The soldiers of Haven fired guns, but their bullets could not penetrate the creatures' hardened skin. They too fell to the claws and fangs.

War.

Marco ran around the corpse of a mother huddling over her child.

Death.

A baby's stroller burned beside him, a charred skeleton inside.

Genocide.

A skyscraper collapsed in the distance, raining shards of glass and metal and roiling the storm.

Through the inferno, Marco kept running. He knew these creatures. He had seen them drawn in Kemi's leaked reports.

Marauders.

In true life, they were more hideous than anything Marco had read about, had seen in drawings. Creatures of endless hunger and malice. Demons of retribution. Terrors from the darkest pits of space. And they were everywhere. And they fed upon the dead.

For years now, memories of war had haunted Marco. For years, in army bases, in subways and elevators, in hives of desks and phones, he had remembered the hives of the scum. A ringing telephone, the screech of a subway's wheels, the cries of a baby— all would set him shaking, sweating, overwhelmed with terror.

Now, as true war flared around him, his legs did not shake. His head did not spin. Now, as war returned to his life, his old training kicked in. The strength Ben-Ari, Sergeant Singh, and Corporal Diaz had given him returned. Once more, running through desolation, he was a soldier.

"Civilian, I need you to stand back!" shouted a soldier ahead of Marco, firing an assault rifle at a marauder on a balcony.

"I'm a staff sergeant in the reserves!" Marco said, running toward the man. "I'm looking for my friend! A tall woman, blond, with a—"

The marauder on the balcony squealed, hammered with bullets, and leaped down toward them.

The soldier cursed, firing in automatic, and emptied his magazine. The marauder landed on the man, and its jaws dug deep. The soldier fell apart, gobbets of flesh thumping onto the ground. His rifle clattered across the road.

As the marauder fed, cracking open the skull, Marco knelt and lifted the weapon.

A T57. The same assault rifle he had used in the war.

A second magazine was strapped to the rifle's side. Marco inserted it, loaded, aimed.

The marauder turned toward him, fangs bloody. Bits of the soldier's skull and brains coated its tongue.

No fear. You are a soldier.

Marco fired.

A bullet slammed into the creature, doing it no harm. It bounded forward, and he fired again, stepped back, fired a hailstorm of bullets.

The marauder slammed into him.

Marco fell. He raised his assault rifle, jamming it into the marauder's mouth, keeping its jaws open. He fired again, and the bullet rang out, and he grimaced. The creature spat the rifle out, laughed, and slammed a leg against Marco. Its nostrils flared. It inhaled and trembled as if savoring the scent.

And the creature spoke.

Its voice was deep, grumbling, unearthly, each word blasting out the stench of rotten meat.

"I smell your fear . . . I will enjoy your—"

Bullets rang.

One of the marauder's eyes exploded.

The creature squealed, a sound so loud Marco's ears rang.

He freed himself, grabbed his fallen rifle, and fired again. Another eye burst. He kept firing, and more bullets came from the shadows. The marauder screamed.

Finally, when Marco's magazine was empty, the alien fell down dead.

A voice rose from the clouds of dust.

"You have to shoot them in the eyes, Poet. Only way to kill the fuckers."

She stepped out from the swirling dust—Addy, pistol in hand, wearing her security guard uniform.

"Addy!" He ran toward her. "God damn it, Addy, it's a fucking alien invasion."

"Captain Obvious saves the day again!" She grabbed his hand. "Now come on! We're sitting ducks out here, you idiot. Come with me if you want to live."

He winced. She had spoken those words before—fourteen years ago, when they had been children, when she had pulled him away from his mother's corpse.

Once more, they ran together.

They ran as they had as children, fleeing the death of his mother and Addy's parents.

They ran as they had in boot camp, training side by side.

They ran as they had on Corpus, fighting the scum in their hives.

They ran as they had on Abaddon, invading the enemy's homeworld.

For so many years, since we were children, we ran together, Marco thought. *But it was here, on Haven, on a world at peace, that I drove Addy away. That I fell apart. That I lost her. I never want to lose you again, Addy.*

Another marauder leaped toward them. They fired their guns together, slaying the beast. A ravager ship streamed overhead, slammed into a Firebird, and the human jet fell and crashed into a tower. Far above, a human warship was firing its cannons, barely visible through the storm, then tilted, tipped, and slammed down onto the city. The ground shook. A mushroom cloud rose where it had fallen, where its armaments burst, the sound deafening, and Haven trembled.

Addy pulled Marco along, and they raced into one of the buildings that still stood. A marauder lurked in the lobby, feeding on human corpses. The skulls had been sawed open, the brains removed. Blood splashed the lobby, and the creature raised its head, leering. A child's severed arm dangled between its teeth.

A nightmare, Marco thought. *A nightmare risen into reality.*

He and Addy fired their guns. The marauder laughed, bounded toward them, nearly reached them. They hit its eyes only a meter away, and it crashed down.

Addy spat onto the corpse.

"They're ugly bastards, these new guys," she said. "Fuck me, I never thought I'd miss the scum." She discarded her empty magazine and loaded another. "Now come on, follow me."

She took him down a staircase. They plunged several stories underground, finally reaching a doorway. Addy unlocked the door, and they stepped into a cramped apartment, barely larger than a closet. There were no windows. Marco saw a bed, a Maple Leafs poster, and a table covered with weapons. Mold covered the walls.

He frowned, looking around. "Addy, do you . . . live here?"

She glared at him. "It's fine and cozy. And rent's cheap. I can't afford a nice place anymore on my salary alone, all right?" She snorted. "Especially when those bastards keep docking my pay every time I punch somebody out."

Marco noticed that fresh bruises coated her knuckles. "You're not supposed to fight the bad guys? I thought that was your job."

Addy stared at the wall. Her fists tightened. "Marco, I never fought bad guys. I stand guard at a fucking subway station."

"But . . . the bruises! The black eyes! You always came home hurt, and I thought—"

"I fought the other guards, all right?" Addy refused to look at him, and she blinked away tears. "The other damn security guards. But I won every fight." She finally turned toward him, eyes red. "They bullied me, all right? They bullied you too. They made fun of us. Called us names. Murderers. War criminals. So I beat the shit out of them." She wiped her eyes with her bruised knuckles. "Besides, none of that matters anymore. The whole damn planet is overrun with space bugs. We're unemployed now, Poet."

"No." Marco shook his head. "We have a job. We're soldiers."

Addy sniffed. "We're soldiers," she whispered.

The muffled explosions and screams of war still sounded above. The basement apartment shook and dust rained from the ceiling. Marco took Addy's hand.

"Addy, I'm sorry. I'm so, so sorry. I was a complete idiot."

She nodded. "You were."

"I acted like an ass."

She nodded. "You did."

"I . . ." Marco lowered his head. "I didn't know how to be anything but a soldier. I didn't know how to live as a civilian. I didn't know how to deal with the trauma, the memories, the nightmares, the feeling of being trapped, useless, purposeless. So I drank, I slept around, I sank into a pit, and worst of all, Addy, I was a bad friend to you." He wiped his eyes. "I drove you away. And that's the worst thing I ever did. Because I lost my best friend."

She smiled tremulously. "I'm right here, Marco. You found me again. Or, more correctly, I found you and saved your ass."

He still held her hand, and he looked into her eyes. "Addy, I love you. I don't care how that love works. I don't care whether

I love you as a friend, a brother, or something more. All I know is that I love you more than anyone, more than anything. I almost died, Addy. I don't just mean from the marauders. I almost died before they ever invaded. Because I couldn't live without you. I love you—always, fully, completely." His voice shook. "You're the most important person to me in the world. Can you forgive me? Can you let me back into your life?"

Tears filled her eyes. "Fuck you, Marco Emery. Fuck you, because you're making me all emotional and shit." She sniffed, her tears falling. "I forgive you, you asshole. Because I need you. Because I love you too, even though you're an idiot. I love you. I love you. Now hug me, you moron."

He hugged her for a long time. She squeezed him against her. They stood, silent, holding each other.

A boom shook the building. The weapons rattled on the table. Addy pulled away from Marco and pointed at the weapons.

"I've been collecting these for a while now," she said.

"It's a goddamn armory," said Marco. "You're a nut."

She nodded. "Aren't you glad you're my best friend?" She tossed him a grenade. "Now stock up!"

They stocked up. An assault rifle and two loaded pistols each. Spare magazines. Grenades. Bulletproof jackets. Battle knives. Marco didn't dare ask where Addy had bought all this stuff; he didn't want to know.

But yes, tonight, I'm grateful that I'm best friends with this nut.

"Now are you ready to go out there and kick alien ass?" Addy said.

"No," Marco said. "I want to hide here underground. I never want to see war again. But I'll fight with you. Like we used to."

Because maybe that's all that I am, he thought. *All that I know how to be.* And he didn't know if that comforted or horrified him.

They walked up the staircase and back into the lobby. Through the shattered doorway, they saw the battle raging across the street. Barely any humans were still fighting, and the city swarmed with the marauders.

"For Earth," Addy said.

"For humanity," Marco said.

Addy cocked her gun. "For hot dogs."

Marco nodded, smiling thinly. "And rakes."

They ran outside, bullets firing.

The terrors of the galaxy rose before them. Hundreds of the marauders filled the street, climbed the buildings, cast their foul webs over cars and homes. Corpses of humans littered the streets, and only a handful of Firebirds still fought above against thousands of black, spiky ravagers.

The colony has fallen, Marco knew, heart pounding against his ribs. He bared his teeth. *Then I die—not like a coward, defeated and weak. Like a soldier. Not alone. With Addy.*

He roared, firing his T57. Addy stood at his side, firing her own assault rifle. Marauders ahead screeched, the bullets slamming against them, and turned toward Marco and Addy. The aliens advanced, sneering, laughing, snapping their jaws. One fell. Another. A third marauder screamed and died. More replaced them, and hundreds were soon advancing over corpses toward Marco and Addy. They were the last two humans still alive on the street, maybe on the planet.

"Goodbye, Poet!" Addy shouted, firing her gun. "See you in Hell!"

"I'm going to Heaven!" he shouted, knocking back another marauder.

"Wuss!" Addy said, lobbing a grenade. It burst, shattering a marauder's legs.

The aliens moved closer. Their claws lashed. Marco screamed, fired his gun, emptied his magazine. Claws thrust toward him. He swung his gun, knocking them aside. More claws lashed, slicing across his arm. Addy screamed at his side, firing into a marauder's open jaws, then falling as an alien spewed webs at her feet. Webs shot from another marauder's tail, and the net caught Marco's legs, wrapped around them, and knocked him down.

This is it. He grimaced. *The end. With Addy.*

Engines roared above. A shadow fell. A ravager ship lowered itself over the street. Plasma heated up in its cannon, and Marco winced, prepared to burn. Perhaps that was preferable to being torn apart by claws.

Plasma rained, and he closed his eyes.

Marauders screeched.

Marco waited to die.

The aliens screamed, and heat bathed Marco, but he didn't feel the searing pain of death.

He opened his eyes to slits.

The ravager ship was raining its flames onto the marauders.

The aliens burned. They fled from the inferno. The plasma streamed across the street, knocking the aliens aside. The ravager's engines roared, and the ship kept moving from side to side, burning the aliens, sparing Marco and Addy.

When the last marauder on the street was dead, the ravager thumped down before them, knocking over electrical poles.

The ship faced Addy and Marco, its plasma cannon still hot.

"What the hell?" Marco said, rising to his feet.

A hatch opened in the alien vessel, and a figure emerged.

"Need a lift?" the figure said.

Marco gasped.

"Einav!" he said. "I mean, Captain Ben-Ari! I mean, ma'am!"

She stepped down the ramp, wearing a bloodstained orange jumpsuit. "I received your letter." She reached down her hand. "Climb aboard, Sergeant Emery and Sergeant Linden."

Marco cursed his damn eyes. It must have just been the smoke that made them water. He took his captain's hand, and he climbed aboard. He was entering an alien starship, but for the first time in a very long while, he was home.

CHAPTER THIRTY-THREE

Marco looked around him at the innards of the ravager. For the first time, he got to see an alien warship from the inside.

This wasn't like a scum vessel, constructed of flesh and skin and shell. Like human ships, ravagers were made of metal. Yet there was no true floor, walls, or ceiling here, just a roughly cylindrical fuselage. Black webs hung everywhere, hundreds of strands. They were thickest at the front of the ship, where the strands were attached to what looked like electrical outlets.

A chair—a human chair—was lodged into the webbing at the front of the ship. Several glass spheres clung to the web like dewdrops the size of watermelons. Shower curtain rings hung from several marauder strands, and paper notes were attached to them, labeled with words like "thrust" and "brakes" and "altitude" and a dozen other commands.

"We had to make some tweaks," Ben-Ari said, climbing into the seat. "But a human can pilot her now." She grabbed one of the curtain rings that dangled from a strand. "I don't know if the marauders ever named this ship, but I've named her the *Anansi*. The name of an old spider god from Earth."

Addy looked around, scratching her chin. "Where's the cup holder?"

Ben-Ari smiled wryly. "Hold on to something, soldier. She's a bumpy ride." She yanked a shower curtain ring, and the engines roared to life.

Marco and Addy swayed, reached out, and grabbed the strands that dangled everywhere. These ones weren't connected to any controls, it seemed. They were rubbery, sticky, and warm. Marco hung on for dear life as Ben-Ari piloted the *Anansi*, raising the ravager above the city roofs. The spheres in the web crackled to life, showing images of the world outside.

They're monitors, Marco realized. *Spherical monitors.*

He watched the view in the spheres as the *Anansi* soared. Many other ravagers flew around them, still raining plasma on the city. A handful of human ships were still engaged in battle, flying close together, but thousands of enemy vessels surrounded them; Marco doubted the human resistance would last much longer. One sphere showed a view of the colony below. Haven lay in ruins, many of its skyscrapers fallen, and marauders were swarming through the city, rounding up prisoners. Thousands of colonists, bound in webs, were being marched down roads.

Marco felt queasy. He thought of Anisha, wondered if she still lived, and guilt filled him.

I'm sorry, Anisha. I'm so sorry for how I treated you. I'm so sorry for what you must be going through now.

"There's a house we have to go to," Marco said. "A friend of mine lives there."

Ben-Ari shook her head. "No, Marco. The colony is too dangerous now."

Marco inhaled sharply. "Then put me down. Let me off. I have to save her. She's . . . important to me."

He felt Addy looking at him, felt her hand on his shoulder.

Ben-Ari paused for only a second, though it seemed like a year. Finally she nodded. "Show me the way. We'll do it quickly."

"It's fifty kilometers north of the city," Marco said. "I'll guide you."

They flew between the other ravagers. The marauders, it seemed, were flying as a horde with no organized units. No other ship challenged the renegade *Anansi*. They flew, unmolested, for several moments until they hovered over the suburbs. Marco pointed the way, and they lowered themselves to fly over Anisha's street.

Except her street was gone.

The glass domes had shattered. The houses, the trees, the meticulous yards—all had burned. Charred corpses lay among the ruins. Marco wasn't sure which house was Anisha's, which corpse was her. He lowered his head.

Addy's hand returned to his shoulder. "I'm sorry, Marco."

He nodded, throat tight, unable to speak.

Ben-Ari gave him a soft look, then increased altitude. They kept flying. They left the burnt suburbs and flew through the wilderness, hidden in the storm. Finally they reached a mountain, and Ben-Ari gently guided the *Anansi* into a large cave. They landed on the rocky floor beside a second starship: a small human vessel, its hull black, dented, and emblazoned with the words *HDFS Saint Brendan*.

"Your friends are waiting to see you," Ben-Ari said. "They're aboard the *Brendan*. Go see them."

Marco and Addy leaped out of the *Anansi*. The cave was dark, but lights shone in the *Brendan*'s portholes. The airlock slid open. Marco and Addy trudged through the soupy atmosphere, covering their mouths, and stepped into the human vessel.

A woman stood in the shadowy airlock, wearing a blue Space Territorial Command uniform. Black curls haloed her head. She stepped into the light, revealing a young face, brown skin, and large warm eyes. She smiled.

"Hi, Marco."

"Kemi!" He approached her, hesitated, then pulled her into a hug.

Kemi laughed and mussed his hair. "You need a haircut." Her eyes softened. "And you're too skinny."

Marco gasped. "Your hand . . ."

She smiled and flexed it—a metal hand, its gears whizzing. "It dices, it slices—it even gives haircuts!"

"What happened?" Marco whispered, touching her metal fingertips.

"I got overeager when biting my nails," Kemi said.

Addy ran up and squeezed them both between her arms. "Look at us! The three amigos together again. Just like in high school."

Kemi grinned. "Those were good days. Though if I recall correctly, you mostly hung out with the hockey players."

"And you and Marco were always in the library studying," Addy said. "Nerds." Suddenly she frowned. "Say, Kemi, did you know that you lost your hand?"

Kemi gasped. "I had no idea!" She examined her prosthetic, curling and uncurling the steel fingers. "That would certainly explain all those ripped gloves."

Soon the three of them were laughing, shoving one another, and arguing about who was the biggest nerd or knucklehead. And even here, on a distant world, with war raging outside, it felt almost like home. Almost like the old days. Almost like three kids, not three war veterans caught in another hell.

Addy was busy retelling the story of Marco's famous all-night *Dungeons and Dragons* game—proof of what a nerd he was!—when a hesitant voice rose from deeper in the ship.

"Addy? Marco?"

Addy fell silent, rubbed her eyes, and bolted forward. Marco followed. They ran into a corridor, and there Marco saw her.

"Lailani," he whispered.

"Tiny!" Addy bellowed, grabbed the little woman by the waist, and lifted her. She spun Lailani around, then crushed her in a hug. "What the hell are you doing here too?"

"Let me go, you crazy Canadian beast!" Lailani laughed, shoving Addy off. "I had to come get you. Noodles insisted." She jerked her thumb, pointing at a scrawny young man who entered the corridor.

"Hello, ladies and gentlemen," Noodles said.

Addy gasped. "You!" She pointed. "I know you! You were at boot camp with us! For a few weeks, at least. You're the other dragon nerd, Marco's twin!"

Addy ran toward Noodles, and the two began reminiscing about boot camp.

Marco turned toward Lailani. She stood, biting her lip, looking at him.

"Hi," Marco said.

Lailani gave him a hesitant wave. "Hi."

They stood facing each other, silent. Marco could barely believe it. There she stood, right before him—Lailani. The woman Marco had met at boot camp, had fallen in love with. The woman he had made love to. The woman he had proposed to. The woman he had thought he'd live with for the rest of his life. The woman who had left him, choosing to travel with another lover to do charity work in the Third World. The woman who had broken his heart.

It was two years since Marco had left Earth, since he had last seen Lailani, but she looked the same. She still sported a messy pixie cut. She wore cargo shorts, a tank top, and sandals, and tattoos of flowers still coiled around her wrists, hiding her scars. Her old army dog tags hung around her neck. She was still beautiful. She was so beautiful.

"Lailani, I—" he began.

"You don't have to say anything," she whispered. "I know. Everything that you're feeling, I know."

He nodded, throat tight. "How is Sofia?" he finally said.

Lailani lowered her head and stared at her feet. "She fell. The marauders."

"I'm sorry, Lailani. Truly, I'm sorry for your loss."

She nodded, still staring at her feet. "Come on. You look hungry. There's some food."

Within a few moments, the crew was sitting in the kitchen of the *Saint Brendan*, eating microwaved lasagna. Only Kemi had not joined them; the lieutenant stood outside the ship, guarding the cave entrance.

As they ate, Lailani spoke of the Ghost Fleet, of studying it from the Oort Cloud, of tracking down its location behind the Cat's Eye Nebula. She spoke of thousands of alien warships, undefeated in battle, an armada that could defeat the marauders, that could save humanity.

"The marauders won't exterminate us," Lailani said. "They want to enslave us. To breed us like cattle for food. But we'll find the Ghost Fleet. And we will defeat them."

As Marco listened, he thought of the girl he had seen in Haven, the one with the kabuki mask.

Ghosts, he thought, a chill running through his bones.

For a moment, they were all silent, lost in their thoughts.

"You know what we need?" Addy finally said. "A name."

"We have names," Marco said.

"We do, individually," Addy said. "But our team needs a name. We're not the Human Defense Force anymore, not really. Ben-Ari, Kemi, and Noodles were stripped of their ranks.

Everyone else here is a veteran. So we need a name. A superhero-team name."

"The Fellowship of the Ring!" said Noodles.

"Handsome Marco and the Fab Five," Marco suggested.

"The Little Rascals Plus Addy," Lailani said. "Given that Addy is the only one who's a giant."

Addy rolled her eyes. "Your names are all stupid. We need a *real* name. How about: The Alien Asskickers."

They all groaned.

"What?" Addy bristled. "The Alien Asskickers is a good name!"

As they were tossing lasagna containers at her, Ben-Ari spoke softly. "The Dragons. Our name back at basic training."

They turned toward their captain. They nodded, one by one.

"Not bad," Addy said. "Not as good as Alien Asskickers, but I could live with it."

Marco raised his cup. "To the Dragons!"

They all raised their cups of water. "To the Dragons!"

As their cups were raised, Marco felt that something important, something almost holy was happening here, even among all the devastation and fall of humanity. In despair, they found hope. In darkness, they found light.

I thought that boot camp would be the darkest days of my life, Marco thought. *But there I forged my greatest friendships. And when I fell into shadows, when I was lost, they pulled me back into the light.* He smiled, eyes damp. *I'm home again.*

In the silence, Noodles gave a sudden loud sniff. His glasses fogged up, and tears rolled down his cheeks.

"Noodles!" Addy said. "Are you okay? Did you lose your retainer again?"

Noodles wiped his eyes. "It's not that."

Marco patted the young man's shoulder. He remembered Noodles back from boot camp. The boy had come to Fort Djemila scared out of his wits, his limbs so thin and wobbly the others had called him Noodles. Scrawny, half-blind, and constantly trembling, Noodles had spent his time apart from the others, jumping at his own shadow. Marco, himself studious and awkward, had seemed like an action hero in comparison. Noodles had lasted only several weeks at boot camp, unable to complete any obstacle course, not or even do a single push-up. After Ben-Ari had dismissed the boy, Marco hadn't seen him until now.

"It's all right, Noodles," Marco said. "You're one of us now. You deserve to be here."

Tears were still rolling down his cheeks. "I never thought I'd be one of you. Not truly. Not after what happened back at boot camp." Noodles looked at them one by one. "I always thought you were heroes. True heroes. The brave soldiers who invaded Abaddon, who defeated the scum. Who saved the world. And I couldn't be there with you. I couldn't even finish my training. I spent the war behind a computer monitor. For so many years, I hid from the world. Over and over, I read fantasy novels about brave heroes—knights, elves, dwarves, dragon-slayers. But you are all true heroes, heroes in real life. And what we're about to do—this quest to find this fleet—it's like something from the stories. But it's real. And for the first time, I'm not just reading about it. I'm here with you." Noodles removed his glasses and squared his shoulders, and for a moment, he stood as tall and noble as any soldier. He saluted. "I'm proud to be here. I won't let you down."

Addy rose from her seat, walked around the table, and kissed Noodles' cheek. "We're glad to have you."

Noodles blushed. "Aw, shucks. Kissed by the maiden fair! Now I'm truly a hero."

"I'm no damsel to save," Addy said. "I'm a warrior, and I'll fight by your side." She turned toward the rest of them. "I'm proud to be a Dragon. We'll find this fleet, and—"

A shout rose from outside the ship.

Gunfire blazed.

They all froze.

"Kemi," Marco whispered.

They grabbed their weapons. They ran.

Marco led the way. He rushed down the corridor of the *Saint Brendan*, burst out of the airlock, and leaped into the cave.

Terror shattered him like a shock wave.

Marauders. Dozens of marauders filled the cave. One of the aliens, larger than the others, seemed fused of two smaller aliens, a twisted conjoined twin with two faces and a dozen legs. It was busy moving its two front legs, weaving a cocoon around a human figure. Marco glimpsed black curls poking out of the web.

"Kemi!" he shouted and fired his gun.

The other Dragons burst out from the *Saint Brendan* behind them.

"Fuck, it's a goddamn alien army!" Addy shouted, cocked her assault rifle, and sprayed bullets.

"Kemi, God!" Noodles shouted, running toward her.

"Wait!" Marco shouted at him. The young soldier was getting in Marco's line of fire. Reluctantly, Marco lowered his gun and ran too.

The marauders leaped toward them. A claw lashed across Lailani, and she screamed, her arm bleeding. Other creatures raised their spiky tails like scorpions, and they fired sticky black webs. A net hit Ben-Ari, slamming her against the hull of the *Brendan*. Marco leaped over one strand, but another web hit his legs, tangling around them. He hit the cave floor, bloodying his elbows.

More marauders entered the cave. Lying facedown, Marco struggled to rise. He glimpsed ravagers hovering outside, a fleet of them.

Does our quest end now? he thought, struggling to free himself from the webs as marauders approached, fangs bared, eyes filled with hunger.

"Poet, get up!" Addy knelt beside him, drew a knife, and began to cut him free. A web slammed into her, knocking her back, and she screamed.

Laughter filled the cave, deep, booming, echoing. The marauder with the dozen legs spoke in an alien tongue, all clatters and grunts, then turned to stare at Marco with its two faces. Still holding Kemi, the creature grinned.

"We know you," the alien hissed. "You are those who killed the centipedes. We will take you alive. We will take you to Lord Malphas on Earth. Your pain will be legendary."

Marco stared, still trapped in the web, unable to move. The alien eyes stared into his soul, burning him from the inside, and he seemed to fall into an abyss.

CHAPTER THIRTY-FOUR

The monsters filled the cave.

The heroes were falling.

The maiden was trapped, cocooned in the spiderwebs.

Noodles stood in the darkness, legs trembling, gun shaking in his hands.

I can't do this. I'm not a hero.

Addy was shouting behind him. Ben-Ari was firing her gun, unable to free herself from the webs. Marco was down, and Noodles couldn't see Lailani anymore.

Ahead of him, the marauder with the two faces—a conjoined twin with many legs and eyes—lifted the bound Kemi. She was wrapped with so many webs only her hair was visible. The creature began carrying her away, out of the cave and toward a waiting ravager ship.

No.

Noodles shouted.

"No!"

One marauder turned toward him. The creature blasted webs his way. And for the first time in his life, Noodles fired his gun in battle.

A hailstorm of bullets blasted through the flying web, tearing it apart. The kickback nearly knocked Noodles down. He kept firing. He emptied one magazine, loaded another, fired again, and his bullets crashed through the marauder's eyes. It fell.

I killed one. I killed one!

But there were a hundred others here. And the large, twisted one was still carrying Kemi away.

Noodles ran after her, firing his gun.

For nearly two years, he had lived with Kemi aboard the *Saint Brendan*, two outcasts, AWOL from the HDF, hiding on the fringe of the solar system. Within the first day, Noodles had fallen madly in love with the beautiful, courageous pilot, and his love had only grown throughout their time together. His attempts to impress Kemi always failed. He smirked when he should have smiled. He quipped when he should have joked. He hid behind haughtiness when he should have imparted kindness. In truth, he had always feared Kemi, feared that she saw him as nothing but a scrawny nerd, and so he had built the armor around himself.

But now they were taking her away.

Now he would lose her, just before he could prove his true worth. Just as he had signed up to become a hero.

But I won't let them take you, Kemi. I love you. I will prove my worth now.

He ran, shouting, firing his rifle.

"For the Shire!" he cried, then reconsidered. "For Earth!"

Marauders leaped at him. His bullets hit their eyes, knocking them back. He lobbed a grenade, and a marauder crashed down, severed legs flying. A claw scraped against Noodles' leg, and his blood gushed, but he kept running.

They had taken Kemi out of the cave. Noodles followed, bursting out into the storm. He winced, barely able to see. The wind buffeted him, thick with dust. The foul air of New Earth filled his lungs—lungs already asthmatic, weak. He coughed, retched, kept moving.

"Kemi!" he shouted.

He saw her ahead in the storm. Several ravagers hovered above, and one stood on the mountainside, its hatch open, a ramp extended. The marauder with two faces was carrying Kemi into its ship.

"Hey, you filth!" Noodles shouted, firing at the ship. "You like brains, do you? Well, I have an IQ of 171! Come get some!"

The marauder on the ramp saw him, sneered, and dropped Kemi. She landed on the ramp with a thump.

Noodles ran, screaming.

The marauder leaped toward him.

Noodles fired his rifle. Bullets flew. They slammed into the alien's eyes, and the creature squealed, bled, and crashed into him.

Noodles fell. The massive alien—as large as a horse—landed atop him.

All around, more marauders were advancing.

They were approaching Kemi.

With strength Noodles hadn't known was in him, he shoved the dead marauder off.

"That's the trouble with having two faces, you troll," he said. "Many eyes for me to hit."

Leg bleeding, Noodles leaped over the corpse, ran up the ramp, and stood over the cocooned Kemi. He loaded another magazine and spun in a semicircle, firing bullets, holding the marauders back. More gunfire sounded inside the cave; his friends were still alive, still fighting, but out here in the storm, Noodles stood alone. He loaded another magazine, his last, and shattered another creature.

In the brief respite, as the marauders regrouped, Noodles lifted Kemi. He was lighter than her, but he barely felt her weight. She was still wrapped in the cobwebs, and he slung her across his shoulders.

Above, the other ravagers gathered plasma in their cannons.

Noodles ran, and the inferno blazed behind him, burning his back. He kept racing, moving back toward the cave, carrying Kemi.

A marauder rose before him. Noodles fired a bullet, hit an eye.

A creature leaped from his side, and claws tore into his torso, and Noodles screamed.

A gash opened on his belly. Noodles fired, and the marauder screeched and scurried back, claws bloodied.

Noodles fell to his knees, his stomach slashed open.

The cave was still several meters away.

His blood pooled.

Up. On your feet, soldier! Onward! Kemi needs you.

He rose. He kept firing. A marauder leaped toward him, and a fang sank into Noodles' back.

He fell again.

And again, he rose.

He took another step, carrying Kemi.

Don't you fall now. Don't you fall!

A meter away from the cave, a marauder closed its jaws around his arm, bit deep, and ripped off the limb.

Noodles kept walking, carrying Kemi into the cave. He placed her down among dead marauders.

Shadows leaped forth. Ben-Ari and Lailani, finally free from their webs, lobbed grenades. Marauders screeched and fell back.

Noodles was missing one arm. A wound stretched across his belly. Shaking, losing blood fast, he worked with one hand, sawing through Kemi's webs with his knife. He freed her face, and she coughed, gasped, gazed at him.

"Noodles," she whispered.

Kneeling before her, he caressed her cheek. "Kemi. My lady."

He tore off more webs, freeing her arms, then fell. He landed at her side. His blood kept spilling, and everything was cold.

Kemi ripped off the last strands of webbing. She knelt above him.

"Hang on, Noodles! It's going to be all right." Yet her tears splashed him.

"Are you hurt, my lady?" Noodles whispered.

"I'm fine. You'll be fine too. I'm taking you into the ship."

Yet the others were fighting around the airlock. The way was blocked. Noodles knew that he would not see the Ghost Fleet, that he would not see Earth saved, but he could think of no better way to die.

"I'm finally proud," he whispered. "Goodbye, Kemi. Remember me when Earth is saved, when the sky is blue, when flowers bloom. Remember me when there's no more pain."

His own pain was fading now. He held her hand. He closed his eyes, and after a lifetime of reading about heroes, David Min-jun "Noodles" Greene wrote the end to his own story.

CHAPTER THIRTY-FIVE

"They have Addy!" Marco shouted, running across the cave. "Ben-Ari! Lailani! They have Addy, come, help me!"

He ran. He leaped over a human corpse, realized it was Noodles, and kept running.

"Addy!" he shouted, bursting out into the storm.

She was struggling ahead. A marauder was gripping her, a burly beast with a crown of black horns and a twisting parasitic twin growing from its side. Addy kicked and screamed but couldn't free herself, and the marauder spun his web around her, cocooning her. Marco raised his gun, tried to aim at an eye, but the deformed alien was moving too quickly. He couldn't fire without risking a hit to Addy.

"Marco!" she cried, kicking in the alien's grip. It coated her face with sticky webs, muffling her cries.

Marco ran down the mountainside. He leaped over corpses. He had a clear shot, fired, missed. The marauders cast their webs at him, and he fell down hard, tearing his knees. Another web flew, grabbed his rifle, and yanked it from his grip. Bullets sprayed, and one grazed Marco's thigh, and he screamed.

"Addy!"

He tried to rise, fell again. Ben-Ari, Kemi, and Lailani ran past him, firing their guns, but they were too slow.

Ahead, Marco saw it as in a nightmare. The marauders scuttled into a waiting ravager, taking Addy into the ship. The hatch slammed shut, sealing her within. The ravager, with the cocooned Addy inside it, began to rise.

Marco unhooked a grenade from his belt and hurled it. It exploded against the ravager's hull, raining shrapnel. He leaped back, narrowly dodging the shards. The blast had barely dented the ravager. The alien ship kept rising. It joined a hundred other ravagers above, and still more came flying from the storm.

Marco stood outside the cave, firing his gun up at the ravager. It grew more distant, vanishing in the haze.

"Addy!"

The other ravagers turned toward him, opened their claws, and their plasma rained.

Hands grabbed him, pulled him back into the cave. The inferno rained down where Marco had stood.

"Sergeant Emery!" Ben-Ari said. "Follow me. Into the *Brendan.* That's an order!"

He glanced back outside at the storm.

Addy . . .

Jaw clenched, he followed his captain. They raced through the cave, leaping over the dead marauders. Lailani stood at the *Saint Brendan,* bleeding, carrying Noodles' body into the airlock. Kemi fired a bullet into a crawling marauder, knocking it down. Webs still hung around her shoulders and legs.

"Lieutenant Abasi!" Ben-Ari cried to her. "Step into the *Anansi*. You know how to fly it. I'll fly the *Brendan* myself. Home onto my beacon and follow me."

Kemi nodded. "Aye, Captain!"

The marauders had slung webs across the *Saint Brendan*'s wings, but there was no time to saw through them. Already more marauders were leaping into the cave, screeching for blood, and more webs shot out.

Kemi stepped into the *Anansi*, the ravager ship they had commandeered, and started its engines. Smoke and heat filled the cave. Marco and Ben-Ari, firing bullets back at the marauders, leaped into the *Brendan* and slammed the airlock shut.

They ran down the ship's corridor. The hull rocked as marauders slammed against it.

"We have one of you!" boomed an inhuman voice from outside. "Lord Malphas will torture her himself. Her screams will please us!"

Marco clenched his jaw, refusing to surrender to the terror. He leaped onto the bridge. Ben-Ari hopped into her seat, hit controls, and bullets shot out from the *Saint Brendan*'s guns. These bullets were larger, more powerful than what their assault rifles fired. Marauders fell.

"Lieutenant Abasi, do you read me?" Ben-Ari said into her communicator.

Kemi's voice emerged from the speakers. "Ready to go. You fly, I follow."

The *Brendan*'s engines roared to life. They rose to hover inside the cave.

Outside, a ravager lowered itself to block the cave. Its claws opened, and its plasma gurgled.

"Emery, man the weapons as I fly!" Ben-Ari shouted.

Marco had never controlled the guns of this model starship before, but he had enough experience from fighting aboard the *Miyari* and the *Urchin* during the last war. He hit the right controls. A missile blasted out from the *Brendan* and hit the ravager in its flaming heart.

The enemy ship exploded.

The *Saint Brendan* shot out from the cave, slammed through the shards, and burst out into the storm.

An instant later, Kemi followed, flying the larger, bulkier *Anansi*.

The two vessels—a human stealth ship and an alien fighter—flew into a sky full of ravagers.

There were hundreds. Marco didn't know which one Addy was in, if it even still flew here. His hands trembled at the controls.

Addy . . . Oh God, Addy . . . Hang in there. I'm coming for you.

Plasma blasted their way. Ben-Ari soared higher, dodging the flames. Marco wanted to fire more missiles, but he couldn't. He didn't know which ship Addy was on. Ben-Ari increased their speed, tugged back the joystick, and soon the *Saint Brendan* was soaring skyward in a straight line. Kemi followed in the *Anansi*.

Within moments, they breached the atmosphere, and the stars spread out above them. No more human warships flew here, only the endless vessels of the enemy.

"There must be a way to find what ship she's on," Marco said, trying to stop his voice from shaking. "Captain, can we run a scan for human lifeforms?"

Ben-Ari was clicking buttons. Engines deep in the ship began to hum and rattle, and a blue glow filled the viewport. Marco knew that glow. They were priming up the warp engine.

"We have no such capability on the *Brendan*, soldier," Ben-Ari said. "Addy is lost for now."

"She's not lost!" Marco leaped to his feet. "She's out there. Right now!" He pointed out the viewport at the thousands of ravagers. "She's in one of those ships, and if we have to board them one by one to find her, we—"

"Get back into your seat and man the cannons!" Ben-Ari said. "That is an order, soldier. Now!"

Ahead, the ravagers fired plasma their way. Ben-Ari yanked the controls, and they swerved sideways. A blast hit their side, and they careened.

"Captain, our azoth engine is fully primed!" Lailani said, turning from a control panel.

"Emery, fire those cannons, dammit!" Ben-Ari said.

Marco sat back down. He fired. He sent shells into space, purposefully missing. He would not fire on any ship Addy might be in.

"Captain, we cannot leave without Addy," he said. "She wouldn't leave without us. You cannot—"

"Engaging azoth engine . . . now!" Ben-Ari said. "Hold on!"

"Captain, no!" Marco cried. But his voice sounded hollow, echoing, coming from outside the ship.

He floated over his body.

The starship curved inward, and the stars streamed as spacetime warped.

With a boom, they blasted into the distance, zooming through streams of starlight at many times the speed of light. The *Anansi* followed, only meters away, sucked into their warp.

Marco rose from his seat. His wounds ached. A stray bullet had sliced his leg, and he could barely stand. Yet he came to face Ben-Ari.

"You left her." His voice shook. "You left Addy. We must turn back now."

Ben-Ari hit a few buttons, then rose from her seat. She glared at him. "Soldier, Addy is gone. She was gone the instant they closed the hatch on their ship. The only way to save Addy now is to find the Ghost Fleet and win this war."

"By then Addy might be dead!" Marco's eyes burned. His fists trembled. "You left her behind!"

"And I would leave you behind!" said Ben-Ari. "And I would leave my lieutenant behind. And if I were trapped, I would expect you to leave me behind." The captain's cheeks flushed with rage. "Those are the choices soldiers must make. And I made this choice, and I do not regret it. If we had pursued Addy, just two ships against hundreds, we'd have died. All of us."

"You don't know that. We saved Kemi. We could have—"

"Noodles saved Kemi, and Noodles died." Ben-Ari glared at him, and her voice shook the slightest, though he couldn't tell if it shook from fury, grief, or fear. "I lost two soldiers down there, Emery. I would not lose more. Not when we're the last people in the galaxy who can find hope." Her voice softened. "Sometimes we must leave soldiers behind."

"Captain!" Lailani said from her control panel. "My scanners are showing ravagers hot in pursuit. Fifty of them, maybe more. They're far behind us, but they're moving fast." She shook her head sadly. "Our stealth cloak took a beating on Haven. It's blasted. The fuckers can see us. We stick out in space like a stripper in a nunnery."

Ben-Ari nodded. She turned back toward Marco. "Sergeant Emery, are you fit to man the cannons? If not, relieve yourself from duty right now."

Marco fumed. How dared Ben-Ari do this? How dared she issue commands? She was no longer an officer! She had been demoted to private, stripped of her rank and commission, and he didn't have to listen to her. He was still a staff sergeant in the reserves, outranking her, and—

He forced himself to take a deep, shaky breath.

No, he thought. *The Human Defense Force is gone now. It fell to the marauders. What remains now is us. The Dragons.*

If he sat down now, if he manned those cannons, he would be accepting Ben-Ari's command. He would be acknowledging her as the commander of this ship, as the leader of their crew. And there would be no turning back.

He stood for only a second, staring at Ben-Ari, a second that seemed to last an eternity. A young woman, only a couple years older than him, still wearing a bloody prison jumpsuit. Broken handcuffs still dangled from her wrist. The woman who had left Addy behind. The woman Marco had written to. The woman who had fought all her life for Earth. The woman who had led Marco through the darkness of Corpus and the searing heat of Abaddon. The woman who had met a scared boy, the son of a librarian, and turned him into a soldier. The woman who, more than any other person in Marco's life, had shaped him. Had saved him. No, not an escaped prisoner. Not a mere private. She was his captain.

He tightened his lips, and he gave a salute. "I'm sorry, Captain. Reporting for duty."

He took his post.

Ben-Ari stared at him. The ghost of a smile touched her lips, and when she nodded, he saw the pride in her eyes.

They flew on. In the *Saint Brendan*: Captain Einav Ben-Ari at the helm, Staff Sergeant Marco Emery at the guns, Staff Sergeant Lailani de la Rosa at the scanners. In the *Anansi* nearby: Lieutenant Kemi Abasi, piloting the alien vessel with a rig of shower curtain rings.

Once more, they were together. Once more, they were soldiers.

And Marco realized that despite the fear, despite the agony of losing Addy . . . he felt like his old self. For the first time in two years, his mind was clear. The storm of Haven was gone, no longer lashing his body, no longer clouding his thoughts.

The starlight streamed at their sides.

After several moments, Lailani broke the silence. "The ravagers are still following us. They're faster than we are. But we leaped into warped space a few seconds ahead of them. That gives us several hours, maybe even several days, until they catch us. I just hope they give up by then."

"Not likely," Ben-Ari said. "But we have a breather. I'm putting the *Brendan* into autopilot. De la Rosa, rig an alarm to sound if those ravagers come within a million kilometers. Emery, you're hurt. Report to the medical bay. Meanwhile I'll see what I can do about fixing that stealth engine; we'll need it before the enemy catches up to us." The captain's voice dropped. "In one hour, meet me in the airlock, both of you. We're going to have a funeral for Noodles. He'll receive a promotion and full military honors before we send him back into the cosmos."

Marco limped off the bridge. In the medical bay, he found antiseptics, painkillers, and bandages, and he treated his wounds. The ugliest one was a gash on his thigh, a gift from a stray bullet.

When his wounds were bandaged, he sat down. He took a deep breath. He closed his eyes.

For years now, whenever he had closed his eyes, Marco had seen his old battles, seen terrors, seen death. But now he saw Addy smile. Tears gathered under his eyelids.

I'm sorry, Addy. I'm sorry. I'm sorry.

CHAPTER THIRTY-SIX

The cosmos spread out like a dark ocean, eternal, ancient, all that was, all that had ever been, all that would ever be. In the darkness and light, in the vast arena of emptiness, they sailed alone. Two ships. Both small. Faster than most. Scarred with memories of war and hardship and heartbreak. One ship was named after an ancient goddess. The other was named after an old patron saint of travelers who had navigated a different ocean on a faraway world. Today, these ships—the *Anansi* and the *Saint Brendan*—sailed this infinitely vaster black sea. Fleeing despair. Seeking hope.

Aboard the ships—four souls from a new species, one that had just woken from a long sleep, blinking, gazing around with curious eyes at the cosmos. Finding it beautiful. Finding it good to explore and bountiful with life. Yet also finding it fraught with many dangers, many challenges, many other species that would challenge them in a galactic Darwinian struggle.

Still, like curious toddlers rising from a fall, they reached into the unknown. To explore. To see what their species was capable of. Even as they suffered, even as their world burned, these four souls sailed the cosmic ocean.

Captain Einav Ben-Ari. Lieutenant Kemi Abasi. Staff Sergeant Lailani de la Rosa. Staff Sergeant Marco Emery. They had named themselves the Dragons, seeking courage in that mythological monster as they fled monsters of flesh and blood. Aboard the *Saint Brendan* and the *Anansi*, they streamed across the interstellar sea, out of humanity's shallow waters and into the unknown.

Marco stood in the *Brendan*'s hold, staring out a porthole at the streaming stars.

"We set out to save the world," he said softly. "We set out to save humanity. But you mean more to me, Addy. You mean more than anyone else, more than anything in this cosmos. Stay strong. Strong like I know that you are. You didn't forget me when I was lost. I will find you." His voice choked. "We'll live together again, and it will be better this time. I promise. We'll roast hot dogs on a rake. And we'll laugh. And we'll tell old stories and hold each other when the nightmares rise. I miss you. I will never stop fighting for you. I will bring you home."

He tried to see the ravagers who still pursued them in the distance, but they were still too far, detectable only with their scanners, not the naked eye. But Marco knew they were following. Fifty enemy ships. Within them—those bastards that had grabbed Addy, that had killed Noodles, that had destroyed the world.

We must find the Ghost Fleet before they catch us, he thought. *And then we'll kill every last one of them.*

He lowered his head, because he recognized that thought, that feeling. Hatred. Bloodlust. A side of himself that he hated. He had sought peace; he had failed to find it. Perhaps war was all that remained for him now. And perhaps that was more terrifying than the war itself.

Footsteps padded behind him, and he turned to see Lailani. Her uniform, a spare found on the *Brendan*, was too large, hanging off her small frame. Her hair was tied behind her head in a ponytail, and her eyes were soft. She hesitated, then stepped closer to him and touched his arm.

"Hi, Poet," she said.

"Hi, Tiny."

She looked out the viewport with him. Beyond the curve of spacetime, they could see a smeared view of the Milky Way's spiral arm. They were heading farther than any human ship had ever traveled. What kind of dangers and wonders awaited in this darkness?

"It's strange," Lailani said. "Sol is too far to see from here." The starlight reflected in her eyes.

"Do you think it's real?" he said. "The Ghost Fleet?"

She turned toward him and looked into his eyes. "I believe. I don't *know*, but I believe." She took his hands in hers. "Addy is strong, Marco. She's the strongest woman I know. If anyone can survive this, it's her. We'll come back with help. We'll save her."

Marco finally cracked a smile. "She'll never forgive me for it—for saving her ass. She'll somehow twist it around to prove that she saved us."

Lailani laughed and wiped her eyes. "That sounds like her."

"Do you remember how Addy stole a can of Spam from boot camp?" he said.

Lailani nodded. "She carried that thing around for weeks!"

"For *years*," Marco said. "She used it as a paperweight. We finally ate it about a year ago. Best damn meal I ever had."

Lailani laughed again. "Not better than that feast from the vending machine you and Addy found."

"Did I tell you that Addy once roasted hot dogs on a rake? She did!" He thought for a moment. "Somehow all the funny stories about Addy involve food."

"The girl can eat," Lailani said. "I saw her scarf down an entire pizza one day. Not a personal pizza or anything. A large family pizza. She said she was full, but an hour later, I saw her digging into a tub of ice cream. Yet she never gained any weight."

"She burned all the calories by jabbing me with her elbow. My spleen developed a callus over time. I could take a marauder claw there now and be fine. Might yet come in handy."

Lailani leaned against him. Silently, she slipped her hand into his.

"We'll make more memories," Lailani said, gazing out at the stars. "With Addy. With all of us." She looked at him. "I'm sorry, Marco. I'm sorry."

"For what?" he said, throat tight.

"For leaving you. When you needed me."

He shook his head. "Don't be sorry. You did what you had to do."

Lailani nodded and embraced him. "I'm glad you're with me, Marco Emery."

He held her in his arms. The starlight streamed through the viewport, filling the cabin. Outside, the cosmic ocean spread into the horizons. The *Anansi* flew nearby, Kemi piloting it onward. The two starships sailed on, seeking a legend, aid for a friend, and hope in darkness.

The story continues in . . .

Earth Shadows (*Earthrise* Book 5)

DanielArenson.com/EarthShadows

NOVELS BY DANIEL ARENSON

Earthrise:

Earth Alone
Earth Lost
Earth Rising
Earth Fire
Earth Shadows
Earth Valor
Earth Reborn
Earth Honor
Earth Eternal

Alien Hunters:

Alien Hunters
Alien Sky
Alien Shadows

The Moth Saga:

Moth
Empires of Moth
Secrets of Moth
Daughter of Moth
Shadows of Moth
Legacy of Moth

KEEP IN TOUCH

www.DanielArenson.com
Daniel@DanielArenson.com
Facebook.com/DanielArenson
Twitter.com/DanielArenson

72702818R00280

Made in the USA
Lexington, KY
02 December 2017